LUCKY

A NOVEL

BY V. R. STREET

D1565296

For Neil, Jessica and William.

I couldn't have written this novel without the support of my awesome family. I love you all so much. Thank you for always being there for me.

CHAPTER 1

MARIA

"You have five minutes," said Neil Charles, the head of programming at A+M Networks. Maria Gonzales noticed him glancing down at his watch with a frown on his face before turning his attention back to her.

'Showtime,' Maria thought as she straightened a cuff on her lucky shirt and tried to smile confidently. This was it, the pitch that could save her career.

Maria's career had once been on the fast track when she was promoted from associate producer to producer on *Redneck and Rowdy*, a reality show about two identical twins living in the Bayou who liked to drink moonshine and raise hell. Things had been going well for the first three episodes but production ended abruptly when one of the twins, Derek, was sent to prison for assault and battery after a bar fight. Maria felt a little guilty because she had encouraged Derek to throw the first punch.

Now that *Redneck and Rowdy* was a bad memory, Maria quickly needed a new gig if she wanted to prove to her father that she hadn't made a mistake with her choice of a career.

"*Lucky* is the name of the show and think of it as lifestyles of the newly rich and soon to be famous," she began, starting to get excited as she talked. "It's a reality docudrama where we film the life of a person who wins the BonusBall and becomes a millionaire overnight."

Neil just raised an eyebrow, so Maria continued, hoping he was interested in the concept.

"Each week, we cover a different theme. One week, the show will be like *House Hunters*, where we film the winner looking to buy a new home with the winnings. We'll work with a realtor to film different mansions and see the house that is finally selected, when the winner moves in."

Maria glanced at Neil and could see that she had his full attention.

"Another week, it will be like *What Not to Wear*, where we team the winner with a stylist, throw out their old clothes and then film them buying a new wardrobe.

"We'll follow the winner around 24/7 and cover the changes to his or her life. We'll edit and post a short clip to YouTube, each week after filming, to build an audience while we wait for the series to be broadcast. People will love seeing the winner living the dream!

"The audience for the show will depend in part on the winner. If a woman wins, the audience will skew female. If a man wins, we can focus on a male audience."

"The basic premise is interesting;" said Neil slowly, "but I see a couple of problems. What if the winner is an octogenarian, living in Iowa, who just wants to set up trust funds for the grandkiddies? Nobody is going to be interested."

Maria had worried about this very scenario but she tried to sound confident as she responded.

"Even Grandma is going to want to splash the cash, if the prize is big enough, plus we'll have the drama of seeing the rest of the family suck up to her, once she's rich."

"What does William think about the concept?" Neil asked Maria.

William Livingstone was the executive producer at 'One Ring to Rule Them All' productions, and Maria's boss.

"William is on board with the concept," said Maria. "That's why he's letting me pitch while he's in Los Angeles this week. He thinks we can keep it lean and mean – just one camera operator and an editor. As the producer, I'll work with the camera person and follow the winner around everywhere. We'll also install hidden cams in the winner's house, so we capture every moment."

"What's the BonusBall up to currently?" asked Neil.

She took a moment to look around Neil's office and gather her thoughts. The June sunlight poured in from the windows overlooking East 45th Street in Manhattan, but the office was on a floor high enough not to hear the noise from the street below. Four television monitors were hung on the wall adjoining Neil's desk, each showing a different station with the volume muted. A large photo, taken from *Pawn It* hung in back of Neil's desk, showing Sam and Charlie with big smiles on their faces. She turned back to Neil.

"We just had a winner last week," said Maria, somewhat reluctantly. "The current pot is only $50 million."

"After taxes, that's enough to change someone's life but not enough to make good TV," Neil pointed out. "We won't be seeing the winner buying a private jet."

"The pot is only going to keep growing, while we're in preproduction, assuming someone doesn't win," said Maria. "We'll wait until the payout is at least $300 million before we start shooting."

"What happens if the winner takes an annuity payout each year instead of a lump sum?" asked Neil, drumming his fingers on the desk.

"Then we don't start production," said Maria, twirling a lock of hair around a finger. Her stomach tightened at the thought. If the winner didn't take the lump sum, if the pot was won by multiple people, or worse, if the winner didn't agree to be on the show, her big chance was over before it had begun.

"I've worked with William a long time and he's had a few hits," said Neil, "so I'm going to take a chance and greenlight a pilot. If I like what I see in the first episode, we'll let you keep shooting the remaining twelve episodes. Just make sure the winner keeps spending big, so we can fuel viewers' fantasies."

"Thank you so very much," said Maria, jumping up to shake his hand. "I'll give you a great pilot. I can't wait to tell William."

She practically skipped out of Neil's office, her brain spinning with ideas about how to help the winner spend a fortune. She wouldn't care if the winner blew through all of it, as long as it made for great TV.

KAT

It was pouring, the November rain chilly, and Kat was grateful for her umbrella when she stepped out of her apartment building into the wind. The sidewalks spattered with raindrops, making it feel even colder and wetter. It was thirteen blocks uptown, and three avenues over, to get to the ad agency where she worked in Midtown Manhattan. She could have taken the subway one stop, to cut down on the walk, but Michael was always encouraging her to get the extra exercise because she didn't go to a gym. She knew she had gained some weight, since their marriage two years ago, but she wished Michael would stop with the helpful suggestions. Kat felt guilty enough about gaining the weight without having to worry about whether Michael still found her attractive.

She put her head down to brave the cold and started to walk. As usual, the sidewalks during rush hour were busy and people seemed more rude than usual as they pushed by her to get to work.

Two blocks from her apartment, Kat walked by a homeless man sitting on the sidewalk, with a damp cardboard sign in front of him.

"Please help," read the sign "I'm hungry."

He looked miserable in the rain, a ratty blanket pulled around his shoulders. His sparse gray hair was soaked and rivulets ran down his wrinkled face.

Kat stopped to look at him and he held out a cup hopefully in her direction. None of the other people rushing to get to work paid attention, as they walked around Kat and the man. Kat remembered what it was like when she was first starting out in New York and struggling to make ends meet. She had always been one paycheck away from being homeless herself.

Kat reached into her purse and pulled out her wallet. Extracting a couple of dollars, she placed them in the man's cup.

"Thank you," he said gratefully. "God bless."

Kat looked at him a moment longer. Giving a couple of dollars seemed so inadequate compared to his need.

'What the hell,' she thought to herself. 'I can always dry off at work,'

She held out her umbrella to the man.

"Here," she said. "You look like you could use this."

A huge smile lit up the man's face as he took her umbrella and covered himself, blocking the rain.

"You're an angel," he said with wonder in his voice.

"You're welcome," she said, feeling a little bashful. The rain started to pelt down harder and she was beginning to get soaked.

"Take care of yourself," she said and started to walk quickly to work, getting wetter with each step. By the time she reached the office, she was freezing and drenched, but the memory of the man's smile stayed with her.

———

Kat loved the Target conference room at the ad agency's headquarters. Each conference room was named for a different agency client and it was easy to tell that Target was a very important client just from the space. Kat enjoyed the juxtaposition between Target's reputation for discount shopping and the conference room's luxurious décor. The huge blond wood conference table was surrounded by beige chairs made of leather so soft that Kat wished she had a jacket made from one of them.

The room was expansive and bright, even without natural sunlight, thanks to the numerous spotlights that beamed down from the ceiling. Even though her hair was still damp, the faux sunny room matched Kat's sunny mood as she waited for her boss to come in. She enjoyed her job and wondered what the new assignment would be.

The door to the conference room opened and the creative director, Harold ("Call me Rufe") Rufian, walked in. Kat had to keep from smiling as she noticed he had added blue streaks to his long brown hair.

Although he was well into middle age, as the creative director, Rufe felt a responsibility to look 'creative.' He wore mirrored sunglasses, even though they were indoors. His form-fitting t-shirt was black, and he wore combat boots. Despite the questionable fashion choices for a man in his mid-forties, Kat enjoyed working with Rufe because of the enthusiasm he brought to every project.

"Hey, Kat, good to see you. I think you're going to love your new project. I asked you to come here a few minutes before the rest of the creative team so we can discuss it.

"As you know, we just landed Mattel account. It's a big win for us and we've been talking to them about the best way to promote their toys. One of the things they want us to do is to take over the Barbie Twitter feed. They want to show Barbie as a strong role model for little girls and I thought it would be the perfect assignment for you."

Rufe looked very pleased and Kat had to stop herself from wincing as her sunny mood started to evaporate.

"Rufe, really? I've never been a big Barbie fan and I don't love the idea of promoting her to a new generation of girls."

"But Kat, you can become the voice of Barbie. Think of the influence you could have."

The voice of Barbie. Kat could just picture it.

'Hi, I'm Barbie,' she thought to herself. 'You can dress me up as an airline pilot, or a doctor, but my real job is to give little girls an unrealistic body image.'

She hated the idea but her job as a senior copywriter was to come up with copy, no matter what she thought about the client or the product.

"Why me, Rufe? I'm not exactly a fashion icon."

Kat thought about the way she looked in the mirror, that morning as she got ready for work. Her strawberry blonde hair was pulled into a messy top knot and the only makeup she put on was a little mascara. She wore jeans which were now too tight, thanks to the twenty pounds she had gained since marrying Michael. She was wearing her favorite red sweater but it was only her favorite because it did a good job of hiding her muffin top. Definitely not Barbie material.

"That's just it. Mattel wants to move away from Barbie being so focused on fashion. They want her to become a role model for little girls – Barbie does math, Barbie does physics, Barbie does anything boys can do. I thought of you because you're a strong woman and the other copywriters look up to you."

Kat wondered whether her coworkers would consider her to be a strong woman if they could see her at home around Michael. In the apartment, she stopped being an ambitious professional and tried to be everything Michael wanted – cook, cleaner, lover and cheerleader whenever he didn't get a call back from an audition. It was exhausting, working 55 hours a week for the agency, along with being the perfect wife. Kat felt like a fraud.

Now she had to be a strong role model for little girls everywhere. Kat would just have to continue faking it. She tried to feel more enthusiastic about the project.

"Thanks, Rufe. It's nice to hear that I'm respected. I'll try to do a good job with the Barbie Twitter feed and give Barbie a new image."

"Girl power!" Rufe said, holding his fist up to be bumped.

"Girl power," Kat responded as she bumped his fist.

As the rest of the creative team started coming into the conference room, Kat noticed a small tear in the leather of the chair she was sitting in. She started to worm her finger into the hole, then felt guilty as she realized she was ruining the chair. She quickly stopped and inspected the damage. Luckily, it didn't look too bad. She tuned back into what Rufe was saying to Eric, the art director.

"Eric, you'll be responsible for updating the hero image on the Barbie Twitter feed. We want it to be pink, but not too pink. It's Monday and I need three concepts to show the client by end of day Thursday."

"I would love to get you concepts by Thursday, but I plan on being independently wealthy by Wednesday night," said Eric with a grin.

"You're gonna win BonusBall?" said Rufe with a smile, "Good luck with that!"

"Yes, sorry Rufe, but I'm quitting on Thursday and then sailing the world on my yacht."

"Okay," said Rufe, "I'll play along. What would each of you do if you win? Let's get the fantasy out of our systems before we get back to the meeting."

"I would buy a stable of racehorses," said Bethany, the project manager, "and then I would win the Kentucky Derby."

"Double fantasy," said Rufe approvingly. "I like it!"

"How much is the jackpot?" asked Kat.

"$379 million!" said Scott, the graphic artist. "I plan to buy my own private island in the Caribbean!"

"That's too much money for one person," said Carla, the associate creative director. "I would create a charitable foundation for people in third world countries."

"I would start my own agency," said Rufe. "Kat, what would you do?"

"I would write the great American novel and then have a baby," said Kat, surprising herself. The entire team started laughing.

"Kat, someone should explain to you how baby-making works," said Carla. "You don't need to be a millionaire to have a baby. I have three kids and we live paycheck to paycheck."

Kat felt herself start to flush, her face reflecting the color of her sweater.

"The thing is, I can't imagine having that much money. I guess I need to think bigger – right?"

"You don't need to think bigger right now, Kat," said Rufe. "Enough with the daydreams. Let's get back to Barbie."

Kat wasn't able to focus on Barbie, or much of anything else, during the rest of the day. In her mind, she kept replaying Carla's comment about not needing to be a millionaire to have a baby.

She had been dropping hints to Michael, that maybe it was time to start a family, but she had been afraid to ask him straight out. She knew he would list all the reasons why having a baby wasn't practical.

'The thing is,' Kat thought, 'having a baby isn't a practical decision, it's an emotional one. If we really wanted a baby, we could make it work somehow.'

At thirty-four, Kat was very worried about getting older. It was fine for Michael to put off having children; he could be middle-aged and still father a child. If she waited for Michael to bring it up, she thought they would never have kids. She made up her mind to talk to Michael over dinner.

When she was back home in her apartment, Kat lit the candles on the dining room table, the soft glow illuminating the good china, the crystal glasses and silver-plated flatware that she inherited from her mother. The white tablecloth was spotless and the yellow daisies added a touch of color. She wanted everything to be perfect when she talked to Michael.

The smell of the roast pork wafted in from a kitchen so tiny, it was little more than a large closet in their shoebox of a Manhattan apartment. She added butter to the mashed sweet potatoes, his favorite, and opened a bottle of white wine.

The sound of the key in the lock told her Michael was home from his acting class. She looked at him, as he walked in the door. Even after two years of marriage, she wondered how she had been so lucky to marry such a good looking man.

He smiled as he caught sight of their little dining table.

"What's the occasion? Did I forget our anniversary or something?"

"Nothing like that," Kat said, giving him a hug, "I just wanted to have a nice dinner. I made pork roast and sweet potatoes, just for you. Go wash your hands and I'll start serving."

Kat's nerves kept her from eating too much during dinner but Michael made up for it by having seconds. As he was pouring them both a second glass of wine, she decided there was no time like the present.

"Michael, I've been doing a lot of thinking," she said tentatively.

"Sounds serious," said Michael, as the smile left his lips, "is everything okay?"

"Everything is okay, but I'm thirty-four and we've been married a couple of years. We've always talked about having a family someday and I think it's time to get started." Kat knew she was speaking in a rush but her nerves were getting the better of her.

"So that's the reason behind the nice dinner and the fancy table settings? You want a baby? This seems manipulative, Kat." Michael scowled.

"I'm not trying to be manipulative, Michael. I just wanted to have a nice discussion over dinner. I'm not getting any younger and I'm worried if we wait too long, I might have a hard time getting pregnant. Sarah, at work, waited until she was thirty-five and now she and her husband have to try in vitro fertilization to get pregnant. I don't want to go through that."

"Kat, you know it's not a good time. We talked about having a baby when we were established in our careers. You're doing well at the agency but I'm not having an easy time finding parts. It's bad enough that I feel like you're supporting me. How are we going to afford a baby?"

"I think we can make it work. We can cut back on some of our expenses."

"What expenses?"

"Well, there's your acting classes and gym membership – do you think you could give them up?"

"You know I can't, Kat. I need to keep practicing, in class, so I can get roles when I audition. And giving up the gym doesn't make sense because I need to look as good as possible. Why am I the only one who needs to give up things? How are you planning to economize?"

"We don't need to live in Manhattan. We could get an apartment somewhere in Queens. We could stop going on vacations. We could cut back on the cable and phone bills. We could stop eating takeout food. There are lots of ways we could save money."

"Kat, you're not even making sense. If we lived outside of Manhattan, I would spend all my time on the subway, traveling in for auditions and classes.

And if we stay in this studio apartment, where would we raise a baby? Where would we even put a crib?"

"If we rearranged the furniture, we could make room for a crib. Please, Michael? Just consider it. I want a baby so badly."

She thought of how beautiful Michael's baby would be. She thought of how much closer a baby would bring them together. The longing to have his child was like a physical hunger.

"Who would take care of the baby when you're at work?"

"I thought you could take care of the baby, since you're not working right now."

Even as she said the words, Kat knew she was making a tactical mistake. Michael frowned as he threw down his napkin.

"So what am I supposed to do, Kat, stop going on auditions? So I can take care of your baby and be a house husband?"

"It would be our baby, Michael, not my baby. We could get a sitter when you need to go out."

Michael's frown softened a little. "We don't have money for sitters, Kat. You know that. If we had more money coming in, you know I would say yes. But it's just not doable right now. Let's see how the next year goes. If I get some roles, maybe we can try for that baby."

Kat wanted to keep talking, to convince Michael that he would love the child, once the baby became a reality. She wanted to persuade him that they could find a way to afford a child, if they both tried. But she knew he wouldn't agree unless they had more money coming in. She tried not to cry, as she cleaned up the dinner dishes.

MICHAEL

Michael handed his headshot and resume to the casting director seated at the folding table in the back of the room. She was in her mid-fifties with frizzy hair and too much eyeliner.

The casting director looked at Michael. He hoped she could see that his looks were leading man material: square jaw, straight nose, full lips. His wavy brown curls contrasted with his pale skin. His big green eyes had the type of long dark lashes that women were always envying.

"Hi there, Michael," she said, glancing at his resume. "It looks like you've done a couple of commercials and you were in an off-Broadway production of Othello. We want you to read for the role of Dr. Christian Parker. He's an emergency room doctor here on *Days of Our Lives*.

Please take a moment to look over this script and then take your cue in front of the camera. I will read the role of Nurse Emily."

Michael quickly reviewed the script. The scene was one where Dr. Parker tries to convince Nurse Emily to leave her husband and run away with him. Taking a deep breath, he tried to focus and walked over to the line that was taped to the floor.

Facing the camera, he waited.

"And action," he heard. Michael looked at the camera.

"Christian, you know I can't leave Jack," he heard the casting director say. "He's just started walking again."

Michael glanced at the script.

"But Emily, what about us?" he said plaintively. "What about Paris?" He held out an arm, as if reaching out to Nurse Emily.

"Paris was wonderful but it wasn't real. What I have with Jack is real. I love both of you and I hate having to choose."

"So choose me," Michael said, adding as much warmth to his voice as he could. "Choose love over duty. What we have is special, you know that."

'Who writes this drivel?' he thought to himself, momentarily losing his focus.

"What we have is special, but Jack is my husband and he needs me," the casting director said, as Michael glanced at the next line.

"But I need you too, Emily." Michael looked straight into the camera, trying to project love and desire.

"Cut."

Michael was startled. He had just been getting into the role.

"Thank you, Michael," the casting director said. "We'll call your agent if we want you to come back in."

Michael had to keep himself from shooting the casting director a dirty look, as he left the audition room. He wondered why they bothered having him come in, if they were only going to let him read a couple of lines.

As he was leaving the building, he pulled out his cell phone to call Alan, his agent. As usual, Alan wasn't picking up, so Michael left a voicemail, letting him know that the audition hadn't gone well.

He walked to the subway, so he could get to his class uptown, his mood getting blacker with every step.

CHAPTER 2

KAT

On Tuesday morning, Kat stopped by a bodega on her way to the office to get a much-needed cup of coffee and a buttered roll. After giving her order to the woman behind the counter, she noticed the advertising for the multiple lotteries offered by New York State. Mega Millions! BonusBall! Scratch and Win! Super Draw!

She remembered that Scott said the BonusBall jackpot was up to $379 million.

"How much is a BonusBall ticket?" Kat asked the woman.

"Two dollars," said the woman. "You want to add a ticket to your order?"

"Why not?" Kat said. "I can afford to lose two bucks."

"What are your numbers?" asked the woman.

"How many numbers do I need to give you?"

"Five," said the woman, sounding exasperated, as the line behind Kat grew longer, "plus the BonusBall number."

'What are my lucky numbers?' Kat thought to herself.

"6 – 15," she said, giving the date of her wedding anniversary.

"32 – 34," she added, giving Michael's age and her age.

"57." The year her mother had been born.

"2 for the BonusBall," she finished, giving the number of years she had been married.

"Good luck," said the woman. "Your total comes to $7.95."

Kat gave the woman ten dollars, and pocketed the change, then grabbed her coffee, the bag with the roll and her ticket.

She slipped the ticket inside her purse and hurried to work, so she wouldn't be late.

At work, she stopped by Scott's desk, so she could view the Barbie images for the Twitter feed and start writing the tweets. The glow of his monitor reflected in his glasses, as they viewed the screen. As expected, the Barbie images from Mattel featured a lot of pink.

"I bought a BonusBall ticket today," she told him as they were finishing up.

"Just one?" said Scott, "I bought ten."

"How does it work?" Kat felt a little foolish asking but this was her first time buying a lottery ticket. "When do you find out who wins?"

"BonusBall draws happen twice a week. The next drawing is Wednesday night at 10:59 P.M. They have a drum that blows all the balls around before blowing the selected balls into a tube. First they pick five white balls out of sixty-nine, then one red BonusBall out of a different drum. I plan to watch it on TV."

"What if you don't want to watch?" asked Kat. Usually, she liked to be in bed reading around 11:00 P.M.

"You can always check the BonusBall site the next day. It lists the winning numbers."

"Good to know," said Kat, "even if I don't think I'll win. The odds are pretty bad."

"I know," said Scott, "but it's still fun to play. For a few days a week, I can dream about what it's like to be filthy rich. Then I get a dose of reality when I see the winning numbers and they're not mine."

Kat spent the work day trying to imagine what she would do if she won. She pictured quitting her job and getting a bigger apartment. She thought about what it would be like to get a vacation home in the Hamptons or on Fire Island. She pictured having children, with enough money to afford private schools in Manhattan. She fantasized about having time to write a novel, instead of working at a job.

Then she had to stop daydreaming because it was making her dissatisfied with her real life. She didn't need millions in the bank; she just needed enough money to convince Michael they should start a family.

MARIA

At a preproduction meeting, Maria Gonzales and William Livingstone sat at the oval conference table in the 'One Ring to Rule Them All' production company's meeting room. Normally, Maria found the cool beige décor of the room soothing but she was getting more agitated, the larger the BonusBall jackpot grew. At some point, there would be a winner and she knew they might be starting production soon, if she could get the winners to agree to be on *Lucky*.

William looked cool and collected in his ivory fisherman's sweater and faded jeans. His dark brown hair was shiny, but she noticed he was starting to get a little gray in his carefully trimmed beard. When William smiled at her, it helped to take some of the edge off her nerves.

Maria hoped she looked as calm as William seemed to be. She had dressed in her favorite blue sweater and black jeans, along with ankle length boots. The outfit looked fine but looking at herself in the bathroom mirror, before the meeting, she noticed the start of a frown line between her eyebrows. She couldn't afford the cost of Botox, so she made a mental note to stop frowning so much.

"It's great that we have a greenlight for a pilot but this is going to be tricky to produce," said William thoughtfully, as he looked at Maria. "We don't know the cast, we don't know when production will be starting and we don't know the location. Despite that, we have to be ready the second someone wins the BonusBall and the pot is now over $300 million. Are you up for the challenge?"

"Yes," said Maria, hoping she didn't sound as stressed as she felt. "What we need to focus on is the spending. As long as the winner spends big, we'll have something the audience is going to want to see. Everybody wishes they could win the lottery. We need to show our winner living the fantasy."

"So let's talk about the beats and how you're going to get them spending," said William.

Beats were predetermined scenes, designed to capture specific pieces of needed footage. On a show like *Lucky*, they could be staged but not scripted. Maria would have to set up the shots and then hope that the BonusBall winner would deliver the goods.

"We know we need to recreate the scene of buying the winning ticket," said Maria, going over the list she had put together. "That should be easy. We can have the winner buy a BonusBall ticket anywhere, as long as he or she asks for the winning numbers.

"Then we can shoot at the BonusBall press conference, where they announce the winner. We'll get a shot of the winner standing next to the big check."

"Okay, that sets things up," said William, "what next?"

"I figure the first thing the winner is going to want to do is move into a better house," said Maria, looking to William for confirmation.

He nodded, so she continued talking.

"My strategy is to offer help at every situation, as long as the help encourages him or her to spend. If the winner wants to house hunt, we'll find a realtor who will show the most expensive houses.

"We'll encourage the winner to get an entourage. If he or she needs to go anywhere, we'll get a limo and make sure it's stocked with enough booze to start a party.

"If he or she wants to get a new car, we'll steer him or her towards the sports cars and away from the SUVs.

"We'll encourage the winner to travel, so we can get footage in exotic locales. I'll make sure the winner travels first class, or in a private jet."

"If we shoot over a three-month period, there's only so much the winner is going to spend," said William. "Will you have any conflict? Anything else to keep viewers interested?"

"We'll get users to care about the winner and then show the story of how that person's life changes, as a result of winning the money.

"Some of that is going to depend on the circumstances of the person who wins. We'll look for drama in the winner's relationships. Are other family members jealous? Are they looking for a handout? If the winner is married, does the money affect the relationship with his or her spouse? We'll look to increase the conflict, wherever we find it."

"It's going to be tricky, with so many unknowns," said William, "I know this was your concept but are you going to be able to deliver a strong pilot? Should we assign a more senior producer to help you out?"

That was the last thing Maria wanted. She wanted her father to see her name in the credits when the show was broadcast. David Gonzales, Maria's father, was a highly respected Circuit Court Judge and hadn't wanted Maria to go into show business. He hoped she would go to law school and follow in his footsteps. But Maria had wanted to work in the film industry for as long as she could remember. She needed to prove to her father that she made the right choice.

"No, I will be able to handle it, no matter who the winner turns out to be. Trust me to manipulate things to get you great TV," she said to William anxiously.

"Well, if you're certain," said William with some doubt in his voice. "Okay, I'll let you run with it. Just make sure to use the production assistants here, if you need help with anything."

"I will and thank you," said Maria. "I think I can create a pilot with enough interest to get us the greenlight for the remaining episodes. The key will be to encourage as much spending as possible."

KAT

After work, Kat was sitting on the Ikea futon in her tiny apartment when her phone rang. She noticed the call was from her sister, Karen, and she pressed the answer button.

"Hey, Ren," she said, "How are you doing?"

"I'm good, Kat. I just wanted to remind you that Dad's birthday is next week and he would love to hear from you." Kat noticed a ragged cuticle on her thumb and bit it, tearing the skin a little.

Kat paused for a long moment before responding.

"Kat? Still there?"

"I'm still here, Ren. The thought of talking to him makes me physically ill."

"Dad is the only parent we have left. Even if you're mad at him, I still think you should speak to him."

"It wasn't the heart attack that killed Mom, it was finding out about Dad's latest girlfriend. He was always a womanizer and she put up with it for years. No matter what, she took him back every time. I just can't forgive him for hurting her."

"He's not in great health. No matter how he treated Mom, you don't want something to happen to him while the two of you aren't talking."

"So the booze and the cigarettes are finally catching up with him? Seems like justice."

"I know you still love him. He's our dad."

"That doesn't mean I want to be around him right now. The pain of losing Mom is still too raw."

Kat got up off the futon and went in search of a Band-Aid for her bleeding cuticle before speaking again.

"Ren, how can you stick up for him? He used the insurance money to take his girlfriend on a cruise, three weeks after Mom's funeral. It's like he didn't even grieve over her death."

"He grieved, I know he did. He just has a hard time being alone."

"Is that woman still living in the house with him?"

"Yes," admitted Ren. "But I've met Annika. She's not so bad when you get to know her." Kat winced, thinking about Annika cooking in Mom's kitchen.

"Ren! Where's your loyalty to Mom? I never want to meet that woman, let alone get to know her."

"You don't have to meet Annika. Just call Dad. I know it would mean the world to him. No matter how he treated Mom, he always loved us."

"Sure, he always made me feel special, when he was around. But that's what he was like. He was charming but not really there when you needed him."

"He thought about us while he was on business trips. He always brought home little presents."

"I would have traded all those presents for someone who was around for birthdays and swim meets. Let's face it, Ren. He was a lousy dad and an even worse husband. If it wasn't for Uncle Charlie, we wouldn't have had a father figure in our lives."

"I wouldn't say he was a lousy dad," Ren protested. "Maybe he wasn't the best dad but he did love us. And he wants to be close to us, now that he's getting older."

"You can be close to him, Ren. And close to Annika too, if that's what you want. But leave me out of it. Listen, I have to run or I'm going to be late for book club."

"Okay, Kat, just promise me you'll think about calling him," Ren said before hanging up. "Love you."

"Love you too, Ren," Kat said and disconnected the call.

———

Kat loved going to Jessica's apartment for book club. The apartment was a lot like Jessica: warm and homey. The walls of the living room were peach and the couch was chintz and overstuffed. The matching chairs framed a real working fireplace − a rarity in most New York apartments. Kat noticed the living room was almost too warm, thanks to the fire Jessica had started to chase away the chill of the November evening.

Kat looked at Jessica, as she sat down on the couch. Jessica's steel-gray hair was pulled into a bun, although a few wisps were falling down around her ears. In her mid-sixties, Jessica worked as a project manager for a firm that made software for the financial services industry.

Angela had arrived before Kat. As usual, she was in a tailored suit, which looked fantastic on her model-thin frame. A stunning black woman in her late thirties, Angela was an investment banker who was also passionate about books. She added a unique perspective to their literary discussions.

Sharon was the last to arrive. An editor in her early forties, who worked at a major publishing house, Sharon had red hair and very pale skin, beneath all the freckles. She often brought galleys to their meetings, so they could read books before they were published.

They did discuss books during their book club meetings but it was also an excuse to drink wine and enjoy talking to each other. The four women had been meeting every Tuesday for about two years, and it was one of the highlights of Kat's week. This month, they were reading Mary Shelley's *Frankenstein*. After they had finished discussing the book, they started talking about how they each met their partners.

Jessica, Sharon and Angela all shared the stories of how they met their significant others before turning towards Kat.

"I guess you could say it was a speed relationship," she said, a little self-consciously. "Michael and I met when I went to an off-off-Broadway production of *Othello*, where he was playing Iago. I couldn't take my eyes off him, he was so good. I stayed around, at the end of the show, so I could meet him.

"We started dating and I knew, right away, he was the one I wanted to be with. After we had been dating a couple of months, he was going to lose his sublet, so we decided to move in together.

"Then the Othello run ended and his visa was about to expire. We were worried that he would be deported back to England. We went down to City Hall and got married, so he could get his green card.

"It was quick, but we've been happy," she said, sounding a little defensive.

"Well, I think it sounds romantic," said Jessica, pouring them all another glass. Kat was relieved. She always worried that people would judge her relationship, after hearing how quickly she and Michael got married.

CHAPTER 3

MICHAEL

Michael had to reach up and across Erica to pick up the slim gold ring that was on the bedside table. He slipped it back on the third finger of his left hand and sat up.

He looked around the bedroom, something he didn't have a chance to do when he was busy tearing her clothes off. The walls were painted a dingy white and the bed was just a mattress and box spring against a wall of the little room, covered with bedding. In an effort to decorate the space, someone had hung a print of Monet's water lilies, opposite the bed. Michael was willing to bet that Erica bought it from a museum gift shop.

The mattress took up most of the space in the room. There was a brass lamp on the bedside table, with a red scarf draped over it, to cast a dim red glow across the bed. A desk chair stood in the opposite corner, although there was no place to house a desk.

Michael's and Erica's clothes lay in a heap on the small sisal carpet that covered the wooden floor.

Michael felt like taking a shower, but he didn't want to deal with Erica's roommates. He could hear them talking through the paper thin walls. He could also hear the sound of the traffic, from the street outside Erica's Brooklyn apartment in Bushwick.

Michael's phone chimed again and he felt a momentary irritation. Kat was probably wondering why he was late, coming home from class.

"Do you think you should check your phone?" Erica asked as she sat up and stretched her arms over her head. "It sounds like she's trying to reach you."

"It's nothing," said Michael, as he reached out to cup one of her full breasts in his palm. He felt his penis stir and he wondered if they had time for a quickie.

"Enough of that," said Erica with a smile, as she removed his hand. "Why don't we snuggle for a bit? Tell me how things have been going with your auditions."

Michael felt exasperated. He was already late and if more sex wasn't in the picture, he just wanted to head home. He grabbed the bottle of scotch off the night table and took a swig to give himself time to think.

Even if he did want to talk, talking about his acting career wouldn't have been his topic of choice. Things hadn't been going well and Michael was getting tired of the constant rejection. Still, it was nice that Erica asked. Kat hadn't been showing much interest in his acting career these days.

"My agent sent me to an audition for a soap," he said, "but I didn't get a callback. I've been starting wonder whether I should go back to off-off-Broadway productions."

"My agent sent me to an audition last week," said Erica, "but the casting director told me I didn't look maternal enough to be cast in a Pampers commercial."

He turned to look at Erica. The sweat on her skin made her glisten in the dim lighting of the bedroom, as she lay on top of the blue plaid comforter. Her mascara was smudged and her dark brown hair was somewhat tangled around her face, but it just made her look sexier.

"You definitely don't look maternal," said Michael, "I don't see you as a mom at all."

"What role were you auditioning for in the soap?" she asked, as she stroked the hair on his chest.

"It was for an emergency room doctor in a hospital. It wasn't a big role but maybe they didn't want a guy in his early thirties."

"I could see you as an emergency room doctor. You would have looked great in a white lab coat."

Michael could see himself in the lab coat. It would have set off his dark hair and green eyes. Women were always telling him how handsome he was and Michael knew he was a good actor. He had studied acting at the prestigious Royal Academy of Dramatic Art in London. He couldn't understand why he didn't get more callbacks.

"I feel like I just need the right role. Something to get people's attention."

"What made you want to be an actor?" asked Erica.

Michael paused a moment before answering and held Erica's hand in his.

"My parents were killed in a car accident when I was seven and I was raised by my grandmother, who was very strict. Even though she provided for all my material needs, she wasn't very loving. I always felt like a burden.

"Then, when I was eight, I was cast as the lead in our school play. When the audience applauded at the end of the play, I could feel the love coming in waves from them. I became addicted. I've wanted to be an actor ever since. My grandmother disapproved but I didn't care."

"Applause is a like a drug," agreed Erica, squeezing his hand. "Have you ever considered moving to L.A? Maybe New York isn't working out for you. Steve moved out there last year and I hear he's starting to get roles."

Michael briefly fantasized about moving but knew that Kat would never agree. She loved New York and her career at the ad agency was doing well. Suddenly, Erica's small bedroom felt claustrophobic and he wanted to leave.

"Erica, I've got to get going," he said, getting out from under the covers and reaching for his shorts on the floor. "Kat is probably frantic by now."

"That's it? You've had your fun and now you want to run home to wifey?" She jumped out of bed and started getting dressed in a hurry.

"Erica, don't be like that. You've always known about Kat. I've never tried to hide my marriage."

Erica stopped in the middle of putting on her bra. "I know, Michael, but I hate being the girlfriend. It makes me feel cheap."

Michael hugged her from behind, and then helped her hook her bra strap. "You're not cheap, Erica. You're very special but I have a wife."

"Why not leave? You're not happy with her or you wouldn't be seeing me."

"Erica, I don't have time for this argument right now. I've got to go."

"Don't go just yet," said Erica, turning around to face him. She pressed her lips to his and gave him a long lingering kiss. Her body leaned into his, promising more if only he would stay.

Michael broke off the kiss and finished putting on his clothes. He left her pouting and half-dressed as he closed the bedroom door. Michael exited the apartment, nodding to the roommates on his way out.

Once he was outside the apartment building, he felt like he could breathe. The sky was dark and a light November drizzle had started. He opened an umbrella, which provided a cone of privacy as he quickly walked the crowded streets, to the L Subway, to take him back to Manhattan.

KAT

Wednesday, 10:30 P.M.

Kat checked her phone again to see if Michael had responded to her texts. Logically, she knew that she would have heard a chime but she checked anyway, in case her phone had somehow gone on mute. Still nothing.

11:00 P.M.

Kat sent a third text to Michael's phone.

'Starting to worry. Please text me back to let me know you're okay. Love you.'

11:15 P.M.

Kat checked the clock again and felt her stomach tighten into a knot. Maybe Michael's phone battery had died and he was unable to text her back. She paced across the oriental carpet that covered the floor of the little apartment, going from the futon to the small dining room table and back again.

11:47 P.M.

Kat jumped up as she heard Michael's key in the lock, her fear quickly turning to anger, now that she knew he was safe.

"Jesus, Michael, where the hell have you been? Why haven't you returned any of my texts?"

She took a step back, as she took in Michael's appearance as he stood in the doorway. His clothes were disheveled and his eyes were bloodshot. Even from a distance, he smelled like a bar at last call.

"You went out drinking after class again? I texted you. Why didn't you text me back, to let me know you were going to be late?"

"I'm sorry, Kitty Kat. It was so loud in the bar that I couldn't hear my phone. I didn't know you texted me."

"Well you could have let me know you were going to be late. I've stayed up worrying and I have to get to the office early tomorrow."

"You're right, sweetheart. I should have let you know. It was a last-minute decision, after class, and I didn't mean to stay as long as I did."

He walked over towards the red futon, a little unsteadily, to give her a hug and an apologetic kiss.

Kat stiffened as he put his arms around her. Underneath the stink of Jack Daniels, she smelled something distinctly floral.

"Michael, you smell like perfume! Have you been with another woman?"

Michael's big sloppy grin quickly changed to a grimace.

"Of course not! Kat, you know I hate it when you start acting paranoid."

Worry that she was being paranoid wrestled with the worry that Michael had been with another woman. Worry about the other woman won.

"Why do you smell like perfume?" she said, holding her ground. "Who did you go to the bar with?"

"I don't know, Kat, there was a group of us," Michael said as he sat down heavily. "Mostly guys but a couple of the women came too. You probably smell Erica. She douses herself in perfume."

"You must have been pretty close to Erica, to start smelling like her." Kat stood in front of Michael, arms folded over her chest and tried to control her breathing.

"Some of her perfume must have rubbed off when we were dancing."

"You were dancing? I thought you just went to the bar?"

Michael ran his hand through his hair and responded slowly. "Well there was music and some of us started dancing. It's nothing to stress about. Just a little harmless dancing."

Kat wanted to grill him, to get all the details about the dancing and find out if he had really been with some other woman. As she opened her mouth, to start the interrogation, she remembered a fight between her parents when she was ten. They had been arguing in the kitchen but their loud voices had carried into the family room where she had been sitting.

Her mother had been interrogating her father, after he was late coming home from the office. Kat remembered being scared as they screamed at each other. The fight had ended when her father told her mother that all her paranoia was smothering him and chasing him away. Her father had stormed out the door and left her mother sobbing in the kitchen.

Kat didn't want to become a paranoid wife who would chase her husband away. She tried hard to push down the fear that Michael had really been with someone else.

"Maybe next time you can text me and I can join you," she said, trying hard to smile. "It would be fun to go out dancing."

"I didn't think that you would want to join us," said Michael with surprise. "Usually you just want to go to bed early because you have to work the next day."

Kat wanted to respond that if he was working, he might want to go to bed early too, but she knew that would just start them arguing again. Michael was sensitive about not working.

It was getting late and she just wanted Michael to hold her and tell her she was the only woman in his life. She needed to feel his arms around her.

"I would love to go dancing with you, even during the work week. I guess I can be a little tired at work the next day."

"That sounds good to me, Kitty Kat. It would be great to go dancing with you." With that, Michael put his arms around her and she leaned into his hug.

Kat promised herself she would be more fun. Anything to make sure he wouldn't go out dancing with other women.

CHAPTER 4

KAT

Although she wanted to believe Michael's explanation about dancing with Erica, Kat still felt a knot in her stomach, when she arrived at the office Thursday morning. After drinking some coffee at her desk, she decided to shake it off and throw herself into her work. No matter what was going on in her personal life, Kat felt confident at the office.

She started by searching for "Barbie," just to see what came up, and if it could inspire her. She was surprised to discover that Barbie had a last name (Roberts) but what really caught her eye was an article about a human Barbie.

Human Barbie was a model who looked just like a Barbie doll through diet, makeup and plastic surgery. Kat thought it was one of the most disturbing things she had ever seen. She didn't want to write Barbie promotional messages, if making little girls want to look like a Barbie was the end result.

But writing the Barbie tweets was the assignment and Kat couldn't think of a way out, short of quitting. She decided to focus on the positive messages for little girls and downplay the fashion and beauty.

After a couple of hours, she had some tweets that didn't make her feel like a total sellout. She decided to take a break and walk by Scott's desk to see how he was doing with the images.

"Hey, Scotty, how's it going?" she asked, peering over his shoulder at the large monitor. As expected, it was filled with images of Barbie, against a background of pink and flowers.

Scott turned to face her. "Could be better Kat, how are things with you?" Scott was usually a cheerful person but today he was pouting a little.

"I'm fine but what's the matter? You seem down."

"It's nothing, Kat. I'm being stupid."

"It's not stupid if it's bothering you. Do you want to talk about it?" Kat gave Scott a little smile of encouragement, in case he wanted to spill.

Scott gave her a woeful smile. "It really is stupid. All yesterday, I had this feeling it was my lucky day. The stars were aligned and I just knew I was going to win the BonusBall. Last night, I put my tickets on the coffee table and turned on the TV to watch the drawing.

The first ball came up, and it matched one of my tickets! I was so pumped. But then they called the remaining balls and there were no more matches. I wasn't the big winner. In fact, I had just wasted twenty bucks."

Kat gave his shoulder a squeeze to commiserate. "Scott, nobody ever wins those things, you know that."

"Somebody actually did win. Just not me."

"How do you know somebody won?" asked Kat.

"I looked it up on the BonusBall site this morning. It shows that there is a winner who bought their ticket in New York."

"I should check my ticket," said Kat. "Then we can be bummed together." She gave him another smile.

"Well if it can't be me, Kat, then I hope it's you."

"It won't be me, Scott. Let's focus on reality. Unfortunately, that means getting back to Barbie.

I came by to see how you're doing with the images. I've written some tweets that actually leave my self-respect intact. I'll email them to you and you can pick the images to go with them."

"Sounds good Kat. I'll try to find something that doesn't make you want to vomit pink."

Kat laughed and walked back to her desk.

Sitting in her swivel chair, she pulled up the BonusBall site in a browser; then reached in her desk for her purse. Placing the purse on her lap, she started digging through the contents, looking for her ticket. She finally found it at the bottom, a little wrinkled. She held it up to her monitor and started to compare the numbers.

She saw 6 on the screen and looked down to see 6 on her ticket. 15 was the next number on the screen, another match with her ticket. The month and day she got married.

32 – 32, Michael's age. Match.

34 – 34, her age. Match.

She saw 57 on the screen – the year her mother had been born. It matched what was on her ticket.

Then she looked at the BonusBall number. It was 2 – the number of years she had been married. She looked at her ticket, scarcely breathing. Sure enough, the ticket showed 2 for the BonusBall.

Kat blinked, convinced she was imagining things. She held the ticket closer to the screen and started comparing again.

She looked at the screen and read the numbers aloud to herself. "6-15-32-34-57 and 2."

She looked at her ticket and read again "6-15-32-34-57 and 2."

"Hi, Kat."

Kat nearly jumped out of her chair. She quickly minimized her browser so no one could see what was on her screen before turning around. Her boss, Rufe, stood behind her.

"Hi, Rufe, what's up?" Kat said in a shaky voice.

"Can you come into my office a second? Mattel wants to change the focus of the Barbie Twitter feed and I wanted to discuss the changes with you."

Kat stood up to follow him and felt dizzy for a second. She slipped the ticket into her back pocket, frightened at the idea of letting it just sit on her desk. Her legs were trembling as she walked and she was having an almost out of body experience.

'I won,' she kept thinking as she walked to Rufe's office. 'I think I've won the BonusBall!'

They got to Rufe's office. In contrast to Rufe himself, his office was incredibly organized and neat. He had a desk with two large monitors, a small refrigerator in one corner, and printouts of projects he was currently working on were pinned to the walls. He indicated Kat should sit in one of his guest chairs while he pulled up the email from the client on one of his monitors.

Kat tried to clear her head so she could focus on what he was saying.

"Let's see here," he said, while staring at the screen. "This comes from the marketing manager. She says that third-quarter sales were not as good as anticipated and they need to increase sales during the Christmas season.

She wants you to push the Barbie merchandise and focus less on the empowering messages for girls."

Kat felt momentarily dismayed. Working on the girl power tweets were the only thing that made this assignment tolerable. If all she would be doing was pushing the pink, she would feel like she was letting down little girls everywhere.

Then she remembered, she had just won the BonusBall. She was rich; beyond rich. She was seriously wealthy. She didn't need this job. She never had to work at a job again.

No more Barbie tweets!

Rufe was staring at her, waiting for her to respond to the Mattel email.

"Rufe, I quit."

Rufe looked confused. "What do you mean?"

"I mean I am handing in my resignation, effective immediately."

Rufe looked crestfallen.

"Ahh, Kat. I'm sorry to hear that! Listen, if you're getting a better salary somewhere else, at least give us a chance to make you a counteroffer. I'm sure we can match your new salary."

'I doubt it,' thought Kat as she tried not to giggle.

"I don't have another offer, Rufe, I've just decided not to be a copywriter anymore."

"Is this because you don't want to write the Barbie tweets? You don't need to quit over that. I can take you off the Mattel account. You've been with the agency three years and we don't want to lose you."

Kat was touched and didn't know what to say. She wasn't ready to start telling people she had won the BonusBall, especially since she hadn't even told Michael.

Then Kat had a disturbing thought and for a moment, and she could hear her heartbeat drumming in her ears. What if she hadn't won the BonusBall? What if she just imagined seeing the winning numbers on the screen, because that's what she wanted to see?

She was quitting her job, a job she needed if she wasn't rich. She wanted to take the ticket out of her back pocket and check the numbers again, to be sure.

Rufe looked at her, from behind his monitor.

"Kat, are you okay? You've gone as pale as a ghost."

"I'm fine, Rufe," said Kat, not really feeling fine at all.

"Listen, go home and think it over. Take the day off. Take a couple of days to decide if quitting is really what you want to do. I'm hoping you change your mind. Just give me a call and let me know what you decide."

"Thank you, Rufe. I'll go home and think it over." She walked out of his office on shaky legs; feeling in her back pocket to make sure the ticket was still there.

She decided not to check the numbers again at her desk, when she got back to her cubicle, because she didn't want to risk being interrupted a second time. Kat opted to go home and check the numbers with Michael by her side. If she wasn't the winner, Kat would tell Rufe she planned to stay at her job.

If she was the winner, she and Michael could decide what to do next.

Kat grabbed her coat and purse and walked home. She kept checking her back pocket every other block to make sure the ticket was still there.

"Michael, I'm home," she yelled, after unlocking her apartment door. Glancing across the studio, she saw that the futon was unfolded and Michael was still asleep under the covers.

She walked over to him and shook his shoulder.

"Michael, wake up! It's important!"

Michael rolled over and opened one eye to look at her.

"Kat, what are you doing home? Are you sick?"

"No, I'm fine but get out of bed. I think we've won the BonusBall!"

Michael sat up slowly and looked at her. "What are you talking about? You're not making any sense."

"I bought a BonusBall ticket the other day and they had the drawing last night. I checked the BonusBall site today at work and the numbers matched!"

Michael stared at her, a confused look on his face. "You must be mistaken, Kat." With one hand, he grabbed his laptop off the table that was next to the futon, and ran the other hand through his tousled hair. Still sitting under the covers, he opened up the laptop and pulled up the BonusBall site.

"Let me see the ticket," he said, holding out his hand.

Kat reached into her back pocket and gave him the ticket, her hands shaking as she handed it over. Then she sat next to him on the futon and looked at his screen.

Ticket in hand, Michael started comparing.

"6-6," he read aloud, "15-15."

"That's our wedding anniversary," Kat said.

"32-32 and 34-34."

"Our ages," Kat said, feeling her excitement starting to grow.

"What is 57?" asked Michael.

"The year my mother was born."

"It's a match! And the BonusBall number is 2."

"The number of years we've been married!" said Kat triumphantly.

"Holy shit," said Michael in a whisper. His eyes grew wide as he kept glancing between the screen and the ticket. "Holy shit! The numbers match!"

Kat jumped off the bed and spun around with her arms held out wide. "We won! We won!"

Michael jumped out of bed, put the ticket on the table and grabbed her in his arms, spinning her around again.

"We're rich!" he shouted, "We won the BonusBall!" They started jumping up and down while holding onto each other.

"We're millionaires!" Kat screamed at the top of her voice. She didn't care if everyone in the apartment building could hear her.

Michael stepped away from Kat and turned to look at her. He was grinning from ear to ear.

"We're rich, Kat! Stinking filthy rich! We can buy everything we ever wanted. We can get a mansion and a yacht and maybe a private jet!"

"We can set up trust funds for our children and grandchildren," said Kat, as she grinned back at Michael. "This money is enough to take care of our family for generations."

"We can go to auctions and buy artwork," said Michael gleefully. "I've always wanted to have a Pollock or maybe a Warhol."

"We can donate to charity," said Kat eagerly. "We could do so much good for so many people. Just look at what Bill and Melinda Gates have been doing with their foundation. Maybe we can set up a foundation too."

"We could get a fleet of antique cars," said Michael. "We could buy a private island! Maybe we should get a castle in Ireland."

"I don't need a castle," laughed Kat. "I would be happy with having a real house instead of this tiny apartment."

"We can travel, Kat. We can see the world! With so much money, the possibilities are endless," said Michael happily. He reached out to hug Kat again.

"Endless," agreed Kat, hugging him back. She was overjoyed. In a single day, all their problems had been solved and anything was possible.

MICHAEL

Later that afternoon, Michael and Kat went to the Lottery Customer Service Center on Beaver Street to claim their prize money. The large office building had two big BonusBall posters in the windows and a set of double glass doors.

Michael was thinking hard, as they walked up to the building. It was amazing that Kat won the BonusBall but she was the one who was going to be a multimillionaire whereas he was just a man with a very rich wife.

He put a hand on Kat's arm before she walked through the doors.

"Kat, it's great that you'll be rich but people are going to see me as your penniless hanger-on of a husband. I don't want to share what's yours. I want to share what belongs to both of us."

"But we do share and everything does belong to both of us. That's what being married means. We share a checking account, and our apartment, and everything we own. That will include the millions."

"Do you really mean that, Kat? You want to make sure it belongs to both of us?"

"Of course I mean it, Michael." Kat looked uncertainly at Michael.

"Then let's tell the BonusBall people that we both bought the ticket. That way, they'll award the prize to both of us and we can make sure that the money will really be ours." Michael felt as if he had come up with the perfect solution.

"What do you say, Kat? We'll be rich together and I won't be dependent upon you for everything."

Kat looked bewildered. "I don't understand, Michael. Why can't we share the money, even if it's all in my name?"

"Kat, I feel emasculated having you support me. Even before winning, I had to rely on you for everything. I don't want to start resenting you, once you become rich."

"I don't understand, Michael. Why would you start resenting me? It's not like I care whether you bring in any money."

"You may not care, Kat, but I care. I don't want to have a rich wife who has to support me. If the money was in both of our names, I would feel like we were really sharing it."

Kat bit on her lip and thought for a moment. "I don't want you to start resenting me."

"I don't want to start resenting you either." Michael held his breath while Kat thought some more.

"Okay, Michael. We'll say we both bought the ticket, if it makes you happy. All the money is going to go into a single account anyways." Michael was very relieved that she agreed to his suggestion.

"Thank you, Kat. It makes the most sense to share it this way."

They entered the building and looked around. Posters for all of the New York state lotteries were pinned to the walls. Michael and Kat saw a middle-aged black woman in a gray sweater, who was behind a sleek silver counter. 'My name is Michelle' it said on her name tag.

"Good afternoon," Michelle said cheerfully, "Have you come to claim a prize?"

"Yes," said Michael, holding up the ticket while Kat stood next to him. "We're the BonusBall winners!"

"Lordy, congratulations!" the woman beamed at them. "This is so exciting! You must be thrilled."

"We are," said Michael, beaming back at her. "How do we claim the prize?"

"Let me walk you through the claims process," said Michelle. "The first thing you need to do is sign the back of the ticket. Which one of you is the winner?"

"We both are," said Michael. "We bought the ticket together." Michael was perspiring a little, despite the fact that the room was slightly chilly.

The woman handed over a pen. "Well, both of you sign the back of the ticket right now. Anyone can claim the prize if they have the ticket and you haven't signed."

Michael put the ticket down on the counter and signed the back before handing the pen to Kat. Kat quickly put her signature under Michael's.

"Next you each have to fill out a claims form," said the woman, handing the forms to them.

It took Michael and Kat several minutes to fill out the forms, entering their ticket number and their names and address, before signing the forms.

"Please give me your ticket, and I'll staple it to the first form, and staple the two forms together. Then I'll make copies of the forms and the ticket for you to hold on to."

"And then do we get the money?" asked Kat, handing over the ticket and the paperwork.

"Not quite yet, Sugar," said the woman with a smile. "The forms go to Schenectady to be processed. It can take up to fifteen business days for processing. And of course, we need to schedule the press conference."

The woman walked over to a copier behind the counter, and made copies of the forms and the tickets, which she handed to Michael and Kat.

"Someone from Schenectady should be contacting you later today, or first thing tomorrow," said Michelle. "You need to start thinking about whether you want to take the annuity or the lump sum."

"We would rather take the $379 million as a lump sum," said Michael, even though he and Kat had not discussed it.

"If you take the lump sum, you don't get the full $379 million," said Michelle. "The only way to get the full prize amount is to take the annuity.

The annuity is thirty payments that are spread over twenty-nine years. Each year, the annual payment is increased by 5 percent. By the thirtieth payment, you'll have collected $379 million. The average annual payment is over $12 million."

"How much do we get, if we take the lump sum?" asked Michael.

"You'll get almost $235 million. But don't forget that federal, state and New York City tax will be taken out of the prize." Michael was bummed that they wouldn't get the full $379 million as a lump sum.

"How much are the taxes?" asked Kat, looking anxious.

Michelle pulled a calculator out from beneath the counter. "We take out 25 percent to cover federal taxes before we give you the payout," said Michelle, "but BonusBall and lottery winnings are taxed as income, which means you'll be at the highest income tax rate of 39.6 percent. You'll have to make sure you can cover the remaining 14.6 percent at tax time.

"New York state taxes are another 8.8 percent and New York City taxes are 3.9 percent. It's too bad you don't live in a state without state income tax. New York City is an expensive place to win."

"So what do we walk away with?" asked Michael.

Michelle tapped at the buttons and peered at the calculator screen. "If you take the lump sum, after paying all the taxes, you'll wind up with roughly $112 million, which is still a fortune."

"Michael, maybe we should take the annuity," Kat said, tugging on his arm.

"You'll still pay taxes with the annuity," said Michelle, "but your average annual payment, after taxes, will be over $6 million."

"What do you think, Michael? It will give us the chance to get used to being wealthy. We won't be like those people who blow through a fortune and wind up broke."

"That will never happen to us," said Michael, as he gently pushed away her hand. "We're too smart. I think we should take the lump sum payment. If we work with a good financial planner, we'll wind up with more than $379 million after 30 years."

"Well I think we should take the annuity," said Kat, folding her arms over her chest. "Financial planners can make mistakes. If we blow through $6 million the first year because of bad investments, or spending too much, we get another fortune the next year, and the year after that. It's the gift that keeps on giving."

"Kat, don't you want to be super rich?" asked Michael. He felt impatient with Kat's anxiety. "$112 million in one lump sum puts us in the top 1 percent. We can hang with tech billionaires and media moguls."

"I never wanted to be super rich," said Kat.

Michael glanced at Michelle, who had a bemused look on her face, as she watched the two of them argue.

"I don't want to hang with Mark Cuban or Mark Zuckerberg," Kat said. "The annuity is more than enough to get everything on my wish list, and then some."

"But with $112 million, we could become venture capitalists, and wind up even richer. We could have homes around the world and visit them by flying in our private jet. We could buy a yacht."

"I don't need a yacht or homes around the world. With $6 million, we could buy a large apartment, here in New York, and a home in the Hamptons, the very first year."

"Kitty Kat," said Michael, as he took her hand, "trust me. We should take the lump sum. It gives us so many more options. I promise we'll be smart and won't wind up broke.

Please, Kitty Kat?"

Michael could see that Kat was indecisive. She bit her lip while she thought for a minute about their options.

"Kat, I promise we won't go broke. $112 million is so much money we could never go through it all."

The frown left Kat's face.

"Okay, Michael, you win," she said, smiling up at him. "Let's take the lump sum and be super rich, right from the start."

"Thank you, Kat, I promise you won't regret it!"

"Congratulations again!" said Michelle, looking relieved that they were no longer arguing in front of the counter. "We'll see you at the press conference. Then, after Schenectady has processed your claims we'll wire the funds into your bank account."

"Don't we just deposit the big check?" asked Kat.

"The big check is just for show – it makes for better TV."

"I'm really looking forward to the press conference," said Michael with a grin. "It should be fun!"

He couldn't wait to be in front of all the cameras.

KAT

When they got back from the Lottery Customer Service Center, Kat realized that she needed to call Rufe and let him know she wouldn't be returning to work. She sat down on their futon and hit the speed dial on her iPhone.

She was expecting to get his voicemail but was surprised when he picked up.

"This is Rufe. How can I help you?"

"Hey, Rufe, it's Kat."

"Kat! How are you doing? I've been worried about you since our conversation – is everything okay?"

Kat smiled at his concern.

"Everything is fine. More than fine, actually. The reason I'm calling is because, because we won the BonusBall! I won't be returning to work." Kat stood up and started pacing. She had too much energy to keep sitting.

There was dead silence on the line for several seconds.

"Kat, you're shitting me."

"No, Rufe, it's true. Michael and I went to the Lottery Customer Service Center this afternoon. We're the winners."

"You won over 300 million dollars?" Kat could hear something like awe in his voice.

"It's less than that," Kat admitted. "We're taking the lump sum, and taxes get taken out, but we will be getting around $112 million dollars." She walked over to the small kitchenette and poured herself a glass of water because her throat had suddenly gone dry. For some reason, talking to Rufe was making it more real.

"Jesus fucking Christ, Kat! Excuse my language. That's fucking unbelievable!"

"I still can't believe it myself. I wanted to let you know because I won't be coming back to the job."

"No wonder you said you didn't want to be a copywriter anymore. I can't blame you! I wouldn't keep working either. Are you going to come in to clear out your desk and return your ID badge?"

"I haven't thought that far," said Kat. "I'll mail in the ID badge but I won't be coming into the office."

"That makes sense," said Rufe, "although we'll be sorry to lose you. Have you thought about what you're going to do with the money?"

"Not yet," said Kat. "We're still trying to wrap our heads around the fact that we're the winners. It's a bit overwhelming."

"Your head is probably spinning right now," said Rufe. "But let's have lunch sometime next week, when things have calmed down a little. I have a business proposition I want to discuss with you."

Business proposition? Kat felt her stomach drop.

"What business proposition, Rufe?"

Rufe chuckled. "I think we should start a new agency. With my contacts, and your backing, we could go after some big clients right away. Within a year or two, we could become major players in the ad industry. I have a business plan I've been working on, which I would love to go over with you."

"I don't know, Rufe. Going into a new business seems risky." Kat wished Rufe would stop talking about going into business together.

"Wait 'til you see the plan, Kat. It's not that risky. I know a few account execs here that would join us and they could bring their clients. You could be the CEO. I would be the Chief Creative Officer.

"We would find office space, here in Manhattan. Maybe down in Soho! It'll be awesome!

"Just think about it, Kat. You don't have to decide anything right now. I'll call you next week."

"Listen, Rufe, I've got to get going. Thank you so much for being such a great boss these past three years."

"Kat, this is just the beginning. We're going to do great things together. Let's talk soon." Rufe disconnected the call.

'I need to change my phone number', Kat thought to herself. 'I don't want everyone I know to start hitting me up for money.' She made up her mind to get a new cell phone as soon as possible.

CHAPTER 5

MARIA

At the BonusBall winner press conference, Maria Gonzales was glad they had teamed her up with Dan Murray as her cameraman because he was a consummate professional. Dan had the rare gift of being able to fade into the background with his camera, so after a short time, the subjects tended to forget they were being filmed. At forty-five, although going bald, he was still trim and able to lift the heavy handheld cam.

Dan smiled at Maria. "Time to make the magic happen," he said. "Let's get something good."

"Let's hope the winner looks good on camera," said Maria, smiling back at him.

It was crowded in the small press room at the lottery headquarters. Cameramen and women, reporters and producers were all there to get some footage of the newest multimillionaire. Maria noticed people from all the major networks, as well as the cable news networks.

For a small woman, Maria was physically aggressive and she managed to elbow their way to the front of the pack of photographers and producers who were waiting to get a glimpse of the BonusBall winner.

She could see the big check positioned on a stand, next to a podium. The check read "Pay to the order of BonusBall Winner!" The amount of the check was $379,000,000.

"Get a shot of the check," she instructed Dan.

"On it!" he replied and moved in closer.

"Down in front!" Maria heard someone protest from the back of the room.

"Ignore them, Dan," Maria said, "get all the footage you need."

"Roger that," he said cheerfully, ignoring the pleas to sit down.

The room, which had been noisy, got quieter when the BonusBall press secretary walked into the room, followed by two people. The three went up to the podium, while flashbulbs went off in unison and photographers jostled each other to get closer.

The press secretary beamed. "I would like to introduce to you our BonusBall winners – Michael and Katherine Davidson."

Maria appraised the two people at the podium. She noticed how photogenic the man was, with dark curls and a strong jaw.

"Oh my God, would you look at him," gushed Maria. "He's absolutely gorgeous." She practically hopped up and down in her excitement.

Then she turned to look at the man's partner and was less impressed. She saw an attractive but slightly overweight strawberry blonde in her early thirties.

"How did she ever manage to wind up with him?" she asked Dan.

"Yeah, the model and the mouse," answered Dan, as he zoomed in for a close-up of the winners' faces.

Maria noticed that Michael Davidson was beaming in front of the cameras, while Katherine looked distinctly uncomfortable and kept wiping her hands on her pants.

The press secretary brought the couple over to the big check, while the cameras whirred and clicked around them. Then she brought them back to the podium and asked if they would like to say a few words.

Michael stepped up to the microphones.

"Kat and I would just like to say how excited we are to be winners. This has been the biggest thrill of our lives."

Maria noticed the slight British accent. This guy was perfect. She just hoped he would say yes to starring in *Lucky*.

"Where were you when you found out you won?" someone asked from the crowd.

"Kat, do you want to take this one?" asked Michael as he put an arm around her and gave her a quick squeeze.

"I was at work, when I looked up the winning number on my computer. I couldn't believe it. I had to run home and tell Michael that we won," the woman said in a tremulous voice. She avoided looking at the cameras and looked at her husband instead.

"What's the first thing you're going to buy?" Maria shouted out.

"I don't know," Michael said. "Maybe a penthouse? Maybe a sports car? We're going to take a few days and figure it all out."

This guy was a natural – handsome and he wanted to spend. Maria could barely wait for the press conference to be over so she could approach him.

There were a few more questions before the press secretary announced the press conference was over.

"I have one request," she said, looking over the crowd. "Give our winners some time and privacy to let them figure out what they want to do next. I would encourage the press to leave them alone. Thank you all for coming."

With that, she ushered the winners behind a curtain in back of the podium.

"Wish me luck," Maria said to Dan, as she pushed her way through the crowd to the exit. She saw a security guard standing near the door.

"Is there a back way out of this building?" she asked, while slipping him a twenty. He smiled while pocketing the bill.

"As you exit the room, take a left. There are stairs that will take you down to the back entrance. The door to the outside has an emergency sign but there's no alarm."

"Thanks!" she yelled, while flying down the hallway. She found the door to the staircase and ran down the steps in her high heels, then pushed through the exit door to the street. She waited, panting a little from the exertion. After five minutes, her patience was rewarded. The press secretary opened the rear door and led the BonusBall winners outside.

The press secretary spent a couple more minutes talking to them and then shook their hands before going back inside the building.

Just as the winners were about to get into the waiting limo, Maria ran up to them.

"Michael! Katherine! Can I talk to you for a moment? We're shooting a television show for A+M Networks and would like to feature you." It wasn't strictly true. Maria had the greenlight for a pilot, not a show, but now was not the time to split hairs.

Katherine shook her head no and started to get into the car, but Michael froze for a second with a slight smile on his face.

"Let me start again. My name is Maria Gonzales and I'm shooting a show called *Lucky*." She held out her hand, which Michael shook. "It's a reality show about BonusBall winners and I would love to make you famous."

She had him at famous; Maria could see it on his face. He wanted to be a star.

"Look, we don't need to talk about it here on the street. Here's my card. Please give me a call and we'll discuss it." She handed him one of her business cards, which he glanced at and then slipped into his pocket.

"That sounds very interesting, Maria, and I would love to find out more. I'll give you a call," said Michael.

As he turned to get into the limo, Maria could hear Katherine say, "Michael, no!" but she wasn't worried. The look on his face said it all.

MICHAEL

Once they were back at their small studio, after the BonusBall press conference, Michael sat down on the futon and pulled Maria's card out of his pocket to look at it.

Maria Gonzales
Producer
One Ring to Rule Them All Productions
212-555-3746
MariaG@OneRing.com

Kat came over and sat down next to him, to see what he was looking at.

"Michael, no. You can't be serious. The last thing we need is to be on some reality TV show. They would just exploit us to entertain their viewers."

Michael felt stressed as he turned to look at Kat. Couldn't she see that this could be his big break?

"Kat, we haven't even talked to the woman to find out what the opportunity is. Why are you saying no already?"

"I don't want our private moments to be recorded for everyone to see."

"But this could be the chance for me to break out. If the show gets a large enough audience, it might lead to me getting other roles in television and movies."

"Michael, we're rich. You don't need to get roles in television or the movies. We never need to work again!"

"I'm not going to give up my career as an actor, just because we won the BonusBall. It's great that we don't need to work but I still want to work. Being rich doesn't change that."

Michael stood up and started pacing around the studio.

"This show could be a chance for me to become known, to get my name out there. It could be my big break."

Kat stood up and walked over to him, and put her hand on his arm to get him to stop pacing.

"Michael, I didn't realize you still wanted to work. I'll support you but we don't need to do a reality TV show. We have enough money to finance an off-Broadway play, if that's what you want to do. You could do Shakespeare again. Would you like that?"

Michael pushed her hand off his arm impatiently and started pacing again.

"Kat, I want to be bigger than just an actor in an off-Broadway production. This TV show could reach millions of people. It could lead to the type of roles I've always wanted."

"But Michael, I don't want to be on a reality TV show. I don't even like having my picture taken, much less being on camera all the time. The thought of it makes me feel ill."

Michael stopped pacing and looked at Kat. She had gained some weight since they got married but she was still pretty. He could see the two of them starring in a show.

"Kitty Kat, you're beautiful. You shouldn't shy away from the camera."

"I hate the way I look in pictures. The last thing I want is a camera person in my face, capturing every intimate detail of our lives. We would have no privacy at all." Kat sat back down on the futon.

"There is no such thing as privacy anymore, Kat. Your every move is tracked across the internet. Each time you use social media, someone is watching your behavior and using your data to sell you something."

"But that's not the same as having millions of people watch everything we do and say. And I've never been a big user of social media anyways. I don't want to let people know what I'm doing every second of the day. Please, Michael, stop pacing and sit down."

Michael stopped pacing for a moment, although he opted not to sit down next to Kat. He turned to look at her holding the pillow from the futon in her lap and nervously stroking the fringe with her fingers. He thought about what she said about millions of people watching.

"Kat, I supported you, when you wanted to do well at the agency. I didn't give you a hard time when you needed to work late. I need you to support me."

Kat looked stunned. "I do support you, Michael. I paid for all those acting classes and the gym membership. I supported us financially while you chased your dream. It's not fair for you to act like I wasn't supportive."

Michael walked over, sat down next to Kat and put an arm around her shoulders.

"Sweetheart, I didn't mean you weren't supportive before. You were, and I have always appreciated it. It's just that this could be my chance to breakout and I want to take advantage of it. If millions of people like the show, I could develop a fan base, which would lead to other roles. Surely, you can see what a great opportunity this is."

"Michael, I thought you wanted to be a serious actor. Being on a reality show isn't acting."

"Kat, you're being naïve. Those shows are totally scripted and the people on them are acting out for the camera."

"Acting out isn't acting. And I don't want us to act out on camera. To be honest, I haven't been comfortable with all the attention we've been getting since we won. My hope is that we can go back to a normal life, just one where we have a lot more money."

"Kat, people who have $112 million don't lead normal lives. They live extraordinary lives. I want us to have homes all over the world and to use our private jet to go places. This is our ticket into a new life, a much better life. I want to take advantage of every opportunity that comes along."

"I want a better life too but I was thinking we could just get a larger apartment and maybe a house on Fire Island. I would settle for a nice car – we don't need a private jet. I think we should invest the bulk of the money and set up trust funds for our children." Kat stopped playing with the fringe and put the pillow back down on the futon.

"Kat, we don't have any children yet and we should enjoy the money before we think about setting up trust funds. We can live like millionaires and still have enough left over to fund a legacy." Michael got up from the futon.

He thought about what to say next while he walked over to the small kitchenette and got a Guinness out of the fridge. He wanted to discuss being on the show, and this had turned into a discussion about how to spend the money. There was time later to figure out the money but the show was an opportunity he wanted to jump on right away.

"Kat, do you want one too?" He held out a bottle in her direction but Kat shook her head no. Michael thought about what to say next.

"We don't even have the money yet, so we don't need to worry about what to do with it. If you want a larger apartment and a house on Fire Island, I'll make sure you get them. Making you happy is important to me. If making me happy is important to you, at least consider doing this show."

Kat got up and gave Michael a hug.

"Making you happy is important to me, you know that Michael. I want you to get work as an actor, if that's what you want."

"It's what I want more than anything. Kat, what do you want to do, now that you don't have to work?"

Kat smiled. "I enjoyed being a copywriter but I've always dreamed of being a real writer. Now that I won't be spending all day at an office I thought I would try to write a novel. I have an idea that I want to develop and see where it goes."

"Kat, I fully support you, as you follow your dream of becoming a published author. I need you to fully support my dream of being an actor. Let's at least talk to this producer and see what she says."

Kat leaned into his embrace and put her head on Michael's shoulder.

"Okay, Michael, we can talk to her and find out more. But if I'm uncomfortable, we won't say yes. Deal?"

Michael tilted his head to the side to give Kat a kiss on her cheek. "Deal. I'll give her a call and see what she says. I love you, Kitty Kat. I really do."

He got up, off the futon and went to get his phone.

"Maria Gonzales? Hi, this is Michael Davidson. We met at the press conference and you wanted to talk about a show you're producing." It wasn't a great connection and he felt a little anxious as he heard some static on the line.

"Michael? Hi! I'm so glad you called. We want to shoot a show named – static, static – and I would love to – static – as soon as possible."

"Maria? You're breaking up. Could you repeat what you just said?"

"We have a terrible connection. Hold on, I'll stop using my headset. Can you hear me now?"

Maria's voice came through the phone more clearly.

"That's much better – can you repeat what you said?" Michael held the phone closer to his ear, wanting to catch every word.

"We're shooting a show named *Lucky* about a BonusBall winner and I would love to star you and Katherine. I don't want to go into a lot of details on the phone. Can we arrange for a time to meet? I can come by your apartment in the morning if that works for you."

"Hold on a second, Maria. I'll be right back." He put his phone on mute and looked at Kat.

"She wants to come by the apartment in the morning and tell us about the show. Is that okay with you?" His hand holding the phone trembled a little, while he waited for her response.

Kat rolled her eyes. "Okay, but not too early. Let's hear what she has to say."

Michael put the phone back on unmute. "Maria, are you free at 11:00 tomorrow morning?"

"Sure, 11:00 A.M. would be great. Give me your address."

Michael gave her directions for getting to their building and hung up. He could hardly wait until tomorrow.

MARIA

Maria's calves were aching by the time she reached the sixth-floor walk-up where Michael and Katherine lived. She knocked on the door and waited impatiently for someone to answer.

This was her chance to get them to sign the contract, agreeing to be on the show, and she was determined to get their signatures as soon as possible.

Michael answered the door.

"Hi, Maria, good to see you again," he said, holding out his hand.

"Good to see you too Michael," she responded with a firm handshake.

Up close, he was even better looking than he had looked at the BonusBall press conference.

"Come on in," he said, holding the door open wider. Maria saw Katherine standing behind him, with a slight frown on her face.

'Time to turn on the charm,' thought Maria.

"Katherine, hi!" she said, "It's very good to see you again." She held out her hand. Katherine hesitated before shaking it.

"Hi, Maria, please call me Kat."

"Of course, Kat. How are you doing, now that the press conference is over?"

Maria didn't bother listening to Kat's response. She was busy checking out the tiny studio apartment and thinking about how it would look on camera. The studio was no bigger than 700 square feet. It just had room for a raggedy futon, a coffee table, a small dinette table with two chairs and a kitchen no larger than a hall closet.

It would be a total rags-to-riches story if she could contrast their current digs with the palace she hoped they would buy, now that they were rich.

'I would watch the shit out of that,' she thought to herself gleefully.

"Why don't you sit down?" said Michael, guiding her over to the futon. He pulled the two kitchen table chairs over, so they were facing her. He sat in one chair and waved his hand to indicate Kat should sit in the other chair.

"Please tell us about this show," he said with a big smile on his face.

'Showtime!' Maria thought to herself, as she smiled back.

"The name of the show is *Lucky*, and we want to focus on the life of a BonusBall winner. In your case, it would be focused on the two of you, since you're both winners. We want to show how your lives will change, now that you're rich.

"Currently, we have the greenlight for a pilot. If A+M likes what they see, they'll give us approval to shoot the remaining twelve episodes for broadcast."

"What would A+M be looking for?" asked Michael. "What would convince them to broadcast the rest of the show?"

"They want to see great TV," said Maria. "What interests viewers is stories

– they'll want to see what it's like for someone to live out the fantasy of being super rich. Our viewers will want to see how you and Kat change as a result of winning all that money."

"But I don't think we'll change," exclaimed Kat with a startled look on her face. "Not really. We'll still be ourselves but with a lot more money."

'What planet does she live on?' Maria thought as she plastered an insincere smile on her face.

"Maybe you won't change where it really counts Kat," said Maria talking slowly, as if to a child. "But your circumstances are going to change. I mean, are you planning on staying in this apartment?"

"Of course not," Michael said. He wrinkled his nose as he looked around the small space. "We plan on finding a new home as soon as the money comes through."

"Our viewers will want to go through that house hunting process with you. What are you planning on getting? A loft in Soho? A penthouse on Park Avenue? A mansion in Greenwich, Connecticut?"

"We haven't really talked about it yet," said Kat, "but I'm not sure I want a camera filming us as we look for a new home. To be honest, I don't know if being on a reality show is right for us."

Maria's heart sank. This was her biggest fear: that the winners wouldn't agree to be on the show. She looked at Michael, to see if he felt the same way. He was looking at Kat with his mouth set in a grim line.

"Maria," he said, "Kat and I are not on the same page about this. I'm very interested in being on the show."

He was on board. Now Maria just needed to convince Kat.

"Kat, what's your objection to being on the show? Let's talk about it."

Maria shifted her butt on the uncomfortable futon.

"I'm a very private person and I don't like having my picture taken."

Maria looked at Kat objectively for a moment. She wasn't a looker, like Michael, but she wasn't bad either.

"Why don't you like having your picture taken Kat? You're a very attractive woman." Maria figured it wouldn't hurt to butter her up.

"I guess I never like the way the photos come out," admitted Kat, tucking a lock of hair behind an ear.

"You've probably never been shot by a professional," said Maria. "We can team you with a videographer who can make you look really good."

"That's what I've been trying to tell her," said Michael, jumping in. "Kat is really pretty and she shouldn't shy away from letting other people see it." He leaned over and stroked Kat's arm.

Kat gave him a smile. "It's not just about how I look in photos. I hate the idea of letting everyone in the world learn about our personal business. Michael's the one who wants to be famous, not me."

"You want to be famous?" Maria turned to look at Michael who seemed a little embarrassed.

"I'm an actor. It's not so much that I want to be famous as I'm hoping exposure on a show like this could lead to other roles."

So he was an actor? That explained a lot.

"Being on *Lucky* could definitely raise your profile," said Maria. "If we build an audience and you get to be well known, it could really help your career."

"That's what I think too," said Michael, "but Kat doesn't feel the same way."

"Michael, that's not fair!" said Kat. "I do want to help your career. I'm just not sure that we have to be on a reality show to help it."

"I have an idea," said Maria. "We've only budgeted for a single camera person. What if we shot the show around Michael? Kat, we could limit your exposure on camera to those times when you're interacting with your husband."

It seemed like the perfect solution. They wouldn't need to get a second camera person and they could focus on Michael. He was really the one with star quality. Kat's time on camera could be limited.

Michael started beaming. "What do you say, Kat? I'll be the one they're following around. You can maintain some privacy when we're not together."

"I don't know," said Kat, biting down on her lip. "I would still be on camera when Michael and I are in the same place. I was planning on being together a lot, now that I don't need to work."

"There are lots of times when we're not together," said Michael. "When I'm in class, when I go to the gym and when I go on auditions. Now that we have money to fly, I can go to auditions in Los Angeles, in addition to auditions in New York. Maybe even London. We won't be together when I'm on the road."

Kat looked dismayed and Maria wished she had a camera person with her to capture Kat's face.

"I didn't realize you were planning on traveling for auditions," said Kat slowly. "Maybe we can go together."

"We aren't joined at the hip," said Michael, leaning away from Kat. "Plus, if I travel alone a lot, you won't need to be on camera as much. Maybe they can even shoot the whole show without you, if you really don't want to be on camera."

"That's an idea," said Maria, thinking it over. "Of course, we would want to put cameras where Michael lives. Kat, what do you think about getting a separate apartment, just while we shoot the show? Michael could come visit you in your apartment and we wouldn't film him, but we could get footage while he's in his apartment."

Kat looked upset. "I don't want to live in his-and-her apartments. Michael and I live together."

Maria pursed her lips. "It will be hard to get the video we need if the two of you are together and we can't shoot you too. I don't see how this is going to work."

Michael stood up and walked over to Kat and started massaging her shoulders.

"So say yes to the show, Kat. We'll live in the same place and people can see that we have a great relationship."

Kat's shoulders sagged under Michael's hands. Her face was a mask of indecision. Maria held her breath for a full minute while she waited for Kat to respond.

"I don't know," said Kat. "I don't really want to be on the show but I don't want to stand in your way Michael if this really could be good for your career."

"It could be just the career boost that I need. Please say yes." He looked at her like a little boy asking his parents for a puppy. She slowly smiled when she saw the look on his face.

"Okay, Michael. You win. We can be on the show."

Michael wrapped his arms around her, from behind, and gave her a hug. Maria felt like hugging her too.

"Thank you, Kat. It's going to be great, you'll see," said Michael.

Maria opened her briefcase and brought out the contract and the nondisclosure agreement. "Here is the contract and the NDA, giving us permission to shoot the pilot. Once we start filming, you agree not to discuss what we film with anyone. We'll be paying you $2,000 each for the pilot and $2,000 per episode if the show is picked up."

Maria laughed. "Not like you need the money, right?"

Michael grinned. "A month ago, $2,000 per episode would have seemed great, now it's just a rounding error."

That was exactly the type of attitude Maria was hoping for. If Michael considered $2,000 to be chump change, she would have an easy time getting him to spend on luxury items. She continued talking.

"Dan is our cameraman. We'll follow Michael around during the day and evening. We'll also put hidden cams in your home, to capture conversations if there are times when the Dan and I are not around."

"Do we really have to have hidden cams in our home?" Kat asked as Michael took the contracts out of Maria's hand and started looking at them.

"It's pretty standard and it's not like we'll have cameras in the bathroom," said Maria. "You won't be on camera 24/7 if that's what you're worried about. Plus, we edit out most of the footage."

Kat bit down on her lip and looked at Michael.

"Do you have a pen?" he asked Maria. Maria pulled a pen out of her briefcase and handed it to Michael.

"Michael! Don't you want to have a lawyer look over the contracts?"

"We don't even have a lawyer, Kat," said Michael. "I'm sure it will be fine. Maria – it's all pretty standard right?"

"It's mostly boilerplate," said Maria. "You give us the right to shoot you and we can use whatever footage we get."

"Don't we have editorial control?" asked Kat.

The small apartment was overheated and Maria could feel herself start to sweat a little.

"Not exactly, Kat," admitted Maria. "If you're not comfortable giving up control, we can just shoot Michael and make him the star of the show. Maybe we should consider the two apartments?"

Maria relaxed a little as she saw Michael start to sign the contracts.

"Sign here and here, Michael," Maria said, showing him the sticky notes with the arrows. "And initial here and here, and here."

"Your choice, Kat," said Michael, holding out the pen and the contract to her. "We can do this together or I can do it on my own, in my own apartment."

Kat sighed and reached out for the pen. "Where do I sign?"

Maria showed her the spaces on the contracts and Kat put her signature under Michael's.

Victory! Maria felt like dancing as she put the contract and NDA back in her briefcase.

"I'll bring Dan by tomorrow, and introduce him to you. We'll also send the electricians to wire up the house with the hidden cams. When do you get the money?"

"Probably not for another couple of weeks," said Michael.

"Great," said Maria. "That will give us some time to shoot you here. We'll want to show the contrast between your apartment and whatever home you wind up with. But don't start discussing your dream home until we're here tomorrow. We're going to want to capture the discussion."

"We won't," said Michael, giving her a big smile. Maria was thrilled just looking at him. He was going to be amazing and she had a feeling that *Lucky* was going to be a hit.

Maria stood up, glad to get off the futon that was putting her butt to sleep, and shook their hands before leaving quickly. Even though she had signed contracts, she didn't want to risk having Kat change her mind.

Outside their apartment door, she whipped out her phone and called her boss William.

"We're a go," she said and then hung up. She had so much to do, to get ready.

CHAPTER 6

KAT

Kat was somewhat anxious before book club on Tuesday night, because she worried about how her friends Jessica, Sharon and Angela were going to react to her winning the BonusBall. Standing in Jessica's hallway, she thought about some of the reactions she had been getting, after winning the money.

There had been Rufe, who wanted her to invest in his new agency. His happiness for her had been fueled by self-interest.

Her Uncle Charlie had jokingly asked if she would buy him a Rolls. At least, she hoped he had been joking.

And then there was her sister Ren. Ren seemed genuinely happy for her about the money, but deeply concerned when she heard about the reality show. Kat thought back to their phone call earlier that afternoon.

"Kat, how are you going to be on a reality show? You're a complete introvert!"

"It's the last thing I want to do, Ren but it's important to Michael because he thinks it could be good for his career. He'll be the focus of the show. I'll only be on camera when we're together."

"Isn't this just another example of you taking care of Michael's needs, without considering your own?"

"Why are you always so critical of him, Ren?"

"I want you to be happy, Kat. You've spent years supporting Michael, and his career, and sometimes he strikes me as selfish. I just hope he appreciates you."

"He does appreciate me. He loves me."

"I hope so, Kat."

Kat stopped thinking about her conversation with Ren, as she knocked on Jessica's door.

Jessica was grinning from ear to ear, as she opened the door and enveloped Kat in a big hug. Jessica's maternal hug reminded Kat of her mom.

"Kat! Congratulations! We are so happy for you. Come on in." Jessica stopped hugging her and stepped to the side so Kat could enter the apartment.

Kat looked at Sharon and Angela, who were seated on Jessica's couch. They jumped up when they saw Kat and came over to hug her.

"Oh my God, Kat," squealed Sharon, "It couldn't happen to a nicer person! We're thrilled for you!"

Kat looked at Angela, who had a big smile on her face. "Absolutely thrilled! How are you feeling? Come sit down and tell us everything." She grabbed Kat's hand and pulled her over to the couch.

Kat sat down on the couch. Jessica sat down next to her, while Sharon and Angela grabbed the chairs facing the couch. Jessica opened a bottle of champagne that was sitting in an ice bucket on the coffee table. After pouring, she handed each of them a champagne flute.

"To Kat!" she said, raising her flute in a toast.

"To Kat," said Sharon and Angela, raising their flutes as well.

"The first thing I want to know," said Jessica, after putting her flute down, "is where you and Michael were, when you bought the ticket?"

Kat paused for a moment, while she thought about what to say.

"We didn't actually buy the ticket together," she said slowly, while looking down at the couch instead of looking at her friends. "We just told the lottery people that so they would award the prize to both of us, instead of just me.

Michael was threatened by the idea of having a rich wife that he was completely dependent on. By having the lottery administrators award the money to both of us, he feels like we're really sharing it."

Angela stopped smiling. "Didn't you tell us that Michael has a green card?"

"Yes," said Kat, wondering where Angela was going with the discussion.

"Currently, U.S. husbands and wives can give each other unlimited amounts of money without any tax implications. But I think the tax laws are different for foreign nationals. Maybe it's good that you said you both bought the ticket. That way, they'll divide the money between the two of you. Otherwise, all the money would be in your name."

"So where were you when you bought the ticket?" asked Jessica.

"It was at a bodega, on the way to work," said Kat, feeling relieved that they stopped talking about how the money would be divided. "I gave the woman at the counter my lucky numbers."

"Lucky being the operative word in that sentence," said Sharon with a big smile.

"So what now?" asked Angela, "What are you going to do in your retirement?"

"There are two things I want to do," said Kat as she started to smile again. "I want to write a novel and I want to have children."

"What type of novel do you want to write?" asked Sharon. "Do you have a premise yet?"

"Not really a premise, more of a germ of an idea," said Kat. "I was hoping to get your feedback, since you work in publishing."

"Let's hear your idea," said Jessica.

"Before I quit my job," said Kat, "they had me working on a Barbie Twitter feed."

"No wonder you quit," said Angela, laughing. "I would quit too."

"Yeah, it wasn't my favorite assignment but while I was doing some research, I came across an article about a woman who turned herself into a human Barbie."

"What do you mean, a human Barbie?" asked Sharon.

"Hold on a sec," Kat pulled out her phone and searched for 'human Barbie'. She held up a picture for the group to see. The picture showed a young woman who looked eerily like a Barbie doll, right down to the heavy eye makeup, tiny nose and impossibly small waist.

"I think that is the sickest thing I've ever seen," said Jessica, frowning. "Who does that to themselves?"

"I know, right?" said Kat. "That's what I want to write about. The story of a woman who starts out normal and turns herself into a human Barbie."

"Do you have an antagonist?" asked Sharon, leaning forward on her chair. Kat was pleased to see she looked interested.

"Not yet," admitted Kat. "That's why it's just a germ of an idea. But now that I have time, I can work on the concept. It's an amazing feeling, knowing that I can do whatever I want to do, instead of being tied down to a job."

"Cheers to that!" said Jessica, raising her flute in Kat's direction.

"And you guys are going to start your family?" said Angela. "How many kids do you want to have? Boys or girls?"

"I don't know," said Kat with a smile. "I would love to have a little boy, but I guess I would be happy with either gender, as long as the baby is healthy."

"The day I gave birth to Isaiah was the happiest day of my life," said Angela with a big smile. "Fingers crossed that you'll have more good news for us soon!"

"Are you going to move out of your apartment?" asked Jessica, as she stood up and refilled their flutes.

Kat's happy mood immediately took a nosedive as she remembered Maria and how she wanted to shoot Kat and Michael looking for a new place to live.

"I forgot to tell you guys about the other thing I'll be doing. Michael and I have agreed to be on a reality TV show." Kat stopped smiling and started running her finger around and around the rim of her flute.

"A TV show?" said Jessica with surprise. "Tell us about it."

"This producer came up to us after the BonusBall press conference. The name of the show is *Lucky* and they want to show how someone's life changes after winning the BonusBall.

I wasn't interested but Michael thought the exposure could be good for his career, so we've agreed to be on it. He'll be the one they'll follow around with the camera. They'll only shoot me when Michael and I are together.

They only have the greenlight for a pilot, so I'm hoping they decide not to keep filming after the first episode."

"If you didn't want to be on it, why did you agree to it"?" Jessica asked gently.

"Michael made it clear that he was going to do the show with or without me. The producer suggested that we live in separate apartments, if I didn't agree to be on it. I didn't want to be separated, while they filmed the show, so I said yes."

"The producer actually suggested separate apartments?" said Jessica, sounding shocked. "What an absurd idea!"

"When do they start shooting?" Sharon asked.

"The producer is bringing the cameraman around tomorrow, and they're going to put hidden cameras in the apartment, so it looks like they plan to get started right away."

"Let's just hope that the pilot is so boring, they decide not to shoot the rest of the episodes," said Angela.

"To a boring pilot," said Sharon, raising her glass in a toast.

"To a boring pilot," the group responded, raising their glasses too.

"So you didn't answer my question," said Jessica. "Are you going to look for a new place to live?"

"Yes," Kat's mood started to brighten again. "We're going to start looking even before the money is deposited into our account."

"What will you be looking for?" asked Sharon.

"I don't know," said Kat. "Michael and I are going to talk about it tomorrow. The producer wants to capture our discussion for the show. I just want a place with enough bedrooms for kids."

The group spent the rest of the evening discussing their dream homes, hoping to give Kat some ideas. By the end of the night, Kat still wasn't sure what type of house she wanted to buy, but she knew that no matter what changes the money would make in her life, she wouldn't be changing her friends.

MARIA

Maria knocked on Michael and Kat's door at 8:00 A.M., with Dan and the two electricians standing behind her.

"Start shooting," she instructed Dan, while she waited for Michael or Kat to answer the door.

"Rolling," he answered, pointing his handheld cam towards the front door.

Maria was pleased to see that Michael answered the front door. Although it was early, he looked like he just stepped out of the pages of a Ralph Lauren ad. His navy blue V-neck sweater showed off his broad shoulders. He wore faded jeans on his long legs and brown loafers with blue and white striped socks.

"Maria, great to see you! Come on in." He opened the door so they could enter.

Maria saw Kat as they entered the studio. She was also wearing jeans and a blue sweater but she didn't make it look as good as Michael did.

"Kat, Michael, I want to introduce you to Dan. He will be our cameraman while we shoot *Lucky.*"

"It's very nice to meet you," Dan said, smiling at both of them. He put down the camera to shake their hands. "While I'm shooting, I want you to ignore me – just forget I'm even here. At first it may seem a little strange to have me around but you'll get used to it pretty soon."

"I doubt it," said Kat, rolling her eyes while Dan picked up the camera again.

Maria decided to ignore Kat's comment. "These two men are electricians. They're here to install the hidden cams in the apartment. I suggest we get out of the apartment while they work. I noticed a diner down the street. Do you want to get breakfast?"

"Breakfast sounds great," said Michael, smiling in the direction of the camera. "I haven't eaten yet. Kat, is that okay with you?"

"Where will they be putting the hidden cams?" asked Kat, instead of responding to the breakfast suggestion.

"We want to get a 360-degree view of the apartment," said Maria, "so we'll be positioning them to view the front door, the dining table, the kitchen and the futon. Everywhere except the bathroom."

"But the futon is where we sleep," exclaimed Kat with a dismayed look on her face. "We won't have any privacy."

"Kat, that's what we agreed to," said Michael, massaging Kat's shoulders. "Don't worry. It's not like they're making sex tapes."

"Yes," agreed Maria. "We're not HBO. *Lucky* will be PG entertainment.

We'll edit out anything that would be inappropriate."

"But I don't want an editor to see us making love, even if it doesn't get broadcast."

Maria felt irritated. Was Kat going to be difficult about everything? For a moment she was sorry that they agreed to have both of them in the show, instead of just him.

"Kat, please don't worry," she said soothingly. "Our editors are total professionals and there's nothing they haven't seen before."

"Maybe they've seen other people having sex," said Kat, shrugging Michael's hands off her shoulders, "but I don't want them to see us having sex, no matter how professional they are."

Michael turned to face her. "Kat, it will be okay," he said. "We can keep the lights down low, or we can make sure we're under the covers when we're fooling around."

Maria was pleased to see that Dan was filming the argument but she noticed that the electricians seemed to be getting impatient just standing around.

"Maybe we should just stop fooling around, if you would rather be on camera all the time," snapped Kat. "Is that what you want?" She shot Michael a dirty look.

"Of course not, Kat, don't be ridiculous," said Michael, frowning at her.

Maria smiled. First day and already there was drama.

"After a day or two, you'll forget the cameras are even there," she said, noticing that Kat was scowling.

She turned to Dan. "Close-up on Kat." He moved the camera to within three feet of her face.

Kat waved an arm, as if to swat away Dan. "Are you serious? How am I going to forget about the cameras with him in my face like this?"

"Trust me, you'll get used to it," said Maria soothingly. "Just give it a chance, Kat."

"I don't want to give it a chance," said Kat.

"But this is what we agreed to, when we signed the contract," said Michael. "You agreed to be on the show. We don't want to be in breach of contract on day one."

Kat threw up her hands in disgust. "Okay, fine. You win as usual, Michael. Wire up the whole apartment and capture every private moment if that's what you want. Just don't expect me to feel romantic any time soon."

"It's going to be okay, Kat. I promise," said Michael. "Soon, you won't even notice the cameras are around."

'Thank God Michael has a clue,' Maria thought to herself. 'I can work with him, even if Kat turns out to be a problem.'

She spent a few minutes giving instructions to the electricians about where she wanted the cameras before turning back to Kat and Michael. They were standing, facing each other, scowling. She was glad to see that Dan was filming both of their angry faces.

"So how about breakfast?" she said brightly. "Let's start talking about the new home you want to buy." She still had her coat on and was starting to get too warm in the overheated apartment.

Kat and Michael got their coats and followed her downstairs and outside, with Dan shooting them as they walked. She was disappointed to notice they weren't talking to each other but hoped she could do something with the footage of their argument in the apartment.

They passed a deli with a sign for the NY Lottery out front. That reminded Maria about a beat she needed to shoot.

"Listen," she said. "Could I ask you guys to go inside and buy a BonusBall ticket, using your winning numbers?"

"Why," asked Kat with an exasperated look on her face. "Do you think we'll win again?"

"Of course not," said Maria. "It's just that we weren't able to film you purchasing the winning ticket and we want to recreate that moment for our viewers. It will only take a couple of minutes."

"We don't mind," said Michael jovially. "Do we, Kat? Let's buy a ticket and then we can go get breakfast."

It took more than a couple of minutes because Maria had to get people inside the deli to sign waivers, agreeing to be on camera, but they were finally ready. Kat and Michael bought a new BonusBall ticket, with Michael giving the woman behind the counter their winning numbers.

Once the ticket was purchased, they left the deli and walked to the diner, a few blocks down the street from Michael and Kat's apartment. It was old-fashioned, with a long Formica counter framed by stools, and red leather booths. This time of morning, it was crowded with people eating eggs and bacon, and enjoying coffee.

"Give me a sec," said Maria while they waited to be seated. She went up to the manager and the waitress and gave them agreements to be on camera. The waitress seemed particularly pleased to sign the waiver.

"I'm an actress," she said happily to Maria, giving her a big smile.

"Of course you are," Maria said.

She got Kat and Michael settled into a booth, while she stood next to Dan, facing them. The other patrons seemed interested for a few minutes, but being jaded New Yorkers soon stopped paying attention to the filming.

"Do you want to order a beer with breakfast?" Maria suggested. It wouldn't hurt to loosen Kat up a little.

"No thanks," said Michael, "I'm just waking up."

"I'll just have coffee," said Kat, looking at Maria as if she had lost her mind. "It's pretty early in the day for a beer."

'Bummer,' thought Maria. 'No harm in trying,'

Kat and Michael gave their orders to the waitress, who kept positioning herself in front of the camera. After letting them drink their coffee for a few minutes, Maria thought it was time to get started.

"Why don't you tell us about the new home you want to buy," she asked them. "Tell us what it feels like to be able to get any home you want. Michael, what do you want?"

Maria's goal was to give them prompts, to get the conversation flowing. Later, the editor working on *Lucky* would edit out Maria's questions, leaving the discussion between Kat and Michael.

"I've been thinking a lot about this," said Michael excitedly, grabbing Kat's hands in his. "What do you think about a huge loft in Soho? Imagine one vast space with twenty-foot ceilings, hardwood floors, white pillars and a huge wall of windows. We could fill it with artwork and it would be amazing. I've already been looking at spaces on Realtor.com."

Maria was happy to see Kat looked dismayed. "Eyes on Kat," she whispered to Dan. He moved the camera in a little closer.

"I was thinking about a house," Kat said to Michael. "Someplace with rooms for our children and a lawn for them to play on."

Michael laughed. "Kat, we don't have children yet. We have plenty of time to buy a house later. I want to enjoy being young and rich in the city. A loft would be perfect. Think about the parties we could throw."

"Michael, we're not in our twenties. I don't want a space for throwing parties. I want a home where we can grow old together."

"So what were you thinking?" said Michael, frowning slightly as he sipped his coffee.

"I was thinking we could buy a house in Westchester, close to where my uncle lives. Maybe a place in Scarsdale? It's only a forty-minute train ride to Grand Central."

"Kat, I don't want to become a commuter," said Michael. "I still need to be in the city for classes and auditions."

"Why don't you buy both?" prompted Maria, hoping to get them to start spending. "You could have a loft in the city for during the week and go to Scarsdale on the weekends."

"We could do that," said Michael slowly, as if thinking aloud. "Kat, you can go to Scarsdale on the weekends if you want to. I would probably prefer to stay in the city. I have no interest in the suburbs."

"That's no good," said Kat, looking upset. "We need a place where we stay together, not where I go alone on weekends."

"Here's your breakfast," said the waitress cheerily as she came by with the dishes. She turned to face Dan and the camera and gave him a big smile.

"I have a Western omelet for you," she said, putting the plate down in front of Michael. "And scrambled eggs and toast for you." She put Kat's breakfast down in front of her. She turned to face the camera again.

"Can I get you anything else? Maybe more coffee?"

'You can get out of the way,' thought Maria with annoyance. 'You are so getting edited out of this clip.' There was conflict over the new home and this stupid twat had interrupted the discussion. She just hoped she could get the conversation back on track.

"So Kat, what did you want in a new home?" Maria prompted.

"We can get a home in the city, if you don't want to be in the suburbs," said Kat to Michael, as she took a bite of her scrambled eggs, "but I want something with lots of rooms, instead of one big space."

"No loft?" said Michael, looking disappointed.

"No, let's look for something else. Maybe we could get a large condo. We can get one in Soho, if that's where you want to be."

"No, being in Soho was all about the loft. If we're not going to get a loft, I would probably rather be on the Upper East Side, close to Central Park."

"What about a penthouse?" suggested Maria. "Maybe the entire top floor of a building?"

"Yes, what about a penthouse, Kat?" Michael asked eagerly.

"I don't know, Michael," said Kat with a slight frown on her face, as she put down her fork. "How much were you thinking of spending?"

"That's the amazing thing, Kat, price is no object. We can afford anything we want!"

"I have a suggestion," said Maria. "I can team you guys up with a realtor to start looking at properties on the Upper East Side. "He or she can show you a range of places so you can decide what you want to get."

Maria would make sure that the realtor only showed them properties costing tens of millions. After they had seen the best, they wouldn't be satisfied with a three bedroom somewhere in the East 90's.

"What do you say, Kat?" said Michael with a big smile on his face. "Won't it be fun to start looking?"

Kat's face brightened. "Yes, it will be a lot of fun to start looking. Thank you for the suggestion Maria."

"Leave it all to me," said Maria. "I'll find you the best real estate agent in the city."

She would get the production assistants at 'One Ring to Rule Them All' productions working on it right away. She needed the most exclusive broker in the city, preferably one who was also photogenic.

CHAPTER 7

MICHAEL

Michael, accompanied by Dan and Maria, took a limo to his acting class on West 54th Street in the theatre district. Dan was filming Michael during the ride. Maria was asking Michael questions while the aggressive limo driver cut off traffic and beeped his horn, but Michael could barely hear her because he was so focused on the problem of Erica.

'What the fuck am I going to do?' he thought to himself as the limo pulled up to the building.

He was sure Maria would love a philandering twist for her reality TV show, but he wouldn't develop a loyal fan base if people saw him cheating on his wife.

The problem wasn't breaking up with Erica; it was how to do it without giving away, on camera, the fact that they had been sleeping together. He needed to talk to her after class, but wasn't sure what to say.

The acting class met in the studio space above a Thai restaurant. Michael led Maria and Dan through a side door and up the stairs to the second floor. The smell of green curry permeated the air as they climbed the steps.

When Michael walked through the door of the acting studio, with Dan and Maria trailing him, his classmates broke into spontaneous applause.

"It's our big winner!" Michael heard someone say. There was a Greek chorus of people wishing him congratulations. Michael spotted Erica in the far corner of the room. She was beaming at him.

"Michael, congratulations on winning the BonusBall!" Barry, his acting coach, came bounding up to him, to shake his hand. "What's with the camera?"

Michael spent a few minutes explaining about *Lucky* before Maria asked if the students in the class would mind signing waivers, agreeing to be on camera.

The other students were absolutely thrilled to sign the waivers. It took fifteen minutes to get everyone's signature, but Barry didn't seem to mind the delay in getting started.

As usual, Barry started the class with breathing and acting exercises, before they broke out into separate groups to practice the scenes they were working on.

"Michael, Erica, let's see that love scene that you've been working on," said Barry enthusiastically as he took a seat in front of the raised dais that served as a stage in the front of the room.

'This is going to be awkward,' thought Michael, wincing as he took his position and put his arms around Erica.

"Hey there," she whispered in his ear, before going into character. "Why don't we celebrate your win after class?"

Michael didn't answer her but started reciting his lines instead. Erica seemed surprised that he didn't respond to her invitation but she took his cue and said her lines. They worked through the scene, which culminated with a passionate kiss. As he kissed her full lips, Michael felt a momentary pang of regret at the idea of giving up Erica – she was the best lay ever.

"That was fantastic," said Barry as the class applauded. "You two have amazing chemistry together."

"Thanks, Barry," said Michael as he got down off the raised platform, the wooden boards bouncing a bit from his weight. He took one of the empty chairs facing the stage. Erica promptly sat down next to him.

"So what about after class?" she asked with a big smile, before the next scene started. "I've never fucked a multimillionaire before."

"We should talk, after class," said Michael. He noticed Dan zoomed in on the two of them and hoped the mic hadn't caught Erica's last comment. Michael could feel a bead of sweat, running down his neck.

The other students went through their scenes on the stage and all too quickly, the class was over.

"So what did you want to talk about?" said Erica, as the other students started leaving.

"Not here," said Michael, waving a hand around the studio space. "Let's wait until we get outside."

"Okay, we can wait," said Erica. She looked a little apprehensive. "Is everything okay?"

Michael didn't answer her as he walked out of the studio. They gathered their coats from the lockers in the hall outside the studio and took the stairs down to the street level. When they were outside the building, Michael turned to face Erica. He could see Dan was only three feet away, with Maria standing next to him.

"Erica, your friendship has meant a lot to me," Michael began slowly, taking one of Erica's gloved hands in his own. "But now that I'm being filmed all the time, I don't want Kat to misinterpret our friendship and become jealous. I think we should stop seeing each other after class."

Erica's eyes widened. "We're more than just friends, Michael." She pulled her hand out of his.

"I know you wanted to be more than just friends, Erica. I'm sorry if I ever gave you reason to believe that I had more than friendship to offer you."

'Please get it,' prayed Michael. 'And please don't cause a scene.'

Erica looked over at Dan and then slowly back at Michael. Michael could see she got it.

"So that's it? You become rich and famous and you want to dump me? Fuck you, Michael, you selfish prick."

"I wouldn't call it dumping you," said Michael desperately, "Erica, we can't be friends anymore. You know how insecure Kat is. I wouldn't want her to see footage of our friendship and come to the wrong conclusion. You know how jealous she gets."

Michael felt sorry to be breaking up with Erica. Not only was she phenomenal in bed, she understood his need to be an actor in a way that Kat never could. But with a camera following him all the time, a relationship with her was impossible. He needed to make a clean break.

"I bet she would come to the wrong conclusion if she could see footage of our 'friendship'," hissed Erica, as she took a step back from Michael. Tears started to glisten in the corners of her eyes.

"Dan, are you getting this?" Michael heard Maria say. Dan didn't respond but he moved the camera closer to Michael and Erica.

"Exactly," said Michael, "she might come to the wrong conclusion. I wouldn't want her getting upset." Even though it was cold outside, he was sweating heavily in his coat.

"You wouldn't want Kat getting upset?" said Erica, her voice rising in pitch, as the tears started rolling down her face. "What about me getting upset? Michael, I love you. I don't want to break up." She held her arms out to him.

Michael felt guilty but couldn't think of a way to comfort her without the camera capturing everything.

"Erica, I don't want to upset you. You've always known that I was married and couldn't offer you anything more than friendship."

Erica put her arms down and wiped her face.

"Fuck your friendship and fuck you, Michael. You don't want to be 'friends' anymore now that you have a camera following you around? Fine. We'll stop being friends. But I'm not giving up this acting class, so you're going to have to drop out if you want to stop seeing me." She turned to Dan.

"Get your camera out of my face," she said with disgust before walking quickly away.

"Michael, how do you feel about giving up Erica's friendship?" asked Maria as Dan zoomed in on Michael's face.

Michael wasn't paying attention to Maria's question. He was busy wondering if Barry would give him private acting lessons now that he had to drop the class.

KAT

Kat was apprehensive about working with a money manager but Michael seemed enthusiastic when Maria had pitched the idea, so she and Michael were meeting with Len Applebaum in his Park Avenue office on East 38th Street.

"You'll love Len," Maria had said. "He'll take care of everything, so you won't have to deal with money at all."

Len's waiting room was very tasteful, with a studded maroon leather couch and matching armchairs, and a glass coffee table with a selection of upscale magazines. A blue and red cubist oil painting of a woman's face hung on the wall, in back of the mahogany reception desk. Kat wondered if it was a Picasso.

'How much does this guy charge?' Kat worried, as she looked around. Len's attractive young assistant asked them to take a seat, before asking if they wanted water or coffee. Kat and Michael said no, but Maria asked for a glass of water.

After a few minutes, the door to the office opened and Len came out to welcome them. Kat was a little reassured when she looked at him. He reminded Kat of her Uncle Charlie – his suit was somewhat strained across his large stomach and he had white curls around the back and sides of his head, although he was bald on top. He had a pair of glasses perched on his nose and a big smile on his face as he shook their hands.

"So very nice to meet you, Michael and Katherine! Please call me Len. Come into my office."

He stopped smiling and nodded hello to Maria and Dan, with a slight frown on his face.

Kat and Michael walked into Len's office but Len blocked the doorway as Maria and Dan tried to follow them.

"Sorry but this meeting will just be Katherine, Michael and I. No cameras please. We'll be discussing their personal finances."

'I think I like this guy,' Kat thought approvingly.

"But our viewers are going to want to hear about the investment strategies you propose to Kat and Michael," protested Maria. "This could really help publicize your business."

"My investment practice is very exclusive," said Len, "and I don't need to publicize to find new clients. I won't sign a waiver agreeing to be on camera, so you wouldn't be able to use the footage even if I were to let you in my office. Sorry, but this meeting is going to be private. Please wait here."

With that, Len followed Kat and Michael into his office and closed the door in Maria and Dan's faces.

"Please sit down," he said, indicating the chairs in front of his desk. Len's office wasn't as luxurious as his waiting room. His desk was maple, as were the frames of the guest chairs which were upholstered in a blue plaid fabric instead of leather. He had a large bookcase and a wooden credenza which matched the desk. He had two monitors, positioned to one side of the desk, along with a phone. It was all neat but somewhat utilitarian.

"So let's talk about your goals," he said, as he seated himself at the desk and looked at them. "You're going to be very wealthy. What do you want to do with the money? Is the long term goal to make it grow?"

"We do want to make it grow in the long term," said Michael, "but we're also going to want to spend some of it."

"We can help you with both goals," said Len, smiling at the two of them. "We can put together a long term investment strategy designed to work with your risk tolerance and we can also help make any spending frictionless."

"What do you mean frictionless spending?" asked Kat. The very term made her nervous.

"We pay for everything, on your behalf, so you don't have the headaches. Just call us and we'll arrange the financing for whatever you want to purchase. If you hire staff, we'll pay their salaries. If you buy a house, we'll deal with all the paperwork. We handle your taxes. All your bills will come through us."

"That sounds great!" said Michael.

"I don't know," said Kat slowly. "It would be great to not have to deal with bills but how do we keep track of what we're spending?"

"Our office would send you an itemized report at the end of each month," said Len. "The first part of the report shows the spending for the previous month. The rest of the report shows your investment portfolio."

"How would you invest our money?" asked Kat. "I'm worried about bad investments."

"Totally understandable," said Len in a soothing tone of voice. "We discuss what level of risk you're comfortable with and invest accordingly. If you want less risk, we'll invest more in bonds and less in stocks. Your money won't grow as fast but you'll be more protected from the swings of the stock market."

"Less risk sounds good," said Kat in a somewhat shaky voice. She looked at Michael, hoping he would feel the same way. To her relief, he agreed.

"I'm with Kat," Michael said, nodding. "It would be great if our portfolio grows but we don't need to be aggressive about it. I would rather focus on safer investments."

"Then I would recommend a mix of 60 percent bonds and only 40 percent stocks," said Len. "And to make for even less risk, we'll invest in stock funds, rather than individual stocks. Stock funds invest in hundreds of stocks, which spreads out the risk more than owning individual stocks."

"I like the sound of that," said Michael. "What rate of return can we expect on our investment?"

"My clients, with a portfolio mix like the one I'm recommending for you, usually see around 6 percent returns annually, but to set expectations, I tell people not to expect more than 4 percent a year. That will allow for the fluctuations of the market."

"So how much can we expect a year?" Kat asked as she tried to do the math in her head.

"What are you expecting, after the taxes are taken out of the prize money?" Len asked as he pushed his glasses further up the bridge of his nose. He looked at them expectantly.

"The woman at the BonusBall claims center said we could expect around $112 million," said Kat.

"Let's see," said Len, pulling a calculator out of a desk drawer. "If you get a 4 percent rate of return on $112 million, you can expect $4.4 million a year."

Kat was thrilled. The portfolio was so large that they could buy anything they wanted with the interest alone. They wouldn't need to touch the principal at all.

"Yes, but don't forget," said Michael, "We won't be investing the full $112 million. We'll be using some of the prize money for purchases, like a new place to live. Our portfolio will actually be smaller."

"How much were you thinking of setting aside for purchases?" asked Len, smiling at the two of them. The idea that they wouldn't be investing the full amount didn't seem to faze him at all.

"I don't know, maybe half?" said Michael.

Kat's jaw dropped. "Are you serious?" she said to Michael as her voice squeaked. "What do you think we'll be purchasing that we would need to spend $56 million?"

Michael turned to her with an impatient look on his face. "Kat, we're going to be in the top 1 percent. I want to live in a place that reflects that. I'm not looking to just purchase a two-bedroom apartment on the Upper East Side.

"If we can't get a loft, I think we should buy a penthouse. Those places cost serious money. I'm going to want to get more than one home, and maybe a jet to fly from one home to another. All of that will cost money. We can spend $56 million and still have $56 million left over to invest.

"Len, what's the rate of return on $56 million?"

"That would be $2.2 million a year," said Len, as he tapped at his calculator again.

"See Kat, we can spend $56 million and still make a fortune each year on our investments."

"Michael, it's irresponsible to spend so much," Kat protested, her head spinning.

"It seems clear that the two of you need to discuss this further," said Len smoothly. "Here's what we can do. We'll invest $56 million in bonds and stock funds and put $56 million in a money market account, where the interest rate will be approximately 1.6 percent. The $56 million will still earn a healthy income while you decide what to do with it. If you want to spend it, the money is there. If you decide not to spend all of it, we can roll the remainder back into your investment portfolio."

"What do you think, Kat?" asked Michael. "Does that sound like a plan you can live with?"

"I guess so," Kat said, although she didn't really feel reassured. Spending $56 million seemed insane to her. She didn't want to be the voice of no, every time Michael wanted to buy something, but it looked like she was going to have to keep a close eye on the spending when Len sent out his monthly report.

"Do you have additional questions about the services our firm can provide?" Len asked, smiling at the two of them. He folded his hands as he put them on his desk.

Kat thought about the maybe-Picasso in the waiting room.

"What do you charge for your services?" she asked apprehensively. If Len was going to take care of investments and paying all the bills, she bet his services didn't come cheap.

"We charge on a sliding scale, according to a percentage of the assets we manage for you. The larger the portfolio, the smaller percentage we charge," he explained.

"For portfolios of $10 million to $50 million, we charge 1 percent a year. For portfolios of $50 million to $100 million, we charge 0.5 percent a year. Since your portfolio is over $100 million, we would charge the lowest percentage of 0.25 percent a year."

"But that's over $250,000 a year," said Kat in dismay. She didn't need a calculator to figure out the fee.

"True," said Len confidently, "but our goal is to make your money grow. The larger we grow your portfolio, the more you pay us, so our interests are aligned. Unlike some other financial planners, we're not paid on commission, so you can trust us not to invest in something unless it's in your best interests."

"Can we think about it?" asked Kat. "Do you have any references we can talk to?"

"Of course," said Len. "It's a big decision, so take all the time you need. I can ask my assistant to get you the number of some clients who have agreed to be references. We can have you talk to Billy Samuelson."

"The quarterback?" said Michael with a big grin, "We would be happy to talk to him. Do you have any other references?"

"Yes," said Len. "You could also talk to Alina Cox, the actor." Michael sat up straighter in his chair.

"I don't know Alina," said Kat. "What's she been on?"

"You do know her," said Michael. "She's the lead on that show *Copycat*."

"Oh, right," said Kat. Now that she thought about it, the name did ring a bell.

"Finally, we'll get you the number of Scott Wilton."

"The New York Times bestselling author?" said Kat, feeling a bit more enthusiastic. "I would be happy to call him – I love his books!"

"So call the references and think it over," said Len, patiently. "We're not going anywhere. I would be happy to work with the two of you, if you decide this is right for you."

He got up from behind the desk and ushered the two of them out of his office, before shaking their hands to say goodbye.

"So how did it go?" said Maria, as soon as they got out of the door, Dan was filming them, while walking backward.

"Well, we still need to check references," said Michael, smiling for the camera, "but assuming everything checks out, I think we've found our money manager. Right, Kat?" He turned and looked at Kat.

Kat was still uneasy but she realized that it had more to do with Michael wanting to spend $56 million, and less to do with Len. She didn't have any real objections to Len – his easy demeanor inspired confidence. She hated the idea that it would cost a quarter of a million dollars a year to retain his services but she guessed you had to spend money to make money.

"Right, Michael," she opted to look at him and not at Dan. "I think we've found our money manager."

CHAPTER 8

KAT

According to New York Magazine, Tremors was the hottest restaurant in New York City, at the moment, and Kat had been happy when Maria had been able to pull a few strings and get them a reservation to celebrate their BonusBall win, on Friday night.

"You'll be in one of the private dining rooms," explained Maria, "and the chef will prepare an exclusive tasting menu."

Ren and her boyfriend, Dylan, would be meeting them at the restaurant. At Maria's insistence, a stretch limo went to Yonkers to pick up her Uncle Charlie and her Aunt Jan, before driving to the apartment building to pick up Kat, Michael, Dan and Maria. After Kat introduced her uncle and aunt to Dan and Maria, they all got into the limo. Once they were inside the luxe black leather interior, Maria poured them all a glass of champagne while Dan filmed them making a toast.

"To winning," said Kat with a grin, raising her glass.

"To winning," the group responded, raising their glasses in response.

Kat glanced at her Uncle Charlie. He had a crown of white curls but was balding on top, and she noticed he had on his best suit. Even at 64, although a little chubby, he was still a good looking man. He caught her looking at him.

"How's our kitten?" he said, giving her his signature wink and a smile.

"I'm doing good, Uncle Charlie," she said, smiling back, before looking out the window, as they drove in the limo, west to Hudson Yards.

'Is this really my life now?' Kat thought happily.

At 7:00 P.M. on a Friday night, the traffic was terrible, but they were immune from the noise of the streets in their cocoon of luxury. Kat looked out the window at the skyscrapers that were all lit up and the pedestrians rushing by. She loved New York, especially at night.

'Maybe Michael is right about not moving out to the suburbs,' she thought. 'We can afford to have children and stay in Manhattan.'

The restaurant was in an old converted warehouse, with a wall of lighted windows facing the street. A discrete green awning was over the door with the word "Tremors" written in gold lettering.

They entered the restaurant and Maria gave her name to the hostess in the reception area, who then escorted them to the private dining room. As they walked through the restaurant, Kat noticed the soaring ceiling and the green walls with antique maps in gold frames. The lighting fixtures were large glass globes, encased in golden cages. The restaurant was packed, every table full, and the noise of the diners echoed throughout the space.

Once they were seated in the private dining room, it was quiet again. Kat looked happily around the room, which had bouquets of fresh flowers on the table, on the sideboard, and standing in large vases in the corners of the room. Although it was November outside, she felt like she just walked into spring.

The hostess seated the six of them, while Dan and Maria stood, facing the table.

"Don't mind us," Dan said from behind the camera. "Just pretend we're not here."

"Here is the tasting menu our chef will be preparing for you this evening," said the hostess, handing each of them a printed card with gold edging. "I'll send in our sommelier to help you with your wine pairings."

The sommelier came and made several suggestions, which the group agreed to.

"And please bring a bottle of your best champagne with dessert," added Michael. "We're celebrating."

"Very good, sir," said the sommelier. "We have a Charles Heidsieck Brut champagne. It has a noticeable citrus note, on both the nose and the palate, which I think you'll find very pleasing."

"That sounds great, thank you," said Michael. He looked very happy.

"This is amazing," said Kat's uncle, looking around the room. He seemed impressed by their surroundings. "Thank you for inviting us."

"It's our pleasure," said Kat. She smiled as she looked at her family gathered around the table.

"Yes, thank you," said Aunt Jan. She was a small dark-haired woman with bright, inquisitive eyes which widened as she looked around the luxurious private dining room. "This is very fancy."

Before Kat could respond to her Aunt Jan, a waiter brought the first course of crudo, which included razor clams, tuna belly, scallops and sea urchin. It was delicious.

The crudo was followed by a radicchio salad and Chilean sea bass. The group started talking about their plans for Thanksgiving.

"You guys should come to our house in Yonkers," said Uncle Charlie.

"I think we're going to be with Dylan's family this year," said Ren regretfully. "But maybe we can come at Christmas?"

"Not a problem," said Uncle Charlie, "although we'll miss you!"

"We'll be there – right, Michael?" said Kat.

"Of course," said Michael. "Do you want us to have the meal catered?"

"I think your Aunt Jan was planning on cooking the meal," said Charlie looking over at Jan for confirmation.

"That's okay," said Jan, while beaming at Michael. "If Michael wants to have the meal catered, that's fine with me. I don't really cook much. Charlie and I usually eat takeout."

"So that's settled," said Michael. "Just let us know how many people and we'll find a caterer."

"Thank you very much. That will be fantastic," said Jan. "Now if you could only do something about the size of our dining room."

"What do you mean?" Kat asked in surprise. Aunt Jan had always been able to host large Thanksgiving dinners by bringing in an extra folding table, which extended from the dining room into the hallway. Some of the kids, at the kids table, were actually sitting in the hall but it was family and no one seemed to mind.

"Our dining room is so small and dark," complained Jan. "Actually, the whole house is so small and dark. And Yonkers has become so down-market."

"Jan, stop," said Uncle Charlie, looked embarrassed.

"No, Charlie, let me finish. Kat, we were thinking now that you and Michael are so rich, maybe you could help us out by getting us a new house."

"Uncle Charlie, is that what you want?" said Kat, feeling dismayed. She loved her Uncle Charlie's house. It never seemed small and dark to her.

"No, kitten, I'm perfectly happy in our house." He turned to Jan with a frown on his face.

"Jan, stop. I want Kat and Michael to focus on getting their new home, not a house for us. We're fine in Yonkers."

Jan pouted. "But we could live someplace much nicer, like on the Hudson River in Dobb's Ferry. They're so rich now that it won't make a dent in their net worth."

"Jan, I said stop," said Kat's uncle, raising his voice.

"It just seems selfish for them not to share the wealth," insisted Jan, laying down her utensils.

"We don't mind helping out if you want a new house," said Michael. Kat wished he had kept his mouth shut because his comment seemed to energize Jan.

"See," she said to Charlie, raising her voice in return. "They don't mind and we could find someplace bigger with a view."

Kat's uncle put down his napkin. "That's it, we're leaving Jan. We'll discuss this at home."

"No, Uncle Charlie, please don't go," pleaded Kat. They had been having such a wonderful time before Aunt Jan spoiled the evening. "We won't get you a new house, if that's not what you want."

"We'll stay," agreed Kat's uncle, "but only Jan shuts up about a new house – can you do that, Jan?"

All eyes turned towards Jan, including Dan's camera.

"Okay, I'll stop talking about it tonight," said Jan reluctantly. "But Charlie, this conversation isn't over."

"Yes, it is," said Kat's uncle, looking furious. He put his napkin back on his lap and resuming eating.

They discussed neutral topics, like the weather, during the rest of dinner. The remaining courses were wonderful, but Kat's enjoyment of the meal had been ruined.

'We don't even have the money yet,' she thought sadly, 'and so many people have their hands out.'

She thought about the letters which had been arriving lately, in the mail, from desperate people begging for money. She read them all, and some of the letters broke her heart.

'I want to do more with this money than buy houses,' she thought. 'I want to do some good with it. Something that will make a difference in people's lives.'

She made up her mind to talk to Michael about donating some of the money to charity, once the funds were available in their account. Just the thought of it helped to brighten her mood again.

"Who gets the check?" the waiter asked, as they were finishing up their desserts and champagne.

"I'll take it," said Michael, holding out his hand for the bill. Glancing over his shoulder, Kat was stunned to see the amount was over $3000 for the six of them.

'I hope the money comes through soon,' she thought nervously. The amounts they had been charging to the American Express card were really starting to add up.

———

Kat was somewhat intimidated when she saw the realtor Maria recommended, at the offices of the Corcoran Group the next day.

Carley Cavanaugh looked straight out of central casting: she was in her thirties, petite and almost too slender. She was dressed in a pink suit with a very short skirt, and beige Jimmy Choo's with three-inch heels. Her short brown hair was expertly highlighted and framed her elfin face. When she held out a perfectly manicured hand for Kat to shake, Kat was embarrassed by her own ragged cuticles.

"So very nice to meet you, Kat and Michael," she said warmly. "I understand you're looking for a new home?"

"Yes," said Michael as they were seated in front of Carley's desk, "We would like to find a new place as soon as possible."

Kat noticed Michael smiling at Carley and felt a pang of jealousy as she worried about whether he was checking her out.

"I would be happy to help you find your dream home. Why don't you tell me a bit about what you're looking for? Let's start with your budget. What is the range we should be looking in?"

"We don't really have a fixed budget in mind," said Michael. "Price is no object."

The professional smile Carley had on her face slipped for a second, replaced with a look of pure greed, but she quickly recovered.

"Well," she said pleasantly, "That gives us lots of options to work with.

Please tell me what you are thinking about. Are you looking for a duplex? A penthouse? A townhouse?"

"We want someplace that will be a home for a family," said Kat. "But I wouldn't say the budget is unlimited."

"How large is your family?" asked Carley.

"It's just the two of us," said Michael, a touch impatiently.

"Yes, but we plan on having children," said Kat. "We want a home that can handle a growing family."

"Are you looking for good schools or a specific neighborhood?"

"We were thinking about the Upper East Side," said Michael, "but we're open to the rest of the city if we find something perfect."

Carley picked an iPad off her desk and tapped on the screen a few times. "We have a number of beautiful homes I would be happy to show you. Do you want to take my Mercedes?"

"We need a car with enough room for Dan, myself and the camera," interrupted Maria, "so we have a limo waiting outside."

"Even better," said Carley smoothly, "Let's get started."

They exited the Corcoran offices and got into the waiting limo, where Maria insisted on pouring everyone a glass of sparkling rosé as Carley gave the address to the limo driver. Maria had suggested that Michael and Kat order a bottle of wine with lunch, earlier in the afternoon, and Kat was already feeling more than a little tipsy, as she quickly finished her glass of rosé in the limo.

It turned out that the first home on 62nd Street, off 5th Avenue, was only a couple of blocks away from the Corcoran offices.

"Our first home is a 1903 Beaux Arts landmark that was designed by John Duncan, the legendary architect of Grant's Tomb," said Carley with pride, as they got out of the car.

The white limestone building was impressive. Kat and Michael, trailed by Dan and Maria, followed Carley up the steps to a set of double glass doors that were covered in gilded filigree ironwork. Over the main entrance, there were ten-foot windows that opened to a small balcony which overlooked the street. Carley opened the front doors and ushered them inside.

"The property is approximately 15,000 square feet with six bedrooms and nine baths on six stories," said Carley, as Kat and Michael looked around the entrance hall.

The first thing Kat noticed was that the ceiling was over seventeen feet tall and the floors were a mosaic of white marble inlaid with small black rosettes. There was an enormous white fireplace which was taller than she was, with an elaborately carved malachite mantel. There was a magnificent marble staircase with more filigree ironwork for the banisters. The walls were white, with decorative carved white lintels over the doors leading out to the street. The only color in the hallway was a large romantic painting of a young girl in a white dress which filled one wall. There was no doubt that it was impressive, but Kat found the entrance cold instead of inviting.

"Let's view the downstairs quarters before I take you in the elevator upstairs," said Carley, leading them through a gallery with modern paintings before taking them into a vast living room with a baby grand piano in one corner and a crystal chandelier. The walls in the living room were covered in white striped silk, which matched the white modern, minimalist furniture with steel frames. There was one black leather couch, which helped to break up the white on white motif. The focal point of the room was the artwork over the white marble fireplace mantel. The painting reminded Kat of Edvard Munch's The Scream.

"As you can see, the building has been beautifully restored, with painstaking attention to detail – it's opulent but with ultra-modern amenities," Carley gushed, while walking them into the formal dining room. The dining room also had white walls and a massive round glass table with sixteen chrome and white chairs around it. White pillars were around the corners of the room, each holding a modern wire sculpture. The paintings on the walls looked as if the artist daubed charcoal on white canvases. As with the other rooms, there was a huge fireplace with a white marble mantel.

'Another cold room with white walls and furniture,' Kat thought to herself as she looked around.

"No surprise the architect did Grant's Tomb," said Kat. "This place is a mausoleum."

She noticed everybody staring at her. "Did I say that aloud?" she asked in surprise, suddenly embarrassed.

"Yes, you did," said Michael, sounding surprised. "This place is magnificent and we haven't even seen most of it– what possible objection could you have?"

"It's just that everything is white," said Kat. "There's no warmth. I can't imagine raising a family here."

"Don't let the furniture sway your decision," said Carley. "You can have your own designer bring in antiques, if that's more to your taste. You can make it very warm and homey." She sniffed as if the concept offended her.

"I can't see how any furniture is going to make that marble hallway homey," said Kat.

"Should I stop showing you around?" asked Carley. "There are many other properties we could look at, if this won't work for you."

"No!" exclaimed Maria. Everybody stopped and looked at her. "Our viewers are going to want to see the rest of the home. I'm sure it's very impressive – right, Carley?"

"Yes, it is impressive. You haven't seen the sauna or the rooftop entertainment terrace with the full outdoor kitchen. There's a closet in the master bedroom with lighted shelving for handbags, and a temperature controlled vault for furs."

"Oh my God," exclaimed Maria, as her eyes got wider. "Please, please, Kat, let's finish the tour."

"Please, Kat?" Michael pleaded. "I would really like to see the rest of the house, even if we don't wind up getting it. We can compare it to other homes on the market."

"How much is this house?" asked Kat.

"The price is $79,500,000," said Carley. "But it's been on the market nearly six months so I'm sure we can negotiate with the owner to bring the price down, if you want to make an offer."

"Eighty million dollars?" said Kat. "That's insane. There's no way I want to spend eighty million on a house."

"I'm sorry," said Carley, looking confused. "I thought price was no object."

"Price is no object," Michael said quickly, as if to reassure Carley. "We could afford to purchase this house if we wanted to, but it's not the right fit for Kat. We just need to keep looking. But, I really would like to see the rest of this house, if you don't mind giving us the tour."

"Of course I don't mind," said Carley smoothly, "but I don't want to waste your time if you're not interested."

"You won't be wasting our time," said Maria, "and we won't be wasting your time. The publicity of being on the show is bound to be good in helping sell this house."

"That could be true," said Carley thoughtfully. "I'll be happy to show you the rest of the house. Please follow me."

As promised, the rest of the house was impressive. Kat could see Michael practically drooling over the gym, and the indoor pool with the fitted glass rooftop to let in the daylight.

As they walked back outside, Carley told them about the heated sidewalks to melt the snow in the winter.

"Are you sure we couldn't work with a good designer, Kat?" Michael asked as they got back in the limo. "I'm sure we could make this house into a warm and welcoming place. We could fill it with antique wooden furniture and flowered prints."

She thought about paying $80 million for a house that seemed cold to her. Kat thought about children running and possibly falling on that hard marble floor. She wasn't even tempted.

"No, Michael, let's keep looking. And let's make sure the next place doesn't cost $80 million. That's an obscene amount of money."

Carley overheard them talking. "What range should I be targeting with the next home?" she asked Kat.

"I don't know," Kat said. "I was thinking we could get a nice condo for $5 or $10 million." Even that price seemed like an obscene amount of money to her.

"Kat, you're thinking much too small," said Michael as he drank more rosé. "Think about our net worth. We can afford something much more impressive. I don't want a three-bedroom somewhere. I want a place with room for a gym, and offices for each of us. You wanted a house in the suburbs. Right?"

Kat nodded, not sure where Michael was going with his line of thinking.

"Well, I don't want to be in the suburbs. But what if we got a house here in the city? It doesn't have to be a marble mansion, like the last place, but what if we got a nice townhouse with multiple floors and a yard? Would that make you happy?"

Kat thought about it for a moment. It would be wonderful to have a real house, someplace with bedrooms for the children and a small yard for them to play in. She turned to Carley.

"How much do townhouses cost, here in Manhattan?" she asked.

"It depends on the neighborhood," said Carley, "and the amenities. Technically, the house we just looked at was a townhouse but it was at the upper end of the range. You could find something reasonable for $15 million, or something more luxurious for $60 million. It all depends on what you want. Should I still be targeting the Upper East Side?"

"Let's start there," said Michael, "and branch out if we don't find something we like."

"Sounds like a plan," said Carley cheerfully, tapping at her iPad again. "I have another place I can show you in the East 70's. She gave the address to the limo driver as Maria poured everyone another glass of wine.

"Cheers!" Carley said. "I'm sure we can find you the perfect home!"

MARIA

Maria had been happy with the eye candy footage of the white marble mansion they just filmed but wanted more drama between Kat and Michael, while they were looking for a new home.

'Time to amp things up,' she thought as they exited the limo when they got to East 76th Street.

"Carley, can I talk to you a second?" she said, grabbing the realtor and pulling her aside on the street.

"Of course," said Carley, looking surprised. "Is there a problem?"

"Not at all," said Maria, glancing over at Kat and Michael, who were looking at the entrance to the property. "I just want to make your life a little easier.

As you can probably tell, Michael is the real decision maker. He's the one you have to impress. I also happen to know he likes flirtatious women. You may want to turn on the charm, while showing him the houses."

"Are you sure?" asked Carley. "I wouldn't want to offend Kat."

"Trust me, she's used to him flirting with attractive women and just puts up with it. Maybe that's how she stays married to him."

"I did wonder about the two of them together," said Carley slowly, looking at Michael. "He's so attractive and she's so..." Carley didn't finish the sentence.

"Exactly, and he likes women who respond to his looks. You should let him know you find him attractive. It will help you sell him a house.

Let me ask you a question, Carley. Are you single?"

"Yes," said Carley in surprise. "I've recently gone through a divorce and now I'm a single mom, trying to make ends meet."

"Well I wouldn't be surprised if Michael wants to find someone new, now that's he's wealthy. You never know what could happen, if he becomes interested in you."

"Really?" Carley said. "Thank you for the tip, Maria. I'll keep it in mind." She walked over to where Kat and Michael were standing.

"Here's the entrance on East 76th Street, near Central Park," Carley said, once she reached them, pointing towards the front of the building. "As you can see, it is the tallest townhome on the block and fronted with a solid-bronze gated entrance. It was built in 1904 by the architects who also built the Mark and the Surrey hotels. Let me take you inside and out of the cold."

"Focus less on the house and more on the interaction between the realtor and Michael. I also want to get Kat's reactions watching the two of them," Maria instructed Dan, as they followed Carley, Kat and Michael into the house.

"What is the price of this home?" Kat asked, once they were inside the house. Like the first house, this house had a huge fireplace and marble staircase in the front hallway.

"The price is $29,950,000, or $45 million if you pay in Bitcoin," answered Carley. "Michael, what do you think about reception gallery? These are the original mosaic tile floors; they have a European patina."

"You mean they're cracked?" said Kat, looking down at the cracks running through the mosaic floor.

"Yes, they're original to the house," said Carley, looking impatient. "The patina gives it a certain charm."

"I don't think cracks are charming in a house costing $30 million dollars," said Kat.

"Dan, get the floor," Maria told Dan. He promptly pointed his camera downwards to get the shot.

"Kat, you can always redo the floors if you purchase the house," said Carley, sounding a little bit snippy. "Maybe put in marble, to match the staircase. Please don't focus just on the floors."

"Yes," said Michael, "Kat, we can always put in new floors. Just look at this hallway – it's magnificent."

"Let me tell you a bit more about the home," she said, turning to face Michael and putting a hand on his arm. She gave him a dazzling smile and used her other hand to sweep her hair back from her face. Michael smiled back and stood a little taller.

Maria was glad to see Dan was getting a shot of Kat wincing as she watched Carley and Michael.

"This home has over 12,000 square feet of living space, with thirteen-foot ceilings and twelve wood burning fireplaces. The house has seven bedrooms and nine-and-a-half bathrooms." Carley slid her hand down Michael's arm and grabbed his hand.

"Please follow me and I'll give you the tour." Carley started walking in the direction of the hallway, leading Michael by the hand. Dan and Maria quickly positioned themselves, so they were walking backward, in front of Carley and Michael.

Michael had a big grin on his face. Maria could practically see the steam rising off Kat, as she followed them.

"Here in the living room, the walls have been painted a robin's egg blue to show off the exquisite white crown moldings on the walls and over the fireplace. You can see that the mosaic floor from the entrance hall has been extended into the living room."

"I can see that the cracks from the entrance hall have been extended into the living room," said Kat, looking annoyed as she looked at Carley and Michael. Carley caught her looking and dropped Michael's hand, as she continued the tour.

Carley took them through the dining room and into the library on the first floor. The library had dark wood paneling and floor to ceiling bookcases with a ladder on wheels to access the top shelves.

"Michael, tell me what you think of the library," Carley said. "Do you like to read?"

"I love to read," said Kat to Carley but Carley ignored her and kept smiling at Michael.

"I'm an actor," said Michael, smiling back at Carley. "I mostly read scripts."

"Do you also model, in addition to acting? You look like you could be in an Armani ad." Carley lowered her voice, so Michael had to move closer and lean in, to hear what she was saying.

"No, I don't model but maybe I should consider it." Maria was happy to see that he stayed closer to Carley while responding to her question.

"I definitely think you should consider it, Michael," said Carley, still speaking in a low voice.

"Carley, what did you say? I couldn't hear you," said Kat, walking up to the two of them. Michael took a step backward, away from Carley.

"Nothing really," said Carley. "I was just telling Michael he should consider modeling in addition to acting."

"What made you say that?" Kat asked with a sour look on her face. She crossed her arms across her chest and glared at Carley.

Maria didn't have to tell Dan to focus in on the three of them. He moved in closer, without prompting.

"It was just an observation because Michael has the look," said Carley smoothly, smiling at Kat. "Don't you think so too?"

Kat just snorted, without answering the question.

Maria was worried that Carley would pick up on Kat's annoyance, but she was so focused on Michael that she seemed oblivious to everyone else in the room.

"Let's see the kitchen next," said Carley, smiling at Michael. "It's a chef's dream."

"Get some footage of the kitchen," Maria directed Dan. "It's the kind of thing that viewers love to see."

They walked out of the library, through a hallway hung with modern paintings, and into a huge kitchen with a gray marble counter and gleaming white cabinets. The kitchen had a stainless steel Viking oven and range, and a Sub-Zero refrigerator. A full sized dining table and chairs were positioned behind a breakfast bar with stools. Light poured in from the windows.

"Wow," said Michael appreciatively. "This is certainly a step up from the kitchenette we have in the apartment. Our kitchen is so small and cramped." He pulled at his shirt collar, as if the thought of the small kitchen was constricting.

Carley laughed, while looking up at him. "Michael, now your collar is crooked. Here, let me help."

She stood in front of him and straightened his shirt collar, brushing the side of his neck with her fingers while she did so.

"That's better," she said, taking a step back and licking her lips.

Maria looked at Kat, to see if she noticed. Kat's face was bright red. She walked over to Michael and put her arm possessively around his waist. Michael glanced at Kat with a look of annoyance on his face.

"Let's continue the tour," said Carley, ignoring the nasty looks that Kat was sending in her direction. Kat took her arm away from Michael's waist but stayed close to him as they walked. Carley finished taking them through the downstairs rooms, before taking them in the elevator to the upper floors.

Upstairs, Maria was disappointed that Carley seemed to have stopped flirting with Michael but things got better when they went to the room with the gym equipment. Carley walked into the room, followed by Michael. Kat got stuck behind Maria and Dan as they entered.

"As you can see this house has room for a complete gym," said Carley. "You look like you work out, Michael. Do you lift weights?"

"Yes," said Michael with pride. "I can bench press 280 pounds. Feel this bicep." He lifted and curled his arm in the direction of Carley.

She squeezed his bicep and looked impressed. "Wow, you're really ripped, Michael. You must look amazing with your shirt off." Carley looked him straight in the eyes and put her hand on his chest while giving him a mysterious little smile worthy of the Mona Lisa. Michael looked as content as a cat whose fur had been stroked.

"Michael, let me give you my private number," Carley said, reaching into her pocket and pulling out a card. "Feel free to call at any time – I would love to hear from you."

"Get the fuck away from my husband," yelled Kat as she strode over to Carley and Michael. Maria noticed that Kat was a little unsteady on her feet. "What the fuck do you think you're doing?"

'Jackpot!' Maria thought as she turned in Kat's direction. She was pleased to see that Dan was capturing every moment. For a moment Maria wondered what her father would think about her manipulating people, just to get reactions for a reality TV show, but she pushed the thought back down.

Carley jumped back as if she had touched a hot stove. "I wasn't doing anything Kat - just giving you and Michael my private number."

"What about what you were doing before that? All the touching and the compliments? You were coming on to Michael."

"I may have been engaging in a little harmless flirting," Carley shot an accusatory look in Maria's direction, "but I didn't think it would bother you."

"Not bother me? When you're blatantly throwing yourself at my husband? What kind of a slut are you?"

"Kat," Michael said as he turned towards Kat and started frowning. "Why are you causing a scene? Carley wasn't doing anything. You're being paranoid."

"I am not being paranoid! She was hitting on you, Michael. Anyone could see it. Right, Maria?" Kat looked over at Maria and Dan, to get confirmation.

"It looked that way to me," said Maria gleefully. She wanted to keep the drama going.

"You bitch," said Carley, looking furiously at Maria. "You set me up." She took a step in Maria's direction.

"I don't know what you're talking about, Carley," said Maria, backing away slightly. "I never told you to throw yourself at Michael."

"I refuse to have you as our real estate agent," said Kat shrilly, still glaring at Carley. "We need to find someone new."

"Kat, what are you talking about?" protested Michael. "There's no reason to stop working with Carley. She's been a great agent so far. I want to keep working with her."

"I bet you do," said Kat, turning to face Michael. "You probably loved all the attention she was giving you."

"Kat, you don't need to stop working with me," said Carley, sounding a little desperate. "I apologize if my flirting bothered you and I can assure you I'll be strictly professional from now on. I wouldn't want you to take your business away from the Corcoran Group."

"I don't want to see you ever again," said Kat, "much lesh, I mean less, work with you. Why on earth would I help you earn a big fat commission after you've come on to my husband?"

"Well, I do want to keep working with Carley," said Michael. "This is just you being paranoid again, Kat. Carley wasn't coming on to me – she's done nothing wrong."

"Nothing wrong? She told you she wanted to see you with your shirt off! She's a house whore."

There were days when Maria loved her job.

"Kat! There's no reason to insult Carley. Maybe Carley was complimenting me, but that's just because she was being friendly. Charming clients is probably part of the job. Right, Carley?" Michael turned to Carley, as if to get affirmation.

"That's right, Kat. I'm so sorry if I was too heavy-handed with the compliments. I never meant to offend you." Carley clasped her hands nervously and looked contrite.

"Maybe Michael found you charming, but I certainly didn't. We won't be working with you again. As a matter of fact, I don't want you riding in the limo with us, when we leave this house. Take an Uber back to your office and let them know we need a new agent – preferably a man next time."

Kat turned towards Michael. "Don't even think about changing my mind.

We're getting a new agent. And while we're at it, give me that card she handed you."

"Kat, you're being ridiculous," said Michael frowning, but he pulled the card out of his pocket. He placed it in Kat's outstretched hand.

Kat ripped up the card into small pieces and threw them on the floor. "We're out of here. I definitely don't want to buy this house – it already has bad memories." Kat walked out of the gym and into the hallway. Michael sighed and gave an apologetic look to Carley before following Kat out.

"Eyes on Carley," Maria whispered to Dan. He zoomed in.

Carley looked utterly defeated as she bent down to pick up the pieces of the ripped up card. She collected the small pile and stood up to face Maria and Dan.

"I guess you got what you wanted," she said with a sour look on her face. "Are you happy?"

"I don't know what you're talking about," said Maria cheerfully. "Excuse me, but we have to follow Michael and Kat."

With that, Maria left the room, followed closely by Dan. It would take some editing, but she just scored ratings gold.

CHAPTER 9

MICHAEL

Maria had been pouring them shots of tequila all evening, while encouraging them to talk about their dream home, and Michael was pleasantly buzzed when Maria and Dan left the small apartment at 9:00 P.M. Now that he and Kat were alone, Michael was feeling a little horny and wondered if he could entice Kat into fooling around.

He looked over at Kat. She was sitting at the small dinette table in front of her laptop, staring intently at the screen but not typing.

"What's up, Kat?" he asked, getting up off the futon and going to the fridge to get a Dos Equis.

"Now that we have some privacy, I wanted to get some writing done but I'm not feeling inspired. I thought the alcohol might loosen me up but I can't find my muse."

"Maybe I can be your muse," Michael said, putting down the beer and walking over to where she was sitting. He started rubbing her shoulders before leaning down and kissing her slowly on the neck.

"Michael, not now. I'm trying to write." She gently pushed him away.

"I'm trying to inspire you," he said. He leaned over and ran his tongue down the length of her neck, before burrowing his nose in her hair. "Kat, you smell so good. Sweetheart, turn around and kiss me."

"I said not now, Michael." Kat pulled away from him.

His happy mood quickly turned to annoyance and he walked away from her chair. "It's been over a week since we fooled around. Why have you been pushing me away?"

"I haven't been pushing you away, Michael."

"Yes, you have. Every time I try to touch you, you give an excuse about why it's not a good time. What is going on?"

Kat turned around with an exasperated look on her face. "It's the cameras that are all over this apartment. I told you I didn't want to make love with other people watching. I'm too self-conscious to fool around."

"So that's it, Kat? Our sex life is over because we have cameras in the apartment?" Michael felt his irritation grow. "We're never going to make love again?"

"Maybe you should have thought about that, before agreeing to let Maria wire up this apartment. There are cameras everywhere."

'Not everywhere,' Michael thought suddenly. "Hey, sweetheart, we can go in the bathroom – there are no cameras in there."

"What am I – some cheap hookup you met in a bar?" said Kat, looking annoyed. "I don't want to make love in the bathroom."

"Kat, you're punishing me because I agreed to let them put cameras in here. You're angry because I wanted to be on the show. You're not being fair!"

"I'm not punishing you, Michael, but you didn't take my feelings into account when you agreed to let them put hidden cams in here. Now I'm not feeling horny and you're just going to have to deal with it."

Kat's rejection had made Michael's happy, horny mood completely evaporate. It was bad enough being rejected when he auditioned for a role. Being rejected at home really stung.

"Fuck this," he said suddenly, walking over to their closet to get his coat. "Sit here and write if it makes you happy. I'm going out."

"Where are you going?" asked Kat. He was pleased to see she looked dismayed.

"Just out. I'll figure out where, when I get there. Don't wait up." He slammed the door on his way out.

Once outside their building, Michael walked aimlessly, the cold helping to sober him up a little. When he got to 14th Street, he headed underground to the subway. It wasn't until Michael was on the L train that he figured out he was going to see Erica.

He got off the L at the Myrtle–Wyckoff exit and walked the seven blocks to Erica's apartment building. When he got to her row house, he paused before pressing the buzzer.

What if Erica didn't want to see him? The way he broke up with her was pretty harsh. What if she wasn't at home? What if she was with someone else?

He could feel his heart beating more rapidly, as he pressed the button and waited a minute for someone to answer.

"Hello?" Michael could hear Erica's voice through the intercom. He was glad she answered and not one of her roommates.

"Erica? It's me, Michael. Can we talk?" He held his breath, waiting for her response.

"Michael? What are you doing here?" Her voice sounded somewhat tinny, coming through the speaker.

"Erica Sweetheart, I miss you so much." As he said the words, Michael was surprised to realize they were true. He really did miss Erica.

"Erica, can I come up? I just want to talk." There was a long pause.

"Do you have the camera crew with you, or are you alone?" Michael could hear the anger in her voice.

"I'm alone. I managed to ditch them for the evening. Please, Erica, let me come up. It's freezing out here and I don't want to talk to you through an intercom." He could see his breath condense in the cold air as he talked.

She didn't respond but he heard the door buzz. Michael opened the door and was grateful to get out of the cold, into the warm hallway. He walked quickly up to the third floor; as he reached her apartment, the door opened. Erica stood in the doorway, arms crossed across her chest and a furious look on her face.

Michael looked at her. Even angry, she was so sexy. She was wearing a tight pair of jeans and a wraparound sweater that accentuated her curvy body. Her feet were bare and he could see the siren red polish on her toes. Her full lips were pursed and she looked beautiful despite her scowl. He wanted to take her in his arms and kiss her but her body language suggested that would be a bad move.

"Michael, what the fuck do you want?" She continued to block the door.

"I just want to talk, Erica. I've missed you so much. Please, can I come in? I don't want to talk in the hallway."

Her look softened slightly and she stepped to the side to let him in. He entered her apartment and saw Brad, one of Erica's roommates in the small living room, watching TV.

"Hey, Brad," he said, trying to be friendly.

"Hey, Michael," said Brad, looking over in his direction, but not smiling. Michael could only imagine what Erica must have told him about their breakup.

"Erica, is there someplace we can talk in private?" he asked, looking over at Brad.

"Don't mind me," said Brad, frowning in Michael's direction.

"We can go in my room," said Erica, opening the door and walking into her small bedroom. Michael followed her and shut the door behind them. Erica sat down in the desk chair, leaving Michael with nowhere to sit, except the edge of the mattress on the floor.

"So what did you want to talk about?" Erica asked. "You made things pretty clear after class when the cameraman was filming us. As I recall, your exact words were that I've always known you couldn't offer me anything more than friendship." She stopped looking angry for a second and looked sad.

"I'm so sorry about that. I didn't know what to say with the camera there and I didn't want Kat to find out about us." Michael winced, remembering how awkward things had been.

"Yeah, I figured that out. So why are you here now?"

"I've missed you so much. I've missed holding you, and kissing you and being with you. Since breaking up with you, I haven't been able to think about much else."

This wasn't strictly true. There had been lots of things to distract Michael but he really had missed Erica. Sitting on the mattress, he was at a height disadvantage, but he reached up and ran one hand along her ankle.

Erica pushed his hand away. "So what are you saying, Michael? You want to get back together? What about the camera that's following you most of the time?"

Michael thought for a second. Maybe there was a way he could keep seeing Erica.

"Erica, I was able to sneak away tonight, after the cameraman and producer left for the evening. Maybe we could continue to see each other late at night. I can always come up with some excuse for Kat about why I need to leave the apartment."

"Fuck you, Michael, you selfish prick," said Erica, glaring at him. "It was bad enough sneaking around so your wife wouldn't find out. Now you want to sneak around so your producer won't find out. I want a man who is proud to be with me. Not someone who treats me a like a dirty secret."

"Erica, you're not a dirty secret. You know I adore you."

"Do you love me, Michael? You've never said it." Beneath the angry look, there was hope in her eyes.

Michael paused, while thinking about what to say. Did he love Erica? He didn't feel about Erica the way he felt about Kat. Kat was a safe haven for when his ego was bruised by the constant rejection of being an actor. She represented home and security.

Erica represented danger and excitement. He loved how she made him feel, virile and desirable. But was that the same as loving her? He guessed maybe he did love Erica, in a way.

"I do love you, Erica," he said softly, reaching out to stroke her leg again.

"Oh Michael, I love you too," she said with tears in her eyes. "I've missed you so much." She got off the chair and sat down next to him on the mattress.

Michael put an arm around her and leaned in close to kiss her full, soft lips.

He worried that she would reject his kiss, the way Kat rejected him earlier in the evening but Erica responded by facing him and kissing him back passionately. Although he was getting excited, Michael's strongest emotion was one of relief that Erica still seemed to want him. He didn't think he could stand being rejected twice in one night.

As they kissed, Michael stroked her thigh softly and then moved his hand over her hip and up to the curve of her waist. He pulled back from kissing her, to gauge Erica's reaction. She had her eyes closed and a small satisfied smile on her face, so he reached beneath her sweater to fondle the warm skin of her stomach before moving his hand under her bra.

He could hear her starting to breathe heavier as he circled her nipple with his fingers. Suddenly, she stopped kissing him, and pushed his hand away.

"No, Michael. You can't just come in here, tell me you love me and expect me to fall into your arms."

Michael could feel his erection start to shrink and he pulled back.

"Erica, I'm not expecting you to fall into my arms. I just had to see you because I've missed you so much." He tucked a lock of hair behind her ear and ran his fingers softly down her neck. He could feel her shiver under his fingers.

"So what are we going to do? I don't want to see you just late at night," she said, looking at him.

"I don't know, Erica. I'll try to think of something. But I'm here now, so let's not waste our precious time together arguing."

She looked at him for a moment. "I don't want to argue either. All I've been thinking about, since you broke up with me, is how much I want to be with you."

"I want to be with you too, Erica." Michael cupped his hand under her chin and pulled her towards him to kiss her again. As she kissed him back, he moved his hand to the back of her neck and cradled the base of her head in his hand.

'Come on, Erica,' he thought as he continued kissing her, 'don't push me away again.'

Michael pulled Erica gently down, so she was lying on the bed with him on top of her. He moved his mouth off hers and started kissing her neck, while untying the strings of her wraparound sweater. Erica pushed his hands away once, but he could hear her starting to breathe heavily, so he went back to taking her sweater off.

He continued kissing down her body until he reached the top of her jeans. The salty taste of her skin inflamed him, as did the thought that she was going to let him make love to her without any more protests. Unlike Kat, Erica really seemed to want him. She moaned slightly, as he unzipped her jeans and slid them off her hips, and removed her thong. Once she was undressed, from the waist down, he turned his attention to taking off her bra, before taking both nipples in his mouth.

"What about you?" she panted. "You still have all your clothes on." Erica started fumbling with his belt buckle. After undoing his belt, she unzipped his jeans and pulled them off. His shorts came off at the same time.

"Now your shirt," she demanded. Michael took his mouth off her, to undo his buttons. His hands were shaking with excitement from the thought of how much she seemed to want him.

Once they were both naked on the bed, he went back to kissing every inch of her body. As she was moaning, he slipped a finger inside her to see how wet she was. She was dripping, so he spread her thighs, and got ready to enter her.

"Hold on a sec," she panted, placing a restraining hand on his chest. "Aren't you forgetting something? You need to put on a condom."

Shit. After breaking up with Erica, he hadn't made another trip to the drugstore to pick up more condoms.

"I don't have any," he said, sounding out of breath. "Maybe you should just give me a blow job."

"But I love you, Michael. I want to feel you inside of me," she protested.

"Where are you in your monthly cycle?" he asked. The idea of not using a condom excited him but he didn't want the consequences.

Erica thought for a second. "I think it should be okay. I don't think I'm ovulating right now."

"Are you sure?" asked Michael.

"Pretty sure," said Erica. She grabbed his penis and guided him inside her. It felt amazing to be inside her without the condom.

He started grinding against her, finding a rhythm that seemed to excite both of them. Erica's panting got faster and faster until she started screaming in ecstasy. Her passion ignited Michael and he exploded inside her, moaning aloud as he came.

"I guess we were pretty loud," Erica laughed a couple of minutes later, as he lay on top of her, waiting for his breathing to get back to normal.

"Do you think Brad heard us?" laughed Michael.

"I think all of Brooklyn heard us," she said, smiling up at him. He rolled off of her and she snuggled up, against his shoulder.

"I've missed this," said Michael. He stroked his finger over the tip of her nose.

"I've missed you so much," said Erica. "Does this mean we're not broken up?"

"I want to keep seeing you, Erica, but I'm not sure how. I've got the cameras following me all the time and Kat breathing down my neck. You know how paranoid she gets."

"So leave her and be with me," pleaded Erica, stroking his arm. "You said you love me."

"I can't leave Kat, especially not now," said Michael. He was starting to get cold, so he pulled the comforter over the two of them.

"Why not? Is it because of the money?" said Erica. Her eyes narrowed, as she looked at him.

"No, they're awarding the money to both of us," said Michael. "It has more to do with the TV show. I want to develop a big fan base and it won't look very good if I dump Kat the second the money comes through."

"So you're staying with her because of the optics?" Erica's voice rose in pitch as she sat up to look at him.

"Well, I guess you could say that. I don't want to be cast as the bad husband." Michael felt annoyed that Erica was making a big deal out of this.

"But you are a bad husband. You're cheating on your wife and staying with her because it makes you look better on TV." Erica glared at Michael.

"What type of husband I am is really none of your business," Michael said, as his annoyance grew.

"What the fuck do you mean it's none of my business?" Erica said.

"We may have a relationship, but my relationship with my wife is none of your business."

"Fuck you, Michael. Okay, let's stop talking about Kat." Erica paused to take a breath. "What I want to know is whether your TV show is more important to you than my feelings."

"Erica, can't you understand that this could be my big break? I don't want to risk blowing it"

"Oh, I understand, Michael." Tears started to form in her eyes as she looked at him. "I understand that you're a bad husband, and a bad boyfriend, and a totally selfish prick. I think you should leave." She pulled away from him.

Michael threw off the comforter. "If I leave now, Erica, I'm not sure when I'll be able to come back."

"So don't come back, Michael. You say you love me but the only one you really love is yourself."

Michael threw on his clothes and took a last look at Erica, as she lay on the mattress, under the comforter. She was crying but she also radiated fury as she watched him leaving.

Michael was sorry to be giving her up, because she was so good in bed, but he didn't need the extra aggravation. His life was complicated enough.

He didn't bother to say goodbye to Brad, as he left Erica's apartment.

CHAPTER 10

KAT

They were all gathered around the Thanksgiving table. Kat's Uncle Charlie sat at the head of the table with Aunt Jan at the other end. Kat was next to Michael, with her adult cousins, Brian and Gina in the middle of the table.

Her Uncle Charlie was wearing his celebratory red sweater, which was stretched tightly over his pot belly. His white tonsure of curls contrasted with his somewhat flushed face. Kat thought he looked jolly, as if Santa Claus had started balding.

Her Aunt Jan was dressed in a yellow oversized sweater which somewhat dwarfed her tiny frame. Brunette and petite, Gina took after her mother, rather than her father, whereas Brian was starting to look more like Charlie every day.

Dan and Maria stood at one corner of the dining room, facing the table.

"Don't mind us," said Maria, as they got set up. "Just enjoy your celebration."

The dining room was crowded but Kat thought it was nice having so many people at the table. The lights were dimmed to accentuate the candles in the silver candlestick holders. The table was covered with a tablecloth patterned with autumn leaves. Her Aunt Jan knew how to make the table look good.

The table was laden with the food prepared by the caterers Michael had hired. They started with rolls, butternut squash soup and goat cheese salad. The traditional main course included a golden brown turkey, stuffing with chestnuts, mashed potatoes, a sweet potato casserole and a green bean casserole.

Kat was reaching for a second helping of sweet potatoes when she saw Michael glance at her with a disapproving look on his face, so she immediately withdrew her hand. Even though she had worn her loose pants, the waistline was tight after the big meal and she felt guilty about all the calories she had consumed.

'I'll start cutting back tomorrow,' she promised herself. 'Maybe I could even start going to a gym.'

The dinner conversation had been conflict-free, thanks to an agreement not to discuss politics or religion during the meal, when her Uncle Charlie asked how the house hunting was going.

"Initially, the Corcoran Group teamed us up with a horrible realtor," Kat said, putting down her fork.

"I wouldn't say she was horrible," protested Michael, turning to Kat.

Kat silenced him with a sharp look and continued.

"But then they assigned us Philip and he has been wonderful to work with. We've seen some amazing houses but there's one I just love. It's on East 65th Street, between Lexington and Third."

"What do you love about it?" asked her Aunt Jan.

"It's not as grand as some of the houses we've seen, but it feels cozy, even though it's over 8,500 square feet. There are five bedrooms, so it has lots of room for a growing family."

"It doesn't have a gym," said Michael, "but we can always convert one of the bedrooms."

"When you walk into the house, there's a wood-paneled study with a fireplace to the right. Then you walk through a hallway to this large kitchen which has room for a full sized table and chairs. The kitchen back door opens to a beautiful little back yard that was designed by a curator at the Brooklyn Botanical Gardens."

"The basement has a full wine cellar and an apartment for live-in help," said Michael.

"The second floor has the living room, the dining room and a conservatory with floor to ceiling windows and ceiling fans," said Kat. "We could fill it with plants and patio furniture."

"There's a terrace on the top floor which has a fire pit," said Michael, rubbing his hands together. "We could have some great parties out there."

"The third floor is a master suite," said Kat. "It has the master bedroom, a sitting room and his and her bathrooms. No more fighting over who needs to use the bathroom sink!

"The fourth and fifth floors have more bedrooms, a library and a solarium. The house is amazing. I just hope it's still on the market when the money is wired to our account. I would be really bummed if someone else bought it."

"So how much does this palace cost?" Jan asked with a frown on her face.

Kat suddenly remembered that Aunt Jan had wanted a new home in Dobb's Ferry. She felt reluctant to share that the house on East 65th cost nearly $20 million because it would only increase her aunt's resentment about having to stay in Yonkers.

"The house is on the market for…shit, Kat." Michael started saying until

Kat kicked him hard under the table.

"It's expensive but not nearly as expensive as some of the other homes we looked at," Kat said quickly.

"I'll bet it's expensive," said Aunt Jan. "A house like that, in Manhattan, probably goes for $30 million, at least."

"No, it's not $30 million," said Kat, hoping they weren't going to start playing a guessing game about the price. She noticed her cousins were looking at her with interest.

Her discomfort must have shown on her face, because her Uncle Charlie joined the conversation.

"Hey, Jan, money and finances should be private matters. Kat and Michael don't have to share the cost of their new home, unless they want to discuss it." Kat gave her Uncle Charlie a grateful smile.

"I don't mind," Michael began when Kat kicked him again. She was annoyed that he was being so obtuse. Couldn't he see that the price of the new house could lead to her family resenting them?

"Kat, stop that," said Michael, scowling at her. "That hurts!"

"Stop talking about the price of the house," Kat hissed quietly at Michael. She hoped no one else had heard her.

"I didn't think house prices were a private matter," said Jan, frowning at Charlie. "Anybody can look up the price on the internet as long as they have the address."

"Asking somebody what their house cost is a little like asking what their salary is," said Charlie. "You're being borderline rude."

"I certainly don't want to be rude," said Jan, looking displeased. "It's just that a house that is five times the size of this one, in Manhattan, must be a fortune. I was just curious, that's all."

"Jan, stop," said Charlie, while glowering at Jan. "You agreed that we wouldn't discuss our house during dinner."

"I'm not discussing our house, as cramped as it is. We're discussing the mansion they plan on buying now that they're rich."

"Well, why shouldn't they buy a mansion, after winning the BonusBall?" asked Gina. "That's what anybody would do."

"It just seems selfish for them to buy a huge house in Manhattan and leave us in a tiny house in Yonkers. You would think Kat would want to take better care of her family."

'Not this again,' Kat thought with dismay. Thanksgiving had been going great until they started talking about the house. She glanced over at Maria and Dan. Maria wasn't saying anything but she had a big grin on her face.

"I don't want Kat to take care of me," said Charlie. "If this house is too small for you, maybe you shouldn't be here."

Jan froze for a second. "Charlie, what are you saying?" she said with a nervous look on her face.

"I think I was pretty clear," said Charlie. "If you're not happy with what I make, or the size of my home, then there's the door." He pointed to the front door for emphasis.

All eyes and the camera turned towards Jan.

"I'm happy with what you make and this house is fine," said Jan, back-pedaling furiously. "I didn't mean to imply I wasn't happy here. Charlie, I'm very happy here with you." She took a large gulp from her wineglass.

"Then I don't expect to hear anything more about Kat and Michael buying us a new house. Is that understood?" Charlie stopped pointing at the front door.

Jan didn't reply.

"I said, is that understood, Jan?" Charlie continued to frown at her.

"Yes, it's understood," said Jan in a conciliatory tone. "I won't mention a new house again." She looked around the table. "Why don't we all get back to this lovely meal?"

Everyone resumed eating and there was no more conversation for a couple of minutes until Brian interrupted the silence.

"Where is Uncle Andy this Thanksgiving?"

Kat winced at the mention of her father.

"I'm not sure," she admitted. "I think Ren said that Dad and Annika went to a restaurant to celebrate."

"They didn't want to be here with us?" asked Gina. She looked confused.

"We didn't invite Andy this year," said Charlie after an awkward pause in the conversation. "Kat didn't want to be here if Annika was going to come."

"Why not?" asked Brian, looking over at Kat with a curious look on his face.

"I don't want to discuss it," said Kat, glancing over at Maria and Dan. She couldn't see Dan behind his camera but Maria looked very interested in the conversation. "Can we discuss something else?" Kat could feel the back of her neck start to tense up.

"Of course," said Charlie. "Do you have any other plans, beyond buying a new house?"

Kat was grateful to her Uncle Charlie for bringing up a new topic of conversation. She took a look at Michael. "I haven't really discussed this with Michael, but I would like to donate some of the money to charity. Michael, what do you think?"

"I think it's an interesting idea," he said thoughtfully. "Which charity and how much were you thinking of donating?"

Kat thought back to the homeless man she had given her umbrella to. It would be wonderful to do more than just give away an umbrella.

"What do you think about giving money to one of the homeless shelters in New York City?" she asked, warming to the idea as she talked. "There are so many people who need shelter, especially when it's cold out. This close to winter, people can die of exposure from sleeping outside. We could help provide housing for at least some of them."

"I think it's a wonderful idea," said Gina. "You could really make a difference in people's lives."

"I would be open to doing that," said Michael. "We've been so lucky and it's good karma to pay it forward. How much were you thinking of donating?"

Kat had been thinking of maybe as much as $1 million but she didn't want to name the amount in front of Jan, because it would trigger her resentment again.

"We should discuss the idea with Len and see what he recommends," said Kat, evading Michael's question. "I'm sure this has tax implications."

"Who is Len?" asked Charlie.

"Len Applebaum," said Michael. "He's our money manager. You're right, Kat. Giving a donation may even help us at tax time. Let's discuss it with Len."

Kat gave Michael a big smile. She was thrilled at the idea that their money could do something good, for someone other than themselves.

She was able to relax and enjoy the rest of the meal, including a piece of butterscotch pecan pie, with a scoop of vanilla ice cream, for dessert.

"I am definitely going on a diet tomorrow," she thought contentedly at the end of the night, as she surreptitiously unbuttoned the top bottom of her pants, to give her stomach a little more room.

———

It was a week after Thanksgiving when Kat got out of the shower and found she had missed a call from Len Applebaum.

"Hey, Kat, It's Len Applebaum.

"I've sent emails to you and Michael so you can check the accounts we've set up for you. The email has a link to our portal and your username. I'll send you each a text with your password. I recommend that you change the password as soon as you've gotten into the account.

"I've also put $32,897,200.00 in a separate account, so you can pay the IRS the remaining 14.6 percent tax that you owe. I need to pay your estimated taxes on January 15th.

"Please call me if you have any questions or if you're unable to access the accounts.

Talk to you soon."

A few minutes later, her phone pinged with the text from Len containing her password.

She glanced at Michael, who was still asleep on the futon.

Quietly, so as not to wake him, she got her laptop and opened Gmail. Kat saw the email from Len, with a link to the account portal and her username. She clicked on the link and entered her credentials.

At the top of the page, she saw "Portfolio for Katherine and Michael Davidson." Under the heading, in a large font, it said "Total Assets: $112,085,460.00."

Below that was a pie chart showing 50 percent in a money market account, 30 percent in bonds and 20 percent in indexed stock funds. There was a link at the bottom of the page to "Balances and Holdings."

Kat just stared at the page, unable to wrap her head around the fact that she and Michael had a net worth over $112 million dollars.

She was just about to wake Michael, to tell him the money had arrived when she heard the buzzer for the front door of their apartment building. The sound woke up Michael.

"Is that Maria and Dan?" he asked sleepily as he opened his eyes, "Better let them in."

"Let them wait a second," said Kat, "Michael, the money has arrived!"

"How do you know?" asked Michael, sitting up in bed.

"Check your email. Len sent us credentials for accessing our account. Look!"

She handed her laptop to Michael as the door buzzed again. Kat walked over to the intercom and pressed the button.

"Maria, is that you?"

"It's us, Kat," she heard Maria's voice. "Can you let us in?" Kat pressed the button to open the front door.

"Holy shit," Michael said, staring at the screen with his eyes wide. "It's over $112 million dollars."

Kat sat down next to Michael on the futon and looked at the screen again.

$112,085,460.00.

She thought for a few minutes about spending $20 million for a townhouse. It would bring the total down to $92,085,460.00. Even though she loved the house, Kat felt a sudden reluctance to see the portfolio number go under $100,000,000.

"Hey, Michael, what if we didn't buy that townhouse and found something a little cheaper? Maybe something costing $10 million, instead of $20 million? What if we tried to keep the portfolio above $100,000,000 and just lived off the interest?"

"But Kat, I thought you loved that townhouse?" Michael looked surprised.

"I do love the townhouse – it's fabulous. But if we keep $100,000,000 in our account and the returns are 4 percent a year, that's $4,000,000. We could live like kings off the interest and wouldn't have to touch the principal."

Maria and Dan must have walked up the six flights because Kat heard them knocking at the front door of the apartment; she left Michael with the laptop and let them in.

She looked at Maria, as she walked in the door. Maria always looked so pulled together that Kat felt dowdy in comparison. This morning, when she took off her coat, Maria was wearing skinny jeans and a tailored gray jacket that looked expensive. Kat was wearing black yoga pants and an old white sweatshirt that had a coffee stain on the front.

"Hey there, Kat and Michael," Maria said, sounding upbeat, as she got settled. "What's going on this morning?"

"The money has arrived," said Michael. "We were just checking the account on Kat's laptop."

"Dan, get a shot of that," said Maria. "Michael, can you face the laptop screen to the camera?"

"Michael, don't…" Kat started to say, but Michael held the laptop up to Dan with a big smile on his face.

Maria whistled when she saw the number on the screen. "Congratulations! You guys are officially millionaires. What are you going to buy first? Are you going to make an offer on the townhouse you liked?"

"We were just discussing that," said Kat. "I was wondering if we wouldn't be better off finding something cheaper and leaving more money in the account to let it grow."

Kat saw a look of dismay flit across Maria's face, as she turned to look at Michael.

"I like our original plan," said Michael. "Let's leave $56 million to grow but I want to use the rest to ensure we live like millionaires."

"I have an idea," said Kat. "What if we put $10 million down on the townhouse and got a mortgage for the rest? We could pay the mortgage off each year and leave more of the principal untouched."

"Kat, the last thing I want to do is go into debt for $10 million, even if we can afford it. Paying off the interest, on that size mortgage, is a waste of money when we can just buy the house outright.

"Kitty Kat, don't you want that house? You said it was perfect."

Kat thought about it. She really did want the house and they would still have over $92 million after purchasing it. $100,000,000 was a nice round number but $92,000,000 was still a fortune and would generate a lot of interest to live on. They could spend $20 million out of the $56 million that Michael had asked Len to set aside. Maybe she could work on Michael to not spend the remaining $36 million in what she was starting to think of as the world's largest slush fund.

"Yes Michael, I do want the house. Let's put in an offer," she said happily.

"No point in wasting time," said Maria. "Why don't you call Philip now? You don't want someone else to offer above the asking price. You'll lose the house."

"Good point," said Michael. "I'll call him as soon as I've gotten dressed. Now, if you'll excuse me." He walked over to the closet to get some clothes and went into the bathroom.

"So Kat, how do you feel about putting in an offer?" asked Maria, as Dan moved in closer.

"I feel very happy," said Kat, looking at Maria, instead of the camera. "It's an amazing house and I just hope we get it." She went to get another cup of coffee while she waited for Michael to get out of the bathroom.

After he was dressed, Michael picked up his phone to call Philip. He put his phone on speaker.

"Hi, Philip? It's Michael Davidson."

"Michael, good morning! How are you doing?"

"I'm good, how are you?"

"I'm great." Philip's voice sounded cheery over the speaker.

"Kat and I would like to put in an offer on the townhouse on East 65th Street. The asking price is $19,950,000. How much do you think we should offer?"

"Will this be an all-cash purchase or will you be arranging financing?"

"This will be an all-cash purchase."

"Let me think. The house has only been on the market three weeks and I know there's been some interest. If you want to make sure you get the house, I would go in with an offer that is slightly above the asking price. What do you think about $20,050,000?"

"I think that sounds fine, Philip. Please put in the offer as soon as possible."

"I'll write up the paperwork right now. Hopefully, I should have some good news for you later this afternoon."

"Thank you, Philip. We'll wait to hear from you." Michael hung up and went over to Kat, to give her a hug.

"So Philip is putting together the offer for the house," he said happily. He beamed at Kat.

"I just hope they accept the offer," said Kat, hugging him back. Now that they had decided to purchase the house, she was worried they wouldn't get it. She would be crushed if someone swooped in with a higher offer.

"So that's your new house taken care of," said Maria. "What other plans do you have for the money? Are you thinking of buying a vacation home?"

"Let's focus on buying one house at a time," laughed Michael, going over to the futon. "Hey, Kat, give me a hand with this?" They straightened the sheets and folded up the futon, so they could sit down.

"So what other fantasies do you have?" pushed Maria. "You must want more than just a new home. Are you thinking about traveling, or maybe buying a new car? Do you want a sports car?"

"I've always dreamed of having a red Ferrari," said Michael, as he walked to the kitchen area to get a cup of coffee. "What do you think, Kat? Can we get a car?"

"Where would we keep a car in the city?" asked Kat. "Parking is a nightmare around here."

"That's no problem," said Maria quickly. "I can have our production assistants find you a garage and the bills will go to Len each month. Do you want a garage near East 65th Street, so it's near your new house?"

"That could work," said Michael happily. "Kat, do you want to go to a dealership this afternoon? We could stop taking limos and Ubers if we had our own car."

"There won't be room for Dan and I if you get a Ferrari," said Maria. "We would want to put cameras in the car."

"I'm sure that won't be a problem," said Michael. Kat just rolled her eyes.

"We can get a car, Michael, but why a Ferrari? Doesn't it make sense to get something a little less expensive, with room for more than two people? We could get a nice Mercedes or a BMW."

"Kat, now that we're millionaires, I want to purchase my fantasy car. Please, Kitty Kat?" He looked as eager as a child asking for a toy before Christmas.

Kat sighed inwardly. She didn't want to say no, every time Michael wanted to purchase something but she also didn't want to blow through their fortune.

'Maybe letting him get a Ferrari will get it out of his system,' she thought.

'Once he has the luxury home and the luxury car, I can put a cap on other spending. Hopefully, he won't want a yacht.'

"Michael, if we get the Ferrari, can we slow down on the spending?" Kat asked him. "We just got the money and I don't want to start going through all of it."

"I promise, Kat. Just let me get the car, and we can stop spending for now."

"Okay, you can have the red Ferrari. Just promise me you won't drive too fast."

"You know I'm a good driver Kat. I won't be getting any speed tickets, especially here in the city."

"So let's go to the Ferrari dealership," said Maria.

They took a limo to the Ferrari dealership in Greenwich, CT.

In the showroom, Kat looked around at all the gleaming sports cars while a dealer, who looked more like an investment banker, took them through the benefits of the different models. Michael seemed to have a hard time deciding between a Ferrari 488 Spider and a Ferrari California T. Both cars looked so similar to Kat that she doubted she could tell them apart.

Michael started to lean towards the 488 Spider.

"Just look at her gorgeous curves," he said to Kat, running his hand over a fender that was so glossy it looked like the red paint was still wet. Michael looked like he was in love. "She's the sexiest thing I've ever seen."

Was it possible to feel jealous about a car? Kat wanted to be the sexiest thing Michael had ever seen.

"Kat, just sit in the driver's seat. See what you think," said the dealer, opening the car door for her.

Kat had to admit that the soft leather racing seat cushioned her body as if made to fit. She looked at the dashboard with its dual screens and shiny knobs. Most of the car controls seemed to be accessible from buttons and dials on the steering wheel. It certainly looked impressive.

"Wait 'til you see how she drives," said the dealer. "You'll love it."

The dealer took Michael on a test drive, while Kat, Maria and Dan waited in the showroom. While they were waiting, Kat's phone rang.

"Hi, Kat? It's Philip. I tried reaching Michael but he's not picking up right now. I wanted to let you know that they accepted your offer on the house. Congratulations!"

"Philip, that's awesome news! I can't wait to tell Michael. What happens next? When can we move in?"

"Send me the contact information for your money manager and we'll get started on the paperwork. I'll also start working on getting you a closing date. When do you want to move in?"

"As soon as possible."

"Okay, I'll coordinate a date with the agent for the sellers. Congratulations again!"

When Michael got back from the test drive, Kat told him the news about getting the house. He gave her a big hug.

"Are you happy, Kitty Kat?" he said with a big grin.

"I'm so happy, Michael," she said, grinning back at him. "I'm thrilled that soon we'll be moving into my dream home."

"And I'm thrilled that we'll be getting my dream car," said Michael. He turned to the dealer. "We'll definitely be getting the Spider. What is the cost of this model?"

"The manufacturer's suggested retail price is $252,800. It comes with a seven-year complimentary contract for service."

Kat was staggered that the cost was over a quarter million dollars. It seemed insane to pay so much for a car but she told Michael he could have his fantasy vehicle. She wasn't about to go back on her word.

"Can I put you in touch with Len, our money manager?" Michael asked the dealer. "He can arrange for payment and insurance."

"That's fine, Michael. I would be happy to work with him and arrange delivery. Congratulations! I think you're going to love the Spider."

"I know I will," said Michael happily, as he put an arm around Kat. "Thank you very much."

Kat was glad Michael was happy but it occurred to her that the money had been in their account less than 24 hours, and they had already gone through more than $20,300,000. She wondered what her family would think, if they knew how much she and Michael had spent in a single day. She knew there would be more expenses to come, when they started furnishing the new home, but after that, she hoped they would slow down on the spending.

CHAPTER 11

MICHAEL

"The first *Lucky* clip was posted to YouTube yesterday in the channel we created," said Maria when they got back from the Ferrari dealership and were in the apartment. "Do you want to see how many views it's gotten?"

'Could this day get any better?' Michael thought happily to himself. First the money, then the house, then the car and now he was the star in a YouTube channel. Michael was confident that if he could get a lot of fans on social media, it would lead to more acting gigs in the future.

He sat down on the futon next to Kat and reached for his laptop. After pulling up YouTube in the browser, he typed "Lucky" into the search box.

He had to scroll through a number of music videos and movie trailers with the word "Lucky" in the title but then he saw a thumbnail image of him and Kat. He read the blurb.

Lucky – Episode 1

See what it's really like to be a BonusBall winner. Follow the story of Michael and Kat Davidson as they go from rags to riches and discover that money can't always buy happiness.

'What do they mean, money can't buy happiness?' Michael thought with a prickle of anxiety. He was pretty happy these days, wasn't he? Michael wondered just what the video was going to show but then he relaxed somewhat when he saw that the video already had 97,000 views and the channel had 7,875 subscribers.

"That's great. We're up to 97,000 views," said Maria, looking over his shoulder. "Our publicity is starting to pay off. If this keeps up, we may start trending."

Michael clicked on the thumbnail so he could watch the episode.

"This is the story of Kat and Michael Davidson," Michael heard a voiceover and saw a *Lucky* title slide with a picture of him and Kat.

"They live in a tiny studio apartment in New York City." There was a shot of the apartment. Somehow Dan had managed to make it look even smaller than it actually was.

"Michael is an actor who is looking for work." There was a close-up of Michael's face. Michael was pleased to see he looked good.

"Kat has a low-level job at an ad agency." Close-up of Kat's face. She looked stressed.

"My job was not low-level," Kat protested, turning around to look at Maria with an annoyed look on her face.

"Sorry, Kat. It makes for better TV," said Maria. She didn't look sorry at all.

"Kat, shush," said Michael. He didn't want to miss the rest of the video.

"Then one day, they bought a BonusBall ticket." The YouTube video showed footage of Kat and Michael buying a BonusBall ticket from the deli.

"The odds were one in 292 million, but they were the big winners!" The video showed them at the BonusBall press conference standing next to the big check for $379,000,000.

Cut to a shot of them at the podium with the BonusBall press secretary. *"Kat and I would just like to say how excited we are to be winners. This has been the biggest thrill of our lives."* Michael watched himself talking to the cameras. He was pleased to see that he looked confident and relaxed. Unfortunately, Kat looked awkward and heavier than she looked in real life.

"Kat quit her job to become a novelist but Michael still wants to be an actor." Cut to a scene of Michael in his acting class, doing the love scene with Erica. The video showed the end of the love scene, where Michael and Erica kiss.

Michael glanced at Kat. She was staring at the laptop with a pained look on her face.

"Is that Erica? You didn't tell me you were working on a love scene with her."

Michael paused the YouTube video, starting to feel irritated. "Kat, it was just acting. I don't even see Erica anymore because I've started taking private acting lessons with Barry. Please don't go all paranoid on me. How am I ever going to act in love scenes if you get freaked out watching?"

"Maybe I just won't watch your love scenes," said Kat, biting her lip. "Seeing you kiss someone else is upsetting."

"Can we get back to the YouTube video now?" asked Michael. He wanted to see the rest of the clip instead of dealing with Kat's insecurity.

"Okay, I won't interrupt again," said Kat but she still looked upset.

Michael clicked on the play button and the video continued.

"You would think with all those millions in the bank, their troubles would all be over but money can't solve all problems, like relatives with their hands out."

The video showed an excerpt filmed from the celebration in the restaurant. In the clip, there was a close-up of Jan saying *"Kat, we were thinking now that you and Michael are so rich, maybe you could help us out by getting us a new house."*

The camera focus changed to Michael saying *"We don't mind helping out if you want a new house."*

Then there was a shot of Kat saying "W*e won't get you a new house.*"

Close-up of Jan again saying *"It just seems selfish for them not to share the wealth."*

Michael was pretty sure Kat had said they wouldn't be buying Jan and Charlie a new house because that's not what Charlie wanted but the editor had left that part on the cutting room floor. Instead, Michael came off as generous, and Kat seemed stingy. He glanced over at Kat. She seemed near to tears.

The voiceover continued. *"No, money can't fix grasping relatives or a jealous spouse."*

The video showed Michael and Erica outside acting class. Michael's stomach started to clench up. He watched himself saying, *"Erica, we can't be friends anymore. You know how insecure Kat is. I wouldn't want her to see footage of our friendship and come to the wrong conclusion. You know how jealous she gets."*

Cut to a shot of Erica, with tears running down her face. The camera switched back to Michael. *"Erica, I don't want to upset you. You've always known that I was married and couldn't offer you anything more than friendship."*

The camera panned back to show both Erica and Michael. Erica said, *"Fine. We'll stop being friends. But I'm not giving up this acting class, so you're going to have to drop out if you want to stop seeing me."*

Michael breathed a big sigh of relief that the clip hadn't shown more. He looked over at Kat. She was staring at the screen with her mouth open.

"Pause the video," Kat snapped, taking her eyes off the screen and glaring at Michael. He clicked on the pause button.

"Erica was in love with you," she said. "Don't deny it. You told me you were just friends."

"But Kat, I told her we couldn't be more than friends," said Michael, hoping desperately that the clip wouldn't show more of his conversation with Erica. "It was a case of unrequited love."

Kat narrowed her eyes, while looking at him. "Why would you be friends with a woman who is in love with you? Were you hoping for something to happen? You were working on that love scene together."

"Kitty Kat, no. You're the one I love. Erica was just a casual friend – we hung out after acting class sometimes but I made it clear that we couldn't be more than friends. There was nothing more. To be honest, she was more like an acquaintance."

"Some acquaintance," Kat hissed. "I'm glad you're not seeing her anymore. " She looked closely at Michael for a minute without saying anything, and then glanced at Dan and the camera. She gave a deep sigh before turning back to the screen. "Okay, Michael, maybe it's not your fault she was crushing on you. Play the rest of the video."

Michael was relieved that Kat was uncharacteristically letting it go. Maybe she didn't want to cause another scene in front of the camera? He let out the breath that he had been holding.

"Go ahead, Michael, play the rest of the video," Maria said.

Michael wasn't sure if he wanted to play the rest of the video. It was a thrill, seeing himself on screen, but the clip with Erica could have led to a huge blowup with Kat, if the entire conversation had been played. Swallowing hard, he clicked on the play button again.

"So Michael had to drop his acting class because of Kat's jealousy over his friendship with Erica. Jealousy reared its ugly head again when Kat and Michael went house hunting."

The film showed a shot of Carley, looking polished in her suit, with Kat suffering in comparison, dressed in her jeans and down jacket. The video showed Carley showing them the features of the first house they viewed and telling them the price was $79,500,000.

The film dissolved to showing Carley in the gym of the second house, giving Michael her card.

"Michael, let me give you my private number," Carley said. *"Feel free to call at any time – I would love to hear from you."*

The camera showed Kat marching over to Michael and Carley and yelling, *"Get the fuck away from my husband. What the fuck do you think you're doing?"*

The camera showed Carley jumping back from Michael. *"I wasn't doing anything, Kat - just giving you and Michael my private number."*

Cut to Kat. *"You were coming on to Michael."*

The camera angle shifted slightly, keeping Kat as the focus. *"What kind of a slut are you?"*

The focus shifted to Michael frowning. *"Kat, why are you causing a scene? Carley wasn't doing anything. You're being paranoid."*

The camera panned out to show the three of them. Carley looked pained as Kat responded to Michael. *"I am not being paranoid! She was hitting on you, Michael. Anyone could see it."*

Close-up on Kat, with a red face. *"I refuse to have you as our real estate agent. We need to find someone new."*

The focus shifted to Michael. *"Kat, what are you talking about? There's no reason to stop working with Carley. She's been a great agent so far. I want to keep working with her."*

The camera pulled back slightly to show Kat and Michael. "*I bet you do*," said Kat.

The camera angle shifted slightly. "*She's a house whore.*"

The camera angle shifted again to show Kat talking to Carley. "*We won't be working with you again. As a matter of fact, I don't want you riding in the limo with us, when we leave this house. Take an Uber back to your office and let them know we need a new agent – preferably a man next time.*"

The camera pulled back again to show Kat and Michael. Kat said, "*Give me that card she handed you.*"

The film showed Kat ripping the card into small pieces and throwing them on the floor. The video showed the back of Kat, as she left the gym with Carley looking crushed as she watched Kat exit.

"Pause the video again," Kat said, turning around to stare at Maria. Michael paused the video.

"Maria, what the fuck was that? You didn't show any of the footage of Carley coming on to Michael. Instead, you made me look unhinged. I come off like the crazy spouse-from-hell."

"I guess the editor thought it would be more dramatic this way," said Maria, looking a little stressed.

Kat got up off the futon and turned to face Maria and Dan. "Don't give me that. You're the producer, Maria. You must have told the editor this is what you wanted."

"The executive producer makes the final editing decisions. My boss, William Livingstone, is the showrunner. He must have decided that a jealous spouse makes for more viewer interest."

"Well, you're certainly getting viewer interest. Nearly 100,000 people have seen me looking selfish and certifiable. I thought Michael was supposed to be the subject of your show. So far, this video seems to be more about me."

"Kat, I'll ask William if we can focus more on Michael in future clips and less on you if it makes you uncomfortable," said Maria with a nervous look on her face.

"You need to stop making me look crazy or I'm going to refuse to let you shoot me in the future."

Michael was worried. Kat could screw things up if she told the producers she wouldn't be in more episodes. Maybe Kat wasn't coming off looking too good, but he liked seeing himself as the star of *Lucky*.

"Kat, this is the first episode and they're just trying to figure out what works," he said a little desperately, getting off the futon and massaging Kat's tense shoulders. "Maria will ensure that the editor doesn't make you look crazy in the future."

"But Michael, this is exactly what I was worried about." She turned to face him and he could see tears starting to form in her eyes. "They're exploiting us to get an audience. Plus, they made me look fat."

"Kitty Kat, you're not fat," he said, turning her around to face him and putting his arms around her. "You're voluptuous and I love your body."

"Well, I hate the way I look on camera," said Kat, starting to sniffle. She left his arms and went into the bathroom, emerging with a tissue a moment later.

"Kat, if you really want to change how you look on camera, we could team you up with a personal trainer," Maria offered helpfully. "With intense training, you could drop any excess pounds very quickly."

"That would be perfect," said Kat sarcastically. "Letting all 100,000 of your viewers see me sweaty, as I do aerobics."

"Kat, our agreement was to only shoot you when you're with Michael," said Maria. "We wouldn't be filming you while you work out. I was only offering the suggestion to be helpful."

"In that case, I may take you up on your offer," said Kat slowly. "Find me a trainer and a gym, and I'll start working out. If I have to be on camera, I want to look thinner. And make sure you don't show me as crazy in the future or I'm off the show."

Michael was relieved. If Kat liked the way she looked on camera, maybe she wouldn't object as much to what they were shooting.

"Of course, Kat," said Maria quickly. "We'll make sure you're a sympathetic character in the future and we'll find you a fantastic personal trainer. Leave it to me."

"Can we un-pause the video?" asked Michael. He sat down on the futon and patted the space next to him. "Kat, sit down and let's look at the rest."

Kat sighed as she sat down next to him, nervously playing with the tissue.

"There's not much more," said Maria. "We just want the YouTube clips to tease interest for the show. We don't want to give everything away, so they're short.

We'll edit the footage differently for broadcast. Kat, we can make sure you don't come off as crazy when we air the first episode. We can show Carley coming on to Michael, which would explain your reaction to her."

Michael felt nervous as he thought about what else might be in the first broadcast episode. He would need to talk to Maria, to make sure she didn't show more of the scene with Erica.

He clicked the play button.

"*Tune in next week*," he heard the narrator say, as the video showed his and Kat's apartment. "*We'll see more of the houses Kat and Michael are considering for their new home, so they can move out of their tiny apartment.*" The screen faded to black.

MARIA

Maria took a quick look at William as they were sitting in Neil Charles' office at the A+M Networks headquarters. As usual, her boss looked polished in a black turtleneck, under a gray jacket with black jeans.

"Nervous?" he asked her with a smile, as they waited for Neil Charles to get off the phone.

"Maybe a little," she admitted. "I really hope he likes the pilot."

"It's a great pilot and you've done an amazing job. I think he's going to love it," William said as Neil ended his call and turned towards the two of them.

"I've cleared my schedule for the next forty-five minutes, so let's see this pilot you've been working on. I liked your premise, so I'm hoping the pilot delivers," said Neil, a bit brusquely.

"I think you'll like what you see," said William smoothly as he picked up the remote. The lights in the office dimmed automatically when William pressed play.

The pilot for *Lucky* started playing on the large screen TV that was located at the back of Neil's office. First was the title sequence, with the music that William had commissioned. Then Maria watched the story play out, from Michael and Kat buying the ticket, to the BonusBall press conference, to their disagreement about what type of house to get. She worried about whether there was enough drama to hold viewer interest. She looked at

Neil, hoping to get a clue about whether he liked what he was seeing.

Neil watched the screen with a completely neutral expression on his face. He didn't comment but he raised his eyebrows a little when he saw the exchange between Michael and Erica, outside the acting class. Unlike the short clip they edited for YouTube, the pilot contained more dialog and it was clear that Michael was trying to cover up the relationship.

The next part of the pilot focused on the mansions that Kat and Michael had looked at when house hunting. Each one was more luxurious than the last. The editor had saved the $80 million marble mansion for the end of the sequence, along with Kat's comment that it looked like a mausoleum.

The final part of the pilot showed Carley coming on to Michael and Kat's extreme reaction to Carley's flirting. At the end of the pilot, they teased some clips for the next episode.

William turned off the TV, which caused the dimmed lights to brighten and light up the room again.

"So what did you think, Neil?" he asked. "I think viewers are going to love it!"

"I think it has potential," said Neil, smiling for the first time. "How many people have viewed the clip on YouTube?"

"We're on YouTube's trending page," said Maria. "Over 300,000 people have viewed the ten-minute video with 49,000 subscribers to the channel."

"And when did you post it?" asked Neil.

"Three days ago," said Maria, feeling some of the tension leave her shoulders for the first time that day.

"That's not bad," said Neil approvingly. "I'm going to greenlight the remaining twelve episodes."

"That's great news!" said William, looking very pleased. "Thank you very much."

"Yes, thank you," said Maria. It was only the start of December but Maria felt like she just got what she wanted for Christmas. She planned to call up her dad and let him know that she was the producer of a show that had been greenlit.

"We will make this show part of the spring line up," said Neil. "That gives you about three months before we broadcast the first episode. It's unfortunate that they won't be purchasing a big-ticket item like a mansion every week."

"What are you thinking?" asked William.

"The show could have the potential to drag if we try to shoot all thirteen episodes in just three months. There are bound to be weeks where not much is going on. But if you continue to film them, even after we start broadcasting, you can edit out the slow parts right before we air each episode."

"We could do that," said William, "but it will be more expensive to produce. Will that be okay?" Maria could see him drumming his fingers on his thigh.

Neil thought for a second. "Right now, it's just one producer and a cameraman, plus the editor – right?"

"That's right," said William. "We've been trying to keep the costs down."

"So we can afford to keep shooting for six months. I think this show has the potential to be a hit and I want to give it the best chance. Plus, we'll have material if we contract for a second season.

"Maria, do you think you can keep them spending? Viewers are going to want to see them living like millionaires."

"He likes to spend and I can work with that," said Maria. She didn't think this was the time to bring up the fact that Kat was always trying to save.

"You should keep building the audience on YouTube with ten-minute weekly excerpts," said Neil. "We can build a lot of anticipation for the show. Just make sure you don't give too much away. Save the good stuff for broadcast."

"Sounds like a plan," said William. He sounded very upbeat.

"There's just one more thing," said Neil, looking thoughtful, as he played with a paperclip on his desk. "Do you think Michael was banging that woman from his acting class?"

"I'm convinced of it," said Maria. "He was trying to break up with her without making it obvious in front of the camera, but anyone could see what he was trying to do."

"That's what I'm concerned about," said Neil. "If you show that scene during the first episode, any filming you do, after we start broadcasting, will be about Kat divorcing him. You should save any mention of his philandering for the season finale, when it can be the surprise twist. Before then, try to make him look like a model husband."

 "I like it!" said William, "We'll get America loving him and then show who he really is. People won't be able to stop talking about it. Maria, what do you think?" He gave her a big grin.

"I think we can make it work," said Maria thoughtfully. "If he cheats again, we'll try to get it on camera for the final episode."

"I have to get ready for my next meeting," said Neil, glancing at his watch. "You've done great work here and I look forward to seeing the next episode when it's ready."

He got up and shook their hands before ushering them out of his office.

Maria felt like she was floating on a cloud. She had the greenlight to shoot the remaining episodes and she was going to have a gig for at least six months. She couldn't wait until her father saw her name in the opening credits. That was assuming she could get him to watch her show.

KAT

John Sanford, of the law offices of Adams, Robertson and Taft, seemed very competent and Kat was sorry they hadn't had him on retainer when they signed the *Lucky* contracts. He looked like he just stepped out a legal drama, in his dark gray suit with white shirt and striped navy blue tie. His silver hair contrasted nicely with his dark skin and the laugh lines around his chocolate brown eyes deepened, when he smiled at Kat and Michael.

"So tell me why you're here," he said in a rich baritone voice. "What can Adams, Robertson and Taft help you with?"

Michael slid the summons and the complaint across John's desk.

"We were served this yesterday, while we were leaving our apartment," Michael said. He looked as stressed as Kat felt.

John picked up the papers and glanced through them, while Kat waited with a knot in her stomach.

"So let's see, it looks like this restaurant owner is suing you for libel because Michael posted a negative tweet on Twitter about his raw chicken dinner."

"But that's ludicrous," said Michael angrily. "We can't be sued for a tweet about raw chicken, even if we mention the restaurant's name."

"In order to win a libel case, the burden of proof is on the plaintiff. He has to prove that a statement is defamatory and damaging. The statement also has to be false. Was the chicken actually raw?"

"Yes," said Michael. "It looked cooked on the outside but when I cut into it, it was dark pink and bloody."

"And what did you do?" asked John. Kat found his calm voice reassuring.

"I sent the chicken back to the kitchen," said Michael, "and then we asked for the check. The waitress was very apologetic and only charged us for Kat's meal."

"Do you have any idea why the restaurant owner is suing you?"

"The owner is probably looking to make a quick buck," said Michael. "Since winning the BonusBall, there are a lot of people who want a payout."

John put his hands on his desk. His fingertips formed a temple, pointing upwards. "How would the restaurant owner know that you're BonusBall winners?"

"We're on a YouTube reality show about BonusBall winners," explained Kat. "You may have seen our cameraman and producer, waiting outside your office.

Because of the show, Michael is starting to get a lot of followers on Twitter. Someone may have seen his tweet and told the restaurant owner."

"There are several ways we can handle this," said John. "Obviously, it would be best if we can get the case dismissed. If you could prove that the chicken was bloody, the restaurant owner wouldn't have a case. Do you think you could get the waitress to make a statement?"

"I don't know," said Michael, looking unsure. "We would have to go back to the restaurant and hope that she's on shift. Then we would have to convince her to give us a statement. If the restaurant owner is there, when we try to talk to her, it could get awkward."

"Another option," said John, "is for us to go to court. The burden of proof would be on the restaurant owner, so that would be to your advantage. Plus, he would have to prove that he was harmed by your tweet.

"The drawback is that it's time-consuming and could get expensive if we have to mount a solid defense. Our firm charges $400 an hour. If we go to court, there's always the chance that the judgment could go against you and you would have to pay him damages."

"How many hours do you think defending us would take?" Kat asked. She had hoped this lawsuit would go away quickly and didn't like the idea of going to court.

"It's hard to say," said John. "Our firm would start with a retainer of $10,000 but that only covers twenty-five hours. I could easily see this taking more time than that."

"For a stupid tweet?" Michael said, scowling. "That seems crazy."

"Unfortunately, in our litigious society you have to be very careful what you say on social media."

"Do we have any other options?" Kat asked.

"Of course, you could always settle with the restaurant owner. That would make this go away quickly."

"Settle with him? The chicken was raw. Why should we have to settle?" said Michael angrily.

John looked at them sympathetically. "You may wind up paying less for a small settlement, compared to what it would cost you to go to court. But of course, the choice is up to you. I'm happy to handle it in any way that you want."

"How much would we have to pay if we settled?" Kat asked. She glanced at Michael. He looked furious at the very idea.

"I would start by offering a very small amount, like $5,000 and let him negotiate up to $10,000. If he wanted more than that, I would consider going to court and making him prove the tweet cost him customers."

"What do you think, Michael? It seems like the fastest way to make this go away."

Michael ran his hand over his face and sighed deeply. "I don't know, Kat. I want this to go away but the idea of paying this bottom feeder makes me furious, especially since the chicken really was raw. Are we going to pay anyone who sues us to make a quick buck?"

Kat felt annoyed. If Michael wasn't so quick to tweet; if he wasn't so in love with his own dry wit, they wouldn't be in this situation.

"I think we should offer a settlement and you should be more careful about what you tweet in the future," she said snippily.

Michael looked at her unhappily. "I'll be a lot more careful about what I tweet from now on." He sighed again and turned back towards John.

"When do we have to let you know what we want to do?"

"You don't have much time," said John. "We only have twenty days to file a response with the court."

Michael looked down. "Okay," he said in a defeated voice, "let's settle with this bastard."

John nodded. "So am I authorized to offer up to $10,000 as a settlement?"

Kat and Michael said "Yes" at the same time.

"Okay, I'll put in the call this afternoon. Please don't worry. His case isn't a strong one and I'm sure he was hoping for a settlement, rather than going to court. I'll call you after I've spoken to his lawyer."

Kat and Michael thanked him.

"One word of advice," John said, as they stood up to leave. "Don't mention on camera that you're settling out of court. You don't want to open a floodgate of lawsuits from other litigants. Just tell your audience that your lawyer is handling the matter. The less said about this, the better."

"Thank you, that's good advice," said Kat, looking meaningfully at Michael. For once, she hoped he would keep his mouth shut. He just nodded.

Maria came running up to them, as they left John's office, with Dan following right behind.

"So what happened?" she asked excitedly. "Are you going to court?"

"Our lawyer will be handling this," said Kat, "and he's asked us not to talk about it on camera."

Kat was pleased to see that Maria looked crushed as she turned to Michael.

"Michael, is there anything you can tell our audience?"

Michael looked pained. "Like Kat said, we're not supposed to discuss the case. Please just edit out anything having to do with this lawsuit."

'At least there's one part of our lives we can keep private,' Kat thought with some satisfaction as they left the Adams, Robertson and Taft offices.

A couple of hours later, they got a call from John. The restaurant owner had agreed to settle for $7,500 and was dropping the case. If they included the $800 to cover John's fee, the total cost to make the lawsuit go away came to $8,300.

'That's a lot of money for a stupid joke about chicken crudo,' Kat thought bitterly. She knew they could afford it but it still aggravated her. 'I hope Michael has learned a lesson about trying to be funny online.'

CHAPTER 12

MARIA

Maria woke up early, so she could call her father before she had to get to work. As she dialed his number, she could picture him drinking his coffee at the breakfast table.

"Maria, how are you doing?" she heard him say, after he picked up.

"I'm good, Dad, how are you?" As always, she felt a little anxious talking to her father. His approval meant so much to her.

"I'm good but I can't talk long because I have to leave for court."

"I know, Dad. I won't keep you. I just wanted to let you know that A+M gave us the greenlight for this show I'll be producing. It's called *Lucky* and it's about a couple of BonusBall winners."

Her father paused before asking "Is it a documentary?"

Maria felt her eyelid twitch. "Not exactly, Dad. It's more of a reality TV show."

"Maria, aren't those shows just trash? Lots of people arguing and having sex on camera? Is that why you studied film at U.C.L.A.?"

"This show isn't about sex or dating. It's strictly PG entertainment. It's about how becoming suddenly rich changes the lives of the people who win the lottery."

"Is that really how you want to spend your career? If you have to work in the film industry, wouldn't you rather be more like Ken Burns?"

Leave it to her father to compare her to one of the most acclaimed documentary filmmakers. There was no way Maria would ever be able to measure up.

"Dad, this show has the potential to become a huge hit. And I would be the producer."

"I don't think you should be wasting your time on reality TV. Maria, you know it's not too late for you to take the LSAT and apply for law school. Maybe you could become a lawyer in the entertainment industry if you wanted to stay in the business."

"Dad, I don't want to become a lawyer. I like being a producer. This show could be a steppingstone for me if the ratings are great."

"A steppingstone to what? More reality TV shows? I'm sorry, Maria, but I really do have to run. I can't be late for court. You can tell me more about your show when you come home for Christmas."

Maria felt crushed that her father wasn't impressed with her show. She wondered what he would think, if he knew how she manipulated Kat and Michael just to create drama for the show. Somehow she had the feeling that he wouldn't approve.

She was about to say goodbye when she realized he had already hung up. She got ready to leave for Kat and Michael's apartment.

———

Dan had been filming Kat and Michael decorating their small Christmas tree when Kat left the apartment to go to her book club.

"So what are you thinking of getting Kat for Christmas?" Maria asked

Michael, as Dan turned from focusing on the tree to shooting Michael.

"I don't know," said Michael with a sigh. "I want to get her something nice but when I asked what she wanted, she said she just wanted a baby for Christmas. I can't exactly wrap that up and put it under the tree. Maria, do you have any suggestions?"

Of course, Maria had suggestions. She had been keeping what she thought of as her 'Big-Ticket' list, just waiting for a chance to suggest spending to Michael and Kat.

"Yes," she said. "Sotheby's is having an auction of important jewels this week. Maybe you can get her jewelry."

"I don't think that's a good idea," said Michael with a pensive look on his face. "Kat and I agreed to a limit of spending no more than $15,000 on Christmas gifts for each other."

"Surely, that doesn't include jewelry. Jewelry isn't really a gift; it's more like an investment."

"Kat doesn't really wear much jewelry," Michael pointed out.

"Maybe that's because Kat doesn't have much jewelry to wear. I notice she only wears a slim gold wedding band. Have you thought about getting her a diamond ring, now that you can afford it?"

Michael thought about it for a moment, and his face brightened with a smile.

"I think Kat would really like that," said Michael. "It seems a little odd, getting her an engagement ring, two years after we've been married, but I think she would love the gesture. Thank you for the suggestion!"

"So let's go to the auction preview tomorrow," said Maria. "If you see something you like, we can go to the auction on Thursday and bid on a ring. Give me a moment and I'll get it set up."

She called Bethany, one of the production assistants at 'One Ring to Rule Them All' productions.

"Hey, Bethany, it's Maria. We're going to want to do some shooting at a Sotheby's preview tomorrow and then again at an auction on Thursday. Can you call them up and get their permission to film? They probably won't give us permission to shoot the other bidders so reassure them that we'll only shoot Michael, the items he plans to bid on, and the auctioneer. Call me if they give you a hard time."

Bethany agreed to get all the necessary permissions, before the preview.

———

On Wednesday, at 10:00 am, Maria and Dan waited outside Sotheby's, on York Avenue, while Michael was parking his Ferrari in a parking garage on 71st. The imposing Sotheby's building was fronted with mirrored windows and spanned the entire block between 71st and 72nd Streets.

"Get a shot of the front," instructed Maria. Dan walked across the street so he could get a shot of the big gray Sotheby's sign with the international flags hung over the entrance. When Michael joined them, they went inside the building. A security guard escorted them to the office of Francesca Laurent, the Senior VP in charge of Magnificent Jewels.

Francesca was an attractive woman in her late thirties, dressed in an iron-gray suit with an ivory silk blouse. Her sleek, dark hair was pulled into a bun so tight, it gave Maria a headache just looking at it. Francesca gave Michael, Maria and Dan a cold little smile.

"Here at Sotheby's, we take the privacy of our patrons very seriously," she said. Maria noticed that Francesca had a slight French accent.

"Yes, of course," said Maria anxiously, hoping they would still be allowed to shoot the auction. She fidgeted on her chair.

"You have our permission to shoot the items that Michael is interested in bidding on, during the preview and the auction. You can also shoot Michael while he's bidding."

"What about the auctioneer?" Maria asked.

"We don't want your cameraman moving the camera back and forth between Michael and the auctioneer. You would capture video of the other bidders that way and we can't allow that. If you want to shoot Michael and the auctioneer, I suggest you get another camera for the auction. You can have one camera focused on Michael, and the second camera focused on the front of the room."

Maria knew William would approve the expense of having a second cameraman for the day if it meant capturing the auction. She nodded in agreement.

"We can do that, Francesca. Is there anything else?"

"Yes, Sotheby's would like to get a copy of your film, in case we want to use any of it for P.R. purposes. Would you be open to that?"

"We would need to get approval from A+M Networks but I don't think that will be a problem. Could we agree that Sotheby's wouldn't be able to use the footage until after we've aired the episode with the auction?" Maria asked.

"When are you planning on airing the episode?" Francesca asked, leaning forward in her chair.

"We start broadcasting in March, so the episode would air sometime next spring but I don't have an exact date."

"I think we can work with that," Francesca said. "Let me take you to the room where we're previewing the jewelry. It's a stunning collection and I'm sure you'll find something you love." She turned to Michael. "Are you looking for anything in particular?"

"Yes," said Michael with a big smile, "We're looking for a diamond ring for my wife."

"This sale features a variety of signed jewels from numerous notable estates. We have an impressive selection of classic white diamond and colored stone rings in a variety of shapes and sizes."

"That sounds amazing," said Michael as Francesca stood up.

"Please follow me," she said, leading them out of her office and through the hall to the elevators. They took an elevator down to the ground level.

"Start filming," Maria said to Dan, as they reached the preview room with glass cases full of sparkling jewels. Each case had a Sotheby's employee standing behind it, ready to take items out of the case for potential bidders to examine.

"Let me get you an auction catalog," said Francesca, pulling one from a pile on top of a case, nearest the entrance to the room. "You can see the estimates for each item, along with a detailed description. Please ask if you want to have anything taken out of a case. Enjoy the preview!"

With that, she shook Michael and Maria's hands and left the room.

Michael walked over to the first case, followed by Dan and Maria. Michael gave a long whistle, as he looked in the case. Glittering rings, brooches, necklaces, earrings and bracelets were arranged on light gray velvet. Each item in the case had a number displayed next to it, which mapped to a description in the catalog. Michael stared for a couple of minutes.

"Is there something I can show you, sir?" the Sotheby's employee behind the case asked.

"Could I see that ring, and that one?" asked Michael, pointing at two of the rings.

"Michael, why don't you read the descriptions from the catalog out loud," suggested Maria, "so our viewers will know what you're looking at."

"Lot 21," read Michael. "A diamond and green sapphire ring, by Van Cleef & Arpels. The oval-shaped diamond weighing 3.12 carats, claw-set between oval-shaped green sapphires, the shoulders accented by round diamonds, size 6, signed VCA."

He picked up the ring and looked at it closely.

"Hold it up to the camera," said Maria. Michael held it up and Dan got a close-up of the ring. It was one large diamond, flanked by two large emeralds.

"What's the range?" asked Maria.

"The estimate is $10,000 to $15,000," responded Michael. "It's beautiful. What do you think, Maria?"

Maria thought she wanted Michael to spend more than $15,000 on a ring.

"It is beautiful," she agreed, "but I don't know if Kat will like the two emeralds which are almost as big as the diamond. What do you think about the other ring?"

Michael handed the emerald and diamond ring back to the Sotheby's employee and picked up the second ring.

"Read the description," said Maria.

"Lot 32. Diamond Ring, Van Cleef & Arpels. Estimate $50,000 to $70,000."

'Now we're getting somewhere,' thought Maria.

"This is so much more than the limit we said we would put on our presents," said Michael with a worried look on his face.

"Yes, but jewelry is so much more than just a present," Maria pointed out. "All the really wealthy people invest in jewelry. If you buy something here today, you can always sell it in the future or it can become an heirloom."

'Was jewelry really a good investment?' Maria wondered for a moment. She decided not to let that worry her as she tried to convince Michael.

"What else does it say?" she asked. Dan moved for a close-up of the second ring.

Michael read the rest of the description from the catalog. "Set with a round diamond weighing 10.51 carats, with baguette diamond shoulders, size 7, signed VCA." He turned towards Maria. "Do you think ten carats is too large?"

"You know what they say," she responded flippantly, "size matters. No, Michael, I don't think ten carats is too large. I think any woman would be ecstatic with a diamond that big."

"I don't know," said Michael, handing the ring to be put back in the case. "I'll think about it. Let's see what else they have."

He went around the room, trailed by Dan and Maria, looking at various rings. He spent the longest amount of time with a ring that had a pink diamond center stone, surrounded by round white diamonds.

"Lot 719," he read from the catalog. "Light pink diamond and diamond ring. Estimate $40,000 to $60,000. A rectangular brilliant-cut light pink diamond weighing 1.41 carats, surrounded by round diamonds weighing approximately 1.70 carats in total, mounted in platinum and pink gold. Ring size: 6."

He had spent nearly five minutes looking at the one ring and Maria was starting to get impatient.

"Pink is Kat's favorite color," Michael said. "I think she would love this ring. What do you think, Maria?"

"I think it's a gorgeous ring," said Maria, "I'm sure Kat would love it. Michael, do you think she would like more than just a ring for Christmas? Maybe some earrings or a bracelet to go with the ring? They have so many beautiful pieces here you could consider getting. I'm sure our viewers would love to see you purchase more than one item at the auction. And of course, buying more jewelry would be a good investment."

Michael looked at her thoughtfully. "Do you really think viewers would want to see that?"

"I know it," said Maria. "We could preview the auction on YouTube. Viewers will tune in, just to see what items you win at auction. I've been tracking interest on social media. Viewers love it when you and Kat live like millionaires."

"I want to keep viewers interested," said Michael. "Maybe we should look at some other items, in addition to the rings." He turned to the woman standing behind the case.

"Could I see those earrings, and that necklace, please?"

"Of course, sir," she responded, taking the items out of the case and handing them to Michael.

Maria didn't even have to ask him to read the descriptions, he read them automatically.

"Lot 520. Pair of Cartier Diamond Ear Clips. Estimate $50,000 to $70,000. Of floral design, set with an old European-cut diamond weighing 3.14 carats and an old mine-cut diamond weighing 2.19 carats, accented by variously-cut diamonds, signed Cartier Mtg."

"Lot 523. Diamond necklace from a private collection, Los Angeles, California. Estimate $12,000 to $15,000. The flexible V-shaped design, set with round, baguette and marquise-shaped diamonds, length 15 inches."

The description didn't do the necklace justice. It had diamond baguettes which formed a V-shape. Hanging from the baguettes were diamonds shaped like tree leaves and there was a diamond pendant at the bottom. Maria wished she had the money to bid on it.

After another hour, Maria felt as though Michael had looked at nearly every piece of jewelry in the Sotheby's cases. She excused herself to put in a call, to find a second camera person for tomorrow's auction.

When she came back, Michael was ready to leave. He clutched his catalog with the notes he had written, on the items he wanted to bid on.

"So how many items are you planning on bidding on?" Maria asked him.

"It depends on how the auction goes," said Michael. "If I win the early lots, I won't put in a bid on the later lots. Right now, there are twelve items I would like to bid on."

That sounded very promising. Maria couldn't wait for the auction the next day.

————

They got to Sotheby's about an hour before the auction started and met Francesca to get the cameras set up in the room where Sotheby's was holding the auction. The auction room was a large space with gray carpeting and a coffered white ceiling with spotlights shining down. There were rows of folding chairs facing a wooden podium where the auctioneer would stand. In back of the podium were two large screens, so images of the jewelry could be projected to the bidders. At the back of the room were tables where Sotheby's employees would sit, so they could take telephone bids and monitor the online bidding.

At Francesca's insistence, Michael was seated in a chair to the right of the rows, so Dan's camera wouldn't accidentally film someone sitting next to Michael. Maria was seated next to Michael. The second camera person, Jada, would have her camera focused on the auctioneer. Once Francesca was satisfied the privacy of the other bidders would be maintained, she left the room. Maria, Dan, Jada and Michael waited while the room started filling up with other bidders.

At 11:00 A.M., the auctioneer walked to the front of the room. He looked to be in his fifties, with a full head of silver hair and was dressed in a navy three-piece suit.

"Ladies and gentlemen, thank you very much for attending this Sotheby's auction of important jewels." A photo of an intricate diamond brooch showed on both screens. "Let's get started with our first lot, this magnificent Marianne Ostier diamond brooch. I would like to start the bidding at $10,000."

Maria watched the bidders compete for the brooch. Looking in her catalog, she could see that the estimate was $10,000 to $15,000. The brooch was won by an online bidder for $13,500.

"Which is the first lot you'll be bidding on?" she whispered to Michael.

"Lot 12, a cultured pearl necklace," he whispered back, after looking at his catalog.

"What's the range?" she asked.

"$20,000 to $25,000," he answered. "It should be coming up in a couple of minutes."

Maria watched the bidding on the other items.

"Lot 12," the auctioneer announced as the necklace filled both screens. "A cultured pearl necklace with a jade clasp. We already have some online bids, so I'm going to start the bidding at $22,000. Do I have $22,000?"

Michael raised his paddle.

"$22,000, in the room," said the auctioneer, acknowledging his bid. "Will anyone bid $23,000?"

An Asian man, seated in the front row on the left side, raised his paddle. From her angle, Maria couldn't see much of him except the side of his face and his outstretched arm holding up the paddle.

"23,000 in the front. $24,000 on the phone," the auctioneer said.

The man in the front row raised his paddle again.

"$25,000 in the room Am I bid $26,000?"

"Are you going to let him win?" whispered Maria, hoping she could get Michael into a bidding war

"This was a nice-to-have, not a must-have," said Michael. "I don't want to go above the range for this necklace. He can have it."

"I'm at $25,000. $25,000. Going once, twice? Sold for $25,000."

"What's the next item you want to bid on?" asked Maria.

"Lot 32. The ten-carat diamond ring," said Michael.

Maria waited impatiently until they got to Lot 32.

"Lot 32," said the auctioneer. "An important 10.51-carat diamond ring by Van Cleef & Arpels. I'll start the bidding at $50,000."

Michael raised his paddle.

"Do I have $55?"

The man in the front row raised his paddle.

"$55 in the room, do I have $60? $60 on the phone," said the auctioneer, speaking rapidly.

Michael raised his paddle.

"$65 in the room."

The man in front raised his paddle.

"I have $70,000, thank you."

"Bastard," said Michael under his breath. Maria hoped that Dan's mic was able to capture it.

Michael raised his paddle.

"$75. Do I have $80?"

The same man in front raised his paddle.

"$80 in the room. $85 on the phone. $90 online. Do I have $100,000?"

The Asian man raised his paddle a fraction before Michael.

"Do I have $110,000?" Michael raised his paddle.

"$110, thank you."

The man in the front row raised his paddle again.

"$120,000," said the auctioneer.

"He's winning," said Maria, "Don't you want to go up to $130?"

Michael sighed. "I'll let him win again. The range on this ring was only up to $70,000. I don't want to pay double that, by the time you throw in the buyer's premium of 25 percent."

"I have $120,000," said the auctioneer. "$120 going once. $120 going twice. Sold!"

Maria was getting frustrated. Although the auction process could be entertaining, she needed Michael to start winning to hold viewers' interest.

"You don't have Kat's Christmas gift yet," she pointed out. "Do you think you should start increasing your bids?"

"I know," said Michael. "Maybe I should be a little more aggressive. I just wish that man in the front would stop bidding against me. Quiet, Maria, Lot 57 is coming up."

"Lot 57," said the auctioneer. "A sapphire and diamond bracelet. I'll start the bidding at $12,000." A large picture of a sapphire and diamond bracelet was displayed on both screens.

Michael raised his paddle.

"I have $12,000, do I hear $13?" asked the auctioneer. "$13 on the phone."

Michael raised his paddle.

"I have $14, do I hear $15?" asked the auctioneer. "$15 on the phone. Do I hear $16?"

Michael raised his paddle. Maria held her breath, hoping the bidder on the phone would drop out.

The auctioneer paused for a moment. "I'm at $16, do I hear $17? $16 going once. $16 going twice. Sold for $16,000!"

"Yes!" said Michael, pumping his fist in the air.

"Congratulations!" Maria said, happy he had won something. She had hoped he would win a bigger ticket item, but $16,000 was a good start.

The auction was in its second hour when Michael won a pair of sapphire and diamond earrings for $22,000.

"How are you feeling?" asked Maria. She was wondering if they had enough footage and could call it a day.

"I'm feeling good but I still want to win that pink diamond ring. It's lot 719, so we probably have another hour before it comes up. Hey look, that man in the front is bidding on a diamond necklace. I would love to ruin his day."

Lot 598 was displayed on the monitors at the front of the room. It was a diamond baguette necklace with pear-shaped diamonds hanging from diamond swags. At the end of each swag was a diamond flower, with a round stone and diamond petals.

The man in the front row had just put in a bid for $22,000.

"Do I hear $24?" the auctioneer asked.

Michael quickly put up his paddle.

"I have $24, do I hear $26?"

The man in the front row put up his paddle.

"Do I have $28?"

Michael put up his paddle.

"Sir, will you bid $30,000?" The auctioneer looked at the man in the front row expectantly. The man in front shook his head no.

"I have $28. $28 going once. $28 going twice. Sold for $28,000."

"Take that," said Michael, grinning triumphantly. Maria was thrilled that he seemed to have a case of auction fever.

It was another forty-five minutes before the auctioneer got to lot 719, the pink diamond ring surrounded by white diamonds.

Maria watched as the bidding quickly rose to $60,000. Finally, it seemed to come down to Michael and the man in the front row.

"I have $60," said the auctioneer, nodding towards Michael. "Do I hear $65?"

The man in the front row raised his paddle.

"Do I hear $70?"

Michael raised his paddle and called out "70."

"Do I hear $75?"

Maria turned to look at the man in the front row. He sat still without raising his paddle, staring intently at the auctioneer.

"I have $70," said the auctioneer, pausing for a moment. "$70 going once. $70 going twice."

The auctioneer called out "Sold!" just as the man started to raise his paddle. He put his paddle down again, shaking his head. He was too late. Michael had won the pink diamond ring.

"Awesome!" Michael said to Maria excitedly. "We won!" He leaned over and surprised Maria by giving her a quick hug. Startled, she hugged him back.

As they got up, to arrange for payment, Maria quickly did the numbers in her head. The sapphire and diamond bracelet was $16,000. The sapphire and diamond earrings were $22,000. The diamond swag necklace was $28,000 and the pink diamond ring was $70,000. By the time you added in Sotheby's 25 percent buyer's premium, the total came to $170,000.

"So do you think viewers are going to like seeing the auction?" asked Michael. "Does it make for great TV?"

"I think viewers are going to love it," said Maria enthusiastically. "I'm sure we'll get more subscribers to the YouTube channel, when we post the clip, and people will watch the episode on TV when it airs. You did a great job winning that jewelry in the auction."

"Anything to help the show," said Michael. "Plus, the jewelry is a great investment. I think Kat will be very happy with her Christmas gifts this year."

"I'm sure she'll be happy," said Maria, trying to sound sincere. She wasn't really concerned with Kat's happiness. She was more interested in seeing if William was happy with the footage they filmed at the auction.

KAT

It was December 28th before Kat and Michael were able to open their presents to each other. Dan and Maria had been off for the Christmas holiday but Maria wanted to be able to film the unwrapping, so she had convinced Michael to wait a few days to exchange gifts.

"It's your choice," Maria had said. "You can open your presents on the 25th and wrap them up again, to open while we're filming, or you can just wait until the 28th."

Michael, of course, had agreed to wait until the 28th. Kat supposed it was for the best because she doubted she could fake being surprised, if she had to open her presents for the second time.

Kat got a cup of coffee and waited impatiently while Dan and Maria got set up in front of the small Christmas tree. At least the delay had allowed her to get dressed and put on some makeup before they started filming. She didn't want to be on camera, in her pajamas with serious bed head.

Finally, they were ready. Kat and Michael sat on the floor in front of the small tree.

"Kat, why don't you give Michael his first gift," directed Maria.

Kat felt annoyed. Was Maria going to orchestrate their entire Christmas celebration? Would she be telling Kat how to react to each gift? Kat looked at Michael, to see how he was responding to Maria. He was beaming at Dan and the camera, so she just sighed and handed him his first gift.

"Merry Christmas, Michael," she said, handing him a large box.

"Kat, this is the black leather bomber jacket I wanted before we won the BonusBall. You remembered!"

"Of course I remembered Michael. I knew how much you wanted it but we couldn't afford it back then. It was one of the first presents I bought you."

"I love it!" he said, standing up and slipping the jacket over his sweater. "How does it look?"

Kat wasn't sure if he was modeling for her, or for the camera but she had to admit he looked fabulous in the jacket.

"Michael, why don't you give Kat that present next?" said Maria, pointing to a rectangular package with silver wrapping paper and a red bow.

"Thank you," said Kat, as Michael handed her the gift. She started unwrapping and was very happy to see *Fibonacci*, the latest thriller by Scott Wilton.

"Thank you very much, Michael. I've wanted to read this ever since I read the book review in the *New York Times*. I can't wait to get started."

"Hey, Kat," said Maria. "Do you want to tell me the other gifts you've gotten for Michael, so I can tell you the order he should open them in?"

"That's okay, Maria. I think I can handle the order myself," said Kat. She was trying not to let the filming spoil her enjoyment of Christmas.

She handed Michael his next gift, which was a pair of black leather driving gloves.

"I bought them so you can wear them when you drive the Ferrari," Kat said.

"Thank you, Kat, they're great!" said Michael, placing the gloves next to his jacket.

"The box with the green ribbon next, Michael," said Maria.

Kat unwrapped the package. Her pulse quickened when she saw it was a long thin black velvet box. Opening the box slowly, she saw something sparkling inside. Holding her breath, she saw a diamond and sapphire bracelet in the box. Nestled in with the bracelet was a breathtaking pair of diamond and sapphire earrings with a knotted design.

"Oh my God," she said softly, holding the box up to the light. "Oh, Michael, they're so beautiful. They must have cost a fortune."

"Do you like them, Kitty Kat?" asked Michael with a big grin.

"I love them but they're so extravagant." She looked at the bracelet closely, the way the diamonds refracted the light into tiny rainbows and the deep blue of the sapphires. She had never owned something so beautiful. "Did you stick to the $15,000 limit we put on the presents?"

"Please don't worry about what I spent, Kat. I may have gone a little over budget but jewelry is a solid investment. And I want you to have beautiful things now that we can afford it."

He looked so excited that she didn't have the heart to give him a hard time about how much he must have spent.

"Oh, Michael, put it on." She held the bracelet and her wrist out to Michael. He undid the clasp and put it on, around her wrist. She held her arm up and looked at the bracelet. It was gorgeous.

"It looks amazing," said Michael with a big smile. "Happy Christmas, Kat."

"Merry Christmas, Michael," she said, handing him his next gift. "I splurged on this one but I hope you love it."

The splurge was a Rolex Submariner watch. Michael seemed to really like it.

"We both have well-dressed wrists," he laughed, holding the arm with the watch up for Dan to shoot.

"That green box next," said Maria.

For a moment Kat wondered if Maria had told Michael what to buy for Kat. She loved her diamond and sapphire bracelet and earrings. She hoped the idea came from Michael, not Maria.

"Here you go," said Michael, handing the box to Kat.

"Thank you," said Kat as she tore the paper off. Inside was a MacBook Air.

"I know your writing hasn't been going well," said Michael, "and I thought a new laptop might help inspire you."

Kat was touched. She didn't think a new laptop would help with the wicked case of writer's block she had developed but she appreciated the gesture.

"Thank you, Michael, I can't wait to try it out. Here, open your next gift." She handed him a large box.

Inside was a Brooks Brothers cashmere sweater with a shawl collar. Kat bought it because she thought the beige color would look great on Michael.

"Thank you. It's a gorgeous sweater," said Michael. He pulled off the sweater he was wearing and tried it on. "What do you think?"

"It looks great on you," said Maria. "Dan, move in on Michael."

Dan walked towards Michael, who preened a bit in front of the camera. Kat just rolled her eyes.

Michael turned towards Maria. "Small box last?" he asked.

"Yes," Maria said, nodding her head, "so give Kat the larger box now."

Michael handed Kat a box the size of a large book. For a moment, Kat hoped it would be a pregnancy book, signaling Michael's readiness to start a family.

'I'm being silly,' she chided herself as she started taking off the wrapping paper. To her surprise, it was another black velvet box.

"Michael, what did you get me?" Kat asked nervously as she slowly opened the box.

She was staggered when she saw the diamond necklace inside the box.

It looked like something the Queen of England would wear. Kat wasn't sure if she would ever have an occasion to wear a necklace with so many diamonds.

"Do you like it, Kat?" asked Michael, looking at her closely.

Kat thought the necklace was beautiful but she was upset at what it must have cost. "It's stunning but Michael, we agreed on a price cap for our gifts. This necklace must have cost a fortune."

"I didn't think the limit included jewelry, Kat. I invested in something that should increase in value over time."

"Who told you that jewelry was a good investment?" Kat asked anxiously.

"Everybody knows that jewelry is a good investment, Kat."

"I'm not sure that jewelry is a good investment and I don't know that I would ever wear a necklace like this. It will just sit in the safety deposit box for years at a time. It's beautiful but I already have the bracelet and the earrings. I think you should take this back to the jewelry store where you bought it."

"I bought it at auction," said Michael, frowning. "So we can't take it back." Kat was distressed that the necklace couldn't be returned.

"Michael, even though we're rich, you shouldn't be spending money recklessly on things like diamond necklaces I'll never wear."

"Kat, stop giving me a hard time. We can afford it and it's a great investment. We can probably sell it at auction tomorrow, for more than I paid."

"How much did you pay, Michael? Just how much did all this jewelry cost?"

"Kat, you're not supposed to ask how much your presents cost."

"And you weren't supposed to spend more than $15,000."

"I invested in something, Kat. I didn't just buy you something."

"Did you check with Len, before you 'invested' in the jewelry?"

"Len is our money manager, not my father. I don't have to check with him anytime I want to spend some of our money."

"Well maybe you should have," said Kat hotly. "You've clearly spent tens of thousands of dollars."

"Kitty Kat, it's Christmas. I don't want to fight with you over how much I spent on your presents. I wanted you to have beautiful things and I know they will be good investments. If I promise not to invest in anything from now on, without checking with you, can we stop fighting?" Michael looked at her with such a hopeful expression on his face that it took the edge off her anger.

Kat took a deep breath and tried to put a good face on it.

"Alright, Michael," she said. "The necklace really is beautiful. If you promise not to buy really expensive things without me from now on, I'll stop giving you a hard time. Maybe this necklace can become an heirloom for our children someday."

"Yes, Kat," said Michael, looking relieved.

Kat reached under the tree to get Michael's last present. It was a scroll with a ribbon tied around it.

"Here," she said, offering him a conciliatory smile. "I hope you like this."

Michael slid the ribbon off and straightened out the scroll.

"These are tickets for a Tottenham Hotspur's football match on March 16th!" Michael looked very excited.

"Yes, I thought we could make a trip of it. We can fly first class to London, stay in the Savoy and go to the soccer match. While we're there, we can see the Palace and the Tower of London. We can also go to some great restaurants."

"That sounds excellent. Thank you so much! I love this gift!"

Kat was very happy Michael seemed to like his gift.

"I'll get our production assistants working on all the arrangements," said Maria excitedly. "Just leave it to me. We'll put together an amazing trip for the two of you."

Kat had to admit; sometimes it was convenient to have Maria making all their travel plans.

"Thank you Maria, that sounds great," Kat said.

She looked under the tree, where there was one more gift.

"Michael, why don't you give Kat her last gift," said Maria. "Dan, close-up on Kat."

"Not to spoil the surprise," said Michael, picking up the small box, "but I know you always regretted not getting engaged in the traditional way."

It was true. Kat proposed to Michael when they learned he might be deported. She always felt a little regretful that she didn't give him the chance to propose to her in some romantic way. In some of her more insecure moments, she wondered if he would have proposed at all.

Michael got down on one knee and handed Kat the box.

"Here, Kitty Kat. This is for you."

Kat's hands shook as she unwrapped the paper and saw the small black velvet box. Opening the lid slowly, she was flabbergasted when she saw the pink diamond ring, surrounding by a ring of white diamonds.

"Michael, it's stunning but why did you get me more jewelry for Christmas? Haven't you gotten me enough?"

"This isn't just a Christmas present, Kat. It's the engagement ring I should have gotten you, when we first decided to get married. I couldn't afford it then, but I can afford it now. Do you like it?"

Kat didn't know whether to be aggravated that he had spent even more on jewelry or touched by the romantic gesture. She decided to let herself get swept up in the moment.

"Yes, Michael, it's gorgeous." Michael took the ring out of the box slowly and pulled her left hand towards him. He slipped the ring on the third finger. It fit like it belonged there.

Kat held her hand out in front of her, marveling at the ring. She didn't even mind when Dan zoomed in on her left hand.

"Kitty Kat," said Michael, glancing at Maria and Dan, "will you marry me?"

Kat laughed. "Michael, we're already married."

"We got married at City Hall," said Michael. "I think we should finally plan that wedding you always wanted. We can have a recommitment ceremony."

Kat was moved. "What a lovely idea, Michael. What made you think of that?"

Michael looked a little embarrassed. "It was actually Maria's idea but I think we should do it. What do you say?"

Kat's enjoyment of the idea was a little marred that it came from Maria but she still loved the idea.

"I say 'Yes' Michael. Let's get married."

"What do you think about a destination wedding?" suggested Maria. "We could fly your friends and family to someplace beautiful to have the ceremony."

"What a fantastic idea," said Michael. "Kat, where have you always wanted to go? Should we get married in Paris? Should we have a beach wedding?"

Kat had always dreamed of having a wedding someplace tropical, like Hawaii.

"What do you think about Maui?" she said, warming to the idea. "It's so beautiful there. It would be the perfect spot to have a wedding."

"Maui is it!" said Michael, beaming. Kat noticed he was smiling at the camera instead of at her.

"I'll find you a fantastic wedding planner and we'll make all the arrangements," said Maria. "Just leave it to me."

Kat was very happy. Although in the back of her mind, she wondered what Michael had spent on jewelry, she decided that she wouldn't let the cost ruin her Christmas. After all, she had a wedding to plan!

CHAPTER 13

MICHAEL

Michael was aggravated when his phone pinged for the fourth time in an hour. Checking the screen, he saw it was another text from Erica.

'*We need to talk. Stop ghosting me and call me back.*'

"Who keeps trying to reach you?" asked Maria. Without prompting, Dan moved in closer to Michael. Michael hoped Dan wouldn't try to film the text displayed on his phone.

Kat looked up from the futon where she had been reading *Fibonacci*, the book Michael had gotten her for Christmas.

"Yes, Michael, who keeps sending you so many texts?" Kat asked with a slightly suspicious tone to her voice.

Michael felt exasperated. It was bad enough having Erica hound him. He didn't need Kat's paranoia on top of it, especially not in front of the camera.

"It's just some guys from my old acting class. We're trying to coordinate getting together for drinks."

Kat stared at him for a few seconds, before shrugging and returning to her book.

Maria looked disappointed for a moment but then asked, "So are you excited about the movers coming tomorrow?"

"Yes," said Kat. "We're so excited, right, Michael?"

"Yes, very excited," Michael responded automatically, without really thinking about the question. He was more focused on figuring out an excuse for leaving the apartment, so he could call Erica and find out why she wanted to reach him so badly. Unfortunately, he knew Dan and Maria would trail him, the moment he tried to leave. Although he loved being on camera most of the time, right now it was really inconvenient.

"I have to go out and get some shaving cream," he said. "It will be just a quick trip to the drugstore. I shouldn't be gone more than 15 minutes."

"Okay," said Maria. "Give us a minute to get our coats and we'll be ready to go."

"I don't think you need to follow me for this," Michael said quickly. "I'll be back before you know it."

"We don't mind," said Maria. "Maybe we'll get lucky and we can shoot somebody recognizing you again."

The latest *Lucky* episode on YouTube had 928,000 views and the channel had 230,000 subscribers. Michael and Kat had been recognized a few times on the street and asked for autographs. There had even been one persistent person who kept asking for a $10,000 loan. Maria loved that they were getting recognized and predicted *Lucky* would be a hit when it finally aired.

"It's snowing out and I hate dragging you out in this weather," Michael protested. "Really, I'll only be gone a few minutes."

"That's why we have down jackets," Maria said cheerfully.

Michael groaned inwardly. He wouldn't have the chance to call Erica and now he was stuck going to the drugstore for shaving cream he didn't need.

"Okay, let's make this quick," he said, walking to the closet to get a coat. He wanted to wear his bomber jacket but the January weather was frigid, so he decided to go with his down parka. Glancing out the window, he could see the snow was really starting to come down, so he put on a wool newsboy cap and his driving gloves.

Dan put down the camera, and he and Maria put on their coats, before Dan picked up his camera again. They followed Michael out of the apartment and down the six flights of stairs.

They exited out the front door of the building when disaster struck: Erica was waiting on the street. Michael wondered if he could pretend not to know her but then remembered that the camera had filmed him breaking up with Erica. Anyone who had watched the episode on YouTube knew that Erica was not a random stranger.

'If only Erica had waited a couple of days,' he thought glumly. 'We would be in the new house and she wouldn't have known how to find me.'

Erica walked up to him, an apprehensive look on her face.

"Michael, I'm sorry to stalk you like this but we really need to talk."

Erica still looked gorgeous. Her face was slightly flushed from the cold and her dark hair was tucked into a woolen ski hat that framed her beautiful face. He watched a snowflake settle on her cheek before she brushed it away.

Michael was aware of Maria and Dan walking from behind him, to the side, to get both Michael and Erica in front of the camera.

"Erica, what do you want? I told you we couldn't be friends anymore."

Erica looked close to tears. "I don't want to talk on the street, Michael and it's freezing out. Can we go somewhere and talk?"

"Can't you just send me a text with whatever it is you want to say?" asked Michael. He was feeling desperate to get Erica away from Maria and Dan. If she would just send a text, he could keep the conversation off camera.

"Michael, we really need to talk and I can't just send a text. There's a bar across the street. Can we go there?" Erica pointed to O'Leary's Irish Pub.

A bar sounded like a good idea. Michael could really use a drink and a few minutes to try to gather his thoughts.

"Okay, Erica, let's get a quick drink and we can talk. But after that, I want you to leave me and Kat alone. No more texting and no more stalking."

"Thank you, Michael." Erica turned and headed for the crosswalk. Michael had the urge to run in the opposite direction. Trying to control his racing heart, he followed Erica, trailed by Maria and Dan.

A blast of warm air hit him in the face when he opened the door to O'Leary's. The bar was a bit of a dive and he had never been there before, despite its close proximity to his apartment. There was a long wooden bar with a few drinkers who looked like they had been glued to the stools all afternoon. It was dark and gloomy with some scattered tables that were empty. The bar smelled of stale beer and sweat. He told the middle-aged hostess that they wouldn't need menus.

He and Erica seated themselves at a table in the back of the room. Maria and Dan set up opposite the table. Although there was nothing on it, the scarred table felt sticky to the touch and Michael was faintly disgusted. He hoped the glasses would be clean when the waiter brought his double scotch on the rocks and Erica's seltzer water with lemon.

Michael had a sudden thought.

"Hey, Maria," he said looking hopefully in Maria's direction. "You don't have permission to shoot Erica, so you can't film this conversation, right?"

"Wrong," said Maria. "We got a waiver to shoot Erica when we went to your acting class. She signed the agreement form."

"But didn't that just cover the class?" asked Michael, feeling desperate.

"It was a blanket agreement, so we're good to shoot now. Erica, do you mind if we film this conversation?"

'Please say no,' thought Michael, trying to communicate with Erica by looking in her eyes and shaking his head.

"I don't mind," said Erica, "in fact, it might be a good idea to have a record of this conversation."

Was Erica going to sue him for sexual harassment? Michael's stomach tightened at the thought.

"Erica, why are we here?" he asked. "What did you need to talk to me about?"

Erica looked at him for a long moment. He couldn't read the expression on her face.

"Do you remember the last time you came to my apartment? When we made love without a condom?"

Michael felt suddenly dizzy and like his heart was pounding in his ears. As he was trying to think about a response that wouldn't implicate him on camera, the waiter came by with their drinks. He took a big gulp of scotch. The warmth of the scotch helped to loosen the knot in his stomach a little.

Erica continued talking.

"Well, I'm pregnant and the baby is yours."

All Michael could think was 'Deny, deny, deny.'

"I don't believe you, Erica. I'm sorry you got pregnant but someone else must be the father. Your baby couldn't be mine because we were never more than friends. You're just trying to shake me down because I'm rich now."

Erica looked stunned as she stared at him.

"Are you serious? I'm pregnant and you think this is about money?"

"Are you telling me that you haven't seen any other guys since we stopped being friends?" Michael glanced at Dan and Maria. He couldn't see Dan behind the camera but Maria looked elated.

"I have started seeing someone, after breaking up with you," admitted Erica, "but I went to the doctor. He told me that I'm six weeks pregnant. I've only been seeing Fin for three weeks and we use protection. The baby is yours."

"The doctor must be wrong," said Michael desperately, "but I'm happy to help you even if the baby's not mine. Do you need money for an abortion?" He picked up his scotch and drained the glass before motioning to the waiter that another round was needed.

"Michael, I'm Catholic. I can't have an abortion." Erica looked as if she might cry.

"You never struck me as particularly religious, Erica. Why can't you have an abortion?"

"I just couldn't handle the guilt," Erica said softly. "I don't want to get an abortion, so please stop talking about it."

"So why are you telling me? What do you want?" The waiter brought the second round and Michael took a gulp from the fresh drink.

"What do I want?" Erica's voice rose in volume. "We're having a baby and I want you to step up. You need to take responsibility because you're going to be a father."

Michael didn't want to be a father. He had been ignoring all the hints Kat had been dropping about starting a family. If he didn't want a child with his wife, he certainly didn't want to be the father of Erica's baby. He wanted to be free to focus on his career without the responsibilities of a baby weighing him down.

"What do you mean by stepping up?" he asked.

"What do you think I mean? I want you to be part of the baby's life and I expect you to pay child support. I also want you to help me out while I'm pregnant. I won't be getting too many acting gigs once I start to show."

"So this is about money," said Michael accusingly.

Erica took a sip of her seltzer. "This is about so much more than just money. You're going to be the father of our baby. Doesn't that mean anything to you?" She had a pleading look on her face.

Michael glanced at the camera again and felt like a wild animal, trapped in a cage. He was desperate to get out of this situation.

"Dan," he said, "stop filming."

"Not a chance," said Maria. She looked at Michael with something like sympathy on her face. "This is what you signed up for when you agreed to be on *Lucky*."

There was no way Michael could admit on camera that he was the father. Kat would divorce him the second the episode aired.

'Maybe Fin really is the father,' Michael thought hopefully. That would give him an out.

"Erica," said Michael, turning back to her, "this guy Fin must be the father because we were never intimate. You're living in a fantasy world, where you think we were together but it never happened. I think you're disturbed and need help."

Erica stared at him for a long moment before standing up and slapping Michael hard across the face. Michael couldn't blame her for hitting him.

His face was burning as he looked up at her. Erica stood across from him. Her face was red and her hands were balled into fists. She looked like she wanted to hit him again.

"You're the one who's disturbed, Michael," she yelled. The patrons at the bar looked over to see why someone was shouting.

"Erica, please sit down and stop causing a scene," pleaded Michael. He picked up his glass and held it to his cheek to help cool down his stinging face.

Erica didn't sit down but she lowered the volume of her voice. "Why shouldn't I cause a scene? You're trying to pretend like our relationship never happened, so you don't have to take responsibility for the baby. You sick, selfish bastard."

"Erica, I think you should get a paternity test after the baby is born. It will prove Fin is the father. Then you can accept that we were never more than friends."

"Don't worry, Michael. I plan on getting a paternity test once the baby is born. And then I'm going to hit you with a huge paternity suit."

"See? You're just trying to get me to pay for your baby. Maybe you and Fin dreamed up this scheme together to hustle me."

"Fin doesn't even know I'm pregnant. He'll probably leave me once he finds out I'm carrying another man's child." Erica looked like she was trying to hold back tears.

"Fin won't leave you, if you let him know the baby is his," said Michael hopefully. Maybe Fin would marry Erica and they could leave Michael out of it.

"I'm not going to trap Fin when I'm pregnant with your child. What kind of person do you think I am?" Erica asked indignantly.

Michael didn't respond. He needed to get out of the bar and away from Erica, so he could think clearly. He caught the waiter's attention and motioned for the check.

"Maybe I should tell Kat about the baby. I bet she'll believe me even if you don't," Erica said with a sneer on her face. "Maybe I should go to the press with my story."

Michael froze for a second. He needed to keep Erica away from Kat, at least for the next 24 hours. Once they moved, Erica would have a harder time finding Kat, without knowing their new address. He also had to keep Erica from blabbing to the press.

"Erica, you need to leave Kat out of this. I don't accept that the baby is mine but I'll write you a check to help you out, while you're pregnant, if you promise to leave us alone. No texting and no stalking. And you won't say anything to the press. Do we have an agreement?"

"How big a check?" asked Erica. She sat down again. Michael was relieved to see that she looked a little less angry.

"I'll give you $3,000 a month, for each month of the pregnancy. That's $27,000." It would be worth the money if he could make Erica go away.

"Make it an even $30,000 and I'll leave you alone until after the baby is born," said Erica, "But I plan on hitting you with a paternity suit once I can prove the baby is yours. This isn't over, Michael."

Michael had Len Applebaum on speed dial. He pulled out his phone, hoping Len was available. To his relief, he got Len on the line.

"Hey, Len. I need you to write a check for $30,000 and make it out to cash. I'll text you the address where it should be mailed. In the monthly report, just mark it down as miscellaneous. I don't want a record of where the check has been sent. Can you do that?"

Len assured Michael that he would take care of it, so Michael texted him Erica's address. He would have to come up with some excuse for Kat about why he needed $30,000 for miscellaneous expenses but he had until next month to think about it.

Michael turned back to Erica. "You should have the check in a couple of days. Do we have an agreement? You won't try to contact Kat or me until after the baby is born?"

"We have an agreement," Erica agreed. "I'm glad you're taking some responsibility, but I still want you to admit the baby is yours."

"Erica, stop living in a fantasy. The baby can't be mine because we were never more than friends."

Erica glanced at the camera. "If the baby isn't yours, why are you giving me $30,000? How are you going to explain that to your viewers?"

"I'm giving you the money because we were friends and I want to help you out now that you're in a tough situation. Maybe you can use some of the money to get some therapy. You need help, Erica."

"Don't worry, Michael," Erica said with a scowl. "I'll get help. I'll get the help of a good lawyer once the baby is born. You won't be able to deny the baby is yours once we do a paternity test."

Michael ignored the comment about the lawyer. "Do we have an agreement? You won't contact me again before the baby is born?"

She stood up again. "Don't worry, we have an agreement. I feel dirty taking your hush money but I really need the help right now. In another couple of months, I'll have to stop going on auditions and I don't know if I can keep waiting tables when I'm in my last trimester."

She glanced at the camera again and smiled grimly. "I'll leave you alone with your camera crew. I can't wait to see this episode on YouTube." With that, she stalked out of the pub.

Michael shuddered at the thought of the episode being shown on YouTube, much less on broadcast TV. He drained his glass of scotch and turned to Maria.

"Maria, I don't want you to use any of this on *Lucky*. This isn't about spending our BonusBall money. I want to keep it private."

Maria stared at him for a moment. "Michael, the show isn't just about spending money. Viewers are invested in what happens to you. Of course, they're going to want to see this."

"But this will wreck my marriage. You can't show it!" Michael's stomach clenched in a knot.

"Maybe you should have thought of that before you slept with Erica," said Dan from behind the camera.

"Please, Maria," pleaded Michael. "Don't show this. Kat will leave me."

"As it happens, you're in luck," said Maria. "In terms of the story arc, we've decided to show you as the perfect husband until the last episode. Then we'll show your infidelity as the surprise twist. We'll leave all this for the finale. That will give you some time to figure out what you want to say to Kat."

"When is the last episode supposed to air?" asked Michael, feeling a small ray of hope. At least he could postpone having Kat find out about Erica.

"The first episode airs on March 13th and the final episode airs on June 12th," said Maria. "You have until the early summer before you need to tell Kat." She paused. "I assume you are going to tell Kat, right? You won't let her find out by watching the show?"

"Of course I'll tell Kat," said Michael, feeling insulted. "I'm not heartless. I just need to find a way to break it to her gently."

"And we'll be there when you do," said Maria. "It should make for some great TV."

CHAPTER 14

KAT

After the movers left, Michael and Kat walked through the townhouse, from room to empty room, marveling at the size of the house, which had five floors and a full basement. They started on the ground floor where the foyer led into an oak-paneled study with a large marble fireplace. A big picture window looked out over East 65th Street.

"I'm going to turn this into my office," declared Michael. "It will be a perfect man cave."

The study led to a hallway that contained a staircase. Opposite the staircase were a powder room, some closets and a paneled elevator. The hallway also had folding doors that opened to a huge 18x20 foot kitchen, with white cabinets and a marble island with a double sink and a breakfast bar. Kat was impressed by the Sub-Zero refrigerator and the double wall ovens and range. As much as the kitchen was a chef's dream, she was most excited about having a dishwasher. No more scrubbing pots by hand!

The kitchen opened into a breakfast room. Their small dinette table and two chairs looked absurd in the large space which was designed for a full-sized dining table and chairs. The breakfast room had white shelving, cabinets and a place for a large TV. Double French doors opened to the small garden. Unfortunately, the garden was blanketed in snow, so they couldn't see the plantings that were visible when they viewed the house in November.

"What are we going to do with all this space?" Kat said, looking around the kitchen.

"I can find you a designer who can help you furnish the house," Maria offered. "I'm sure our viewers would love seeing you work with an interior decorator." Kat noticed that Maria was always helpful when it came to spending money.

"That's a great idea," Michael said, giving her a thumbs up. "Thank you, Maria. We would love to start working with someone."

"I'll find a designer you can start working with," said Maria. "Viewers will love it. Just leave it to me."

'Michael would agree to running down the street naked if Maria told him it would get more viewers,' Kat thought with momentary annoyance. Then she decided not to let her irritation distract her from her enjoyment of the new house.

They walked up the stairs to the second-floor dining room with its hand-painted mural of cherry blossom trees. The second floor also had a large living room with a marble fireplace and opened into a marble conservatory overlooking East 65th Street.

"I can't wait until this is furnished," said Kat happily, looking at the afternoon sun pouring in through the conservatory windows. "We should fill it with plants. It will be like having a greenhouse."

The master suite spanned the entire third floor. Their futon was dwarfed by the size of the master bedroom which had a wood burning fireplace, and a set of French doors that opened into a sitting area. The sitting area had built-in bookcases and a desk.

"This could be where you write," suggested Michael. "We can get you a comfortable office chair and you can work for hours."

Kat looked at the cabinets opposite the desk, which had a space for a large TV, with room for a sofa in front.

"I don't know, Michael," Kat said. "I think I would rather convert one of the bedrooms into an office. I would find it a distraction, having a TV in here." She felt a moment of guilt when she thought about how long it had been, since she tried working on her novel.

"Okay," said Michael cheerfully. "We can always use the sitting room for watching TV before bed."

They walked up to the fourth floor which had three smaller bedrooms, two bathrooms and a long narrow library with floor to ceiling bookshelves and a fireplace with a wooden mantel. One of the bedrooms and the library opened onto a small bricked-in terrace.

The fifth floor had a solarium with a wall of glass and a glassed-in ceiling. It had a large bathroom and a large bedroom which opened out on to a large terrace with a fire pit and built-in grill.

They didn't spend much time out on the terrace, because of the cold. Kat was grateful to walk back into the warm bedroom and close the French doors.

Michael looked appreciatively at the large bedroom. "I think this is the perfect place to put the gym."

Kat was dismayed. "Michael, I think this would be the perfect place to put the nursery."

Michael looked at her with a frown on his face. "We don't have children yet, so we don't need to worry about a nursery."

'No time like the present,' thought Kat. 'I just wish Dan and Maria weren't here.'

"Michael, I waited until we were in the new house but I think it's time to start our family. We couldn't afford a baby before but we certainly can now, and we have all this space. Let's not wait."

Michael looked at her for a minute. She was worried to see that he was still scowling.

"Kat, unless you're planning on an immaculate conception, I don't see how you're going to become pregnant."

"What are you talking about, Michael?" Kat started to feel anxious.

"I mean we haven't fooled around since they installed cameras in our apartment. You haven't wanted to."

Kat glanced at Dan. "Jesus, Michael, did you have to say that in front of the camera? Can't we have any privacy?"

"Why shouldn't I say it? It's true, isn't it?" Michael looked angry.

Kat thought back. She guessed it had been a long time since they made love.

"Michael, we don't have to install cameras in the master bedroom in our new house. We can make it off limits." Kat wished Michael would stop frowning.

"Kat, we really should install cameras in every room," said Maria quickly. "We want to capture every conversation."

"I'm sorry, Maria. I'm putting my foot down. We need some privacy and I won't let you put a camera in the bedroom this time." Kat felt determined to win the argument.

Maria turned to Michael. "Michael, please talk to her," Maria pleaded, looking anxious.

Michael turned to look at Maria. "Sorry, Maria. After two months of being celibate, I'm going to side with Kat. If I ever want to have sex again, we can't have a camera in the bedroom. You can have cameras everywhere else but not there."

Kat was elated that Michael was agreeing with her.

"Michael, thank you! Does this mean we can start our family?" Kat looked at Michael nervously while he thought before giving his response.

"Kat, I don't think you want to get pregnant right now," he said slowly with a pensive look on his face.

"What do you mean? It's all I want," said Kat.

"Are you sure, Kat? You've worked so hard to lose the extra weight. Don't you want to look great in your wedding dress?"

It was true that since starting to work with a trainer at the gym, Kat had sweated off fifteen pounds. Her clothes were loose and she loved the feeling of being slender again. She thought about what Michael had said about the wedding dress. It wouldn't look the same if she had a baby bump.

She weighed that against the fact that she was thirty-four and worried she might have a hard time getting pregnant. For a moment, Kat wondered how much of her baby hunger was due to the fact that she was having such a hard time writing her novel. There were days when she despaired of ever becoming a novelist, but at least she knew she could be a great mother.

Maria chimed in. "Kat, I thought you wanted to get your dress at Vera Wang. She doesn't have a maternity line of wedding dresses. Maybe you should hold off getting pregnant, at least until after the ceremony in Maui."

Kat looked at Michael. "Even if we get started now, there's no guarantee

I'll get pregnant right away. I'll probably still look good in the dress by the end of May."

Michael still had a strange look on his face. "Or you could be in your second trimester if it happened right away. I really think you should stay on the pill for now and look gorgeous in the wedding photos."

It was the word gorgeous that changed Kat's mind. Michael had never called her gorgeous before. She was aware that people comparing her looks to Michael's would find her somewhat inadequate. The idea that Michael would find her gorgeous made her want to lose ten more pounds and be the most beautiful bride ever.

"I guess I can wait four more months before we start trying," Kat said. "At least that way I won't have morning sickness when we're in Maui."

"So I can use this room for a gym?" Michael asked with a relieved look on his face. He put his arm around Kat's shoulders.

"You can use it as a gym for now, but once I get pregnant, we're converting it to a nursery. Deal?"

"Deal," said Michael. "It's going to be great. We can cover that wall with mirrors and get a treadmill and an exercise bike. I can put my free weights over there. We can even get a Bowflex machine." He smiled just thinking about it.

It was a large room and Kat wondered where they would put all the exercise equipment, once she was pregnant but she figured that was a problem for another day. For now, it was enough that they wouldn't be putting a camera in the bedroom and Michael would find her gorgeous in a wedding dress. She couldn't wait to get to Vera Wang's.

———

A week later, Kat got a call from Michael on her cell. He had run out on a mysterious errand, followed by Dan and Maria.

"I want you to go into the study and sit down with your eyes closed," he instructed. "I'm outside the front door and I have a surprise for you."

Hoping it wasn't more jewelry, Kat took the elevator down to the first floor. Since they still didn't have any furniture in the room, she sat on the floor and closed her eyes. She heard the front door open.

"Kat, it's us. Do you have your eyes closed?"

"Yes, Michael," she answered a little nervously.

She heard him walk into the room and over to where she was sitting. He put something squirming and wriggly in her lap. She felt a wet nose against her hand.

"Open your eyes!"

Kat opened her eyes and saw a ball of white fluff in her lap with black eyes and a little black nose. A little head with reached up and started licking her face with a wet pink tongue, while making excited whimpering noises.

"Oh my God, he's adorable," Kat said, cuddling the puppy in her arms.

"Do you like him? He's a Samoyed. I got him from a breeder," said Michael, beaming as he stood over her.

"What's he doing here?" asked Kat, while the puppy continued to squirm in her lap.

"I got him for you. Do you like him?"

"He's the cutest thing ever," said Kat, stroking the pup's soft fur, "but why did you get me a dog?"

"Since we're not having a baby right now, I wanted to get you a puppy instead."

Kat felt annoyed at Michael's insensitivity, even though she was charmed by the little bundle in her lap. "Michael, you can't just substitute a dog for a baby. It's not the same."

"I know that, Kat, but I thought he would make you happy. Don't you just love him?"

"Even if he is adorable, I want a baby, not a dog."

"But having a dog makes us seem more like a family. We can walk him together in Central Park every day. And when we do have that baby, he or she can grow up with the dog."

Kat had to admit that the puppy was lovable. She took him off her lap and put him on the floor next to her. The little puppy started nipping at her hand.

"Hey, stop that, you!" she said, laughing while removing her hand from the puppy's mouth.

"What should we call him?" said Michael eagerly.

Kat saw Dan move in for a close-up of the puppy, who was now piddling on the floor.

"If we keep him, we're going to have to start crate training him," said Kat. "Keep an eye on him while I get paper towels to clean up." She walked down the hall to the kitchen to get some paper towels and disinfectant cleaner.

"So what do you want to call him?" Michael yelled from the study.

Kat walked back into the room and started cleaning up. Once the floor was cleaned and she had disposed of the paper towels, she went back into the study and scooped the puppy into her arms.

"What am I going to do with you?" she said, smiling down at the puppy. He gave a little bark in response.

"I think we should call him Max," Kat said while putting the puppy back down on the floor. "Max is a good name for a dog."

"Max, it is," agreed Michael. "I'm so glad you like him."

Kat's family had dogs when she was growing up, so she knew they needed to get some basic supplies to take care of Max.

"Hey, Michael, you need to get to the pet store. We need a crate and food and a feeding bowl and a leash and...Well, I better make a list."

"Sounds good, Kat," said Michael, reaching down to pet the puppy. "Just tell me what you need and we'll get it all. We need to take good care of Max, now that he's part of the family."

Somehow having a puppy did make them seem like more of a family. Kat hadn't thought about getting a dog but she wondered if Michael wasn't right.

'Maybe taking care of Max will make him more ready to be a father,' Kat thought as she wrote up the list for Michael to take to the pet store. She really hoped it would be true.

MICHAEL

"Hey, Michael, can you come here a second?" Michael heard Kat's voice through the intercom that had been installed in the townhouse. He was sitting on their old futon in the master bedroom, watching Tottenham play Everton on TV.

"Kat, can it wait ten minutes?" he said, holding the speaker button down. "It's almost the end of the game."

Tottenham was up, 2-1, and Michael wanted to see if they could hold on for the win.

"Sure, come down when the game is over. I'm in the kitchen."

Everton scored in the last minute of stoppage time and Michael was in a grumpy mood as he squeezed into the elevator with Dan and Maria. His mood wasn't improved at the sight of Kat sitting at their dinette table in the breakfast area of the kitchen.

'Ridiculous,' he thought to himself, looking at the small table in the large space. 'The sooner we get furniture in here, the better.'

His mood brightened as Max came bouncing over to sniff at his shoes.

"Hey there, little guy," he said, bending down to rub Max behind the ears. The shoes must have met with Max's approval because he gave a short bark and went over to lie down beside Kat.

"Michael, pull up a chair," said Kat, peering at her laptop which was on the table. "Sit down next to me so you can see my screen." Dan and Maria stood opposite the table.

"What is it?" asked Michael, sitting down.

"It's the monthly report from Len for our January expenses." Michael could feel his pulse start to race.

"What's up? Are we spending too much?" he asked in what he hoped was a light-hearted tone of voice.

"Last month's million dollar donation to the homeless shelter is listed, so that was a huge expense, but I'm really glad we donated the money," said Kat. "It will benefit so many people and Len said it will help us at tax time. But that's not why I called you down here. Look at this." She pointed to the screen.

Michael peered at the screen and saw 'American Express…$17,238.13'.

"The Amex charges? They're high but we can afford it."

"No, under the Amex charges. What's this $30,000 payment for miscellaneous expenses?"

Michael started breathing more rapidly. He had prepared for this moment and hoped Kat would buy his explanation.

"I hoped you wouldn't see that," he said, trying to sound upbeat. "You shouldn't find out the cost of a Christmas present."

"Which Christmas present?" asked Kat.

"The earrings," said Michael, "They were $30,000." He glanced over at Maria, who was looking at him. He couldn't read the expression on her face.

"But the charges for the jewelry came in last month," said Kat, looking surprised. "You spent $170,000 at Sotheby's."

"The $170,000 was for the bracelet, the necklace and your ring," said Michael, feeling anxious. "I bought the earrings separately."

"Why is it listed as miscellaneous, instead of showing the name of the jewelry store?" Kat asked, starting to frown.

"I didn't buy them from a jewelry store. I bought them from a private collector."

"How do you know someone who owns earrings costing $30,000?" Kat's voice started to rise a little in volume. Max lifted his head to look at her and gave a little whimper.

"It was a private transaction, arranged by Sotheby's," said Michael. He called upon his training as an actor to make his voice sound confident but inside he was quaking.

"Then why doesn't the transaction show payment to Sotheby's?" asked Kat.

"I paid the private collector directly. He wanted to remain anonymous, so I had Len make the check out to cash."

"Michael, that doesn't even make sense. If Sotheby's arranged for the sale, surely they would be getting a commission."

Michael glanced at Maria. She was watching him closely and smiling. Dan moved in for a close-up.

"I don't know, Kat, maybe Sotheby's was doing the collector a favor because he's such a big client or something. All I know is that I bought the earrings directly from him."

"Where did you go to view the earrings before purchasing them?" Kat asked. She crossed her arms over her chest and scowled at him. He knew she wasn't buying the story.

"I viewed them at Sotheby's. Their VP of Magnificent Jewels had them in her office and told me they could be purchased through a private transaction. When I saw them, I knew you had to have them because they matched your bracelet."

"I'm not sure I believe you," said Kat suspiciously. "Your story isn't making sense."

"It's true, Kat," said Michael urgently. "Ask Maria if you don't believe me." He looked over at Maria, hoping she would confirm his alibi.

"Maria, is this true?" asked Kat. She sounded a little shrill.

Maria paused a few moments before answering. Michael could feel his heart racing.

'Please say yes,' he prayed. He nodded his head in Maria's direction, hoping she would take the hint. 'Come on. You wanted to portray me as the perfect husband, so back me up.'

Maria must have decided now was not the time to let Kat find out about Erica.

"Yes, Kat, it's true," Maria said. "Michael bought the earrings from a private collector and Sotheby's helped broker the transaction. The $30,000 payment was for your Christmas present."

'Thank you,' Michael mouthed to Maria while Kat was looking the other way. Maria smiled back at him.

"Seems pretty strange," said Kat. She still had a scowl on her face. "But I guess it makes sense. I can't think what else you would do with $30,000. Just make sure there are no strange miscellaneous charges in the future. Okay, Michael?"

"Of course, Kat," said Michael, feeling a huge sense of relief. When the time came, he would need to keep Kat from watching the episode with the jewelry auction, or she would know his story was a lie.

He also had to figure out what to tell Kat when the final episode aired, showing him giving the $30,000 to Erica, but he would worry about that another day.

MARIA

Maria met with her boss, William, and Sophie, the editor that had been working on *Lucky*, to review the raw footage Dan had captured about decorating the house.

"So what do we have?" asked William, rubbing his hands together. "Anything juicy we can work with?"

"No major conflicts but we got Kathy Canon, that designer from HGTV, to work with them on decorating their house. She wasn't taping her show for a couple of months and had time to take on a private client."

"Getting her was a good idea," said William, smiling at Maria. "We might get her fans tuning in to our show."

Maria was happy William approved. It hadn't been easy getting Kathy but she thought it would be worth it.

"The first scene is where she talks to them about the budget," said Maria. "Sophie, please roll the first clip." Maria and William stood over Sophie, looking at the big monitor at her workstation.

Kat and Michael shake hands with Kathy, standing in the foyer of the townhouse. Kathy is a trim, athletic woman in her thirties with vibrant red hair which hangs in a long braid down her back. She is dressed in faded jeans and her signature plaid woolen shirt. Kathy is holding a large binder and a notebook. Kat seems a little starstruck to be meeting her.

They walk through the hallway and into the large kitchen, which has the dinette table and two chairs.

"Why don't you guys sit?" says Kathy. "I'll stand and take notes. Let's start by talking about your budget since that's going to dictate what we'll be able to do. How large is this house?"

"The house is 8,500 square feet," answers Michael. "We're starting with a blank canvas because we don't plan on keeping any of our old furniture."

"Did you have a budget in mind?" asks Kathy, with her pencil poised over a notebook.

"We don't really," says Kat, "how much should it cost?"

"That depends on whether you plan on buying your furniture from Ikea, or filling the house with rare antiques and artwork," says Kathy with a grin.

"If you want to go with high-end furniture, you can calculate a budget of $50 per square foot. If you want to get antiques and artwork from top dealers, you can calculate the budget based on a percentage of what you paid for the house."

Kathy smiles. "Of course, you could always get pieces from auctions at Sotheby's and Christie's. But if you have to ask about a budget, you probably can't afford it."

"We probably want to go with antiques and artwork from high-end dealers," says Michael.

Close-up of Kat, looking dismayed.

"I don't know, Michael. I was thinking we could go with regular furniture instead of antiques. It doesn't make sense to have really expensive furniture, especially now that we have Max. We wouldn't want him ruining anything valuable."

As if on cue, Max runs into the room, with his little tag wagging, and gives a bark.

"I thought you said there wasn't any conflict," said William as Sophie paused the video.

"Keep watching," said Maria. "Kathy resolves it pretty quickly." Sophie started the video again.

Kathy leans over and scratches the top of Max's head. "What a cutie pie," she says with a smile. She straightens up and looks at Kat and Michael.

"I have an idea," she says. "What if we go with upscale but moderately priced furniture for most of the house but get one or two signature pieces for the living room and the dining room? We can use most of your budget for artwork. You can have well-dressed walls."

"Well-dressed walls," says Michael with a grin. "I like the idea of that. Kat, what do you think?"

"Max wouldn't be able to destroy artwork on the walls," says Kat smiling down at the puppy, "and I would be happy with furniture that doesn't cost a fortune. I think it's a good compromise. Thank you, Kathy."

"So let's talk about what type of furniture you like. Do you like modern with clean lines?" asks Kathy.

"I don't have an opinion," says Michael, "as long as you can turn the study down the hall into an office for me."

"I don't really like modern. I find it cold," says Kat. "I love traditional. I want a home that's warm with lots of wood and prints and throw pillows."

"Warm and traditional. Got it." Kathy handed the large binder to Kat. "Here's my portfolio. Why don't you glance through it and see if there are any rooms that you like."

Kat starts going through the portfolio.

"This is starting to drag a little," said William. He turned to Maria with a frown on his face.

"When Kathy suggested going with more moderately priced furniture, you should have steered them towards the auctions to purchase antiques. It would have made for better TV."

"I know," said Maria apologetically. "It's just that Kat is always trying to save money even though Michael likes to spend."

"Your job as producer is to get them to spend as much as possible in as short a time as possible. In a perfect world, you would be getting them to spend all of it before we end the season."

Maria felt pulled in two directions. On the one hand, she wanted to please

William and produce a show that would be a hit, and would prove her worth to her father. On the other hand, a part of her felt guilty about encouraging Kat and Michael to blow through their entire fortune.

'What would Dad think if he knew I was manipulating this couple to spend all their money?' she asked herself, trying hard to push the guilt aside.

William was looking at her expectantly and she had to respond. "You're right, William. I'll keep up the pressure to get them to spend more in the future," Maria said, feeling like she wanted to take a shower.

"That's what we want," said William. He turned back to Sophie's monitor. "What else do you have?"

"We could look at the video from a couple of days later, when Kathy brings mood boards for Kat and Michael to view," said Maria. "We also have footage of Kathy and Kat looking at paint samples and wallpaper, while Michael stands there looking very bored."

"We might be able to do something fun with that," said William. "Do you have anything that shows them spending big, or arguing with each other?"

"We could show Kathy working with Kat and Michael to purchase artwork. We have them at a Christie's auction buying an oil painting to hang over the living room fireplace."

"What did they get and how much was the price?" asked William. "Are we talking a Monet or a Renoir?"

"They bought a painting of a harbor by Raoul Dufy. He's an impressionist but not as famous. The hammer price was $120,000."

"I don't know," said William. "We've already done the jewelry auction. I don't want to get repetitive."

William turned back to Maria.

"Did you work with Kathy to film a big reveal when the house was finished?"

"Yes," said Maria. "It wasn't easy. We had them stay in a hotel for the last week while the furniture was being brought in and Kathy was adding the finishing touches."

"How did they react when the house was finished?"

Maria smiled. "They were thrilled. Sophie, go to the footage from February 22nd."

Maria and William turned back to Sophie's monitor.

"Are you ready to see your house?" Kathy says with a big smile, standing outside the door to the townhouse.

"We can't wait!" says Kat. She is smiling but seems nervous.

"Let's check it out," says Michael. He is smiling as well.

Kathy opens the door and they walk through the hallway and turn to the right into the study.

"Michael, here's your study," Kathy says. "What do you think?"

The study looks like a 19th century men's club. Hunting prints are hung on the oak paneled walls and an antique map of the world is hung over the fireplace, where someone has lit a fire. There's a red and blue oriental carpet covering the tile floor and a leather couch and love seat. One wall has floor-to-ceiling bookshelves, filled with leather-bound volumes. Michael runs his hand over a large walnut desk which faces the window. The window has a burgundy swag valance and sheer curtains. Brass accent lamps provide additional lighting in the room.

"I think it's incredible," Michael says, looking up from the desk and around the room. "I'm going to love spending time here. Kathy, this is amazing!"

"It's gorgeous, Kathy," Kat says. She is beaming.

"I'm so glad you like it," says Kathy. "Let's go upstairs."

They walk up the stairs which have an oriental carpet runner. There's a painting of a seascape on the second-floor landing. Kathy walks into the dining room, followed by Kat and Michael. Kat gasps when she sees the room.

The dining room's mural of cherry blossom trees can be seen on one wall but the other walls are painted a deep burgundy with white trim on the door frames and window sills. As with the study, there's a roaring fire in the fireplace. The curtains are satin in a deep gold print. There's a large mahogany dining table surrounded by ten Queen Anne chairs. Silver serving pieces can be seen through the glass doors of a large decorative cabinet and a sideboard contains a silver tea service. There are ornate silver candlestick holders on the dining room table and the table has been set with table settings. The utensils are silver and the white china has gold rims.

"Wow," says Michael appreciatively, picking up one of the forks to look at it more closely. "I guess we'll be hosting the next Thanksgiving dinner."

"I can't wait to show this off," says Kat with a big smile. She picks up a crystal wine glass. "Kathy, the table settings are beautiful. Where did you get them?"

"I've been looking in antique shops," says Kathy. "I was able to get the place settings and all the silver from shops in the tristate area. I splurged a little on the decorative elements but I hope you think the end result is worth it."

"Definitely worth it," says Michael.

"I'm glad you agree," says Kathy.

"Why don't we end there," said William, as Sophie paused the video again. "Even if the other rooms are nice, we'll get them in future episodes.

I don't think we need to show them now."

"Makes sense," said Maria, hoping William was happy with what they had captured.

"There's a lot to work with here," said Sophie. "I'll edit for broadcast first and then produce the ten-minute clip for YouTube."

"I don't want to give everything away before the show is aired," said William, looking at Sophie. "Show them starting to work with Kathy but don't show the finished rooms in the YouTube episode."

"You got it," said Sophie cheerfully. "Leave it to me."

"Good work, Maria," said William. "Even without the added drama I think you have a good episode here."

Maria felt happy that William was pleased. Now she just needed to think of other ways to keep Kat and Michael spending big. Hopefully without selling her soul.

CHAPTER 15

KAT

Kat heard the front door buzzer and walked quickly across the living room to get to the intercom. It was her first time hosting the book club in the new townhouse and she couldn't wait to show her friends her new home.

"Who is it?" she said eagerly, while pressing down the button.

"Kat, it's Angela and Sharon."

"I'll be right down," Kat said happily. She quickly walked out of the living room and down the stairs to the first floor.

When she opened the door, she found Jessica had arrived as well.

"Come on in," she said, standing to the side so her friends could enter the hallway.

She noticed that Jessica was holding a house plant with a silver bow wrapped around the pot.

"This is for you," said Jessica with a smile. "I wanted to get you a little housewarming gift."

"Thank you so much," said Kat, taking the plant with a smile.

"We brought gifts as well," said Angela, holding up a bottle of wine with a red bow. Kat noticed that Sharon was holding a gift bag.

"Come on into the kitchen and we can put everything down," said Kat, leading them through the hall and through the double doors that led into the kitchen.

The kitchen had a country motif with wide plank wood floors. The cabinets on the walls were white but the cabinets under the island had been painted a cheery yellow to match the walls. A large farmhouse oak table was placed in the breakfast area, surrounded by eight Windsor chairs painted eggshell white. Framed prints of chickens and roosters decorated the walls. The open shelving in the breakfast area showcased blue and yellow majolica china.

"Wow!" said Jessica appreciatively, looking around once they were in the kitchen. "Kat, this is amazing."

"Your kitchen is gorgeous, like something out of a magazine," said Sharon. She had a big smile on her face.

"Are those Gaggenau wall ovens?" said Angela, walking over to the ovens to get a closer look. "I'm totally envious!"

Kat noticed Colleen was at the counter, putting finishing touches on the hors d'oeuvres.

"Hey guys, I want to introduce you to Colleen, our housekeeper. Colleen, this is Sharon, Jessica and Angela."

Colleen turned around and wiped her hands on the flowered apron that was covering her rounded stomach. Her wiry gray hair was pulled into a bun at the nape of her neck and she had a daub of flour on one cheek. Colleen peered at Kat's friends through steel-framed glasses that magnified the size of her gray eyes.

"Nice to meet you," she said with a big smile, shaking each of their hands in turn. "Kat, where do you want me to put the appetizers?"

"I'm going to give them the grand tour and then we'll be in the living room, so you can put the appetizers in there. Just make sure to keep Max in the kitchen, so he can't get at the food."

"Don't worry, I'll keep the little rascal down here with me," said Colleen, stroking Max's head affectionately. Max nuzzled against Colleen's legs.

"Please give me your coats," said Colleen, "and I'll hang them up in the hall closet."

Jessica, Angela and Sharon took off their winter coats and handed them to Colleen, who walked down the hall to hang them up.

Kat put the plant down on the counter, next to Angela's wine.

"Here you go," said Sharon, handing Kat the gift bag. Inside was a box of chocolates.

"Thank you for the housewarming gifts," said Kat. "These are great! Are you ready to see the rest of the house?"

"We can't wait," said Sharon, as Colleen walked back into the kitchen.

Once they were back in the hallway, Jessica asked, "When did you get a housekeeper?"

"A couple of weeks ago," said Kat. "We got her through an agency. They sent a number of candidates but I picked Colleen because she seemed to get along the best with Max. She does cleaning and cooking during the week but she gets weekends off."

"Does she live here?" asked Angela.

"Yes, the basement level has a complete apartment, including a separate kitchen."

"Is she a good cook?" asked Sharon.

"She's a great cook. Not only that, she does all the grocery shopping. It took a little getting used to, having someone here all the time, but I love not having to do the cleaning myself."

"I would love it too," said Jessica, laughing. "I wish I had a Colleen!"

It took a half hour for Kat to give Jessica, Angela and Sharon the complete tour of the house. They seemed very impressed and she loved being able to share her beautiful home with her friends.

When they were back in the living room, nibbling on Colleen's prosciutto bites and cheese straws, and drinking some of the wine Angela brought, Sharon asked where Michael was.

"He's out for drinks with some of his acting buddies, and the camera crew went with him. I love when they're not around," said Kat.

"You mean you love when the camera crew's not around, not when Michael's not around, right?" asked Jessica with a smile.

"Right, but the only time when the camera crew's not around is late at night. Even then, they have the house wired up with hidden cameras."

"Are we being filmed right now?" asked Sharon, looking up at the ceiling. She looked distressed.

Kat blushed. "Actually there are hidden cameras in this room although they won't use the footage on the show because Michael's not with us."

"Is there anywhere we can go, without the hidden cameras?" asked Sharon.

"Yes," said Kat, standing up. "Follow me to the conservatory. Our producer said they couldn't get good lines of sight in there, because of all the plants, so they didn't install cameras. Michael has agreed not to come into the room unless the camera crew is with him."

The group picked up their glasses and appetizers and walked through a set of French doors leading into the conservatory. The room is filled with standing plants and wicker furniture.

"It's like a jungle in here," said Jessica, looking at all the palms, ferns and the flowering plants in hanging baskets.

"Yes, I love it in here," said Kat, "especially since there are no cameras."

"Do you have cameras in all of the other rooms?" asked Sharon.

"Not in the bedrooms and the bathrooms, although we do have cameras in the room we're using as a gym."

"How do you deal with it?" asked Angela. "I would have a hard time knowing someone is filming everything I say and do."

"I guess I've gotten somewhat used to it," said Kat thoughtfully as she reached for her wine glass. "I'm so used to having Dan and Maria around that I don't notice anymore, unless Dan moves in for a close-up. Then I have to remind myself not to shove his camera out of my face."

"How do you like seeing yourself on YouTube?" asked Jessica, after she swallowed a mouthful of prosciutto. "I watch every episode, just to see you."

"I watched the first episode, which I found very upsetting because they made me look like a crazy person with that real estate broker." Kat nibbled on a cheese straw.

"I remember that one," said Jessica sympathetically. "They made you look unreasonably jealous."

"The second episode was a little better because they focused on Michael going on an audition for a role he didn't get," said Kat. "After that, I stopped watching. I guess don't like the way I look on camera and I find the whole thing exploitative. But Michael watches every episode and tells me each week how many views we've gotten. He can't wait until the show hits broadcast TV."

"Are you starting to get recognized?" asked Angela. "The last episode had 2.3 million views."

"We've been stopped a few times on the street," said Kat with a frown. "I don't mind when they politely ask for an autograph but there have been a few women who have blatantly thrown themselves at Michael, like I'm not even there."

"So he's starting to get groupies?" said Jessica. "That can't be easy to deal with."

Kat's hand shook a little as she reached for her wine glass again. "I know I should trust my husband but I'm always a little worried that a really beautiful woman is going to come on to him and he's going to be tempted. Maybe I should be glad for the camera crew – it's like he has chaperones."

"I'm sure Michael wouldn't be tempted," said Jessica with a smile, reaching out to pat Kat on the hand. "He's married to you and he loves you."

"I hope so," said Kat with a heavy sigh. "The other day I found a large miscellaneous charge when I was checking our monthly expenses. Michael told me it was for one of my Christmas presents. His story didn't really make sense but our producer backed him up so I guess I have to believe him."

"Do you worry that Michael's been unfaithful?" asked Sharon softly.

"There was this woman, Erica, in his acting class that I used to worry about, but he doesn't see her anymore since he started taking private acting lessons."

"Is she the one he was doing that love scene with?" asked Angela. "The one he told he couldn't be her friend anymore?"

Kat could feel herself start to blush. They were her close friends, but it was still a little uncomfortable having Jessica, Sharon and Angela know so many intimate details about her life. If it was this awkward with her friends, she didn't want to think about the millions of anonymous strangers who had been viewing her and Michael, week after week.

"Yes, that was Erica," Kat admitted.

"I'm sure they were just friends," said Jessica loyally, "plus he doesn't see her anymore, so you don't need to worry about her. And don't worry about the groupies either. He's married to you and he loves you. Try to focus on that if you start to feel jealous."

"I know you're right," said Kat gratefully. "I'll try to stop being so insecure. Let's stop talking about me and start talking about the book we're reading. What did you guys think about *The Light Between Oceans*?"

To Kat's relief, they spent the rest of the night discussing the book. She loved her friends but she didn't enjoy discussing her worries about her marriage. At best, it made her feel disloyal to Michael. At worst, she worried that her friends would think he was cheating on her.

She tried to focus on Jessica saying Michael was married to her and loved her. She wondered what was more important to him, adoration from his fans or her feelings.

MARIA

Maria was anxious all day, on Wednesday, March 13th. A+M was broadcasting the first episode of *Lucky* that night and she wondered how the show would do. If the show was a flop, it would be one more failure in her father's eyes and he would start pushing law school again. If the ratings were good, maybe it could prove to her father that she could be successful in her chosen field, despite the fact that she was working on a reality TV show.

Maria had encouraged Michael and Kat to have a second bottle of wine with dinner, hoping to loosen Kat up, before the episode aired. At 8:55 P.M., she got Kat and Michael seated in front of the TV that had been installed in Michael's study. Kat and Michael sat on the couch, with Dan standing opposite them, ready to capture their reactions. Maria sat on the leather love seat, with Max next to her on the floor.

"Ready?" Maria asked. Michael's eyes were gleaming as he nodded yes. Kat didn't respond but Maria thought she looked as though she was waiting to see the dentist.

The show started with a teaser, showing Michael and Kat in their small studio apartment and then cut to them looking at multimillion dollars mansions on the Upper East Side. The title sequence with the theme music played next.

Maria got a shiver of excitement during the credits when she saw her name as the producer, right under William's name as the executive producer.

The narrative unfolded, showing the purchase of the ticket, the BonusBall press conference and Kat and Michael's discussion about what type of house to buy. The way Sophie had edited the episode, Michael was definitely the star of the show, with Kat turning up as a minor character.

Maria could see Kat's shoulders start to relax, as she watched. Maria glanced at Michael. He looked almost intoxicated watching himself on the screen.

The episode continued with the realtor, Carley, showing them houses and then hitting on Michael. Sophie showed Kat's angry reaction but it was clear that Carley's behavior was the catalyst for the blowup.

The show ended by teasing the next episode, showing Michael at the Ferrari dealership and putting an offer in on a house. The teaser didn't show which house they were trying to purchase.

As the commercials started to play, Michael gave a big satisfied sigh, as if he had eaten a large delicious meal.

"So what did you think?" asked Maria, turning off the TV.

"I think it was dope," said Michael. He gave Maria a big smile. "I can't wait to see the next episode!"

"I didn't like seeing the part with that realtor," Kat said, giving Maria a look of disapproval. "But at least you showed her coming on to Michael. Any woman would have reacted the way I did."

"You overreacted to that realtor's flirting," Michael said. "It was really pretty innocuous."

"How can you say that?" Kat asked, looking upset. "She was so obviously hitting on you, even with me right there."

"It's not my fault that women flirt with me."

Kat folded her arms across her chest and glared at Michael. "But you don't have to encourage them. You should let them know you're not interested."

"I wear a ring, so they know I'm married, but they don't seem to care." Michael had a small satisfied smile on his face.

"They need to know you're unavailable, not just that you're married. You don't have to flirt back." Kat's face was turning red.

"But Kat, flirting is harmless as long as I don't take it to the next level."

"Flirting is not harmless, Michael. It hurts me when you do it." Kat reached out to hold Michael's hand.

Michael pulled his hand away. "Flirting is normal; it's even healthy. If you weren't so insecure, you would understand that. It means nothing when I flirt with other women."

"Maybe I am too insecure," said Kat raising her voice a little, "but it's humiliating when I'm standing right there and other women come on to you."

"So what are you saying, Kat? It's okay for me to flirt when you're not around?"

"You're deliberately misunderstanding me. I want you to stop flirting, whether I'm there or not."

"You knew I like to flirt when you married me. I'm not going to change how I behave with other women just because you get jealous all the time." Michael frowned at Kat. "Your insecurity makes me feel suffocated."

"I don't want to make you feel smothered," Kat said. She looked close to tears. "I'm just worried a beautiful woman will start flirting with you and you'll be tempted to take it to the next level."

"How many times do I have to reassure you that I'm not going to cheat? You need to stop being so paranoid." Michael scowled at Kat.

Maria was startled by what an asshole Michael was being. Not only had he been unfaithful, he had knocked up Erica. Now he was telling Kat that she was being paranoid. Michael looked great on camera but Maria was starting to wonder if he was an emotional sociopath.

Maria felt very conflicted. She was sorry for Kat, and wanted to tell her what Michael was really like. But William wanted to wait for the end of the season before revealing to the world what a bastard Michael was. If Maria told Kat about Michael's infidelity, it would ruin the story arc they were trying to develop. She tried to focus on the fact that viewers would probably eat it up, when *Lucky* revealed the real Michael during the final episode.

"Close-up on Kat." Maria said guiltily, as she directed Dan.

Dan moved the camera closer to Kat. Maria could see Kat visibly try to get her emotions under control.

"Okay, Michael, I'll try not to be paranoid. We're married and I know you love me, even if other women try to flirt with you."

Michael smiled and put an arm around Kat.

"Of course I love you, Kitty Kat. You have nothing to worry about. I'll even try to flirt less, especially when you're around. I don't want to upset you."

"Okay, Michael, that sounds good. I love you too."

The conflict seemed to be over, for the night at least, and Maria and Dan started wrapping things up to leave. Once they were outside of the townhouse, Maria turned to Dan.

"What did you think?" she asked.

"About the episode, or about their argument?" Dan asked.

"About both," said Maria.

"Well, I couldn't really see the episode since I was filming them. I've got it saved on my DVR and I plan to watch it tonight, when I get home. From what I could hear, it sounded pretty good."

"I think it was good," said Maria. "Let's just hope viewers think so too. What did you think about them?"

"I think Michael is a stone cold bastard," said Dan. He looked angry. "That poor, poor woman."

"I know. It almost makes me want to show her the footage of Michael and Erica, even before the final episode airs. She needs to divorce his ass and move on with her life."

"So why don't you do it?" asked Dan. "It would be doing her a favor."

"We're not supposed to let anyone know what Michael's really like until we air the final episode. The head of programming at A+M doesn't want this to turn into a show about divorce."

"That's too bad. I want to be there, when she finally finds out about him."

"Let's hope all of America wants to be there when she finally finds out about him," said Maria.

"Yeah, good luck with the ratings. I hope the show's a hit."

"Me too," said Maria, "me too."

She wished Dan goodnight and they went their separate ways.

———

Maria and Dan were filming Kat and Michael having breakfast when Maria's phone rang.

"Have you checked the ratings yet?" William asked.

"Not yet," admitted Maria, holding the phone closer to her ear. Maria had been too nervous to check the Nielsen ratings.

"Are you sitting down?" asked William.

Maria's stomach tightened up in response to William's question. The news was either really bad or really good.

"Give me a sec," said Maria.

She glanced over at Dan, who was filming Michael drinking his coffee. Nothing film-worthy seemed to be going on, so she left the kitchen and walked to Michael's study for a little privacy.

"Okay," she said, sitting down on the leather couch, "I'm sitting. Hit me."

"We got a 1.02 rating in the 18-49 demographic and 2.75 million viewers. Congratulations! You have a hit!"

Maria wasn't sure how to react. She should have been thrilled but her enjoyment of the moment was tainted as she thought of the ways she manipulated Kat and Michael to get the good ratings. She didn't think her father would be proud of her. Hell, she wasn't even proud of herself. Mostly, she felt like taking a long hot shower.

"Maria? You still there?" she heard William ask.

"Yes, I'm still here, William. That's amazing news." Maria tried to sound enthusiastic.

"I had a call from Neil Charles and he's ecstatic. He said he hasn't seen numbers like this since *Diva Dynasty*."

"I can't wait to tell Dan," she said to William.

'I wonder if I should tell Dad,' Maria thought to herself.

"The numbers should go even higher with DVR delayed watching and streaming via the A+M app. Your idea of previewing the show on YouTube has really paid off."

"Thank you so much," said Maria, trying to bask in the glow of his praise. She could hear that he was elated at the numbers.

"Keep up the great work in getting them to spend. I've been checking Twitter and viewers are loving it."

"I will," said Maria, trying to focus. "We have their trip to England coming up and it's first class all the way."

"Are we paying for them to travel first class?" Maria could hear a note of concern in William's voice.

"No, our production assistants booked their trip through a travel agent but the agent sent the bills to their money manager. 'One Ring' pays for me and Dan, but we travel coach."

"Won't that make it harder for you to film on the plane? I can't imagine the flight attendants are going to want you walking up the aisle with the camera."

"That's true," said Maria. She had been worrying about this. "We're just hoping we get a flight attendant who wants to be on the show and will let us film."

"You and Dan should upgrade to first class," said William. "I want to make sure you catch every moment of their trip."

"Should we also stay at the Savoy?" Maria asked, wondering if the budget would cover it.

William laughed. "Why not? You have a hit and I'm feeling generous. Sure, stay at the Savoy. It will make it easier for you to stay up late with them and get to them first thing in the morning."

"Thank you, William," Maria said. She pushed down the feelings of guilt and tried to focus on the positive. She had a hit and they were going first class to London.

CHAPTER 16

MICHAEL

After flying first class, on the British Airways redeye to Heathrow, Michael loved that he would never have to fly coach again. He enjoyed what B.A. called a private suite on the plane, although in reality it was more like a cubicle that walled in his seat to give him a sense of privacy. When it was time to sleep, the flight attendant folded his seat into a full-length bed and added a quilted mattress and a white cotton duvet, along with a pillow. After his bed was ready, Michael went into the bathroom to change into the complimentary pajamas that were given out at the start of the flight.

He didn't get much sleep on the flight, despite the comfort of having PJs and a bed to stretch out in. He was too busy worrying about what to do. It was the middle of March and the final episode of *Lucky* was supposed to air on June 12th. That gave him a little less than two months to figure out how to tell Kat about Erica.

As Michael saw it, he had two options. He could try to convince Kat that Erica had been a dreadful mistake and beg her forgiveness. It would take a lot of work but he thought he could get Kat to stay with him, despite the baby. If he could convince her that he wouldn't cheat again, and if he agreed to give Kat a baby of her own, he could probably keep his marriage. But could he keep from being unfaithful again?

There were so many beautiful women out there. Michael didn't know if he could commit to just having sex with Kat for the rest of his life.

Option two. He could let Kat find out about Erica and sue him for divorce. They would split the money and he could be rich and single. It was good he convinced Kat to say they both bought the BonusBall ticket, so half the money had been awarded to him.

Did Michael want to be single? The truth was that he didn't like being alone and it was always nice to go home to Kat. She was easy going and low maintenance; even if she wasn't the most exciting woman he had ever been with. Erica had been exciting, and look how that ended up.

Michael was leaning towards staying with Kat when the lights came on in the cabin, so the flight attendants could start serving the full English breakfast. He only picked at his eggs, sausage, tomato and beans. The stress of not knowing what to do was killing his appetite.

———————

After they landed at Heathrow, they checked into their suite at the Savoy around 7:30 on Friday morning. Michael was so tired he could barely take in the luxurious living room, before heading into the bedroom to take a nap. He snuggled into cool 600-thread-count sheets, which were like satin against his skin, and pulled the cozy goose down comforter over him. As his head hit the soft pillows, he drifted into a deep dreamless sleep.

He wasn't sure what time it was when he became aware of Kat shaking his shoulder.

"Michael, wake up. You've been sleeping for six hours. It's afternoon and we should do some sightseeing."

Michael felt groggy and disoriented. The last thing he wanted to do was get up and walk around London. He was vaguely aware of Maria and Dan standing behind Kat, filming him in bed.

"Kat, I want to keep sleeping. You should go sightseeing without me this afternoon."

"Come on, Michael, get up. I don't want to go by myself."

"So take Dan and Maria with you. I'm jet-lagged and need to sleep."

"But Michael, we're only here until Tuesday. We have a short trip because you have an audition on Wednesday, so the least you can do is get up, instead of sleeping the day away. Let's go see the Tower of London, or Buckingham Palace."

"I've already seen the Tower and the Palace. I want to keep sleeping."

Kat shook his shoulder again. "Sure, you've seen them because you grew up here, but it's my first time in England. Come on, Michael, get up."

"Kat, I'll take you sightseeing tomorrow, after I've caught up on some sleep."

"We can't go tomorrow, because we're going to the game. Let's not waste this afternoon."

Kat was annoying, like a fly that kept buzzing in his face. He rolled away from her and burrowed deeper into the comforter.

He heard Maria's voice. "Come on, Michael, wake up. Viewers are going to want to see London. We've already filmed the inside of your hotel suite."

Even the thought of pleasing the viewers couldn't motivate him to get up. He was just too jet-lagged.

"Maria, you and Dan should go sightseeing with Kat. Take her to Westminster Abbey or something. I need to sleep."

It was a big relief when he heard them leave the room. He closed his eyes and went back to sleeping.

It was after 6:00 P.M. when Michael finally woke up. He was well rested and starving. He got out of bed and walked into the living room to see if Kat was around. She wasn't but he was able to appreciate the Noel Coward suite, now that he was awake.

The living room had a chandelier, wall sconces and was filled with antiques. Michael sat on the comfortable beige sofa and leaned back into all of the pillows. He put his feet up on a marble coffee table with gilt edge legs. What impressed him the most was not furniture, but the artwork in the suite. A bronze statue of a horse with a rider was on a mahogany sideboard and there was a large porcelain statue of a dog sitting in front of the fireplace screen. A painting of a sailing ship filled one wall, framed by crown molding. He was happy with the way Kathy Canon had decorated his living room, but he would have been equally content if the designer of the suite at the Savoy had worked on his house.

He waited a few minutes but Kat, Maria and Dan didn't show up, so he got up to go to the bathroom. The bathroom was as luxurious as the living room had been, but he opted to take a shower instead of soaking in the claw foot tub.

Michael didn't want to eat dinner without Kat but he figured he would get a drink while he waited. After getting dressed in jeans and the shawl neck sweater Kat had gotten him for Christmas, he made his way down to the American Bar. Michael seated himself at the bar, on one of the blue leather stools and looked at all the bottles on the mirror-backed glass shelves.

The bartender came over and he ordered a scotch on the rocks. When the drink was delivered, Michael was amused to see that the ice cube had been branded with the name of the hotel.

As he was sitting there, nursing his drink and feeling his stomach growl, a young woman approached him. She was stunning, an easy 10, with her wavy blonde hair, long legs and full lips. She was wearing black leggings with tears at the knees and an off the shoulder orange sweater.

"Excuse me, are you Michael Davidson?" she asked.

"Yes I am," he said, as he started smiling. Being recognized was such a rush.

"I'm sorry to disturb you but I love watching *Lucky* on YouTube! I watch each new episode the day it comes out."

"You're not disturbing me. I like hearing from fans, especially beautiful fans."

He was charmed when he saw her start to blush.

"I'm your number one fan! Where is Kat? Is she in London too?" The pleasure of the moment was marred slightly because she had brought up Kat.

"Kat is out with the camera crew, sightseeing. They've abandoned me for the afternoon,"

"You poor thing. Do you want some company?" She licked her lips and gave him a provocative smile. He felt a small flutter inside. She really was gorgeous and couldn't have been more than twenty years old.

"I would enjoy having some company." He indicated that she should sit in the empty stool next to his. "Hey, you know my name but I don't know yours."

"It's Ash Melrose. Ash is short for Ashley." She held out her hand, which he shook. "I can't believe I'm meeting you! Do you mind taking a quick selfie?" She held out her phone.

"Of course I don't mind." She leaned in close to him and held the phone out at arm's length distance. Michael put an arm around her shoulder. The smell of her perfume was intoxicating. She snapped the photo.

"Just let me post this to Instagram," she said, typing rapidly with her thumbs. "My friends will be totally jelly."

Social media taken care of, she put her phone back down on the bar and smiled at him again.

"What are you doing in London, Ash? Are you staying at the Savoy too?"

"I'm in town for a photo shoot but I'm not staying here because it's too expensive. I just wanted to have a drink at the famous American Bar."

"Why don't you let me buy you another drink?" said Michael, noticing that the liquid in her glass was nearly at the bottom. "What are you drinking?"

"Thank you. I'll have another skinny margarita."

Michael caught the eye of the bartender and ordered a skinny margarita and a scotch rocks for himself.

As the bartender was preparing their drinks, Ash turned to Michael.

"Do you mind if I ask you some questions?" she said.

"Go for it," he said, smiling at how adorable she was.

"Do you really live in a mansion in Manhattan and drive a red Ferrari? Or is that just for the show?"

"I do drive a red Ferrari," he admitted, "but I don't know if I would call our house a mansion."

"Yeah, your house is tiny…said no one ever," responded Ash, rolling her eyes.

Michael laughed. "Okay, maybe my house is big for New York City but I don't think of it as a mansion."

Ash smiled and her deep blue eyes brightened. Michael wondered if she was wearing colored contacts, or if her eyes were really the color of sapphires.

"And is it true you bid on jewelry at Sotheby's for Kat's Christmas presents?"

"Guilty as charged."

Ash took a long sip of the margarita the bartender put in front of her. "I wish the YouTube clip showed what you won at auction."

"They'll show what I won, on A+M, when the broadcast episode comes out. You can watch it then," said Michael. His stomach tightened a little at the thought of Kat watching the episode and seeing that he lied about the earrings. Maybe he could convince Maria to edit that part out.

"I won't be able to watch," said Ash regretfully. "Cable's too expensive so I'm a cord cutter. That's why I watch on YouTube. Can't you tell me what you won? I promise to zip it."

"Sorry, Ash," said Michael. "They made us sign a nondisclosure for the show. I can't tell you." He really was sorry. Michael would have liked to see her reaction to knowing he had spent $170,000 on jewelry.

"Are you sure?" asked Ash with a seductive smile, as she reached out and stroked his knee. "I can be very discrete."

Michael got an immediate hard-on. He fantasized about bringing Ash up to his suite, before Kat got back with Dan and Maria, but realized that would be insanity.

"So can't you tell me?" she asked, stroking her hand higher up his thigh.

Michael could barely concentrate on what he was saying, he was so turned on.

"Are you sure you won't tell anyone?" he said in a husky voice.

"Bible," said Ash, her smile deepening. The hand crept a little higher on Michael's leg.

"I'll tell you one thing," said Michael. He was breathing more quickly. "You know that pink diamond ring I was bidding on? Let's just say that Kat now wears an engagement ring on her left hand. But that's all I can tell you – I can't talk about the rest of the jewelry or my producer will kill me."

"FOH," Ash said as her eyes got wide. "I remember the bidding between you and that other guy. It was over $65,000 before they cut the scene." She continued stroking his thigh.

"I won the ring for $70,000," admitted Michael with fake modesty, while really trying to impress her.

On one level, he knew he was being ridiculous because Ash was much too young for him. On the other hand, she was so delicious and her hand on his thigh would suggest she was no innocent.

Michael decided to err on the side of caution, in case she was underage. He gently removed her hand from his leg.

"Hey, Ash, I'm married," he said regretfully. "I think you should stop."

"Are you sure?" said Ash in a soft voice, putting her hand back on his thigh. "We could go to my hotel. It's only a couple of blocks from here."

Michael groaned inwardly. Nothing would make him happier than taking Ash back to her hotel.

"Yes, I'm sure. Kat and the camera crew will probably be back any minute now."

Ash quickly took her hand off his thigh and looked over at the entrance of the room with a nervous look on her face.

"In that case, I better bounce," she said, quickly picking up her phone from the bar. "I wouldn't want to run into Kat. Hey, it was amazing meeting you."

"I enjoyed meeting you too," said Michael. He was both sorry and relieved to see her go.

'No matter how many hours Kat puts in at the gym,' he thought to himself, watching Ash as she walked away, 'her ass is never going to look like that.'

He gave a deep sigh and finished his drink before heading back up to the suite.

———

Kat had gotten amazing seats for the Tottenham-Manchester United game, in the first row on the sideline. The March wind was blowing cold in the stadium but Michael was bundled in his down coat and the weather didn't bother him. He was loving watching the game in person, even if Manchester United was winning 1-0 at halftime.

Tottenham was about to kick off for the second half when Maria swore loudly.

"What the fuck?" she said, while staring at her phone.

"What's up, Maria?" asked Michael.

"Someone leaked about the ring you bought Kat at the Sotheby's auction, using #pinkdiamondforkat. Hundreds of people are retweeting."

Michael felt a little sick, as he thought about talking to Ash the day before.

"Michael, Kat, did either of you say anything to anyone?" Michael couldn't remember seeing Maria look so pissed.

"No," said Kat. "I haven't told anyone. My friends have seen me wearing the ring, but they wouldn't tweet about it."

"Are you sure?" Maria glared at Kat.

"Yes, and if they were going to leak, why would they wait until now to do it?"

"Hmmm," Maria didn't seem convinced. She turned to Michael.

"Have you said anything to anyone? We were saving the pink diamond for the end of the Sotheby's episode. We've been so careful to edit out any scene that shows the ring on Kat's hand."

"No, Maria," said Michael. He was starting to feel anxious. "I would never violate the nondisclosure agreement."

"Well someone has been blabbing and now the info is out there. I just hope that viewers still want to watch you win the ring, even though the surprise factor is gone."

Michael could kick himself for being so stupid the day before. He was just glad he hadn't taken Ash up on her offer to go back to her hotel. Who knows what she would have posted if more had happened?

Harry Kane scored for Tottenham with a brilliant header, but Michael couldn't really enjoy it. He was too busy wondering if the leak could be traced back to him somehow.

As he was worrying, the woman, in the row behind Michael, tapped him on the shoulder.

"Love, aren't you in that YouTube show about winning millions in a lottery?" she said. He turned to look at her. She was a heavyset middle-aged woman with a flushed face that suggested she had been drinking all afternoon.

Michael felt like denying, but realized that it would be hard to convince her she was mistaken, with Dan standing right there, filming him.

"Yes, Kat and I are in a YouTube channel called *Lucky*," he admitted.

"That's what I thought," said the woman with a big gap-toothed smile. "You're Michael Davis."

"Michael Davidson," said Michael, trying to be patient. He didn't want to offend a fan, but she was interrupting him while he was trying to watch the match.

As he was turned around facing her, he heard a roar from the crowd. Turning front again, he saw the entire Tottenham team jumping on one of their players. They had scored and he had missed it.

She tapped him on the shoulder again. "Can I get your autograph?"

"Sure," he said, hoping that giving her an autograph would get her to stop bothering him. He turned to Kat.

"Do you have a pen in your purse?"

"Yes," said Kat, "Just let me dig it out." She rooted around in her bag for a minute before producing a ballpoint pen which she handed to Michael.

He turned back to the woman. "What do you want me to sign?"

"I want you to sign me tits," said the woman cheerfully, pulling up her shirt. Michael stared with distaste at her huge breasts with sow pink nipples and the rolls of fat underneath.

Kat turned to look at the woman. "Is that really necessary?" she asked, looking displeased. "We're not at a concert and Michael's not a rock star. Pull your top back down."

"I just want him to sign me tits," said the woman. "No harm in that, is there?"

"Let me just sign and get this over with," Michael said to Kat. He took the pen and quickly scrawled his name on her breasts."

"Thanks, Love," said the woman, smiling as she pulled her top back down. "It's not every day you meet a YouTube star."

Kat glared at Michael. "Hey, it's not my fault," he said, feeling irritated by her annoyance. "I can't help how fans behave."

"Well you didn't have to sign," she said, speaking in a low voice so the woman behind them couldn't hear. "You could have refused."

"I didn't want to offend a fan of the show," he said.

"What about offending me?" Kat said. "That woman asked you to sign her boobs as if I wasn't even here."

"Why?" said Michael. "Did you want to sign her boobs as well?"

"Of course not, but I'm getting tired of all the attention you get from random women. I thought it would stop, now that we're in England, but you're still getting recognized."

"YouTube is worldwide, even if *Lucky* is only broadcast in the U.S." said Maria cheerfully, "It's great that Michael is getting recognized. We're hoping to syndicate the show in other countries."

"Michael may get recognized all the time, but it hasn't led to any serious acting roles," said Kat peevishly. "And women act as if he's not even married." She took a sip of beer out of her plastic cup.

"But Kat, this is what we wanted," said Michael. "I'm developing a fan base. It's bound to lead to more roles in the future."

"Maybe this is what you wanted," said Kat, "but it's not what I wanted. I'm tired of women throwing themselves at you."

Michael lowered his voice. "Kat, why would you worry because some random woman wants me to sign her boobs? It's not like I'm tempted." He groaned suddenly as Manchester United scored again, making the score 2-2.

"Maybe you're not tempted right now but what if a beautiful woman approached you? Would you be tempted then?"

"Of course not," said Michael, feeling guilty about being turned on by Ash, the night before. "I love you, Kat, you know that."

Kat didn't look convinced. "I hope so, Michael."

"Kat, let's not spoil the rest of the match arguing about this. Let's enjoy the game, okay?" He reached out to hold her left hand in his and gave a little squeeze. He was relieved when she squeezed his hand in return.

"Okay, Michael. I don't want to spoil your Christmas present by arguing about your fans. Let's enjoy the rest of the game."

Michael did enjoy the rest of the game, even though the final score stayed at 2-2.

CHAPTER 17

MARIA

It took Maria days to convince Kat to let them be there while she looked for a wedding gown. Maria had to threaten having Michael come along to Vera Wang's before Kat would agree to letting Dan film her solo.

Maria was relieved, once Kat agreed. William wanted his episode of *Say Yes to the Dress*, and hadn't been taking no for an answer.

Kat's younger sister Ren had come dress hunting with them. Upstairs at the Vera Wang's wedding salon, they sipped champagne and talked with Ana, the Vera Wang's consultant, about Kat's wedding and what she was looking for. Maria instructed Dan to get a shot of the two sisters close together, so the audience could compare how they looked.

Ren had Kat's upturned nose and high cheekbones but that's where the resemblance ended. Ren's hair fell in auburn waves, compared to Kat's straight strawberry blonde hair. She was tall and thin whereas Kat was medium height and still curvy, despite her recent weight loss. If she had been a few years younger, Ren could have easily been a model. Maria was sorry that it wouldn't be Ren trying on the dresses, instead of Kat.

Once she understood what Kat wanted, Ana went off to pull some dresses and encouraged Kat to look around the store while she waited. The walls and carpet in the Vera Wang salon were dark gray, as was the velvet upholstered seating, to showcase the white wedding dresses, which were displayed along the walls. The rooms were like a railway car, going to the back of the store, and displayed dresses according to price. The less expensive dresses were in the front and the most expensive dresses in the back.

"Should we go to the back room?" asked Maria, hoping to get the price tag up as much as possible. Kat and Ren ignored her as they started at the front and worked their way back. Maria and Dan started following them to capture their conversation.

"OMG, that's gorgeous," said Ren as she touched the lace on an ethereal gown that looked as if it were made from a cloud. "Kat, what do you think about this one?"

"It is beautiful," said Kat, "but I want a colored gown, instead of a white wedding gown. I've been married for over two years and would feel silly looking virginal at my wedding. Let's see what Ana comes up with."

"Are you sure?" said Ren, looking a little sad. She seemed reluctant to walk away from the dress. "I think I just found my fantasy dress."

"When you get married, you should come back to Vera Wang's and get that dress," said Kat with a smile. "I bet it would look amazing on you."

"There's no way I could afford a dress from Vera Wang's. This dress probably costs $10,000."

"Don't be silly," said Kat. She put an arm around Ren and gave her a little squeeze. "When the time comes I would be happy to get you a dress from here."

"Do you mean it?" said Ren, looking very excited. "That would be amazing, thank you, Kat!"

"Of course I mean it. Listen, Ren, there's something I want to ask you." Kat wore a big smile. "Would you be maid of honor at my wedding?"

Ren's face lit up. "I would love to be your maid of honor – thank you so much for asking me." She stopped smiling and looked serious for a moment. "But are you going to let Dad give you away? He would be crushed if he missed your wedding."

Kat frowned. "No, I won't be inviting Dad because I don't want to have Annika at my wedding. I've asked Uncle Charlie if he'll give me away."

Maria's ears perked up. There was a story here and she knew William would want her to get to the bottom of it.

Ren sighed. "Are you sure, Kat?"

"Very sure," Kat said firmly.

Ren was about to respond when Ana showed up.

"Have you found anything you want to see?" Ana said to Kat with a friendly smile. "I've put some dresses in the changing room for you to try on."

Maria felt irritated at the interruption. She was hoping to capture more of the discussion between Kat and Ren.

"Let's get started," said Kat to Ana. She didn't look like a happy bride-to-be as she followed Ana into the changing room.

Ren settled herself on a velvet couch, opposite a huge three-way mirror with a pedestal in front. Maria and Dan stood in front of her.

'This is going to take some finesse,' Maria thought to herself.

"So Ren," Maria said. "Were you pleased when Kat asked you to be her maid of honor?"

Ren smiled. "Yes, I was very moved when she asked. Kat and I used to talk about our dream weddings when we were little girls and I always hoped I would be her maid of honor. I want her to be my matron of honor whenever I get married."

"So why doesn't Kat want her father at her wedding?"

Ren gave a long sigh and leaned back on the couch. "I'm not sure I want to go into details, especially not in front of the camera."

"We were there at Thanksgiving. I know it's awkward between Kat and her father right now," said Maria.

Maria thought back to Kat's comment about not wanting Annika at the wedding.

"Who is Annika and why doesn't Kat want to see her?" Maria asked.

Ren didn't answer. She put down her champagne flute on a side table, crossed her arms across her chest and shut her eyes for a moment as if lost in thought.

"Ren?"

'Come on,' Maria thought, 'don't shut down on me.'

Ren gave another long sigh, opened her eyes and picked up her champagne flute again. She took a sip and looked at Maria.

"Does Kat dislike Annika?" Maria asked.

"Kat has never met Annika," said Ren, "but yeah, you could say she dislikes her."

"Why, Ren? Has Annika hurt Kat somehow?" Maria knew she was being intrusive but felt like she had to keep probing.

"I'm not sure I'm the right one to tell this story," said Ren. "This is really between Kat and Annika."

"A lot of viewers are going to wonder why Kat doesn't want a relationship with her father. It doesn't make her look very nice. If you shared the story with us, Kat's viewers might understand her position."

"Do you think viewers are judging her for this?" asked Ren in surprise. "It's not really Kat's fault."

"I think if you explained Kat's side of the story, viewers would understand her better," said Maria in a soft voice, hoping to keep Ren talking.

Ren thought for a moment. "Okay, I'll tell you but just because I don't want America judging her." Ren took a long swallow of champagne.

'Spill it,' thought Maria.

"It was about eighteen months ago when our mom was still alive. She called Kat up one morning, crying because she discovered that my dad had been cheating on her. It wasn't the first time she caught him being unfaithful. All the previous times, she forgave him when he swore he would never do it again. But this time was different. My mom had had enough and said she was ready to divorce him. She was scared at the idea of being on her own, after thirty-five years of marriage, but she was finally ready. Kat told her that we supported her and would be there for her, if she decided to leave him.

"Later that afternoon, she had a massive heart attack. Mom was dead before the paramedics even arrived. They tried performing CPR but they couldn't revive her. I think the stress of finding out about my dad's infidelity is what killed her.

"About three weeks after her funeral, Kat and I were at their house, helping Dad sort through Mom's stuff. He wanted us to have some of Mom's things, to remember her by. We took a break during the middle of the afternoon to have some coffee in the kitchen.

"Dad said there was something important he wanted to discuss with us. He said that although he had loved our mother very much, he didn't want to spend the rest of his life alone. He had invited an old girlfriend to go on a cruise with him and she had accepted his invitation. That's how he spent Mom's insurance money – taking Annika on a luxury cruise.

"We never knew for sure if Annika was the one he was cheating on Mom with, but Kat always suspected it. That's why she doesn't want to meet her – she blames her for our mother's death."

Ren took a deep breath and another sip from the champagne flute.

Maria wanted to keep Ren talking.

"Did your mom have any health problems, before the heart attack?" she asked.

"No," said Ren. She sighed. "But heart disease runs in our family. Her father died of a heart attack at sixty-five. Still, she got regular annual checkups and they never found any problems. It was the stress of my dad's infidelity that triggered her heart attack."

"Did your dad feel guilty, after she died?"

"If he did, he never showed it. He was sad at her funeral but then he just went on with his life. Annika moved into my parents' house six months after my mom's death. Kat hasn't seen our father since then because she just can't forgive him."

Maria knew William would love this unexpected subplot. He would want her to get Kat and Annika at the wedding and capture the drama on film. Maria winced at the thought.

"Excuse me a second," Maria said. "I need to go to the ladies' room before Kat comes out in the first gown."

Maria walked to the front of the store and down the steps to the first level. She called Michael on her cell.

"Hi, Michael. It's Maria."

"Hey, Maria, how's the dress hunting going?" Michael sounded very cheerful.

"It's going fine but I have something I need you to do. It will really help ratings for the show."

"I'll do anything to help the ratings. Maria. You know that."

"I know, Michael. I need you to send Kat's father and Annika an invitation to the wedding but keep it on the DL. I don't want Kat to know."

"I don't know, Maria." Maria could hear the hesitancy in Michael's voice. "Kat doesn't want her father to be there."

"I know," Maria said, grabbing the phone more tightly with her hand. "But nothing makes for drama like a tearful reunion between estranged family members. Viewers are going to love it. Maybe we could even get Kat's father walking her down the aisle, after they make up."

"Do you really think viewers would want to see a reunion between Kat and her father?" Michael asked.

"Of course. And after the reconciliation, they'll probably thank you for bringing them back together. It will make you look great in front of the viewers."

"You think?" asked Michael.

"I know it," said Maria. She felt queasy at what she was asking Michael to do but she could hear William's voice in her head, insisting she set things up. "You should send out the invitation today. It could make for ratings gold."

"Okay, if it will help the ratings, I'll do it."

"Put a note in the envelope telling them not to R.S.V.P. We want it to be a complete surprise when Kat sees them in Maui."

"You got it, Maria. Leave it to me."

"Thanks, Michael. I'll see you later." With that, Maria disconnected and hurried back upstairs. She sat down just as Kat came out of the changing area. She was wearing a strapless silk mermaid gown in a blush color that hugged her curves. The skirt was multi-layered crinkled tulle with a big organza flower. She also wore a tulle veil in a matching blush color.

"Well? What do you think?" she asked nervously, stepping up on the pedestal and twirling around slowly.

"Oh, Kat," gushed Ren, "You look beautiful." Ren gave Kat a big smile.

"Beautiful," said Dan, moving in. "Kat, turn this way." She turned to face him with a small smile on her face.

"I love the color, but I'm just not sure about the flower," said Kat, turning to look at herself in the three-way mirror.

"We can customize the dress any way you want," said Ana. "If you don't want the flower, we can always remove it. We could add a bejeweled belt instead or maybe a grosgrain ribbon."

Kat turned back and forth in front of the three-way mirror.

"I don't know," she said. "Why don't we try the next dress?"

"Sounds good," said Ana. "Let's go back in the changing room."

Maria tried to engage Ren in more conversation while Kat was changing but Ren didn't seem to be in the mood to talk, so after a few minutes

Maria gave up and chatted with Dan.

Kat emerged from the changing room a few minutes later in the most stunning dress Maria had ever seen. It was black and had a sleeveless lace bodice with a sweetheart neckline. Kat's waist was circled with a nude colored grosgrain ribbon. Like the first dress, the skirt was multi-layered crinkled tulle, but black instead of blush. She was also wearing a nude tulle veil.

Maria was much too busy with work to think about getting married. She didn't even have time to date anyone but she had a sudden fantasy of walking down the aisle, on her father's arm.

'Kat's an idiot if she doesn't pick that one,' Maria thought as she waited to see Kat's reaction.

"Ren, what do you think about this dress?" Kat asked, as she stepped on to the pedestal. "I don't know about the color. Do you think it's too severe?"

"It's a striking dress," Ren said. "It looks like it belongs on the red carpet."

"I know what you mean," said Kat thoughtfully. "Despite the veil, I'm not sure it says wedding to me."

"Turn around, Kat," said Dan. "I want to get the dress from all angles."

Kat twirled around obediently. The skirt fanned out while she turned.

"That dress is phenomenal," said Maria, although nobody had asked her opinion.

"Do you think so?" asked Kat. "I'm just not sure about the color. Do you think it makes me look washed out?"

Now that Kat mentioned it, the black dress did make her fair skin look very pale but Maria thought it was an interesting look – kind of heroin chic.

"Maybe a little washed out," said Ren. "Do you want to try on the next dress?"

"Yes," said Kat. "Ana, can you help me out of this one?"

'Goodbye, fabulous dress,' Maria thought, a little sadly as Kat went back in the changing room.

When Kat came out again, she was wearing a coral strapless silk ball gown. The dress had a lace bodice and a full skirt that was draped with floral beaded embroidery. Instead of a veil, Kat wore a coral silk flower pinned into her hair.

Kat twirled around on the pedestal, beaming. "I love it! What do you guys think?"

Maria had to admit that the dress was flattering on Kat. The coral color brought out the pink in her cheeks and the red in her hair. The tight fit of the bodice made her waist look tiny and emphasized her full breasts.

Ren got tears in her eyes. "Kat, you are gorgeous in that gown," she said. "I just wish Mom were here to see you. She would have loved it."

Kat looked sad for a moment. "Yes, I wish Mom were here too. But I'm so glad you were able to come dress shopping with me, Ren."

"Of course," said Ren, "I wouldn't have missed it."

"Do you think this is the dress?" asked Kat, doing a slow twirl on the pedestal. She turned to the mirror and looked at herself.

"I know that's the dress. You look amazing."

"Dan, Maria? What do you guys think?" asked Kat.

"I think you look stunning in that dress," said Dan from behind the camera. He moved in for a closer shot.

Although Maria far preferred the black dress, she thought the coral dress looked better on Kat.

"That dress looks fabulous on you, Kat," said Maria. "I think you should get it."

"I think I should get it too," said Kat happily. "Ana, I want to get this dress for my wedding."

"Congratulations. I can write it up for you," said Ana with a big smile. "You will be a gorgeous bride."

They went downstairs so Kat could pay for the dress and arrange for her first fitting. She looked very happy.

Maria wasn't quite as happy. She had her episode of *Say Yes to the Vera Wang Dress* and she had uncovered a drama that she could exploit at the wedding. She knew William would approve but she doubted her father would approve. In the back of her mind, she was starting to feel like a ratings whore.

CHAPTER 18

KAT

Michael and the camera crew were in Los Angeles because Alan, Michael's agent, had gotten him a couple of auditions. Although she missed Michael, Kat was enjoying being away from Dan's ever-present camera.

After taking Max for his morning walk, Kat took her MacBook Air into the conservatory so she could work on her novel. She sat in one of the wicker chairs and put her laptop down on the glass-topped wicker table before taking an appreciative look around the room. The conservatory was one of her favorite places, because of all the plants and the lack of any cameras. Whenever Michael wasn't around, she spent hours in the room.

After booting up, she opened the Word doc she had been struggling with. Kat read what she had written so far and decided she hated the draft.

When she was a copywriter, she never had a hard time coming up with the copy, even under deadline. But now that she had time to write anything she wanted, she just kept writing the first few pages, over and over. Each draft seemed worse than the one before.

She decided that maybe talking with Sharon would help. Sharon dealt with authors all the time and probably had advice on how to overcome writer's block. Kat picked up her iPhone and tapped Sharon's name in her contacts list.

"This is Sharon Wilson." Sharon's voice sounded crisp and professional.

"Hey, Sharon, it's Kat."

"Kat, how are you doing?"

"I'm fine but I wanted to ask you about something. Are you busy? Is this a bad time?" Kat felt a little nervous talking to Sharon about her novel.

"No, I can talk. I don't have any meetings until this afternoon. What's up?"

"I'm struggling with my writing," Kat admitted. "I just keep writing and rewriting the first ten pages and I hate everything I've written so far. I have a wicked case of writer's block."

Sharon laughed. "Let's see if we can't get you unstuck. Tell me what your premise is."

"A lonely young woman, who doesn't like how she looks, decides to turn herself into a human Barbie through diet, makeup and plastic surgery in order to find a boyfriend. She posts updates on her progress to YouTube and has to deal with feedback from online trolls who criticize her efforts. In the end, she looks like a Barbie, and guys want her for quick hookups, but she comes to realize that the only meaningful relationship in her life is the one with her plastic surgeon." Kat held her breath, waiting for Sharon's response.

"I like the premise," said Sharon. "So what happens when you try to write?"

"I don't know how to begin and I've struggled to write the first chapter."

"I have an idea," said Sharon. "Do you know how you want the story to end?"

"Yes," said Kat, wondering where Sharon was going with this.

"So why not start with the end? Try writing the last chapter instead of the first. Writing the start of a novel can be daunting for some writers, but writing the end can often be easier."

"It's an interesting idea," said Kat, as she thought about it. "Thank you for the suggestion. I'll give it a try."

"How is everything else going?" asked Sharon. "Are you still having a hard time with Michael's groupies?"

"Women are still throwing themselves at Michael," said Kat, biting down on her lip. "You should have been there in England. There was even one woman who asked Michael to sign her boobs."

"Seriously?" said Sharon, sounding scandalized. "Was she attractive? Did he sign?"

"He did sign but she wasn't attractive. She was some heavy middle-aged British woman at the soccer match."

"You poor thing," said Sharon sympathetically. "I would hate it if Frank had groupies but since he's a bald chubby dentist in his fifties I don't think I need to worry."

Kat laughed. "Yeah, dentists don't usually get too many groupies."

"Good thing," said Sharon. "I would kill him if he signed some woman's boobs."

"That's not what's really bothering me right now," said Kat quietly.

"So what is bothering you?" asked Sharon. "Anything you want to talk about?"

"Michael and the television producer want me to get a wardrobe makeover. They want to bring in a stylist to help me get designer clothes."

"That doesn't sound so terrible," said Sharon. "I would love to get new clothes."

"It's not the idea of new clothes that's stressing me out," said Kat. "It's the timing."

Sharon waited for Kat to continue talking without saying anything.

"Michael convinced me to wait until after the wedding to get pregnant so I would look good in the wedding gown. I agreed but I want to start trying as soon as the ceremony is over. Why would they want me to get new clothes now? If everything goes well, I could be starting to show in three months. The new designer clothes won't fit."

"If it wasn't for the potential pregnancy would you want new clothes?" asked Sharon.

"Sure, it would be nice, especially now that I've lost so much weight."

"So why not get the new clothes now? You don't know how long it will take to get pregnant and you can enjoy the clothes until then. Plus, you'll have a fabulous wardrobe waiting for you, after you have the baby and lose the baby weight."

"Maybe you're right," said Kat. "I just worry that encouraging me to get new clothes is Michael's way of discouraging me from having a baby. There are days when I wonder if he even wants children."

"Have you ever asked him if he wants children?" asked Sharon.

"I've never asked him straight out but I've let him know that I want to start trying. He hasn't said no but he keeps putting me off."

"Kat, can I ask you a question?" Sharon said softly.

"Of course," said Kat, wondering what Sharon was thinking.

"What's the driving force behind wanting to have a baby? Is it just that you want kids or is there something deeper going on?"

Kat paused for a moment before responding. "I really do want kids but I also think some of the desire comes from the fact that sometimes I feel lonely. Does that make me a terrible person? I hate to think I want a child to fill a void in my life."

"That doesn't make you terrible," said Sharon. "People want kids for all kinds of reasons. Why are you lonely these days?"

"I think I miss working in an office," admitted Kat. "These days, especially when Michael is on the road, I'm by myself, trying to work on my novel. Maybe if the writing was going better, I wouldn't feel as alone but I miss working with others."

"You don't have to be alone, Kat. You could always get another job."

"I think it would be awkward working with people who would know so much about my personal business, thanks to *Lucky*. Plus I wouldn't want coworkers resenting me because I'm rich."

"I see what you mean," said Sharon sympathetically. "That could get uncomfortable."

"I think I'm better off working on my novel and having a baby. I just wish Michael was more enthusiastic about getting me pregnant."

"What would you do, if he didn't want kids?"

"I don't know. I want them desperately and it never occurred to me that he might feel differently."

"Would you consider leaving him, if he said no to a baby? Maybe try to have a baby on your own?"

"Leaving Michael in order to have a baby seems pretty drastic. I don't know if that's what I would want to do."

"Maybe it's time you talked to Michael about all of this," suggested Sharon. "At least that way you would know where things stand. If he wants to have a baby, you can get started right away. Don't worry about the wedding. Wedding dresses can always be let out. If he says no, you need to think about what you want to do."

"What if he says he wants kids but not yet?" Kat said. "That seems like the most likely scenario."

"You're almost thirty-five, right?"

"That's right," said Kat. "My birthday is in June."

"You don't have that much time to wait," Sharon said. "A woman's fertility starts to decline after age thirty-five. It doesn't mean you can't get pregnant but it may be more difficult."

"Do you think I made a mistake waiting until after the wedding?" Kat asked anxiously.

Kat heard Sharon sigh over the phone. "Kat, please don't stress. I don't think waiting a few months is going to make a big difference in your fertility but waiting a few years could be an issue."

"You're right. I don't have a few years to wait. Maybe I should talk to Michael when he comes home from L.A."

"I think that's probably a good idea," said Sharon. "Wait a sec, Kat. I need to put you on hold."

Kat heard the sound of light Muzak. After a minute, Sharon came back on the line.

"I'm sorry, Kat, I need to run. I've got a small work emergency to deal with."

"But I didn't even have a chance to ask how you're doing," said Kat. She was disappointed that Sharon had to go.

"No worries. We can catch up during Tuesday's book club meeting. Take care, Kat, and try not to stress too much about Michael and the baby. Things will be fine, no matter what you decide."

Kat said goodbye and hung up. She wondered what Sharon had meant about deciding. Her hope was that Michael would say yes to a baby and she wouldn't have to decide anything. It sounded like Sharon thought maybe that wouldn't be the case.

Kat decided she was too anxious to try any more writing. She closed her laptop and went to get a book, hoping that reading would help take her mind off things. It didn't really work. Kat felt anxious for the rest of the day.

MICHAEL

Michael was in the kitchen, relaxing over his second mug of coffee and watching Colleen clean up the breakfast dishes when his phone rang. Checking the number, he saw the call was from Alan, his agent.

"Hi, Alan, what's up?" Michael said when he got on the phone.

"Hey, Michael, how's it going?"

"It's going," said Michael. "How are things with you?"

"Really good." Alan sounded very cheerful. "I have some great news. You know that cop show you auditioned for? *Criminal Streets*? They want you for the role of Lieutenant Frank Wells. It's a limited gig because he gets shot after six episodes but it's a great role."

Michael was elated. "Alan, that's awesome news."

Maria looked over with interest. "Michael, can you put that on speaker phone?" she asked.

"Hey, Alan, can I put you on speaker?" Michael asked.

"Sure," said Alan. Michael put the phone on speaker so Dan and Maria could hear both sides of the conversation.

"They'll want you to do an American accent," said Alan.

"No problemo, I can totally make that work," said Michael, sounding like a surfer from California.

Alan laughed. "I figured you would be able to handle it. They're going to pay you $10,000 an episode."

"That's fantastic," said Michael beaming. It's not like he needed the money but it was an indication that he would be playing more than a bit role.

"There's just one thing," said Alan. "It's going to be a closed set. You won't be able to bring the *Lucky* camera crew with you."

Michael looked over at Maria, who started frowning.

"I understand, Alan." Michael didn't care if Maria was unhappy. There was no way he was going to give up this opportunity.

"They start shooting in eight weeks. You need to be there by May 31st.

I'll send you the script for the first episode, along with the contract. Congratulations! I know you're going to be great."

"Thank you, Alan. You've made my day."

Michael hung up and turned to Maria, who looked peeved.

"Michael, you'll be in breach of contract if we won't be able to film you."

"Maria, it will be okay. You can shoot me when I'm not on set."

"Yeah, but you'll probably go for hair and makeup around 5:00 A.M. and will be working until 10:00 P.M. That doesn't give us a lot of time to shoot *Lucky*, since you'll be asleep the rest of the time. You can't take this gig or we'll be forced to sue you."

"But Maria, I won't be in every scene, so I'll have days off during the six weeks. You can shoot me going around Los Angeles, when I'm not on the set."

"What do you mean, six weeks?"

"You didn't hear the first part of the conversation. The character gets killed off after six episodes."

"Even if it's only six weeks, that's a huge problem for *Lucky*. Our viewers aren't going to be interested if all we get is video of you sightseeing in Los Angeles. If you take this acting job, we'll be forced to get our lawyers involved."

Michael felt an impotent fury. He finally had a gig, a real acting gig, and Maria was telling him he couldn't take it? There was no way he was giving up the opportunity to be on *Criminal Streets*.

"Maria, do what you have to do, even if that means suing me. I'm taking this role."

Maria looked upset. "I need to let William know about this." She pulled out her phone.

"William? It's Maria. We've run into a hiccup on *Lucky*. Michael's been offered a six-week acting gig in California and it's a closed set. We won't be able to shoot him on the days he's working."

Michael couldn't hear William's side of the conversation and he watched Maria closely, feeling anxious as Maria listened to William's response. Even if he could afford to be sued for breach of contract, he didn't need the headache.

"That's what I told him," he heard Maria say, "but he says he doesn't care. He's still going to take the role."

Michael watched Maria frowning as she listened.

"That's what I think, William. Viewers won't be interested just watching him hanging out in Los Angeles."

Maria paused again while William spoke to her.

"No, they haven't purchased anything big in a long time," Maria said. She sounded a little frustrated.

Maria's face brightened suddenly as she listened. "That's a thought. I can run that by him and see what he thinks."

Michael felt suddenly hopeful. Maybe William had figured out a way that he could take the job and not be sued. He waited impatiently for Maria to end the call.

"I think it's a great idea. Thanks, William. I'll let you know what he says." She disconnected the call.

"Well? What did he say?" asked Michael.

"He said that viewers want to see you and Kat living like millionaires and you haven't made a big purchase in a long time. We agree not to sue you over this acting gig if you agree to purchase an impressive house in California. That way we can show you house hunting on days when you're not on set. That will give us a focus for the six weeks you'll be in Los Angeles."

The hope that Michael had been feeling, when Maria ended the call, evaporated. "I think it might be cheaper just to let you sue me," he said to Maria.

"Sure, it will be a big expense but you guys can afford it. Plus, it will let you be bicoastal. All the really big stars have houses on both coasts. Maybe you could even get a jet to fly from one location to the other. Viewers would love to see that."

Michael thought about it for a moment. If he was starting to get acting gigs in Los Angeles, maybe it did make sense to get a house in California. He could see himself on a private jet, going between New York and L.A. Would Kat agree to let him purchase a second home? And a jet?

"Maria, if we get a second home, you agree not to sue me if I take the role on *Criminal Streets*?" he asked.

"Yes, as long as you house hunt on your days off and we can film you looking. We can find you a realtor out there. Leave it all to me."

Michael felt the tension he had been feeling in his shoulders start to relax. He would be happy to get a second house if it meant he could take acting gigs when they came along.

"Alright, Maria, let's look for a place on the beach."

Kat walked into the kitchen with her hair still damp from the shower.

"What place on the beach?" she asked.

"Kat, guess what? I got one of the roles I auditioned for in L.A.! I'm going to be a cop on *Criminal Streets*!" Michael walked over to Kat and gave her a big hug.

"Michael, that's great news! Congratulations! I'm so proud of you."

"I'll be a cop but only for six episodes. My character gets killed after that, but it's a great role. Shooting starts in eight weeks."

Kat looked upset as she sat down at the kitchen table. "But Michael, that's right after the wedding. We were going to be on our honeymoon. When do you have to be on set?"

"Alan said on May 31st."

"We're getting married on May 25th. You'll have to leave Maui just a couple of days after the ceremony!"

Michael felt irritated. Couldn't Kat see that getting this part was a lot more important than just lying on a beach for two weeks?

"I'm sorry, Kat, but I'll have to fly back. You can stay in Maui if you want to." He took a sip of coffee from his mug.

"I don't want to be on our honeymoon by myself!"

"So fly with me to L.A. You can start house hunting."

Kat's eyes widened. "What do you mean, house hunting?"

"I was just discussing it with Maria. Now that I'm starting to get roles in L.A., I think we should be bicoastal. We need to get a house on the West Coast."

"You've gotten one role. I don't think we need to get a second home just yet."

"Kat, we've got $32 million sitting in a money market account that we haven't spent. I told you when we won the money that I wanted to get more than one home. I think we should start house hunting out there. Plus, Maria said that viewers would love seeing us get a second home."

Kat frowned. "You also told me that we were going to slow down on the spending once we got this house and your Ferrari. And I don't care if viewers want to see it. It's not their money."

"That was last fall and we have slowed down since then. But this role is the perfect excuse to get another house. That way, I'll have somewhere to stay when I get other roles in Los Angeles. I don't want to stay in hotels all the time."

"How much time were you planning on spending in Los Angeles?" Kat asked.

"I figured we could split our time between there and here," said Michael with a big grin. "It'll be great."

"But what are we going to do about Max?" said Kat, leaning over to scratch Max behind the ears. "You can't drag him from one end of the country to the other all the time."

Max gave a little bark, as if in agreement.

"Max can stay here with Colleen," said Michael. "You don't mind, do you, Colleen?" He looked over at Colleen, who was wiping her hands on a dish towel.

"Of course I don't mind taking care of Max when you two are traveling," said Colleen with a big smile. She walked over to Max and started stroking his head. "He's such a love."

"See?" said Michael. "It will all work out."

"I don't know," said Kat, looking anxious. "I don't want Max to start thinking Colleen is his owner, instead of us."

"That's not going to happen, will it Max?" Max looked up expectantly at the mention of his name, his little tail thumping.

"Forget about Max for the moment," said Kat. "How's this bicoastal thing going to work when we have a baby?"

Michael felt exasperated. Now that Maria had inspired him, he could picture himself getting roles and going back and forth between New York and Los Angeles. Kat was being such a buzzkill.

"Kat, we don't have a baby yet."

"Yes but I want to start trying as soon as we come back from Maui."

Michael felt trapped. It was bad enough knowing that Erica was pregnant. He didn't think he could handle having Kat pregnant at the same time. Plus, when Kat found out about Erica, she would probably divorce him. He was fooling himself to think he could talk Kat into staying.

Divorcing would be hard enough without the complication of a baby. Without a child, they could just divide their possessions, and the rest of the money, and go their separate ways. With a child, there would be visitation schedules and something always tying him to Kat. Now that his career was taking off, Michael wanted to be free to enjoy his bicoastal lifestyle.

"Kat, I'm not sure I want to try for a baby right now. I would rather focus on my career," he said, wincing in anticipation of Kat's reaction.

Kat's jaw dropped.

"Michael, first we put off having a baby because we couldn't afford it. Then, when we became rich, we put off having a baby so I would look good in the wedding photos. Now you want to put it off so you can focus on your career? Just when were you thinking of having children?"

"I don't know Kat. I do want kids, just not now."

"But Michael, I'm going to be thirty-five in a couple of months. I don't have any more time to wait."

Kat got up from the table and poured herself a mug of coffee. Michael noticed her hands were trembling as she can back to the table and poured milk from the milk jug into her coffee.

"Kat, lots of women wait until their forties to have kids."

"That doesn't mean they have an easy time getting pregnant. And I want more than one child."

"You can still have more than one child if you wait until forty to get started."

"What if we wait and it turns out I can't get pregnant? How will you feel then?"

"Then I'll figure it wasn't meant to be. Kat, I can be happy if it's just the two of us and Max. We don't need a baby to complete us."

He thought for a moment. If he could hold Kat off until Maui, that was just two-and-a-half weeks before the final episode of *Lucky* would be aired. Once Kat saw the final episode, with him giving money to Erica to help with her pregnancy, Michael was willing to bet Kat would no longer want to have a baby with him. Kat would no longer want to have anything with him. He just needed to hold her off.

"Kat, what if we try to get pregnant as soon as I'm done filming *Criminal Streets*? That's just six weeks after Maui. No more delays. We'll work on getting you knocked up. Would that make you happy?"

Kat gave him an uncertain smile. "Yes, that would make me happy."

"It's a deal," said Michael, feeling as though he had dodged a bullet. "And can we house hunt when I'm not on set? I really want to get a second house, maybe in Malibu."

Kat nodded slowly. "Okay, Michael, we can look for a second home if that's what you really want." Michael got the feeling that Kat would agree to anything he wanted in that moment.

"Thanks, Kitty Kat. That would make me very happy."

'Maybe I should move out to the West Coast permanently, after we split up,' Michael thought to himself. 'More roles, better weather and beautiful women. Something to consider.'

Michael could see himself single in L.A. It could be a great life.

CHAPTER 19

MARIA

Michael, Maria and Dan were enjoying the late April weather in the backyard and watching Max run around on the grass. The leaves had recently come out on a beautiful maple tree which provided shade over the patio area, where Michael was sitting, drinking a Dos Equis and studying his *Criminal Streets* script.

Maria instructed Dan to get footage of the backyard. Although not large, it was charming with a fence made of red bricks and evergreen conifers bordering the grass. There was a small fountain and the sound of water splashing into the bowl was like pleasant background music.

Maria leaned back into a cushioned patio chair and gave a contented sigh. She was enjoying this relatively slow period before leaving for the wedding in Maui.

As she was relaxing, her phone rang. Checking the screen, she could see it was William.

"Hey, William, how are things going?" Maria asked.

"Couldn't be better," said William. "Neil Charles called me this morning. A+M wants to sign for a second season of *Lucky*. Audiences can't get enough of Michael and Kat."

Maria paused for a moment, not knowing what to say. She wasn't sure if she wanted to work on a second season of *Lucky*. Despite the stellar ratings, her father had not been impressed with the show. He thought the one episode he viewed was, as he put it, fodder for trailer trash. It had crushed Maria.

Plus, she was increasingly uncomfortable with all the manipulation she had to do, in order to get the strong ratings. But she needed the job if she wanted to keep paying her bills. She tried to sound cheerful as she responded to William.

"Hey, William, that's great. I'll let Dan know."

"A+M wants to air the second season as part of their fall lineup," said William. "I'll send over a messenger with the new contracts for Kat and Michael. We'll be paying them $15,000 per episode."

"Okay. I'll get their signatures as soon as possible."

"I gotta run but I wanted to let you know. Congratulations!"

"Thank you, William," Maria said before ending the call.

"Sounds like good news," said Michael, as Dan walked over.

"Guess what? A+M wants us to produce a second season of *Lucky*. Audiences love watching you and Kat."

"That's awesome," said Dan with a big smile.

Maria looked over at Michael. To her surprise, he wasn't smiling. In fact, he had a small frown on his face.

"Michael? Aren't you happy?"

Michael gave her a long look before responding. "Maria, I'm not sure I want to be on the second season of *Lucky*."

'That makes two of us,' thought Maria. If Kat and Michael didn't want to be on the show, that might let her off the hook. Then she remembered that she needed the job. If she was unemployed, her father would increase the pressure to get her to go to law school.

"Why not?" asked Maria. "The exposure has been great for you. You have a growing fan base and over 600,000 followers on Instagram."

"I initially said yes to being on *Lucky* because I hoped it would help my career."

"And it has helped your career," Maria pointed out. "You just got that role on *Criminal Streets*. You get recognized all the time."

"I know *Lucky* helped me get here but now it's going to ruin my life," said Michael. He looked stressed.

Maria had a feeling she knew why Michael was upset and it increased her ambiguity about working on a second season.

"How is it going to ruin your life?" she asked softly, wondering if there was a way she could fix things.

"You're going to broadcast that episode of Erica telling me she's pregnant. As soon as that comes out, fans will hate me for being unfaithful to Kat." He paused for a moment. "And Kat's going to divorce me."

Maria wondered which bothered Michael more: the idea of losing the approval of his fans, or losing Kat. She noticed he mentioned his fans first, with the divorce as an afterthought.

Michael thought for a minute. "I'll make a deal with you, Maria. I'll agree to be on a second season if you agree not to air anything about Erica."

"But that was going to be our season finale," said Maria. She knew William wouldn't be happy about this development. "How are we going to end the season, if we don't tell the world about the pregnancy?"

"That's your problem," said Michael. "If you want a second season, those are my terms."

'Maybe I can pivot.' Maria thought quickly. 'What if we end the season with the wedding in Maui? It wouldn't have a big twist, like the pregnancy, but *Lucky* viewers would love seeing the wedding.'

"I have to call William," Maria said, grabbing her phone.

To her surprise, William picked up.

"What's up, Maria?" She could hear the sound of traffic in the background. "I'm on my way to a meeting so I don't have much time to talk."

"Michael won't agree to be on a second season of Lucky unless we agree not to broadcast anything about Erica."

"Shit," said William, "The pregnancy was going to be our surprise twist to end the season."

"We could end with the wedding in Maui," said Maria hopefully. "It won't have the same drama but viewers will still love watching it."

"Maybe," said William slowly. "I think I need to check with Neil Charles to find out which he wants more: a second season with Kat and Michael or a shocking season finale. Give me a few minutes and I'll call you back."

"Well?" asked Michael. "What did he say? Do we have a deal?"

"He needs to check with A+M," said Maria. "I'm waiting for him to call me back." She picked nervously at a loose thread in her ripped jeans.

As Maria was waiting anxiously, not knowing if she wanted Kat and Michael to agree to a second season, Kat came out of the kitchen and sat down in one of the patio chairs.

"What a gorgeous day," she said appreciatively, looking around the backyard. Max came running up to her with his ball in his mouth, his little tail wagging.

Kat laughed. "Do you want to play fetch?" She stood up, took the ball out of his mouth and threw it across the backyard. Max went bounding after the ball and grabbed it up. He ran back to Kat and sat down in front of her.

She took the ball and threw it again. As he was chasing after it, a squirrel ran along the top of the fence, distracting Max, who started barking at it. Although Maria usually liked Max, today the sound of his barking was grating on her raw nerves. She wished he would shut up.

Maria needed something to focus on, instead of just waiting for William to call her back. She pulled out her phone and looked at the *Lucky* page on Facebook. Usually, she loved reading the comments left by fans but today it was just making her more anxious. With a sigh, she closed her Facebook app.

After what seemed like an eternity, but in reality was only about fifteen minutes, William called her back.

"I spoke to Neil Charles," said William. He sounded out of breath. "He said we'll agree not to show the episode about Erica if they agree to sign up for a second season."

"Does this mean we're giving them editorial control?" asked Maria.

"God, no!" said William. "Nothing like that. We're just agreeing to keep his dirty little affair out of this season's finale. Neil Charles doesn't see the Michael and Kat story stretching to a third season. He's hoping Erica hits Michael with a paternity suit and we can use that as the finale of season two."

"Nothing like planning ahead," said Maria.

"Promise them anything to sign up for a second season. Once the ink is dry on the contracts, we'll figure out what we want to show in season two."

"I'm on it," said Maria.

"Let me know if you run into any more issues," said William.

"I will," said Maria. "Thanks, William."

She disconnected the call and turned to Michael. "We have a deal."

Michael looked relieved.

"What deal?" asked Kat.

"A+M wants to shoot a second season of *Lucky*," said Michael.

"Yes," said Maria quickly, "and we just got a deal to pay you each $15,000 per episode."

Kat grimaced. "I don't want to do a second season of *Lucky*. One season was more than enough for me."

"I think Michael really wants to do a second season, don't you, Michael?" Maria nodded in his direction. If Michael couldn't get Kat to agree to a second season, they would air the episode with Erica. He had a vested interest in getting Kat to sign up again.

"Please, Kat? I think we should agree to a second season," said Michael.

"But why, Michael? You've gotten what you wanted from the show. You have a fan base and you're starting to get roles. You don't need to be on *Lucky* anymore."

"My role on *Criminal Streets* is great but it's just for six episodes. I need to stay popular on social media if I want to get more roles. If we stopped doing the show, people might forget about me."

"But I was looking forward to a life without cameras everywhere."

Maria had an inspired thought. "Kat," said Maria, "the exposure on *Lucky* could be good for you too."

"I don't care about having fans," said Kat with a bemused look on her face. "I'm not an actor."

"No, but you want to get your novel published one day. Having a large presence on social media could really help with that. Publishers love writers who already have an audience."

Kat frowned. "I have a wicked case of writer's block. I'm a long way from being ready for a publisher."

"But if we teamed you up with a good agent, I bet he or she could help get you unstuck. They might even be able to find you a publisher, based on your outline and the fans you have from being on the show."

Kat stopped frowning as she thought about it.

"Do you really think I could get a publishing contract just based on the outline?"

"With your fans? I'm sure you could," said Maria confidently.

William had said promise anything to get Kat and Michael to sign up for a second season. "We could even tease your novel on the show and build up anticipation for its publication."

"How would you do that?" asked Kat. "It's not like I'll be reading excerpts aloud for the camera."

"We could show meetings with your agent where you discuss the book. We could get your fans excited."

"I don't have an agent yet," Kat pointed out.

"We'll help you find an agent," said Maria. "I would be happy to make some calls." Maria loved the idea of helping Kat find an agent. It would make her feel less guilty for not telling Kat about Michael's infidelity.

"See, Kat?" said Michael. "A second season of *Lucky* could be good for both of us. You could write a New York Times bestseller. Isn't that what you want?" He looked over at Kat with a hopeful look on his face.

"Of course that's my fantasy," Kat admitted, "I'm just not sure if a second season of *Lucky* is the best way to get me there."

"Kat, I follow *Lucky* on social media. You have a lot of fans out there," said Maria.

"Nothing like Michael," Kat said. "He's really the star of the show."

"That's because we've been focusing on him during season one. With the second season, we could put more emphasis on you. We could show your meetings with your agent and your publisher. Fans would get to know your novel as it progresses. When the book is finally published, you'll have a huge potential audience."

Maria saw a look of longing on Kat's face. She had Kat intrigued.

"Please, Kitty Kat?" asked Michael. "Say yes to a second season. It could be great for both of us."

"But I hate being on camera all the time," said Kat with a sigh. "I wanted to go back to a more normal life." Max, having failed to capture the squirrel, came over and sat down by her feet. Kat reached out to pet his head.

"It hasn't been so bad," said Michael. "You've gotten used to having Dan around, right?"

"Yes, I like Dan," said Kat. "It's his camera I'm sick of."

"I'm glad to hear it's not me," said Dan with a laugh.

"Of course it's not you, Dan," said Kat. "I like you, you know that."

"I know Kat. I like you too."

"So say yes, Kat," pleaded Michael. Maria noticed that he sounded slightly desperate.

Kat turned to Maria. "But what if I get an agent and it turns out I still have a hard time writing?"

"In that case, they would probably get a ghostwriter to help you out," said Maria.

"I don't want a ghostwriter working on my novel! I want to write it."

"So let's find you an agent who can help get you over your writer's block. Maybe working collaboratively, instead of writing in isolation, will help," said Michael eagerly.

"I wish I had more isolation for writing," said Kat, looking wistful. "Maybe part of the problem is that I'm on camera all the time."

"We can give you more space to write, Kat," said Maria quickly. "Michael, Dan and I can leave you alone more often. Maybe we could even get you on a writing schedule where you're alone for hours each day."

"That could work," said Kat thoughtfully. "And you would help find me an agent?"

"Of course," said Maria. "Leave it to me."

"Do you really think being on a second season of *Lucky* would help sell the book to a publisher?"

"Yes. Publishers want to work with authors who are famous."

"Being an author who is famous is not the same as being a famous author," said Kat.

"True," said Maria, "but you could be both."

Kat turned to Michael. "This is what you want? Being on a second season?"

"Yes," said Michael. "I really want it. Please say yes."

"Okay," said Kat. "I'll sign on for a second season. But only because it might help sell my novel to a publisher."

"It will help, trust me," said Maria. "The contracts should be here this afternoon. I just need your signatures and we'll be all set."

"This time we're going to have our lawyer look over the contracts before we sign," said Kat.

"Of course," said Maria. "That should be fine."

William would be elated at getting them to agree, as soon as she called to tell him they would be doing a second season. She just hoped he was okay with promoting Kat's book.

That reminded her. She had to start making calls to help Kat find an agent.

KAT

Kat was surprised by how much she enjoyed working with a personal stylist. Maria had teamed her up with Natalie Wendell, who turned out to be warm and personable, despite looking like a runway model with her tall slim frame and penchant for designer outfits. First Natalie interviewed Kat about her lifestyle, what she liked and what she didn't. Then Natalie measured what seemed like every inch of her body. Finally, they went through Kat's current closet to determine what she should keep, what should be thrown away and what should be donated.

Kat was anxious about getting rid of the clothing which used to fit her heavier self.

"What if I become pregnant?" she asked Natalie nervously as they were in the second hour of sorting through her existing clothes.

"If you become pregnant, we'll get you some fabulous maternity clothes," said Natalie confidently. "Mama J makes a line of skinny maternity jeans that are to die for. We can also dress you in some really cute maxi dresses."

"What if I don't become pregnant but I gain the weight back?" asked Kat. That was really her bigger fear.

"We can make an appointment for a wardrobe refresh every three months," said Natalie. "If your weight starts creeping up, we can get new items that fit, no matter what your size is. Finding your personal style isn't about fitting into a specific dress size. It's about finding clothes that make you feel confident and reflect the real you. Please don't worry – I promise we'll make you look great."

Natalie had given Kat the option of going with her to the stores, or having Natalie bring the items she selected to the house. Kat opted to have the items brought to her, so she could try them on in the privacy of her own home.

Natalie and her assistant had shown up with two clothing racks filled with clothes, which she wheeled through the front door and into the elevator. They also brought a massive suitcase filled with designer lingerie and shoes. Kat took her up to the dressing room on the third floor, which had a three-way mirror.

"You said you liked jeans," said Natalie, holding up a pair of skinny jeans. "Why don't you try on this pair from Gucci?"

"I don't know if skinny jeans would look good on me," said Kat nervously. "My calves are too big."

"Why don't you just give them a try?" asked Natalie. "I think you'll be pleasantly surprised by how they fit."

Feeling self-conscious, Kat slipped out of the sweatpants she was wearing and slipped on the Gucci jeans. To her amazement, they fit as though they had been made for her. She looked at herself in the mirror. She was stunned to see that her legs looked amazing.

"Why don't we pair those with the Manolo Blahnik electric blue pumps and this black Givenchy silk blouse?" said Natalie, handing the top and the shoes to Kat.

Kat took off her t-shirt and tried on Natalie's recommendations.

She looked at herself in the mirror and didn't recognize herself. Instead of the somewhat frumpy Kat she was used to, she saw a slim stylish woman staring back at her.

"What do you think?" asked Natalie. "Are these keepers?"

Kat loved the way she looked but she wasn't sure.

"I don't know. These are expensive designers. Where would I wear an outfit like this?"

"That would be a great date night outfit when you go out with your husband," said Natalie.

Kat could see herself on a date with Michael wearing the outfit. She thought he would love it. "Okay, these are keepers," she said with a smile. Kat started to feel more cheerful about the process. "Do you have any sneakers in that suitcase?"

"Of course," said Natalie's assistant, handing over a pair of white Kate Spade sneakers and a pair of Rag & Bone straight leg jeans. "These are good for everyday wear."

"Try those with this Brunello Cucinelli gray cashmere pullover," suggested Natalie.

Kat tried on the outfit and decided it was a keeper.

She spent the next couple of hours trying on everything Natalie had brought. To her amazement, everything fit. There were a couple of tops she didn't like, because she thought the prints were not her style but she wanted to keep the vast majority of the clothes. She even approved of the designer lingerie and hoped Michael would like seeing her in the thongs that Natalie recommended.

She felt beautiful in the new clothes and couldn't wait to start wearing them.

She was exhausted but very happy by the time that Natalie and her assistant left, leaving behind all of her new clothes, underwear and shoes.

She went down to the kitchen and got a glass of wine. Kat was planning to do some reading in the conservatory when her phone rang. She didn't recognize the number but decided to pick up anyway.

"This is Kat Davidson," she said, hoping it wasn't a spam call.

"Hi, Kat? This is Sarah Evans. I'm with the Wordsmith Literary Agency. I got a call from your television producer who said you're working on a book."

Kat could feel her pulse start to race. "Yes, I've been working on a novel, although I haven't written much." Kat felt tongue-tied and hoped she didn't sound like an idiot.

"I wanted to know if you would consider writing a memoir about winning the BonusBall and being on a reality TV show. With your fans, I think publishers would really be interested."

Kat was dismayed. Sarah's proposal sounded like the last thing she wanted to write. It was bad enough being on *Lucky*. She didn't want to write a book about the experience.

"Sarah, I've been working on a literary novel about a woman who turns herself into a human Barbie. I don't think I want to write a memoir right now." Kat winced, hoping she wasn't blowing her chance to get an agent.

"Are you sure about not writing a memoir? I could see it becoming a best seller," said Sarah. She sounded very enthusiastic about the idea.

"I don't want to write a memoir," said Kat firmly.

"That's not a problem," said Sarah. "If you don't want to write the memoir yourself, we could team you up with a ghostwriter who could write it for you. There would be very little effort on your part. What do you think?"

"I already feel uncomfortable with the amount of attention we get from the show. The last thing I want is to let the public in on more of my private life. I wouldn't want to work on a memoir, even if someone else writes it. I'm interested in publishing my novel. Do you think publishers would be interested?"

"I'm not really the right agent to work with your novel," said Sarah, sounding disappointed. "I mostly work with famous people who want to write memoirs or self-help books. If you want to publish a literary novel, there are other agents at our agency who might be able to work with you. Do you have an outline and a sample chapter?"

"I have an outline but I don't really have a sample chapter yet," admitted Kat, feeling very disappointed. She had a chance to have an agent read her work and because of her writers block, she wasn't in a position to take advantage of the opportunity.

"I'll email you my contact information. Let me know when you have something to read and I'll be happy to make a referral."

"I'll do that, thank you," said Kat. She promised herself she would try harder with her novel so she would have something to show an agent soon. She didn't want this opportunity to slip away.

"Sounds like a plan," said Sarah cheerfully. "And please let me know if you have a change of heart about the memoir. I could see it becoming a best seller, given how many fans you have out there."

"I'll think about it," said Kat, before saying goodbye to Sarah and hanging up.

Once she was off the phone, she wondered if she was making the right decision. She didn't really want to write a memoir but what if she just didn't have a novel in her? What if she wasn't meant to write fiction? Should she try to write a memoir that might sell well?

She weighed the desire to have a best seller against her desire to keep some part of her life private. It was bad enough being on camera all the time. She didn't want to let readers know her inner thoughts too. She was making the right decision about not writing a memoir. Kat just wished she could get past her writers block so she could send a sample chapter to an agent. Feeling discouraged, Kat took her wine and book into the conservatory and tried to relax.

CHAPTER 20

MARIA

'It's not the perfect weather or the turquoise ocean that makes Maui so magical,' Maria thought appreciatively as she took a deep breath, 'It's the smell.'

She loved the tang of the ocean combined with the fresh scent of newly mowed grass, overlaid with the heady perfume of jasmine. It was intoxicating.

Not that she and Dan had had much time to smell the flowers since checking into the Grand Wailea Resort for Kat and Michael's wedding. In addition to filming the wedding preparations, she had Dan busy getting b-roll footage of the pristine beach and the gorgeous sunsets.

They had arrived on Thursday along with the wedding party and guests. Everyone who had been invited showed up, thanks, in part, to Kat and Michael footing the bill for all the travel and hotel accommodations.

Kat's guest list included Ren as her maid of honor and Dylan, Ren's boyfriend. Kat's uncle, Charlie, had come along with her aunt, Jan. Kat's friends from her book club were in attendance, along with their spouses. She even had an old friend from high school, and her first college roommate.

Michael jokingly referred to his side of the guest list as his entourage, which seemed to consist of buddies from his acting class. He had asked

Barry, his acting coach, to be his best man. Maria noticed that Michael didn't have any old friends or family attending, although his agent, Alan, had come.

Maria realized she didn't know what Kat's father and Annika looked like so she pulled Michael aside.

"Did you invite Kat's father and Annika? Are they part of the group?"

"No, I spoke to Andy on the phone a couple of days ago. They won't be arriving until tomorrow, but they should be at the rehearsal dinner." Maria didn't know whether to be disappointed or relieved.

Thursday night, after everyone had checked in, there had been a luau on the beach, complete with a lei for each guest, a pig roasted in hot coals, Polynesian dancing and a traditional Samoan Fireknife dancer to end the evening's entertainment. Maria wished she had been able to grab some of the food, but she and Dan were busy, making sure they were capturing everything for *Lucky*.

Friday was the wedding rehearsal, in the Grand Wailea Wedding Chapel, followed by the rehearsal dinner in the Humuhumunukunukuapua'a, a Polynesian thatch-roof restaurant floating on a lagoon, overlooking Wailea Beach.

Maria told Dan not to shoot the rehearsal because she didn't want it to be a repeat of the wedding ceremony. Instead, while everyone else was tied up at the rehearsal, at William's insistence, Maria was busy switching the seating place cards at the restaurant. She needed to ensure that Kat sat near Andy and Annika during the rehearsal dinner.

By 7:00 P.M., the rehearsal had ended and the party was coming into the restaurant and sitting down at the table laid for forty.

"Kat, Ren, come over here." Maria grabbed them as they were entering the restaurant. "I want Dan to get some video of the two of you in your sundresses, with the waterfall as a backdrop." In fact, Maria wanted to ensure that everyone else sat down at the table, so Kat would be forced to sit in the empty seat next to Annika.

Kat and Ren stood by the railing, in front of a man-made waterfall, and beamed at the camera. Dan moved in for a close-up of the two sisters with flowers in their hair and their arms around each other. After a few minutes, Maria looked over at the rest of the party where everyone had been seated.

"That's great — thank you. Why don't you take your seats?" Maria suggested.

Kat and Ren walked over to the large table. Ren sat down in her assigned seat but Kat stopped abruptly when she saw her father at the table, sitting next to a woman in her early sixties with bleached blonde hair.

"Dad," Kat said in a horrified voice. "What are you doing here?" Conversation at the table stopped and all eyes turned to look at Kat.

Kat's father turned around to look with a startled look on his face. Andy was a handsome man in his sixties with a full head of silver hair.

"Kitten, where else would I be? Of course I'm here at the wedding. Annika and I were thrilled to be invited. I'm just sorry we couldn't get here yesterday."

"But I didn't invite you," Kat sputtered. "I didn't think you would be here."

"We got an invitation, along with a card saying there was no need to R.S.V.P."

"How is that possible?" said Kat said. Her face was red and she had her hands clenched in fists.

"Kat, I invited them," said Michael, standing up from his seat and turning to face Kat. He looked a little anxious. "I thought it would be nice if you could patch things up before the wedding."

"Michael, how could you? You knew I didn't want them here," Kat said furiously.

"Kitty Kat, I know you love your dad. I thought a happy occasion like our wedding would be a great time to make up," Michael pleaded with Kat.

"Kat, I thought you wanted us here," said Andy. "I thought the invitation came from you."

"Well, it didn't," said Kat. "And even if I wanted you here, I certainly don't want Annika here."

"But I was hoping you could get to know Annika," said Andy, looking flustered. "She's going to be your stepmother."

Kat's jaw dropped as she looked at her dad. "What do you mean stepmother?"

"Maybe it's because I'm attending your wedding, or maybe it's because Maui is so romantic, but I felt inspired. I asked Annika to marry me, this afternoon, and she's accepted."

"Dad, how could you?" Kat turned pale. "Annika is the reason Mom died."

Annika's hand flew up to her cheek, as if Kat had slapped her.

"Kat, what are you talking about?" Andy sputtered. He stood up and took a step back from Kat to look at her.

"You know exactly what I'm talking about," Kat hissed. "You had an affair with Annika and Mom had a heart attack when she found out. You and Annika killed her."

"Kat, you're not being fair. Your mother had a weak heart. It was a terrible accident when she died but it wasn't anybody's fault." Andy looked as though he was pleading with Kat to believe him.

"Mom died the day she found out about your affair with Annika. Do you think that's a coincidence? The shock was too much for her."

"So that's why you haven't been returning my calls? You blame me for your mother's death?"

"I blame both of you," said Kat. "You should have broken it off with Annika when Mom died. At least you would have been honoring her memory. Instead, you're going to marry…" Kat turned to look hatefully at Annika.

"Kat, heart disease runs in your mother's side of the family. You know that. It doesn't mean I killed her."

"Let's say the heart attack wasn't totally your fault," said Kat, still looking furious. "Her last day was filled with pain because of the heartache you caused her."

Andy shut his eyes for a moment and looked down, sorrow on his face.

"I know, Kat. I'm very sorry about that. I live with the guilt of it every day."

"You have a strange way of making amends. Instead getting rid of Annika, you're going to replace Mom with her."

"Kat, I'm not trying to replace your…" Annika started to say before Kat shut her up with a furious look.

"Kat, of course Annika's not going to replace your mother. No one could."

"You don't need to tell me," said Kat. "Anyways Annika, you're welcome to him. If he cheated on Mom with you, how long before he cheats on you too? Once a philanderer, always a philanderer."

Maria noticed that this last statement made Annika look extremely anxious. Kat's verbal dart must have hit the bullseye.

"Kat, please stop," Andy pleaded. "There's no need to air our dirty laundry in public."

"Andy, maybe you had better go," Michael said apologetically. "I'm sorry I invited you. I think it was a mistake having you come."

"I think you're right," said Andy. "Annika, come on, we're leaving. I don't want to stay if Kat doesn't want us here."

"And don't plan on coming to the wedding tomorrow," said Kat as Annika stood up.

He and Annika walked slowly away from the table. Andy looked upset and Annika looked crushed.

Maria felt guilty that she had ever wanted to get Kat and Annika together on camera. Kat looked incredibly stressed on a night when she should have been completely happy. Maria wanted great ratings but she didn't like what she had to do to get them.

Kat sat down as waiters came and put a Mai Tai in a pineapple in front of each guest. The guests, who had been silent during the exchange between Kat and her father, started talking quietly.

While most people were sipping their drinks, Michael finished his off and signaled to the waiter to bring a second round.

"Hey there, big guy," Barry said jovially, "you may want to pace yourself. We have the bachelor's party after this dinner and I wouldn't want you to get too wasted...too soon." There were some sniggers from the acting contingent at the table.

"I'll be fine," said Michael. "So what have you guys got planned for tonight?"

"We're going to hit a few clubs," said Barry with a grin, "and there may be a few surprises along the way." He raised his voice so it could be heard by the other end of the table. "But don't worry, Kat, we'll get him to the chapel on time."

Kat started smiling for the first time that evening. "You better get him there, Barry," she said.

The waiters placed plates of watercress and mango salad on the table, and poured white wine into everyone's wine goblets. The table was silent for a few minutes while everyone enjoyed the food. Then Barry stood up and banged his fork against his wineglass.

"I would be remiss in my duties as best man if I didn't take this moment to offer a toast to the bride and groom. Kat, Michael, thank you so much for inviting all of us to help celebrate your wedding. I can't think of a more perfect setting than Maui for renewing your vows." He raised his glass. "To the happy couple!"

"To the happy couple" echoed the table, raising their glasses in response.

The toast, although short, seemed to break the ice and everyone went back to talking, in addition to eating the rest of their meal.

There was no more drama, as the table was finishing up their desserts and Kona coffee but Maria didn't mind. She was actually a little relieved.

KAT

The morning of the wedding, Kat woke up at 5:00 A.M. but she couldn't tell if it was from excitement, or jet lag. In a nod to tradition, Michael was sleeping in a separate suite at the hotel, so Kat couldn't ask if he was as excited as she was.

After making a cup of coffee, using the hotel's in-room coffee pot, she made her way into the bathroom to take a quick shower and pull it together. Post-shower, she wrapped herself in one of the hotel's luxurious towels and dug in her toiletries bag for her birth control pills. To her surprise, she couldn't find them. She opened the bag and spilled everything out on the counter – she saw her mascara, blush, facial cleanser and her other toiletries. Everything seemed to be there, except the pills.

Kat tried to remember if she had taken a pill the day before. She thought she had, but then where were the pills now? Was it possible she had forgotten her pills in New York? Kat thought back to when she was packing for the trip. She remembered seeing the pills on the counter in her bathroom when she had been packing her toiletries bag. She remembered putting her toothpaste and toothbrush in the bag but she couldn't remember putting her pills in the bag. She had a strong suspicion that the pills were still on the bathroom counter at home.

Did it matter? Michael said they could start trying for a baby, after he finished shooting *Criminal Streets* but what if they started trying now? Kat thought it would be romantic if she got pregnant on their wedding night. She decided that, as of now, she was off the pill. If she got pregnant in the next six weeks, she would tell Michael about getting a head start. If she didn't get pregnant, he could think she went off the pill when he was done with his acting gig. Kat giggled. Going off the pill was like giving herself a wedding present. She couldn't wait to start trying to have a baby.

Ren arrived at 8:00 A.M. and the stylists arrived by 8:30 A.M. After that, it was a blur of activity as they worked on Kat's hair and face. For the wedding, Kat had opted to have her hair done in a French twist, with red roses and baby's breath woven into her hair.

Once her hair and makeup were done, Ren and the stylists helped Kat into her wedding gown. Kat got the diamond necklace out of the room safe and asked for Ren's help in putting it on.

"Well? How do I look?" she asked Ren nervously, once she was ready.

"Oh, Kat, you look gorgeous," said Ren, pulling her over to the mirror in the room. "Come take a look."

Kat looked at herself in the mirror. She was thrilled with how she looked. The coral wedding gown, combined with the upswept hair and the diamond necklace made her look regal. The expertly applied eyeliner and soft pink eye shadow made her eyes appear huge and almost turquoise in color. She couldn't wait until Michael saw her in her wedding dress.

"What time do you have?" she asked Ren nervously.

"It's just about 10:40," said Ren. "We should get you over to the chapel."

Kat and Ren thanked the stylists, picked up their bouquets and left the room to walk to the hotel lobby. Because the chapel was on the resort grounds, they wouldn't be taking a car to get to the chapel but the wedding planner had arranged for a flower covered golf cart to pick Kat up.

Kat and Ren got to the chapel at 10:55 A.M., five minutes before the wedding was scheduled to begin. Kat's Uncle Charlie met them as they were getting out of the cart. He was dressed in a tux with a white rose in his lapel. Kat noticed that he looked anxious.

"Kat, Ren, you both look beautiful!" he said, helping them out of the golf cart.

"Thank you, Uncle Charlie," said Kat. "You look very handsome yourself.

Are we all ready?"

"Not quite," said Charlie. Kat noticed a sheen of sweat on his forehead.

"What do you mean?" said Kat. She felt a small prickle of anxiety.

"Well, Michael's not here yet."

"What do you mean, Michael's not here? He was supposed to be here no later than 10:30."

"I know," said Charlie looking stressed, "but he's not here yet."

"Is Barry here?" Kat asked.

"Yes, Barry arrived about ten minutes ago."

"Bring Barry out here. I want to talk to him."

"Okay, Kat, wait here and I'll go get him." Charlie dashed into the chapel.

"Don't worry, Kat, I'm sure he'll show up," said Ren. "Michael's always a few minutes late. He won't miss your wedding."

Kat didn't know whether to be anxious or angry. She was furious at Michael for screwing up the choreography of their carefully planned event. She was also worried that something had happened to him. Maybe he was lying in a hospital somewhere. She waited impatiently for Barry to come out of the chapel and tell her what had happened the night before.

Charlie walked out of the chapel a couple of minutes later with Barry in tow. Barry was wearing a gray morning coat with tails over a matching pair of gray pants. His receding hairline emphasized a forehead that was shiny with sweat. He looked as if he was still slightly hungover.

"Hi, Kat, you look beautiful," he said, trying to smile as he walked up to Kat.

"Never mind how I look, where is Michael? He was supposed to be here a half hour ago."

"I know, Kat. I knocked on his door but he never answered. I thought maybe he already left, so I walked over to meet him here."

"As best man, you had one job and that was getting him to the chapel on time. What the hell happened?"

Barry wiped a hand over his forehead. "I know, Kat. I'm really sorry."

"When was the last time you saw him?" asked Ren. She looked furious.

"I think it was when we were at the VIBE Bar. It was the third or fourth bar we went to and we were in a private room in the back of the club."

"What was Michael doing?" asked Kat. She could feel her stomach start to knot with anxiety.

"Kat, it was his bachelor party. I don't know if I should be telling you everything that went on."

"Barry, Michael's MIA. I want to know all the details and I want to know them now."

Barry looked miserable. "Okay, Kat. We were at VIBE around 12:30 A.M. and I had hired a stripper. She started by doing a hula and then removed her costume, piece by piece."

"Barry, I don't need to know what the stripper did. Tell me about Michael." Kat was seething with impatience.

"I'm really sorry, Kat, but the details are fuzzy. I had had a lot to drink by that point in the evening. The last thing I remember was that she was giving Michael a lap dance."

Kat felt a wave of jealousy wash over her. Had Michael gone off with the stripper? Is that why he wasn't at the wedding?

"Barry, what happened next?" asked Ren. She looked like she wanted to shake him.

"That's just it. I can't remember what happened next. Somehow I must have made my way back to my room because the next thing I remember was the alarm going off this morning."

"Barry, you're useless," snapped Kat. "Have you tried calling Michael?"

"I've been trying him every ten minutes," said Barry. "He hasn't been picking up."

Kat had a sudden thought.

"Are Maria and Dan here? They would have been following Michael last night. They can tell me what happened to him."

"The camera crew?" Barry asked. "They're not here yet either."

Kat wasn't sure if this information made her feel relieved or more anxious. Maria and Dan weren't at the chapel which meant they were still filming Michael. He probably hadn't been in an accident, or they would have contacted Kat. On the other hand, what was Michael doing, that they were still following him around? If he had gone back to his room last night, they would have gone back to their own rooms. Where had Michael spent the night?

As Kat's thoughts raced around in her head, the pastor came out of the chapel and over to where they were standing.

"Any sign of the groom?" he asked the group.

"Not yet," answered Ren. "We're sorry about the delay."

"I don't want to add to your stress," said the pastor, "but I have to leave by 12:00 P.M. I have a funeral to officiate at and it's on the other side of the island."

"I understand," said Kat. "We're trying to find Michael." She turned to Ren. "Ren, can you get my phone out of your purse? I need to reach Maria."

Ren handed her bouquet to Barry and opened the small beaded clutch she was carrying to pull out Kat's phone.

Kat tapped on Maria's name in her contacts list. To her relief, Maria picked up right away.

"Maria Gonzales."

"Maria! I'm so glad I reached you. We're at the chapel and Michael's not here. Do you know where he is? Is he okay?"

There was a long pause. Kat could feel her heart hammering fast in her chest.

"Hi Kat. Don't worry about Michael. He's fine. We're here with him."

"Where is here? We're supposed to be getting married. Why aren't you guys at the chapel?"

"It's kind of a long story."

"Did Michael go off with the stripper? Is that why he's not here, because he hooked up with her?" Kat's heart felt like it was pounding out of her chest.

"The stripper? No, she left around 1:15."

"Maria, where the hell is Michael? Please just tell me what happened."

Maria sighed.

"Okay, Kat. I'll tell you. Once the stripper left, Michael was recognized by some fan named Scooter. He insisted on buying Michael shots at the bar. After an hour, they were both pretty wasted. Michael said that he needed something to pick him up, or he was never going to make the ceremony in time. Scooter said he knew a guy they could go see."

"What do you mean, pick me up?" Kat asked.

"Michael wanted to score some coke, to help him wake up."

Kat was dismayed by this new development. She knew Michael liked to party but she had never seen him do more than smoke pot.

"Maria, what happened next?"

"They got into Scooter's car and we followed them in a second car. Scooter was too drunk to drive, so Michael got behind the wheel. In hindsight, maybe that wasn't the best idea, because Michael was weaving all over the road."

"Did Michael get in an accident? Is he okay?"

"No, he's fine but a police car pulled him over."

"So he got a DUI?"

"No, it turned out that the policeman is a fan of the show. He just gave Michael a ticket for reckless driving and took him to the police station to sleep it off. We've been at the police station all night. I'm just waiting for them to release Michael."

"Maria, why didn't you call me?"

"I didn't want to worry you and I thought we would be out of here in time to make the ceremony."

Kat was relieved that Michael hadn't been in an accident, or gone off with a stripper, but she was furious that he was missing his own wedding ceremony. They had been planning the wedding for months, all their friends and family were here and Michael had screwed it up.

Maria interrupted Kat's train of thought. "Hey, it looks like they're letting him out. We're about 45 minutes away. Don't worry, Dan and I will get him to the chapel."

"I'm not sure you'll be able to make it in time," said Kat. "The pastor has to leave at Noon for a funeral."

"We'll get there as fast as we can, without breaking any speed limits. The last thing we need is another ticket."

"Okay, thanks, Maria. Drive carefully."

"We will, Kat. See you soon."

"What happened to Michael?" Ren asked, looking worried as Kat disconnected the call. "Is he okay?"

"He was driving drunk last night and got pulled over by a cop. He spent the night in a cell, sleeping it off. Maria said they just let him out. She and Dan are driving him; they should be here in about forty-five minutes."

"I'm glad it was nothing more serious," said Barry. He looked very relieved.

Kat was too furious with Barry to respond. As the best man, he should have been looking out for Michael and making sure he didn't get into trouble. Instead, Michael had spent the night in the drunk tank and might miss his own wedding.

"I'll go into the chapel and let the guests know that the groom has been a bit delayed. I just hope he gets here in time," said the pastor. He turned and walked back into the chapel.

"Kat, what do you want to do?" asked Ren. "Do you want to wait out here, or do you want to go into the chapel?"

Kat was having a hard time deciding what to do. It was hot outside and it would be nice to go into the chapel, to get out of the sun. But if she did that, it would spoil her grand entrance, assuming Michael got to the chapel in time for the ceremony.

Her perfect wedding was already ruined, thanks to the missing groom, so she decided she might as well be comfortable while she waited for Michael to show up.

"Let's go inside and sit down," she told Ren and her uncle. "There's no point to waiting out in the heat."

Every eye was on Kat, as she entered the chapel with Ren and walked up the aisle, but it was not the way she pictured doing it when she fantasized about her wedding. She didn't look at anyone but she held her head up high as she made her way to the front pew. Jan moved over, to make space for Kat, Ren and Charlie to sit down.

They waited for fifty minutes without Michael, Dan and Maria showing up. The pastor stayed until 12:10 P.M. but finally had to leave with profuse apologies.

Finally, at 12:20 P.M., the chapel doors opened. Dan walked quickly backward, ahead of Michael, so he could film him racing up the aisle. Maria followed behind Michael.

Michael walked over to where Kat was sitting. He looked absolutely terrible. He was wearing the polo shirt and khaki pants he had been wearing the night before, but now they were wrinkled and the shirt was sweat-stained. He was clearly suffering from a monster hangover. His eyes were completely bloodshot and he was pale and sweating. Even at a distance, he still smelled 100 proof.

Michael grabbed one of Kat's hands.

"Kat, I'm so sorry. Am I in time? Is the pastor still here?"

The only emotion Kat had, as she looked at him, was a rage that was all-encompassing.

"Fuck you, Michael," she said in a voice loud enough for everyone to hear. "The pastor left ten minutes ago."

Michael's hopeful look was replaced with a look of total misery.

"Oh Kat, I'm so very sorry, but it wasn't my fault. Some asshole of a cop pulled me over."

"You were driving drunk. Of course it was your fault. Getting pulled over by a cop was probably a good thing. At least you didn't kill anyone."

"Kat, I wasn't that drunk."

"That's not what Maria said. She said you were weaving all over the road."

Michael turned around to give Maria a nasty look before turning back to Kat.

"Maria was exaggerating. I was able to drive just fine."

Kat didn't say anything but she pulled her hand out of his sweaty one.

"Anyways Michael, what were you doing driving anywhere?" She lowered her voice. "Maria said you were going to buy coke. Is that true?"

Michael rolled his eyes. "When did Maria turn into WikiLeaks? We were just going to party. I wasn't going to buy any drugs, I swear."

"Well, no matter what you were going to do, you've ruined our wedding. Fuck you and your juvenile behavior. You're a grown man, not some frat boy on spring break."

"I know, Kat. I'm really so sorry. How can I make this right?"

"Maybe you should start by apologizing to everyone here. You haven't just ruined the wedding for me. You've also ruined it for our guests."

"Maybe there's a way we can fix this," said Maria, inserting herself into the conversation. "Why don't we have the ceremony now? It's a little later than planned but everyone's all here."

"What are you talking about? The pastor already left." Kat glared at Maria. She wasn't just angry at Michael. She blamed Dan and Maria too because they were the ones who let Michael drive drunk. He could have been killed.

"You guys are already married, so we don't need a pastor to perform a wedding ceremony in order to make it official. We can ask one of your guests to officiate and you can say your vows to each other. It would be great to have some type of ceremony for our *Lucky* viewers."

"Michael stands me up and that's what you're worried about? Whether your viewers will get to watch a ceremony? Fuck you too, Maria."

Maria looked a little embarrassed. She looked over at Michael to see what he thought about the idea. He grasped on to it like a drowning man grabbing a lifesaver.

"Please, Kat? I think it's a great idea. I'm sorry I missed the pastor but I still want to have a recommitment ceremony with you. Let me say how much I love you in front of our friends and family. We can ask Noah to conduct the ceremony. He's played a priest in a Lifetime movie. I know he would do a great job."

"I don't want to be married by one of your acting buddies." Kat took a deep breath. "And the last thing I want to do is have a recommitment ceremony with you. You're lucky we're already married Michael because right now, I wouldn't want to marry you."

"Ah Kat." Michael wasn't able to complete his thought as his face turned green. He turned and ran down the aisle and out of the chapel. Kat could hear the sound of him throwing up into the bushes.

'Good,' Kat thought to herself with some satisfaction. 'I hope he feels miserable. I hope he's completely humiliated.'

She looked around the chapel. Everyone was staring at her, wondering what would happen next.

'I'm not going to let Michael ruin the rest of this day,' Kat thought to herself. She stood up and walked to the front of the chapel and turned to face everyone. The room was completely silent.

"I want to thank you all for coming and apologize that we didn't have the recommitment ceremony. This day was supposed to be a celebration of the love that Michael and I have for each other. Instead, I would like to turn it into a celebration of the love that I have for all of you. It means a great deal to me that you traveled to Hawaii to be here for us. You're our friends and family and I treasure having you in our lives.

"I don't see any reason not to enjoy the reception, just because the day hasn't gone as planned. I invite you all to join me on the Beach Courtyard, near the Hibiscus Pool, where we have a tent set up. We have a luncheon planned, and a D.J. I hope you'll have a wonderful time.

"I don't know if Michael will be joining us." Kat paused for a moment, as the sound of Michael retching outside the chapel could be heard.

She smiled grimly. "I think he may be otherwise indisposed. But I will certainly be there and I hope to dance with all of you. Please follow me to the Beach Courtyard."

Kat walked up the aisle, which she noticed had been strewn with flower petals. Ren, Jan and Charlie followed her. After a few moments, the other guests stood up and walked after her.

As she exited the chapel, Kat paused a moment to look at Michael. He was lying on the sidewalk, curled up in a fetal position, holding his head. The smell of vomit was in the air. Kat walked around him without saying a word.

Kat was still so angry with Michael that she didn't miss him at the reception. At her direction, the caterers removed his chair and place setting from the wedding table and spread out the other seats, so it wasn't obvious that someone was missing. Ren was on her right and Barry on her left. They kept up a steady stream of conversation, so there were no awkward silences.

She gazed out at the beach, which was framed by palm trees and tried to enjoy the first course of coconut shrimp. It wasn't the way she pictured her wedding reception but the food was fantastic and the weather was perfect, with soft breezes coming in from the direction of the ocean.

'It's Michael's loss that he's not here,' Kat decided.

She told the D.J. not to play the song she had selected for the couple's first dance but she started things off by dancing with her Uncle Charlie. Then she made a point of dancing with every single man at the reception.

As she ate a piece of wedding cake and viewed the glorious sunset over the Pacific Ocean, Kat reflected on the day. To her surprise, she had had fun at the reception, despite Michael's absence, although she was still furious with him for screwing up the wedding.

She walked over to where Barry was sitting.

"Hey, Barry, I need you to do something for me," she said.

Barry gave her a big smile. "Anything, Kat. What do you need?"

"I want you to book Michael for another night in his suite. I don't want him staying in the Honeymoon Suite with me tonight. Then I want you to go and make sure he's not in my room. I just don't want to see him right now."

Barry stopped smiling and looked troubled. "Okay, Kat. I'll take care of it. Are you sure?"

"I'm very sure. I need some more time to cool off before I see him again."

Kat figured if she spent the reception by herself, she could spend the wedding night by herself. Maybe by tomorrow, she would be ready to see Michael again but she needed some space before she wanted to deal with him.

"You got it," said Barry. "Do you want me to say anything to him?"

"Yes," said Kat, making up her mind on the spot, "you can tell him I won't be going with him to L.A. I would rather stay home with Max. He can film his TV show and go house hunting without me."

Barry's eyes widened but he didn't say anything. He gave Kat an uncertain smile and walked off.

Kat surprised herself with her decision not to go to Los Angeles but the more she thought about it, the more she was convinced that it was the right thing to do. She would rather remain in New York and focus on her writing, instead of just following Michael around.

'Fuck Michael,' she thought to herself. 'I may love him but he can also be an immature asshole at times. I want to focus on myself and my writing.'

That night, Kat had a wonderful night's sleep, despite being alone in the king-sized bed.

MARIA

Maria met with William and Sophie, the editor, to figure out how to cobble together a finale for *Lucky's* first season. Thanks to their agreement with Michael, they couldn't use the footage of Erica telling Michael she was pregnant. Thanks again to Michael, they didn't have a fairy tale wedding to show viewers.

"So what are your thoughts?" William asked Maria, as they stood in front of Sophie's work station.

"Well," said Maria, "we've been showing him as the perfect husband up until now. Buying jewelry for his wife, getting her a puppy, things like that. What if we use the finale to show that he's not so perfect? We can show the audience that he missed the wedding because of his bachelor party. It will also set things up for season two where we show what a bastard Michael really is."

"That could work," said William, sounding cheerful. "Do you have anything else for the finale?"

"There was conflict at the rehearsal dinner. I have Kat accusing her father of killing their mother." Maria flushed a little, remembering how she maneuvered to get Kat's father and Annika at the wedding.

"I love it!" said William with a big smile. "We can definitely work with that." He turned to Sophie.

"Start with some of the b-roll Dan captured, showing how romantic Maui is. I want ocean views, palm trees waving in the breeze and beautiful sunsets."

"You could start with that," said Maria, "and then show the wedding party arriving at the resort and getting welcome leis. You could follow that up with the luau on the beach. Sophie, please find what Dan shot on May 23rd."

They spent a few minutes looking at the footage from the Thursday before the wedding.

"It's perfect," said William. "It looks like something done by the Travel Channel. Sophie, I want the first five minutes of the episode to be about vacationing in beautiful Hawaii."

"Sounds good," said Sophie. "What next?"

William turned to Maria. "Did you get the wedding rehearsal?"

Maria bit down on her lip. "No, I told Dan to skip it because I thought it would just be a repeat of the wedding itself." She worried that William would think she screwed up.

William frowned. "That's unfortunate, especially in light of the fact that there was no wedding."

"I'm really sorry, William."

"Don't sweat it, Maria. It would have been nice to have but we can work without it. Let's see what you got for the rehearsal dinner."

Maria thought a moment. "Sophie, go to May 24th."

William was tapping his foot impatiently while Sophie fast forwarded through the footage of Michael and Kat snorkeling on the beach but he stopped tapping and leaned in close to the monitor while watching the rehearsal dinner. The three of them watched the interaction between Kat and her father.

"I love the tension," William said happily after the clip ended. "Viewers are going to eat it up."

Maria was happy that William was pleased but she felt ashamed that she had exploited Kat's unhappiness for great ratings. She knew her father wouldn't approve.

"When was the bachelor party?" asked William.

"It was right after the rehearsal dinner." Maria answered.

"Let's see what you've got."

If they wanted to portray Michael as a less than perfect husband, the bachelor party footage gave them everything they needed. At the first two bars, Michael and his entourage did shots of tequila. As they got drunker, they started rating the women at the bars on how fuckable they were. There were some great shots of Michael practically drooling over some of the women.

At the third bar, they went into a private room and the stripper showed up.

"Sophie, rewind the video," William instructed after watching the stripper remove all of her clothes.

Sophie rewound the video to the point where the stripper starting dancing the hula.

"Can you show her stripping but blur out the nudity?"

"Sure," said Sophie. "I can make it PG-13 instead of NC-17 if that's what you want."

"That's what I want, thanks, Sophie. Go back to playing the rest."

The worst was yet to come. Dan had captured the naked stripper giving Michael a lap dance, after she finished stripping. He didn't have an orgasm but the expression on Michael's face showed that he was highly aroused.

Lap dance over, the stripper left the club and Michael made his way out of the private room in search of the men's room. He was in the men's room for ten minutes. When he finally emerged, Michael was recognized by a fan, who wanted to buy him a drink at the bar. One drink turned into several drinks and Michael and the fan started discussing how to get some coke to help Michael wake up.

The next part of the footage showed the back of the car that Michael was driving, as he moved unsteadily from one side of the road to the other. There were a couple of times when he nearly had a head-on collision, only to veer out of the way at the last minute. The video showed Michael being pulled over by a cop.

"He really shouldn't have been driving," said William while he was watching.

"I know. Dan and I didn't realize how drunk he was or we would have taken the keys away from him," said Maria.

"I'm just glad he didn't hit anyone. We could have been liable."

"Really?" said Maria nervously. "I didn't think about that."

"You never know. If the injured party got a tough lawyer they might have sued us, in addition to Michael. That cop did us a favor."

William, Maria and Sophie watched the cop speak to Michael. Then the cop helped Michael out of the car and into the back of the police car. Maria was just sorry that handcuffs weren't involved.

"Did you get a shot of him in the jail cell?" asked William hopefully.

"No, the police wouldn't let us shoot inside the building. We'll just have to use the outside shot of the police station and let viewers use their imaginations. Dan stopped filming until Michael was let out of the police station the next morning."

"Let's fast forward to the point where he arrives at the chapel for the wedding."

The footage showed a disheveled Michael running up the aisle to get to where Kat was sitting, looking beautiful in her wedding gown. Dan captured their conversation and Michael running outside of the building to throw up in the bushes.

"Disgusting but good stuff," said William approvingly. "There's nothing like a little barf to titillate the viewers."

The next shot showed Kat coming out of the chapel, followed by the wedding party. Seeing Michael lying down on the sidewalk, the video showed her giving Michael a look of complete disdain, before walking by.

"What next?" asked William.

"Kat decided to have the reception without him," said Maria. "I have to admire her; it was a ballsy move. A lot of brides would have canceled the reception after being stood up, but not Kat."

"So did you follow Kat, or did you follow Michael at that point?" asked William.

"We followed Kat and got footage of the reception. I thought it would be more interesting to viewers instead of watching Michael recover from his hangover."

"Good move," said William. "Let's see what you've got."

The footage showed Kat having fun at her reception. If she was upset by Michael's absence, she didn't show it.

"We can totally work with this for the finale," said William, before giving Sophie instructions on what he wanted.

Sophie agreed to put together the rough cut.

"When do you think you'll have something for us to review?" asked William. "The finale airs in one week."

"I should have the rough cut ready for you tomorrow afternoon," said Sophie. "I'll work all night if I have to."

"Thanks, Sophie, you're the best," said Maria appreciatively.

It wasn't the finale she had planned, showing Erica and the pregnancy. It wasn't the backup finale she had planned, showing Michael and Kat exchanging vows in a flower-filled chapel. But she thought the backup to the backup would get great ratings. Maria sighed to herself. It was great that William was happy but Maria wasn't sure that working on *Lucky* was making her happy. She had a hit but she was having a hard time looking at herself in the mirror.

It was great, being the producer of a hit show, but sometimes late at night, she questioned what she was doing with her life.

CHAPTER 21

MICHAEL

The first five weeks in Los Angeles had been nonstop activity, between shooting *Criminal Streets* and house hunting on his days off. Initially, Michael had been annoyed that Kat opted not to come with him but in the end he didn't mind. He had taken advantage of being away from Dan's camera during the day to engage in some heavy flirting with Olivia Lambert, who played the D.A. on *Criminal Streets*.

Now Kat had flown in, to see the house he wanted to buy in Malibu Colony. Since she arrived, Michael was having a hard time reading her mood. She seemed cool towards him, when they were interacting during the day. But at night, she was passionate and wanted to make love all the time. He was getting a little tired of her schizo behavior.

He couldn't blame her if she was still angry with him. He had really screwed up at the wedding and he knew it. He just couldn't understand what had happened to her libido. It was as if the angrier she was with him, the more she wanted him.

Not that he was complaining. Michael was enjoying all the sex. It was taking the edge off the frustration he felt at not being able to have Olivia.

On his last Monday, he wasn't shooting so they met with a realtor at 23852 Malibu Colony Road. As always, Dan and Maria followed him, when he wasn't on set.

"I think you'll love the house," Michael said to Kat, hoping to get her enthusiastic about the property.

She didn't respond but followed the realtor, Anna, into the house. In an effort to get back in Kat's good graces, Michael had asked Maria to find him a realtor that wouldn't make Kat jealous. Anna was a good choice because there was no way he was attracted to her. It was difficult to tell her age, because her face had been stretched tight by a plastic surgeon and her cheeks and lips had been plumped with fillers. She was rail thin with platinum blonde hair that fell in beach waves over her shoulders. Her chest seemed oddly large, compared to the rest of her. Michael guessed she was in her fifties but trying hard to look thirty.

"I think you'll love the property," gushed Anna, walking Kat into a living room that had a spectacular view of the ocean. The sliding glass doors leading out onto the deck were open and let the sound of crashing waves into the room. "You're in the house but it's almost like you're sitting out on the beach."

The living room had modern furniture and had been decorated in shades of taupe and sand. The house had an open floor plan and the living room was open to a huge modern kitchen and dining room. The outside deck was almost as large as the living room and had wooden sofas and chairs with cream colored cushions.

All of the rooms in the back of the house, the living room, the kitchen and the master bedroom, had floor to ceiling glass doors that opened onto the deck, which wrapped around the house. There was a hot tub on the part of the deck that was near the master bedroom.

Anna took them out onto the deck. "As you can see, there is a gate with steps leading down to the beach. The rest of the deck has a glass barrier so the view of the ocean isn't blocked."

"It's very nice," said Kat. "What is the cost of the house?"

"It's $21 million, or $21.5 million if you want to buy it furnished," said Anna eagerly.

"I was hoping we could buy it furnished," said Michael. "That way, we won't have to work with a designer. I know you don't typically like modern furniture but I think it goes with the house. Don't you agree Kat?"

"Yes, the furniture goes with the house," said Kat thoughtfully. "I can't see traditional furniture in this house." She turned towards Anna.

"Tell me more about the house."

"Of course," said Anna with a big smile. "The house is 4,000 square feet and the lot size is 7,500 square feet. The house was built last year so all the amenities are new and it has a two-car garage. As you can see, you have a view of Catalina, the mountains and the ocean. Best of all, you'll be part of the Malibu Beach community, behind the gates. What do you think about the house, Kat?"

"It's fine," said Kat slowly.

"That's it?" said Michael, feeling slightly annoyed at Kat's restrained reaction. "Fine? I think the house is amazing and we should put in an offer."

"I just don't know how much time I would spend here," said Kat. "And I'm not sure we need a second house. I know you want to spend more time on the West Coast, Michael, but couldn't you just get an apartment?"

Anna's face fell. "Of course there are some lovely condos I could show you, if you don't want to get this house."

"Kat, we got your dream house in New York," said Michael. "I want to get my dream house in Malibu. And what do you mean you won't spend much time here?"

"Being bicoastal is more your dream than my dream," said Kat. "I'm happy with Max in New York. I don't need to fly to California all the time."

"Well, I do need to fly here a lot," said Michael. "I plan on auditioning in L.A. more and getting more roles here. I don't want to stay in hotels all the time and a condo is just like a hotel suite."

"So you want to get his and her houses? That seems needlessly extravagant, even if we can afford it."

"Well, we can afford it," said Michael hotly. "You have the house you wanted in New York, why can't I get the house I want here?"

Kat looked at him for a few minutes.

"I'm not going to fight you on this, Michael. You want this house? Fine, get it. You want to live in Malibu half the time? Fine, live here. Just don't expect me to fly out here all the time with you. I like living in New York and that's where I want to spend my time."

Michael was suddenly uneasy. Usually, Kat was jealous and paranoid if he spent too much time away from her. Since the wedding, she seemed to be fine spending more time solo and less concerned with what he was doing. He wasn't sure he liked this new independent Kat.

Anna looked delighted. "So Michael, are you going to put in an offer on the house?"

He tried to focus on the fact that he would be getting a house in Malibu.

"Yes Anna, please put in an offer for the asking price and we'll be buying the furniture too."

"That's wonderful. I'll put in the offer right away. I'm sure you're going to love it here."

'I should get a car out here, now that I'll have a garage,' he thought. 'Maybe I should get a black Porsche Carrera.'

Then he realized he would be spending a lot of time alone in the Malibu house. It could become more of a bachelor pad. He wondered if he could invite Olivia here.

"Yes," he told Anna. "You're right. I'm going to love it here."

KAT

Kat lay on the beach in Malibu, luxuriating in the warm September sun and digging her toes into the sand. She and Michael had come to the West Coast to close on the beach house and Kat had decided to stay for a week, even though she preferred being in New York with Max. Through Alan, Michael had set up a number of auditions, so he would be staying for four weeks.

Now that the Malibu house was theirs, Kat had to admit it was pretty wonderful having a house right on the beach. She slept in late and spent the afternoons on the beach reading a trashy novel. At the end of each afternoon, she packed up her beach towel and walked up the steps to the house, to rinse off in the master bathroom, which had a massive waterfall shower.

This afternoon, instead of reading, she was thinking about the envelope that had arrived at the New York townhouse the day before she left for California.

It had been addressed to Michael and Kat Davidson, so she grabbed a letter opener and slit open the envelope. Inside had been a birth announcement on cream-colored stock with a blue ribbon. Erica Rosetti had given birth to Michael Andrew Rosetti on September 7. Eight pounds, two ounces and 21 inches.

'Why would Erica send us a birth announcement?' Kat wondered uneasily. There was no mention of a father but, clearly, Erica must have had a man in her life. Where was the father now?

If she was being honest with herself, Kat had been relieved when Michael told Erica they could no longer be friends. Kat chose to believe Michael when he said there was nothing more than friendship between them, but she was glad when he stopped seeing Erica. Clearly, Erica wanted to be more than Michael's friend.

Now Erica was sending them a birth announcement. Kat was worried if she told Michael about Erica's baby that he would want to start up the friendship again. That was the last thing Kat wanted.

'I don't think I'm going to tell Michael,' Kat decided. 'If Erica doesn't get any acknowledgment from Michael, maybe she'll take the hint and leave us alone.'

She felt a little guilty about keeping the announcement from Michael, but only a little guilty, and she went back to reading her book.

Later that afternoon, after her shower, she put on her sexiest lingerie, a crop top and pair of short shorts. She was extra careful with her makeup. Kat wanted to look as sexy as possible before she tried to seduce Michael. The timing was perfect.

Kat's menstrual cycle was like clockwork. She got her period every 28 days, no matter what else was going on in her life. She was 14 days from the date of her last period and according to everything she had been reading, she was at her most fertile. Kat wanted to take advantage of the opportunity before she and Michael would be separated for three weeks.

When he came back from an audition, she met him at the door with a tumbler of scotch.

"Thank you," he said, taking the glass from her hand.

Kat looked behind him and was surprised to see he was by himself. "Where did Dan and Maria go?"

"Maria had a meeting, so she gave Dan the afternoon off."

Kat thought it was like fate giving her a helping hand. She wouldn't have to wait until late this evening to tempt Michael into making love to her.

"So how did the audition go?" Kat asked.

"I think it went okay," he said, walking over to the living room couch and sitting down with a sigh. "It can be hard to tell. This casting director was very complimentary but I won't really know how it went unless I hear from Alan that they want me back."

"I'm sure they'll call you back," said Kat loyally as she walked behind the couch and started massaging his neck and shoulders.

"That feels so good," said Michael, leaning back into her hands.

"Like this?" Kat said kneading hard where she felt some tension in his shoulders.

"Oh yes, please don't stop," he growled. "Just like that."

Kat massaged Michael's neck and shoulders for ten minutes before walking around to the front of the couch and sitting down next to him.

"There are other things I can massage," she said playfully as she reached out and ran a hand over his thigh.

Michael sighed. "I'm not sure I'm feeling horny at the moment. It's been an exhausting day."

"I have no expectations," Kat lied. "Why don't you drink your drink and let me give you a full body massage to relax you? I'm sure I can make some of the tension go away."

Michael laughed as he looked at Kat. "What's gotten into you lately? It's like your libido is in overdrive."

Kat decided to be honest. "That's because I'm fertile right now and I want to get pregnant as soon as possible."

Michael froze as he was reaching out for his drink. "What are you talking about?"

"You said we could start trying as soon as you finished *Criminal Streets*. I've stopped taking the pill. Actually, I stopped taking the pill when we were in Maui."

"So the times we made love, you weren't on the pill?" Michael picked up his drink and took a big gulp. Kat noticed his hand was shaking slightly.

"No, but I didn't think it would make a difference if we started trying a little early. What's six weeks? Anyways I haven't gotten pregnant yet."

"Are you sure?" asked Michael looking anxious.

"Yes, I'm sure. I got my period two weeks ago." Kat couldn't understand why Michael seemed to be so rattled. They had agreed they were going to start trying, so what difference did the timing make?

"And that's why you want to make love all the time? To get pregnant?"

Kat laughed. "It's also because I find you hot. I don't want you to feel like a stud that's being used to breed. Besides, you seemed to be enjoying yourself. So why don't you take me into the bedroom and enjoy yourself right now?"

"I told you, Kat, I'm not in the mood." Michael seemed annoyed.

"So let me change your mood," said Kat seductively, running her hand up his thigh again. She leaned in close to kiss him on the mouth. Michael kissed her back, but there wasn't much passion in the kiss. Kat thought she would have to try harder.

She got up off the couch and stood in front of Michael. "Back when we first got married, you used to love it when I did a striptease."

She ran her hands suggestively over her breasts and slowly removed the crop top. She turned away from him and twerked a little in his direction before unzipping the shorts. She turned around to face him and slowly slid the shorts off her hips and down her legs until they fell to the floor.

"Do you like what you see?" Kat asked, doing a 360-degree turn in her black lace pushup bra and thong. Very slowly, she reached behind her back and undid her bra. Holding it in position against her chest, she slid the straps off her shoulders, before pulling the bra away to expose her breasts. Once her breasts were bare, she cupped them in her hands, as if offering them to him.

Michael watched her with a completely neutral expression on his face. Kat was disappointed. She hoped he would have grabbed her by now. Very slowly, she slid the thong off until she was standing naked before him.

For a brief minute, Kat worried about the hidden cameras but then she relaxed as she remembered that Maria hadn't had the electricians come to the new house yet. Michael was the only one who would see her naked.

Michael still hadn't made a move in her direction so she walked over to the couch and pulled him up by the hand.

"Let's go to the bedroom," Kat said. "I'm thirsty."

Michael didn't say anything but he let Kat lead him by the hand into the master bedroom. Because they had bought the house with the staged furniture, the bedroom was pretty sparse. It had a bed with soft white linens and throw pillows, and a couple of gray chairs which faced a fireplace and a TV. The two bedside tables were glass-topped driftwood.

Kat pushed Michael down on the bed and started taking off his clothes. First, she removed his shoes and socks before reaching up to remove his t-shirt. Michael allowed himself to be undressed, as if he was a baby, but he made no move to help.

Once Michael's shirt was off, Kat eagerly pulled off his jeans and boxer shorts. To Kat's dismay, Michael was completely soft.

"Michael, what's the matter?" Kat asked, reaching out to cup his penis and balls in her hand.

"I told you, Kat, I'm just not feeling horny."

"Let me see if I can change that," Kat said hopefully. She put his penis in her mouth and started sucking on it, while massaging his balls in her hand. Usually, Michael loved this but despite her best efforts, he didn't get hard.

Kat was starting to feel a little humiliated at his lack of response. She wasn't doing a very good job of seducing her husband.

"Kat, stop," said Michael gently, pulling her mouth off him. "It's not going to happen."

"But what am I doing wrong?" Kat asked. She was getting upset. Not only were they missing her most fertile period, she was starting to feel like Michael wasn't attracted to her anymore.

"You're not doing anything wrong, Kat. This just happens to guys sometimes. There's no need to make a big deal out of it. Why don't you come up here and let's just cuddle?"

Since it looked like they wouldn't be making love, Kat stopped trying and curled up in the crook of Michael's arm. Despite his reassurance, she couldn't help feeling a little rejected.

"Isn't this nice?" asked Michael softly. "We don't need to make love to feel close."

'Yes, but we do need to make love to make a baby,' Kat thought to herself. 'Maybe I can try again tomorrow.'

MARIA

While they were in California, Maria and Dan had fallen in the habit of meeting for breakfast at Country Kitchen in Malibu before heading over to the beach house to start filming Michael. Over breakfast burritos and coffee, they organized their day and discussed what they could capture that would interest viewers.

Unfortunately, by late September, they were running out of ideas. They had already filmed the interior and the exterior of the beach house. Michael was going on auditions, but they had shown viewers his auditions in the past and they didn't want to be repetitive.

They needed Michael and Kat to purchase another big-ticket item, or they needed some drama. After Kat left to go back to New York, they had wired up the beach house with the hidden cameras but Michael's activities had been a snooze-fest.

When he didn't have a morning audition, he woke up about 9:00 A.M. and had breakfast on the deck overlooking the ocean. At 12:30 P.M. every day, he went to the gym and worked out before coming home and having a late lunch. Then he lay out on the beach in the afternoons, working on his tan. Post-beach, he would come in the house and make himself a light dinner – usually seafood and salad. By 9:00 P.M., he would get ready for bed and Dan and Maria would leave for the night.

Maria was starting to wonder if they had made a mistake signing up Michael and Kat for a second season.

On September 24, Dan had a big smile on his face, when they met at the restaurant.

"You look cheerful," Maria said. "What's going on?"

"Let's order first and I'll tell you all about it," said Dan. "It's going to make your day."

They sat down and gave the waitress their orders. Once the waitress had brought them some coffee, Maria turned back to Dan.

"Let's have it," she said. "I could use some good news."

"Last night, after we said goodnight to Michael, I was about to start my car when I got a call from my sister. She's in the middle of a messy divorce, so we were on the phone for nearly a half hour."

"I'm sorry," said Maria politely, although she wasn't really interested in Dan's sister's divorce. She wished he would get to the point.

"Just as we got off the phone, guess whose Porsche pulls out of the driveway and takes off?"

"Michael?" asked Maria. "He left the house after we said goodnight?"

"He sure did," said Dan, grinning. "I wondered where the hell he was going, so I decided to follow him."

"Where did he go?" asked Maria, starting to feel more hopeful. Maybe they would have some drama for the second season.

"He went to Moonshadows. You know, that bar on the beach."

"So he's going to bars after we say goodnight? That sneaky bastard."

"That's not all," said Dan. "I left my camera in the car but I followed him into the bar."

"Did he see you?" Maria asked with some concern.

"No, it was crowded in Moonshadows and I made a point of keeping a low profile. He was busy chatting up some pretty brunette at the bar. After about an hour, they left together in his car, so I followed him again. They drove to an apartment complex in Santa Monica and went inside. I'm willing to bet that's where she lives."

"What happened then?" Maria asked impatiently.

"I waited in the car outside the building for a couple of hours. He finally left, alone, and drove home."

"You must be exhausted," said Maria, "but I'm glad you stayed with him."

"Yeah, it was a late night," said Dan with a big yawn. "But that's what coffee is for, right?"

"Right," said Maria. "So our perfect husband is sneaking out late at night for random hookups? We really need a camera crew on him 24/7." She thought for a moment.

"Let me give William a call and see if we can get some help." She picked up her phone and tapped on William in her favorites list.

"Hey, Maria, what's up? How are things going in California?"

"Hey, William. Things have been slow but Dan discovered that Michael is sneaking out late at night, after we leave for the evening. Last night, he went to a bar and hooked up with some woman."

"Did the hidden cams in the house get all the action?"

"Unfortunately no, because he went to her place. I think we need a camera crew on him 24/7 but it will be tricky because we don't want him to know we're on to him."

"Interesting. This could work perfectly with the story arc we want to develop for the second season. We want to show Michael as the unfaithful husband and Kat's reaction when she finds out."

"Exactly," said Maria. "So can we get an associate producer and a camera person to follow Michael late at night, at least while he's in California?"

"I don't know if that's going to work," said William. "Michael will stop going out if he sees a camera person following him around. We need a way to film him, without him knowing he's being filmed. Instead of another camera crew, I think you should hire a private investigator. We need someone who is used to skulking around in bushes, getting shots of unfaithful husbands."

Maria was surprised at the suggestion.

"Don't private detectives usually shoot photos, instead of video?" she asked.

"We can edit in stills, if that's all we get. But I'll try to find you someone who shoots video too. The quality won't be great but it will add to the sleaziness of catching Michael in the act."

Maria thought about it for a moment. The thought of having Michael followed by a private detective made her feel a little slimy but she thought it would probably help the ratings.

"William, I think we can make it work. Can you help find someone we should use?"

"Of course. I think this could tie in nicely with the second season finale."

"What are you thinking?" Maria asked.

"During the season, we show him acting like the perfect husband when he's with Kat but sneaking out at night. Then for the season finale, we show Kat the photos we get from the private detective and expose Michael for the bastard that he really is."

"I thought we were going to use Erica's paternity suit as the season finale," Maria pointed out.

"That's only if Erica decides to sue. If she does, then that's our surprise twist. If she doesn't sue, then we have this as a backup."

"Won't Kat know all about Michael, if she watches the show?"

"The first episode of the second season won't air until October 23rd. Any episode where we show Michael going to bars won't air until closer to Thanksgiving. You should have the filming for the second season wrapped up before Kat can see anything on TV."

"Sounds like a plan," said Maria thoughtfully. "Text me the contact information for the private detective and I'll set up a meeting."

"You got it," said William before disconnecting.

Dan looked over at Maria with raised eyebrows. "What did William say?"

"Instead of a second camera crew, he wants to find a private investigator to follow Michael around at night and take pictures or video. That way Michael won't know we're on to him. As soon as William sends me the name of someone, I'll set up a meeting.

"Once we get the incriminating evidence, our season finale will be exposing Michael to Kat."

"I hope she divorces his dead ass," said Dan with a scowl, "he's such a bastard."

"True," said Maria, "but he's also ratings gold."

————

Maria had expected something seedy but the Century City Investigators' office looked like a law office, with a sophisticated reception area and a handsome young receptionist who offered her coffee when she arrived.

After waiting for a few minutes, she was met by Taylor Milford, who looked as if he was ex-military with his tight iron-gray hair, unlined face and ramrod straight posture. She followed him as he walked quickly to his office.

Once they were both seated, he gave her a small smile.

"So what can Century City Investigators help you with Ms. Gonzales?"

"It's a bit of a delicate situation, Mr. Milford," she said slowly.

"Please, call me Taylor, and delicate situations are what we specialize in."

"Okay, Taylor, please call me Maria." Maria paused for a moment, thinking about how to begin. "I'm the producer of a reality TV show called *Lucky*. It's about a couple of BonusBall winners."

"I'm familiar with your show, Maria. My fifteen-year-old daughter loves it."

"We've been following around our married couple, Kat and Michael, for about ten months. Most of that time we've been in New York, but they've bought a house in Malibu. Michael spends a lot of time alone here, while Kat stays in New York.

"Recently, we have reason to believe that Michael is cheating on Kat. We've caught him sneaking out late at night to go to bars where he meets women."

"My daughter, Emily, is going to be shocked," said Taylor, although he didn't look particularly shocked. "She has a teenage crush on Michael."

"I think a lot of fans are going to be shocked," said Maria. "And of course Kat is going to be devastated. We want to let her know what Michael is doing but we need proof.

"Our camera follows Michael around during the day, usually from 9:00 A.M. to 9:00 P.M. but we can't catch him cheating when he knows he's being filmed. We need someone who can film him or take photos surreptitiously and catch him in the act.

"Ideally, what we want would be proof of him having sex with another woman. Failing that, we want film or photos of him kissing or fooling around."

"Would you be showing the film or photos on your show?" asked Taylor. His expression was completely neutral so Maria couldn't tell if he thought this would be a good thing or a bad thing.

"Yes, we would want to broadcast the proof of his infidelity, along with showing the evidence to his wife. Is that a problem?"

"Not at all," said Taylor. He gave Maria a tight smile. "Our job is to collect the evidence. What you choose to do with it is your business."

'William will be pleased,' thought Maria.

"So would you be able to get someone trailing him at night?"

"Of course," said Taylor, "I'll get one of our best investigators on it. Our rate is $200 an hour. I trust that won't be a problem."

"That's fine," said Maria. "I'll give you the address of my production company where the bills should be sent. Do you think you'll be able to capture video, in addition to photos?"

"That shouldn't be a problem, as long as you're okay with video shot with a cell phone. It won't be the production quality you're used to."

"That's fine. Any video you get would be great."

"Leave it to us, Maria," said Taylor confidently. "Give me Michael's address. We can start trailing him tonight. I'll call you as soon as we have something you can use."

Maria gave him Michael's address and stood up to shake his hand. "Thank you, Taylor. I look forward to hearing from you soon."

"You're very welcome," said Taylor with a broad smile. "Nothing makes me happier than catching some cheating louse in the act. If he's stepping out, we'll get you the proof you need to expose him."

Maria felt very conflicted, leaving the Century City offices. She knew it wouldn't be long before Michael went out again late at night, only this time they would catch him in the act. It would work for the show, but Kat was going to be destroyed.

CHAPTER 22

MICHAEL

At Maria's suggestion, Michael chartered a private jet to fly back to New York, after his auditions in Los Angeles. The price to lease a midsize jet to take Michael, Maria and Dan from California to New York was $49,620, but Michael thought the expense was well worth it, compared to flying first class on a commercial airliner.

There were no security lines to deal with; they were able to get on the jet at the Van Nuys airport in California without waiting. There was no limitation on the amount of luggage they could bring with them. He didn't have to worry about the amount of liquids he could bring on board. As a matter of fact, Michael boarded the flight with a six pack of Dos Equis.

The jet had plush leather seats for six people, high-gloss wooden tables and a leather couch with pillows where Michael stretched out for most of the six-hour flight. They had hired a flight attendant, who brought them a catered lunch of Tacos, complete with guacamole and chips.

Michael spent the trip reading a script he had been given by a producer in California. It was for a period movie, set during the Revolutionary War. The story was one where a young British officer falls in love with the daughter of an American major, serving under George Washington. The script was a total tear jerker and Michael badly wanted to play the role of the young officer. He could see himself winning awards, maybe even an Oscar for the role.

The producer was looking to get the movie financed, which is why he had approached Michael. Michael hadn't thought about forming his own production company but now that the idea had been planted in his mind, he loved the concept. Wasn't that how the big stars got serious movies made? Michael decided to discuss the idea with Kat, once he was back in New York.

The flight landed in White Plains, N.Y., and Michael was really glad he had brought a sweater with him. The weather had been warm when they left California but early October on the East Coast was considerably cooler and he could feel fall in the air. At the airport, Michael, Maria and Dan got into the waiting limo, which brought them to the townhouse on East 65th Street.

"Hey, Kat, we're back," Michael yelled once they had gotten through the front door. Max came running up to them, jumping up on Michael in his excitement.

"Hey there, little guy," said Michael affectionately, scratching Max under the chin. "How's my good boy?" At nearly a year old, Max was almost full-grown and Michael was amazed to see how big he had gotten.

Dropping the bags in the front hall, Michael walked into the kitchen, followed by Maria, Dan and Max. He saw Colleen at the kitchen counter, working on preparing dinner.

"Hey guys, welcome back," Colleen said, giving Michael a big smile. "How was your flight?"

"The flight was great," said Michael. "We chartered a jet and it's the only way to fly."

"What's the only way to fly?" said Kat, walking into the kitchen and over to Michael to give him a big hug. Michael noticed she was dressed in slim black leggings with an off the shoulder cashmere oversized sweater. He was glad that he had talked her into working with a stylist because she looked great.

"We leased a private jet for the flight back to New York," said Michael after he let go of Kat. "It's the only way to fly. Now that we have a house on the West Coast, I think we should buy a private jet."

"You leased a private jet?" said Kat, looking displeased. "How much did that cost?"

"It was $49,000," said Michael, rounding down. "But it saves so much time. You don't have to arrive at the airport two hours before the flight. You just show up at the terminal and get right on the plane. There's room to spread out and we didn't need to worry about Maria and Dan booking seats."

"Michael, that seems like a colossal waste. Even if we can afford it, you shouldn't be blowing money like that."

"Kat, we should buy a private jet now that we have two homes. That way, we won't have the leasing costs." To Michael, this seemed like a sensible solution.

"Michael, do you have any idea how expensive a private jet is? We're wealthy but we're not billionaires."

"I've been looking into this," said Michael. "We can buy a secondhand jet for about $10,000,000. It will pay for itself after 200 flights."

"That's not counting the maintenance or the fuel costs. Michael, I'm putting my foot down. No more leasing private jets and we are absolutely not buying one."

Michael felt frustrated. They hadn't been back more than a half hour and they were already arguing about money. Kat had no idea how to live like a millionaire. If it were up to her, they would be living in a 3,000-square-foot house in the suburbs.

"But Kat, we can afford it and it will make bicoastal living so much easier. I can just hop on the jet whenever I want to go back to Malibu."

"You're just going to have to book a flight on United, whenever you want to go back to Malibu. I mean it, Michael. No more private jets."

"All the big stars fly private jets," said Michael sullenly. He could feel the dream of having his own private jet start to slip away.

"Michael, face it, you're the star of a reality TV show. You're not a big movie star."

That really stung. Michael didn't know why Kat was being such a bitch.

"Fine," he said with irritation. "I'll stop flying on private jets. Maybe I should go back to flying coach if you're so worried about going broke."

"Michael, don't sulk and don't act like a child. I said to stop wasting money on private jets. I never said you needed to go back to flying coach."

"Whatever," said Michael. "I'm going upstairs to unpack. Let me know when dinner is ready."

"That's it?" asked Kat with dismay. "We haven't seen each other for three weeks. I've missed you. Haven't you missed me?"

What Michael actually missed was being in California. He had been getting used to living like a bachelor when Kat wasn't with him in Malibu. Although sometimes it had been lonely, at night he had been able to find women to keep him company. In some ways, sex without strings was preferable to a wife who gave him a hard time about spending his fortune.

"Sure, I've missed you," he said unconvincingly. "I'll unpack and then I'll come back downstairs. Pour me a glass of wine and I'll meet you in the living room."

Unpacking didn't take long because he just dumped all his dirty laundry into a hamper in the master closet. Colleen would get all his clothes when it was time to do the laundry.

Because he was still annoyed with Kat, Michael took some extra time to take a quick shower. He couldn't help comparing the shower in the New York townhouse with the shower in the Malibu house. The shower in Malibu was far superior. In Michael's view, most things in California were far superior to New York. He started to wonder how long he had to spend in New York before he could fly back to Los Angeles.

Once he was back downstairs, in the living room with Kat, sipping a glass of red wine and staring at the fire that Colleen had set in the fireplace, Michael started to feel less agitated. He had to admit that the living room of his townhouse was pretty spectacular, even if it was in New York. He noticed that Dan had set up the camera, opposite the couch.

"So how did your auditions go?" Kat asked brightly, giving Michael a big smile. "Has Alan found you any juicy roles?"

"Most of the auditions were for commercials," Michael said, "but I did get a script for the most fantastic role in a movie called *Lexington and Concord*. It's about a British officer during the Revolutionary War. He falls in love with a woman whose father is fighting on the side of American independence. Think Romeo and Juliet crossed with minutemen and muskets."

"That sounds really interesting," said Kat. "When is the audition?"

"There's no audition," said Michael eagerly. "I met with a producer who is looking for a production partner. If we produce the movie, the role is mine."

"What do you mean, if we produce the movie?" asked Kat, looking confused.

"We would form our own production company and invest in the movie," explained Michael. "We could hire our own director and cast all the roles. Any profits the movie makes would be ours. It could be a great investment."

"But Michael, you don't know anything about producing a movie," said Kat apprehensively.

"That's why we would be teaming up with David Cohen. He's produced a number of big movies and would be the perfect partner."

Kat stared at Michael for a few moments.

"How much would we need to invest?" she asked.

Michael swallowed and tried to prep himself for the rest of the conversation.

"It's a period movie and they tend to be more expensive to produce," he said. "David thinks we can make the movie for around $40 million."

Kat's eyes grew big. "And how much is David putting up?" she asked slowly.

"David is bringing his expertise," said Michael watching her face carefully. "We would be putting up all the money."

"You want us to invest $40 million in a movie?" Kat asked, looking stunned. "Are you high?"

Michael could have predicted that this would be Kat's reaction. He took a deep breath.

"Kitty Kat, a lot of actors form production companies so they can work on serious projects. It's a big investment but you should read the script. It's almost guaranteed to win awards. If I work on such a prestigious movie, it will definitely lead to more roles in the future."

Kats eyebrows were still raised. "We're not going to spend $40 million for you to work on a vanity project."

Leave it to Kat to misunderstand. Michael could feel his enthusiasm wane and his irritation grow.

"Kat, it's not a vanity project. It would be a serious movie and David is a well-respected producer."

"So why doesn't David find the $40 million from some other investor? If the script is as great as you say it is, I'm sure he can line up other financing."

Michael didn't want David to find another investor. If someone else was footing the bill, they would hold auditions for the lead role and Michael might not get the part. But if Michael invested the $40 million, they would have to give him the role. It was the perfect role for him and would make him a movie star, he just knew it. It aggravated him that once again, Kat was standing in his way.

"Kat, this is a great investment opportunity. The movie makes money on more than just the theatrical release. There's also the international release, television rights and streaming rights. We just need to work with the right distributor."

"Or the movie could bomb and we could lose a fortune." Kat's voice no longer sounded quite as high-pitched but she didn't seem to be warming to the idea of investing.

Michael couldn't let go of the idea that this role was his ticket to stardom. He had to convince Kat but he wasn't sure how.

'I guess there's always the nuclear option,' he thought to himself, wondering if he had the balls. He could threaten to divorce Kat if she didn't agree to finance the movie.

For a moment, he felt bad about the idea. But then he thought about Maria and the second season of *Lucky*. During some episode, Maria was going to expose his cheating with Erica for the entire world to see. At that point, it would be Kat threatening to divorce him instead of the other way around. He might as well get something out of it before the divorce papers were signed.

"Kat, I don't think this is working out," he said softly with a serious expression on his face.

"Go tight with the shot on Michael," he overheard Maria say to Dan.

Kat looked confused. "You don't think what is working out?" she asked.

"This. Us. I don't think we're working out." Kat looked alarmed.

"What are you talking about, Michael?" She reached out for his hand, but he pulled away.

"We're not working out," he said. "All we ever do is fight about money. Since winning the BonusBall, we haven't been able to agree on how we should spend the money. I'm sick of all the fighting and I'm sure you are too."

"What are you talking about?" Kat said, with her eyes wide. "I didn't want to get a private jet and I don't think we should invest in a movie but I said yes to this house, and the house in California. I don't think we've been doing a lot of fighting about money."

"We have different ideas about what type of lifestyle we should lead. I want us to live as though we're wealthy and you want us to live as though we're still part of the middle class. I think maybe we should divide the rest of the money and separate."

"You can't be serious," cried Kat. "You want to get a divorce because I don't want to invest $40 million in a movie?" Tears started to form in the corners of her eyes.

"I think we want different things in life," said Michael stoically. "Maybe we don't belong together anymore." The more he thought about it, the more he was convincing himself.

"We do belong together, Michael," said Kat. She sounded frantic. "I love you and I still want us to be together."

"But what we want is so different. I want to be bicoastal and a movie star. You just want to nest here in New York."

"Dinnertime!" Michael could hear Colleen's voice over the intercom.

Michael got up off the couch and walked over to the intercom to press the talk button.

"We'll be down in a few minutes Colleen. Just lay the food out on the kitchen table and don't worry about the washing up. We'll take care of it."

"You got it, Michael."

Michael turned to Kat. "Let's go downstairs and get some dinner."

"I'm not hungry," said Kat, looking highly upset. "How can you eat after telling me we should get a divorce?"

"I'm not saying we absolutely should get a divorce," said Michael slowly. "I'm just saying we want different things. Maybe there's a way we can work this out."

"I want to work it out," said Kat, looking suddenly hopeful. "Tell me what you want."

"I want us to start living like millionaires," said Michael. It was time to reel in Kat slowly.

"But we do live like millionaires," said Kat. "Look around you. Only a millionaire could afford a house like this in New York City."

"Right, but I want to be able to invest in opportunities when they come along. Opportunities like this movie."

Kat's eyes narrowed. "Are you saying what I think you're saying, Michael?"

"What is it you think I'm saying, Kat?"

"That you'll agree stay together if I agree to finance your movie."

"That sounds needlessly crass, Kat. I didn't mean a quid pro quo." Michael didn't like Kat putting it that way, even if that's exactly what he meant.

She looked at him hard for a couple of minutes. Michael was aware of Dan moving in even closer with the camera.

"What about what I want, Michael?"

"What is it you want, Kat?" Michael had a feeling he knew what was coming.

"I want a family and I want to be able to leave them a legacy. At the rate you're spending, there will be nothing left."

"You're being ridiculous, Kat. We'll still have more than $27 million left, after we invest in the movie. And we'll have even more, once the movie makes a profit. That's more than enough to set up a trust fund for a kid."

"What kid, Michael? At the rate we're going, I'll never get pregnant." Kat stopped looking sad and looked a little angry.

"I agreed we could start trying, Kat. What more do you want?"

"Less words and more action. Since you found out I went off the pill, you stopped making love to me. And it doesn't help when we're separated for weeks at a time."

"Kat, you're not being fair. You're the one who wanted to come back to New York. You could have stayed longer in California."

"Not that it would have done me any good. You haven't come near me." Kat folded her arms across her chest and glared at Michael.

"Why don't we make both of us happy, Kat? Agree to invest in the movie and I'll take you upstairs right now to try for that baby."

"Who's being crass now, Michael? Doesn't that make you a whore? Albeit a well-paid one?"

"Jesus Kat!" Michael looked over at Dan and Maria. Maria was staring at them intently but Michael couldn't tell what she was thinking. He flushed, thinking about what Kat had called him.

Kat still looked angry. "You've threatened to divorce me if I don't agree to this movie and you've promised to get me pregnant if I do agree to this movie. Just how important is this movie to you, Michael?"

"Kat, it's the perfect role for me. I just have to have it. How can I convince you to say yes?"

"I'll tell you how you don't convince me. You won't get me to agree by making idle threats or promises."

"Please, Kat? I'll do anything to get that role." Michael was reduced to begging.

"Michael, if I agree to finance this movie, do you promise not to ask for anything else? We agree that the remaining capital stays untouched and we just live off the interest? No more big-ticket purchases? No more private jets? No more houses or jewelry?"

"Yes, Kat, I swear. No more spending. We'll live just on the interest generated by the account."

"And you agree that we can try to have a baby? You'll do more than just provide lip service to the idea?"

"Kat, let me take you upstairs right now and prove that I mean it." Michael held his breath.

Kat nodded slowly. "Okay, I just hope we don't lose money on this. I'll agree to produce your movie if you promise to stop spending. You can call David and tell him we're on board."

"Thank you, Kat. I promise it will be a good investment. You won't regret it." Michael leaned over on the couch and gave Kat a big hug, before they went downstairs to have dinner.

After dinner, they excused themselves and left Dan and Maria in the kitchen while they went up to the bedroom. The idea that he would be a movie star made Michael horny, and he was able to make good on his promise to Kat.

KAT

Kat was trying to write when her phone rang. Glancing at the screen, she saw the call was from Len. Although she hated the interruption, Kat figured she better take the call. Len was in the process of transferring funds for the *Lexington and Concord* movie to the production company that Michael and David Cohen had set up. It had only been a week since Kat agreed they could produce the movie and she had been amazed at how quickly Michael had put things together. She guessed Michael could be super organized when the work involved something he really wanted.

"Hi Len, how are you doing?" Kat asked after picking up her phone.

"I'm good, Kat, how are things with you?" She heard Len's warm voice on the line.

"I'm great. Are you calling about transferring the $40 million to the production company?"

"No, everything's all set and the money should be transferred next week. I'm actually calling about a more delicate matter."

Kat felt her neck tense up. 'When your money manager calls about a delicate matter, it can't be good,' she thought to herself.

"What delicate matter Len? Is everything okay? Is there a problem with our account?"

"Your account is fine, Kat but I wanted to warn you that I don't think you can afford our services once the $40 million is transferred for the movie."

"What are you talking about? We'll have more than $27 million left in our account." Kat could feel her jaw start to clench.

"You'll have $ 27,731,660 left in your account. That may seem like a lot, but you're living beyond your means if you don't want to start dipping into the capital."

"What do you mean, living beyond our means?"

"I'll break it down for you, Kat. Let's say your $27,731,660 million earns 4 percent a year. That's $1,109,266.40 you can expect annually."

"We'll be making over a million dollars a year. Surely we can afford to live on that." Kat couldn't see what the problem was.

"You'll be earning over a million, but your federal taxes will be 39.6 percent. Your New York State taxes will be 8.8 percent and your New York City taxes will be 3.9 percent. After paying all that tax, you'll be left with $529,120.07 to live on."

"So we'll have half a million dollars to live on a year. Maybe Michael can't afford to lease any more private jets but we should be fine. Right, Len?" Kat rubbed the back of her neck.

"I pay all your bills, Kat. You have more than half a million dollars a year in fixed expenses. The real estate taxes on your Malibu house are nearly $220,000 a year. The real estate taxes on your New York house are over $143,000 a year. That's $363,000 in real estate taxes alone. You pay your housekeeper $50,000 a year. Now you're up to $413,000 and that's before any other expenses. I haven't even included the insurance payments on the Ferrari and the Porsche.

"What's putting you over the top is our fee. With the size of your $27.7 million portfolio, we charge you 1 percent a year. That's $277,000. Now your fixed expenses add up to more than $690,000 a year. Your portfolio would need to earn an additional $161,000, just to cover your fixed expenses.

"If you keep spending at this rate, you'll need to dip into your capital and that's a slippery slope. The smaller the capital, the less income it will generate and the more you'll have to reduce your expenses unless you want to keep dipping into more capital."

"So you're telling me we're going broke with $27 million in assets?" Kat asked in dismay. She knew investing $40 million in a movie was going to seriously affect the size of their portfolio but she didn't realize it meant they could no longer afford their lifestyle.

"I'm telling you that after the transfer for this movie goes through, you need to think about how to reduce your fixed expenses. One way you can do that is if you stop using our firm."

"But who will manage our money and keep it growing?" asked Kat. She was starting to feel dizzy with anxiety.

"I would recommend having Vanguard manage your assets. They'll do a fine job and charge less than a third of what we charge."

"Will they pay all our bills the way you do?" asked Kat.

"Unfortunately, no. You'll have to start paying your own bills, Kat. But that may not be a bad thing. It will help you have a better understanding of what things cost. I would also think about selling one of your houses and looking for other ways to reduce expenses if you want to hold on to your capital."

Kat absolutely wanted to hold on to the capital. The money was supposed to provide a legacy for any children she had with Michael. Kat didn't need a multimillion-dollar beach house in California, or a townhouse in New York, as much as she loved it. She could be happy with a two-bedroom apartment in the city, or a more modest home in the suburbs.

"Thank you, Len, for letting me know. I'll discuss this with Michael and we'll start making changes to our lifestyle."

"I think that's a good idea, Kat. Do you want me to find you a contact at Vanguard?"

Kat loved working with Len but she thought his point about paying her own bills was valid. It was time she took charge of her finances again.

"Thank you, I think that's a good idea. It's been great working with you but you're right. We can no longer afford your services."

"It's been great working with you too, Kat, and I'm always here if you have any questions."

Kat thanked Len again and disconnected the phone. Although she would hate giving up the townhouse, she wanted to start living within their means.

She would give Michael the choice of which he preferred. Did he want the $40 million for his movie, or did he want to keep living like a billionaire?

Kat made up her mind to take Michael out to dinner and give him the choice. She had a feeling she knew what he would say.

CHAPTER 23

MICHAEL

He usually enjoyed being on camera, but today Michael was glad for the privacy while Maria was busy working with the editor. He knew his office had a camera positioned above the desk, but it wasn't as intrusive as being filmed by Dan, with Maria at his side. He luxuriated in being alone for a change.

Michael looked around the room he used as an office with approval. The walls had oak wood paneling and floor to ceiling bookshelves that the designer had filled with leather bound volumes. The large windows gave a view of East 65th Street and an expansive walnut desk filled one end of the room. Michael sat down in the hunter green leather desk chair and picked up the pile of mail that the housekeeper left in a wooden tray. He started riffling through the letters.

His stomach tightened as he noticed one from the lab, with the results of his paternity test.

Michael had gotten a letter from Erica's lawyers the week before, hitting him with a paternity suit. The letter had given him the choice: go to a lab and submit to a paternity test, or accept responsibility that the baby was his. On the outside chance that he wasn't the father, Michael had opted to have his cheek swabbed for the test. Now the results were here.

'Might as well get it over with,' he thought, as he grabbed the silver letter opener out of the desk drawer and slit open the envelope.

He glanced at the letter, which was titled 'DNA Test Report.' It showed his name and the name of Erica's baby: Michael Rosetti.

'She named the baby Michael,' he thought with surprise before looking over the rest of the letter.

There were a bunch of numbers listed under Locus, PI and Allele Sizes that he didn't understand, but there it was, at the bottom of the letter. Probability of Paternity: 99.9998 percent.

It wasn't 100 percent but there seemed to be no doubt, Erica's baby was his. He was a father.

"A father," he said aloud, with wonder in his voice. He was the father of a little boy.

He remembered his father, before he died in the car accident, playing soccer with him when he was six. He remembered running with his father and kicking the ball into the net. His father had been so proud.

He had a little boy, a little boy he could play soccer with one day.

His hands were shaking as he pulled out his phone to call Erica. He was glad he hadn't deleted her number, when he broke up with her nearly a year ago.

"Erica? It's Michael. I got the results of the paternity test." He heard a baby crying in the background.

"Is that him?" he asked softly. "Is that little Michael?"

There was a long pause, while Michael put the paternity result on his desk and ran his hand slowly over the paper.

"Yes, that's Michael." Erica sounded angry. "So you got the results of the test and you believe me now? The baby is yours."

LUCKY   359

"I'm sorry I didn't believe you Erica but there were so many people chasing after us with their hands out, once we won the BonusBall. I thought you were just after the money."

"Fuck you, Michael. I wasn't just some random gold-digger. We had a relationship and I got pregnant. How could you not take responsibility for that happening?"

"I'm so sorry, Erica, but I want to take responsibility now."

"You better believe you're going to take responsibility now. That's why I had my lawyer contact you. You're going to provide a lot of child support."

"I want to do more than just provide child support," said Michael, hoping to sooth Erica. "I want to be part of Michael's life. I want him to know he has a dad." He stood up from behind the desk and walked over to the window. Looking out, he could see a man with a stroller walking down the street.

"What are you saying, Michael?" Erica sounded confused. "Are you going to leave Kat? Do you want to be with me and Michael?"

Michael fantasized about being with Erica and the baby for a moment. He could see himself as the guy walking down the street with the stroller, with Erica by his side.

But then he thought about all that he had with Kat – the houses, the cars and producing the movie together. He may have loved the idea of being the perfect father but the truth was that he couldn't afford to leave Kat. Not until after the movie was made. That was assuming he could convince Maria not to air the footage of Erica and the baby until the end of the second season. Once the movie was in production, Kat couldn't pull his funding.

"No Erica, I can't leave Kat right now. But I was thinking we could set up some type of visitation schedule, so I can see little Michael on a regular basis. Don't you want him to have his father in his life?"

"How is Kat going to react to all this?" asked Erica, sounding impatient. "I can't imagine that she's going to be happy with child support and a visitation schedule."

No, Kat wasn't going to be happy. Michael started sweating.

"Erica, is there some way we could keep this just between us? I'll be there for you and the baby, but I don't want Kat to know. Not just yet."

"Michael, you selfish bastard. Our baby is not some shameful secret you can keep on the DL. You don't deserve to be a part of our baby's life. He'll be better off not knowing his father, if you just want to keep him hidden away."

"Erica, I didn't mean he was a shameful secret. I'm proud to have a son."

"Then you had better tell your wife, and get prepared to pay through the nose." With that, Erica hung up.

Michael groaned as he put the phone down and groaned again as he realized that his side of the conversation had been captured by the hidden camera. He thought back to what he had said – was there anything which would implicate him? He winced as he remembered saying he was proud to have a son, right before Erica hung up.

He doubted he could convince Maria not to air the footage. He was going to have to think about how to break the news to Kat before video of him acknowledging his son was broadcast to the entire world.

KAT

The hostess walked Kat and Michael to their table, with Dan and Maria following closely behind them. Kat felt a momentary aggravation that they couldn't even have a private dinner but that's what she agreed to, when she signed up for a second season of *Lucky*. Once they were seated, Dan stood opposite their table; his ever-present handheld cam, focused on the two of them. Maria stood next to Dan, ready to give him instructions on what she wanted him to shoot.

Kat was a little embarrassed but the other diners seemed excited. The buzz in the restaurant increased in volume as a young woman tentatively approached their table with her menu in her hand.

"I'm sorry to interrupt your dinner," she said apologetically while giving Michael a big smile. "I just wanted to say how much I love watching *Lucky*. Would you mind signing my menu?"

Michael beamed as he reached in his pocket for a pen and signed with a flourish. He handed the pen to Kat, who signed, while inwardly sighing. Once the woman went back to her table, she and Michael reviewed the menu.

Kat was nervous about telling Michael they had to make changes to their lifestyle. He had been the one pushing for the multiple houses and the cars. She thought back to what Len had said. If Michael wanted his movie, he was going to need to give up something to avoid dipping into the capital. Kat decided to talk to Michael as soon as their meals arrived.

Kat and Michael had finished giving their orders to the waiter when Michael's phone chimed again.

"Hi, John," Michael said after answering, "No, I get it. We have to deal with this quickly and quietly. I'll be at your office at 10:00 tomorrow morning."

Kat straightened her napkin, trying to get it to cover as much of her lap as possible. She could feel a knot starting to form in her stomach and doubted she would be able to eat much of the mushroom risotto, when it came out of the kitchen.

"Michael, what the hell is going on? That's the third time John has called today. Why are you going to his office tomorrow morning? Are we being sued again?"

Since winning the BonusBall, there had been a few nut cases who had tried to sue them, just to get a payout. Usually, John was able to get rid of them pretty quickly.

Michael took a long breath and reached out to grab Kat's hands.

"Kitty Kat, we need to talk," he said softly.

Kat looked at Michael's serious face and a wave of panic washed over her. She felt as though the room was starting to spin and the only focal point keeping her anchored was the look on Michael's face. She took her hands out of Michael's because she could feel them getting sweaty.

"Michael, you're scaring me," she said softly. "What's wrong?"

"The reason John keeps calling is because I'm being hit with a paternity suit."

"Eyes on Kat!" she heard Maria say excitedly to Dan. "Move in for a close shot."

It took Kat a couple of seconds to deconstruct Michael's sentence. Once she was able to focus on the word "paternity" she started to feel a small sense of relief.

"So some random woman is claiming you fathered her child? John will be able to deal with this – we don't need to worry about it."

She reached out for her wineglass and took a gulp.

"The thing is, it's not some random woman. It's Erica."

The room started to spin more quickly.

"Erica? Erica from your acting class, Erica?" Kat noticed the hand holding her wineglass was starting to shake. "Why would Erica claim you had a baby together?"

"We had an affair and she got pregnant. Now she wants child support. Kat, sweetheart, I'm so very sorry. I never wanted to hurt you." Michael reached out and took the wineglass out of Kat's hands before the wine could start sloshing over the top of the glass.

"When did you have an affair? Was it while we were married?" Kat could hear her voice starting to tremble as her throat tightened up.

She saw Michael glance at Maria and for one horrible moment she wondered if Michael had told her in front of the camera for the shock value.

Suddenly, she felt like she had to know all the details, no matter how much it was going to hurt.

"How old is the baby? Is it a boy or a girl?"

"Michael is two months old," Michael kept talking in a soft voice, as if trying to defuse the situation.

"Michael? She named the baby Michael?" Suddenly Kat remembered Erica's birth announcement.

"Dan, are you getting all this?" Maria whispered but Kat was still able to hear her.

"I'm getting it all," said Dan.

Kat thought she might throw up, right there at the table. All the years she wanted to have Michael's baby and he kept putting her off, saying it wasn't the right time. Now it turned out that he had had a baby with another woman. And, as if it couldn't be bad enough, the baby was named after him.

"Do you love her? Do you want to be with her and the baby?" She held her breath, waiting for his response.

"No, Kat. I love you. Having a fling with Erica meant nothing and I never wanted you to find out."

"Are you sure the baby is yours?" Kat said, holding out a shred of hope. Maybe she could adjust to Michael's being unfaithful but at least there wouldn't be a baby involved.

"Yes, I gave a cheek swab last week and the paternity test confirmed it," admitted Michael.

Suddenly, something in Kat just snapped. She was tired of being lied to, she was tired of Michael's selfishness, and she was very tired of having all of her most intimate moments captured for the world to see.

She glanced over at Dan and Maria. She couldn't see Dan, behind the camera, but Maria was staring at her intently, a sympathetic look on her face.

"Dan," said Kat, "you're going to want to get this."

She stood up and picked up the wineglass in one quick motion, then threw the rest of the wine in Michael's face.

"Kat, what the fuck?" yelled Michael, his hair drenched in wine, which was now dripping down his face.

Kat didn't wait to hear what else he was going to say. She strode out of the restaurant, head held high, in part to get away from Michael, but also to get away from Dan and Maria who were chasing after her.

Kat heard the sound of a key in the lock of the downstairs door and hoped it would be Michael, following her, to see how she was doing. She was crushed when she heard Maria call out.

"Kat? Are you home? Can we come up?"

Of course, it would be Maria and Dan. She couldn't have a private moment to lick her wounds without Dan shoving the camera in her face.

'Not today,' Kat thought grimly. Maria and Dan could go fuck themselves before she would spill her guts on camera.

"Get out Maria and take Dan with you. I'm not interested in feeding your viewers' voyeurism. Go interview Michael, if you want to, but leave me the hell alone."

She hoped that they would get the hint and leave. Unfortunately, Maria was never one to take a hint. She heard them walking up the stairs and cursed the day that Michael had given them the key to the townhouse.

She quickly wiped her face with a tear-dampened tissue as she heard them come in the bedroom and sat up in the bed.

"Kat, how are you doing?" Maria sounded solicitous and she looked sorry for Kat. Dan, as usual, was hidden behind the camera, which focused on Kat.

"I've been so worried about you ever since Michael told you about Erica and the baby. How do you feel?"

"I thought I told you to get out, Maria! Why are you still here?"

"I care about you, Kat. Our viewers care about you too. They want to hear your side of the story."

"My side of the story is pretty simple. My husband had a baby with another woman. How do you think I'm feeling?" A wave of grief washed over Kat and she started crying again, despite her resolve not to cry on camera. She grabbed another tissue from the box on the bedside table and tried to pull it together.

Through her tears, she looked at Maria. Maria looked concerned but not surprised.

"You knew!" Kat said in a whisper. "You knew about Erica and the baby. You knew before I did." She felt like screaming at Maria and Dan. "When did Michael tell you?"

"Michael didn't really tell us but we've been filming the two of you for nearly a year. We have footage of Erica telling Michael she was pregnant."

Kat grabbed on to the bedpost to keep from falling over as a wave of dizziness hit her.

"You have footage of Michael and Erica? You knew about them? Why didn't you tell me?" She felt doubly betrayed. Not only had her husband been cheating but she was the last to know.

Kat thought for a second.

"I don't believe you. I haven't seen Erica in the publicity clips that you've been posting to YouTube."

"We were saving the footage of the other women for the second season broadcast," admitted Maria. "We just wanted to tease on YouTube, not give everything away."

Other women? Kat ran for the bathroom and was just able to make the toilet before the contents of her stomach were voided into the bowl. She kept throwing up until nothing was left except some watery bile. Through her misery, she was aware of Dan at the bathroom door, catching it all.

Grabbing some toilet paper, she wiped her mouth and stood up. She grabbed a cup off the sink and rinsed her mouth out with water before spitting into the sink. Then she turned to face Dan and Maria, hands on her hips.

"I want to know what other women Michael has been seeing and I want to know now. Turn off the camera and start talking."

"Should I stop filming?" Dan asked, turning towards Maria.

"Keep rolling, Dan," Maria said. "Kat, I'll only tell you what I know if we can keep shooting."

"Okay, you can keep shooting. At this point, what does it matter?"

Maria took a folded manila envelope out of her backpack.

"Here, Kat, I think you should look at these."

With shaking hands, Kat opened the envelope. Inside were blurry pictures showing Michael kissing and fondling other women. There was even a shot of a naked man from the back, astride a brunette woman who was lying back on a bed. On his shoulder, Kat recognized Michael's dragon tattoo.

"Kat," said Maria gently, "You know what a handsome man Michael is. As the two of you became famous, women started throwing themselves at him. Women find Michael irresistible."

Kat stared at Maria, who had a guilty look on her face. Kat started to feel like she would throw up again.

"What about you, Maria? Did you find Michael irresistible?"

"What do you mean?" said Maria. She stopped smiling and started to look anxious.

"Were you one of the women who threw themselves at Michael? Did you sleep with my husband?"

MARIA

Maria wiped a hand over her forehead which was breaking out in a sweat. She turned to look at Dan.

"Stop rolling, Dan," she instructed him, before turning back to Kat.

"It was just one time, when we were in Malibu. We were both a little drunk on white wine and we started fooling around. I'm so sorry, Kat. It really meant nothing. I know Michael loves you."

"Jesus, Maria!" she overheard Dan say in disgust.

Kat walked over to Maria and slapped her hard, across the face. The pain of the slap was nothing compared to the shame that Maria was feeling. She put a hand up to her face, which was stinging.

"Get out, Maria, and take Dan with you. As of right now, I am off the show. You can broadcast whatever you've gotten to date but you won't be shooting me again. Sue me for breach of contract, for all I care, but I never want to see you again."

Kat shoved Maria and Dan out of her way and waited by the bedroom door as they walked slowly out. Maria was still holding her face.

Once they were out of the townhouse, Maria turned to face Dan, who had put down his camera.

"Maria! You know what an asshole Michael is. Why on earth would you sleep with him?"

The bewildered look on Dan's face only served to increase her humiliation.

She had a lot of respect for Dan and she wanted him to respect her back. Somehow she had the feeling that he would never respect her again.

"Not that's it's an excuse but Michael and I started drinking one night, after you had left for the evening. I was a little drunk when he started paying me compliments. Then he sat down next to me and started to kiss me. One thing led to another and we wound up in bed. I did the walk of shame, leaving his house the next morning."

"Didn't you think about Kat? About how she would react when she found out?"

"I hoped no one would ever find out. I really regret sleeping with him."

Dan scowled. "If that's the case, why did you tell her? It just seems cruel."

"I thought she deserved to know what type of man Michael really is. Maybe I was trying to make things right by confessing the truth."

"We know what type of man Michael really is. This makes me question what type of woman you really are."

"I know, Dan," said Maria. She became absorbed in looking down at the ground. "I've been doing a lot of questioning myself. This show, sleeping with Michael, the endless manipulation to get ratings. I don't think I like the woman I've become."

The look on Dan's face softened a little. "Maybe it's time you started making some changes."

"Maybe you're right," said Maria, looking up at him again. "Maybe you're right."

KAT

It was an hour later when Kat became aware of Michael standing at the bedroom door.

"Kat, can I come in and explain?" he asked softly. Kat turned to look at him. He looked contrite but Kat didn't believe he was really sorry. She thought Michael was just sorry he had been caught.

"Leave me alone, Michael, I don't want to see you right now. I'm not interested in your explanation."

"Kat, it was just a brief fling and it was unfortunate that Erica got pregnant. I never meant to hurt you."

"Unfortunate? I guess you could say it was unfortunate. Maybe you didn't mean to hurt me but you did. What kills me is that I tried to talk you into having a baby when all along you knew you were going to be a father with someone else."

"Being Erica's baby daddy isn't the same as having a child with you, Kat. You're the one that I love."

"You have a strange way of showing your love, Michael." Kat took a deep breath through her mouth because all the crying had left her nose congested.

"Please, Kat. It happened when you didn't want to fool around because of the cameras in the apartment. Not that it's any excuse, but I was so frustrated that I strayed. I shouldn't have and I'm really sorry."

"That's your excuse? You were unfaithful because you had blue balls? What's your excuse for the other women?"

Kat felt somewhat vindicated when Michael froze with an expression of alarm on his face.

"What other women? What are you talking about, Kat?"

"The other women you fucked. Maria showed me the pictures."

"What pictures are you talking about? How did Maria get pictures?" Michael looked panicked.

"I don't know how Maria got pictures but they're there in the envelope if you want to take a look."

Kat watched Michael closely as he undid the string binding the manila envelope. He pulled out the stack of photos and riffled through them quickly.

"The quality of these photos aren't good, Kat. You can't really tell who's in them. These aren't photos of me."

"Michael, you're such a liar. Of course they're photos of you. You can see your dragon tattoo."

Michael's face fell as he realized he had been caught.

"Kat, these women meant nothing I swear it. I was alone in California and you were back in New York. I was just lonely and looking for some companionship because I was missing you so much."

"Spare me your pathetic excuses, Michael. What I want to know is why you fucked Maria."

Michael visibly shuddered. "I didn't fuck Maria. Why would you think that?"

"I think that because she told me. Of all the women you had to fuck, you fucked someone we've let into our home this past year."

"It only happened one time and we agreed it was a big mistake. It never happened again, Kat."

"So that's supposed to make me feel better? Because you and Maria admitted you made a mistake?"

"All the women were a mistake, Kat. It just happened when we weren't together and making love. I was horny and I let all the fame go to my head. Honestly, Kat, I love you."

Kat had been crying for what seemed like hours and she didn't even feel the pain anymore. She was so exhausted that she just felt numb. It was bad enough, finding out about Erica and the baby. It was too much to comprehend that Erica hadn't been the only one.

"What I want to know," she said softly, "is did you ever really love me, Michael?" She smoothed down an imaginary wrinkle in the ridiculously overpriced peach silk comforter that she had been so thrilled to buy, almost a year ago.

"Of course I loved you, Kat," said Michael, as he sat down and put an arm around her shoulders. "I mean, I do still love you."

"Don't touch me," she hissed at him. He backed off with his hands held up and stood in front of her, next to the bed.

"I love you, Kat, I really do. The other women meant nothing."

"Maybe they meant nothing to you, but they certainly mean something to me." She could see him watching her closely.

"Why do you love me, Michael? What is it about me that you love?"

He gave her a smile. "That's easy, Kat. I love you because you're so good. You're one of the most generous and giving people I've ever known." He sat down next to her on the bed, but at a distance.

She thought about his response for a second while looking at him. Even after hours of fighting, even after the betrayals, he was still so handsome.

She looked at him again closely, tried to look beyond the sculpted cheekbones and the big green eyes with the long dark lashes. In staring at his face, she could see the selfishness, greed and vanity, beneath the beauty. Michael looked good, but only on the surface.

"You love me, Michael, but you're not in love with me."

"Is that a question, Kat?" he asked as a slight frown creased his forehead.

"Not a question, just a statement of fact. You may love what I represent: home and security, but you're not in love with me. Not the way I've been in love with you for the last three years."

She had been so passionately in love with Michael, and so thrilled he wanted to be with her, that she never noticed he didn't feel the same.

She stood up and turned to face him.

"Michael, I want a divorce." She took a small amount of satisfaction in noticing a look of fear on his face.

"Kat, you don't mean that," he said, jumping up off the bed and holding out his arms to her. "I'm so sorry I hurt you but we can put all this past us. I was just immature and let the fame go to my head. It will never happen again – I promise you."

"Oh but I do mean it, Michael. I'll call John in the morning and get the name of a good divorce lawyer."

"But how are we going to divide everything?" he asked, his eyes wide. "What will happen to the movie we're producing?"

There it was. What Michael really loved was everything they had been able to purchase with her winnings. That, and the fame that being on *Lucky* had brought him.

Kat didn't care about the money. All she had ever wanted was a life with Michael and to start a family. The things were just that – things.

"You can have most of it, Michael, and I won't pull the funding for your movie. Don't worry. You'll still be rich after the divorce." It hurt to see how relieved he looked.

"Are you sure, Kat? I want to make sure you're taken care of too."

"I'm sure. You can have the house in Malibu, and the cars. You can even have all the jewelry back. Give it to Erica for all that I care."

"But what do you want? You must want something." He looked at her, the frown back on his face.

"All I want is this townhouse. I'll sell it and buy an apartment. Then I'll have enough money left over to fund me, while I work on my novel. And I want the dog. You never cared about him anyway."

"You can have the townhouse, Kat, and you can have Max. I won't fight you," Michael said, giving her a big smile. "Do you want me to go to a hotel tonight?"

"No," said Kat. "I'll go to the hotel. I'm looking forward to sleeping without Dan and Maria waking me up in the morning."

Kat left Michael in the bedroom and wandered down the hallway, then up the stairs, on her way to the bedroom where she stored all of her clothes so she could pack an overnight bag.

When she was on the landing, she noticed that someone had left the light on, on the fifth floor, in the room that they used as a gym. She walked up one more flight of stairs to the fifth-floor bedroom. The room was the one she had wanted to use as a nursery, but Michael insisted they needed an in-home gym, so training equipment and free weights filled the room, instead of a crib, rocking chair and a changing table. The wall opposite the equipment was mirrored, so Michael could check his form as he worked out.

She stopped for a moment and looked in. The sleek black fittings on the Peloton bike reminded her that she canceled her appointment with the personal trainer that morning. For a moment, she felt guilty. The screen on the bike was dark but she could hear the Peloton instructors in her head, encouraging her to climb that hill, push harder and go faster.

The Peloton bike, where she sweated off twenty-five pounds in an effort to look good for Michael, and to please Maria, who wanted her to lose some weight for the camera.

Kat wandered into the room and sat down on the seat of the Bowflex Home Gym and pulled down the overhead bar. She could feel her arm muscles responding to the resistance as she pulled. She let the bar go back up and thought about all the training sessions, designed to give her the body that would please Michael and keep him from looking at other women. All that work, all that effort and it was all for nothing.

She pulled out her phone and called the personal trainer. Carlos wasn't picking up but she left a message.

"Hi, Carlos? This is Kat. I've decided I no longer need to work with a personal trainer and I'm canceling all my future sessions. You've helped me lose the extra weight and I'm very appreciative. I would be happy to be a reference, if you ever need one. You've been great – thank you."

Kat hung up, stood up and stretched her arms over her head. That simple stretch felt better than all the resistance training she had done on the Bowflex machine.

She didn't want to gain back the weight but maybe she could join a gym and work out with other people around. People of all shapes and sizes who just wanted to get healthy instead of wanting to look perfect.

She left the gym, turning the light off on her way out and walked downstairs until she reached the bedroom she used as a closet. She turned on the light and looked at the racks of designer clothes that Maria and Michael had insisted she purchase. One wall of the room contained lighted shelving for all of her shoes. She looked at all the Jimmy Choo stilettos and Prada pumps that hurt her feet, before selecting a pair of Nike sneakers.

She grabbed a Coach tote from a corner of the room and looked for something comfortable she could get for the overnight stay in a hotel. She looked through the racks before selecting a pair of black leather leggings, and a gray sweatshirt that was as soft as a kitten.

She walked over to the antique maple chest of drawers to get some underwear. Forget a comfortable bra and matching panties from Victoria's Secret. Thanks to her clothing makeover, all she had was couture lingerie, which the housekeeper had sorted by color. She selected a black silk bra and thong from Agent Provocateur, along with a colorful red silk kimono.

Bag packed with her overnight clothes, she walked into the adjoining bathroom to get her toiletries. The light gleamed on the gray and white Carrera marble vanity, as Kat looked in the bathroom mirror. After so many hours crying, she looked like shit. Her eyes were puffy and swollen and her nose was red. The skin around her neck was blotchy and irritated looking, as if she had been scratching.

She told her vanity to take the night off and opened the medicine cabinet to get what she needed. She put the eye makeup remover into a toiletries case, although it looked like she had cried off all of her mascara. She grabbed her facial cleanser and moisturizer, along with her toothbrush and a tube of Colgate. Zipping the case shut, she put it on top of her clothes in the Coach bag.

Turning off the bathroom light, she looked around the bedroom with all the clothes and pulled out her phone to send a text to Colleen.

'In the morning, please call a charity and donate all of my clothes. I want the racks to be empty when I come home. Thanks!'

Goodwill probably didn't get a lot of designer clothing donations but it might make someone very happy.

Kat walked out of the bedroom and took the elevator down to the first floor. When she was in the front hall, she whistled for Max. He came bounding up to her, tail wagging so hard he was almost falling over.

"Hey, Maxie, good boy," said Kat, stroking his head. He put his wet black nose up to meet her hand and whimpered in delight.

"Do you want to go for a walk?" Max gave a little bark to indicate his approval of the idea.

Kat grabbed his leash off a hook near the front door and attached it to his collar. She slipped on a black leather jacket and grabbed her Coach bag before walking out the front door.

Once she was outside, on East 65th Street, with the cars driving by and all of the pedestrians, she took a deep breath. She didn't need designer clothes, she didn't need a townhouse. She didn't even need Michael. As long as she could afford an apartment in Manhattan, someplace where she could keep Max, she was going to be just fine.

CHAPTER 24

MARIA

It was a week before Thanksgiving and the ratings for *Lucky* had been off the charts, since the second season had started. Viewers loved it when Michael and Kat bought the multimillion-dollar beach house but social media really heated up when they started showing video of Michael sneaking out late at night to hook up with women he met in bars.

Almost overnight, Michael had gone from being America's dream husband to the guy they loved to hate. Oddly, even though America was furious with him, Michael was more popular than ever, if the growing number of Instagram followers was anything to judge by.

Maria knew the ratings would only increase when they aired the season finale in January. Not only did they have footage of Michael telling Kat about Erica and the baby, Dan had captured video when Maria showed Kat the pictures of the other women. They had stopped filming after that night because both Kat and Michael refused to be on camera again.

After following Kat and Michael for nearly a year, Maria took a much-needed two-week vacation in Mexico. She spent her time lying on the beach and working on her tan. It had been great but now Maria was starting to get a little antsy, as she looked around the four walls of her studio apartment.

She was reading a magazine when William called.

"Have you checked the ratings?" William asked without preamble.

"Yes," said Maria. "We have 1.15 rating in the 18-49 demographic and 2.90 million viewers. The ratings have been very strong."

"Neil Charles has been very happy with the number of viewers. He wanted to know if you would be interested in producing a third season of *Lucky*."

"I think we've reached the end of the Kat and Michael story," said Maria with some relief. "After Kat found out about Erica's baby, and the other women, they decided they were off the show."

"We weren't thinking about Kat and Michael," said William. "The BonusBall jackpot is up to $550 million. If the winner decides to take the lump sum, it will be $347 million. That's even bigger than Kat and Michael's jackpot. Do you want to start shooting the show again with a new winner?"

Maria thought about attending auctions for jewelry and artwork. She thought about working with realtors to view mansions. She thought about flying first class to exotic locations and staying in world-class hotels. Then she remembered the long days and nights, and the endless manipulation in trying to get the winner to spend.

"I'm out," she told William. "I think it's time I made a career change."

"You don't want to be a reality TV producer?" William said with surprise in his voice.

"No, I want to try something else. I've been thinking about making documentaries."

"It may be prestigious but there's no money in documentaries," William warned.

"I know, but I want to work on something I can feel good about. I have this germ of an idea."

"What about?" asked William.

"I want to make a documentary about lottery winners who blow through their entire fortunes. It will be a rags-to-riches-to-rags story."

"You could call it *Lucky Losers*," suggested William.

Maria laughed. "I think that's a little harsh. I want this to be a sympathetic look at what happened to them. I'm using *Blown!* as a working title."

"Well, good luck," said William. "It sounds interesting. I wish you all the best."

"Thanks, William," said Maria, as he hung up.

She thought it really did sound interesting and she couldn't wait to get started. She didn't even stop to consider whether it would impress her father. She was brimming with enthusiasm for the idea.

'I would watch the shit out of that,' she thought to herself happily.

MICHAEL

It was the third week of November and preproduction had been going well on *Lexington and Concord*. Victor Lindstrom, acclaimed for his work on indie films, had agreed to sign on as their director. Storyboards were being created for the scenes in the script.

This week, they were in the middle of holding auditions for the female lead, Sybil Pitcher.

Michael loved doing the judging, instead of being the one auditioning.

Although he tried hard to focus on their acting, some of the women trying for the role of Sybil had been distractingly gorgeous and he was in a constant state of semi-arousal.

In these days of #metoo, Michael knew better than to hit on any of the women, but there were times when he was sorry that the casting couch was a thing of the past.

They had narrowed the choice down to two finalists. The first was Sienna Williams, a relative newcomer who was pretty, but slightly quirky looking, with dark, heavy eyebrows and a pale, heart-shaped face. The other finalist was Natalie Adams, a classic beauty, well known for her work on the TV show *Countdown*. Natalie was looking for a role in a serious film to help her avoid being typecast as an FBI Agent.

Victor was leaning towards Sienna. He wanted a fresh new face to play his Sybil. Michael was leaning towards Natalie, hoping that her star power would help at the box office when the film was released.

The days had been long, but he loved every minute of working on the movie. At night, he left the *Lexington and Concord* production offices and drove his Porsche home to his beach house in Malibu. Although he didn't miss her during the day, at night, when he was alone in the house, he found himself wishing Kat was still around.

He thought about cruising bars to meet women, but he hadn't been getting the same response from women since the *Lucky* episode aired, showing him cheating on Kat. The women he met these days seemed more interested in telling him what an asshole he had been, and less interested in hooking up. He was already dreading the day when the episode about Erica and the baby would be broadcast. Being single wasn't working out exactly as planned.

Although Kat had threatened him with a divorce lawyer, in the end they worked with a mediator to divide everything. Kat got the townhouse, Max and $13,865,830.00, which had been half the money left in their account, once the funds had been wired to produce the movie. True to her word, she hadn't asked for anything else.

Michael took the beach house, the cars, the jewelry, the production company, and his $13,865,830 share of the account. Although on paper, Michael was a rich man, he was getting a little nervous about cash flow. Life on the West Coast was expensive, to say nothing about property taxes and insurance on his cars. Michael was also paying Erica $20,000 a month in child support and he had put $250,000 aside in a college trust fund for little Michael. Michael had been watching the $13,865,830 number go lower, as he needed to pay bills.

He knew it wouldn't be a problem long term. Once he was well established as a movie star, he would be getting multimillion-dollar contracts to sign up for new movies. He just had to hang on until then.

But there were some bad days when Michael had doubts. What if he didn't get new roles, once his movie was made? What if Kat was right and *Lexington and Concord* was just a vanity project? Michael couldn't bear the thought that he might be an out of work actor again.

On bad days, he called Erica to make himself feel better. He picked up his cell phone and waited for her to answer.

"Hey, Michael, how's it going?" His relationship with Erica had warmed considerably since he started paying child support.

"It's going good. The movie is going great. How are things with you? How's little Michael?"

"You should see him! He's started smiling and cooing. And Michael? He looks just like you."

Michael had an intense longing to see his son. He was about to suggest to Erica that she and Michael visit him on the West Coast when he became aware of a male voice in the background singing *The Itsy-Bitsy Spider*.

"Who's that singing in the background?" he asked Erica.

"Oh, that's just Barry," Erica said breezily. "He likes to sing to Michael."

"Barry comes to visit you?" Michael was a little confused. Why was his old acting coach visiting his ex?

There was a moment of silence before Erica said, "Michael, Barry and I have started seeing each other. We've been dating about a month."

Michael wasn't sure which made him more jealous: Barry starting to date Erica or Barry developing a relationship with his son.

"But Erica, I'm paying for child support."

"What the hell are you talking about, Michael? Do you think I should be celibate because you're paying to take care of our son?"

As a matter of fact, that's exactly what Michael was thinking.

"Erica, it's important for Michael to have consistency. He shouldn't be exposed to just any man you start dating."

"Barry isn't just any man. We haven't been dating long but I have the feeling it could turn into something serious. And who are you to give me parenting advice? Your relationship with Michael has been limited to writing checks."

"Erica, you know I want more of a relationship with Michael but it's been hard when I'm on the West Coast." Michael could feel his stomach being twisted in knots.

"Well, while you've been parenting in absentia, Barry has been providing a male role model for little Michael. I think it's been good for him to have Barry in his life."

Michael's instinct was to hop on the first flight, to go back to New York and claim Erica and Michael for himself. Then he remembered he was in the middle of preproduction and he couldn't leave. Michael felt an impotent rage.

"Erica, if you want me to keep paying child support, I'm going to insist that you stop seeing Barry. Or at least keep him away from little Michael."

"Fuck you, Michael. You can't tell me to stop seeing Barry and you can't keep Barry from seeing our son. You're not Michael's legal guardian." She paused for a moment. "If you stop sending the checks, I'll get my lawyer involved."

Erica threatening to contact her lawyer made Michael cool down a little. He was already in the midst of a P.R. nightmare because he cheated on Kat. If it got out that he wasn't paying child support, he would likely lose any fans he had left. He needed those fans if he wanted to get roles in the future.

"I'm sorry, Erica. Forget what I said about not paying child support. I guess I was jealous and not thinking clearly."

"Okay, Michael." Erica sounded less angry. "But you don't need to be jealous. You're always going to be Michael's father. You can see Michael any time you're back on the East Coast. Nothing would make me happier than for you to have a relationship with your son."

Michael felt a little better. "Thanks, Erica. I'll book a flight back to New York as soon as we're out of preproduction. I can't wait to see him."

As Michael hung up the phone, he realized he wanted to be a great father. He just needed a way to become bicoastal again.

'Maybe I should take some of the remaining money and buy an apartment in New York,' he thought, wondering if he could afford it.

It would seriously dip into his cash reserve but having a relationship with his son would make it worth it.

KAT

Kat sat on the sofa in the living room of her new three-bedroom apartment three weeks before Christmas. She had taken the furnishings from the townhouse and used them to decorate her new place, so it felt like home, even though she had only been in the apartment a couple of weeks. What she couldn't use from the townhouse, she put into storage. If Kat ever decided to buy a house, she had all the furniture she needed.

She heard her phone ringing and saw the caller was Ren.

"Hey, Ren," she said, after answering the phone.

"Hey, Kat, how's the new apartment?"

Kat took a look around her and smiled. "I'm still getting used to it but I think Max and I are going to be very happy here. There's a view of the East River from the living room and I've set up one of the bedrooms as my office. It's not as big as the townhouse but it feels very cozy."

"I can't wait to see it," Ren said enthusiastically.

"Well, you're welcome anytime."

"Hey, Kat, that's not why I called. Uncle Charlie and Aunt Jan are hosting Christmas Eve this year and I was wondering if you wanted to come."

There was a pause. "Is Dad going to be there with Annika?" Kat felt tense at the idea.

"You haven't heard the big news. Dad and Annika broke up last week. He kicked her out of the house."

"That's huge," said Kat, feeling cheerful at the thought. "What happened?"

"Dad didn't go into a lot of details but he discovered that Annika was cheating on him. He said that getting involved with her had been the biggest mistake of his life."

"Really? He said that?"

"Yes. He said he would rather be alone than be with Annika."

"OMG," said Kat. "He actually said he would rather be alone?"

"Yes, he did," said Ren. "But this is Dad we're talking about. How long before he has a new girlfriend?"

"I give it three weeks before he finds someone new," Kat laughed.

"I'm pessimistic," said Ren. "I give it four weeks. But seriously, Kat. Now that Annika is out of the picture, do you think you can come on Christmas Eve? Dad would love to see you."

Kat was silent for a few moments.

"Yes, I can come. I think I'm ready to heal the rift with Dad. It's a bad thing when family members stop talking."

"I couldn't agree more," said Ren sincerely. "I'll let Uncle Charlie and Aunt Jan know that you're coming. Everybody's going to be thrilled." Ren paused for a second before changing topics.

"So how's the writing going?"

"Surprisingly, the writing has been going great. It seems like once I had the time and space to write, without Michael and the camera crew, I found my muse. I sent some sample chapters to an agent, along with an outline, and she's agreed to represent me!"

"Kat! That's amazing. You should let me take you out to celebrate. I just know you're going to get published!"

Kat didn't answer as a wave of nausea hit her. She took several deep breaths and waited for the feeling to pass. It relented somewhat, although she still felt pretty queasy. She took a sip of water from the glass that was on the coffee table.

"Kat, are you still there?"

"Yeah, I'm still here Ren. I just felt sick to my stomach for a moment." Kat took another deep breath.

"Are you okay? Do you have a bug?" Kat could hear the concern in Ren's voice.

"I don't know if it's a stomach bug or a mild case of food poisoning but I've been feeling nauseous off and on for the last couple of weeks."

"Do you have the runs, or any other symptoms?"

"No, just the queasiness. I haven't thrown up but I've come close a couple of times."

"No other symptoms?" Ren asked again.

"No, other than the nausea, I've felt fine. Maybe a little tired, but that's it."

"Kat, when was the last time you got your period?"

Kat had to think about it. Between working with the divorce mediator, selling the townhouse, finding the new apartment and signing on with an agent, she had been too busy to pay attention. Had she missed a month? Actually, now that she thought about it, she might have missed two months.

'It's probably a result of all the stress I've been under,' she thought to herself, taking another sip of water.

"I don't actually remember," she admitted to Ren. "There's been too much going on in my life."

"I know you've been under a crushing load of stress, but I think you should take a pregnancy test. When was the last time you slept with Michael?"

Kat remembered exactly the last time she and Michael had made love. "It was the night I agreed to pay for his movie, not long before I found out about his cheating."

"Kat, I'm going to get off the phone. I want you to walk to the nearest drugstore and get a home pregnancy test. Then I want you to go into the bathroom and pee on the stick. Call me as soon as you get the results."

"Ren, I really don't think I'm pregnant. I just have a bug."

"Promise me you'll take the test, Kat. I'm hanging up now." Ren disconnected the call.

Kat sat for a few minutes on the sofa thinking. Was it possible? Could she actually be pregnant? When she was with Michael, all she wanted was a baby. How did she feel about having a baby without Michael around?

Kat pictured herself as a single mother. She could convert the extra bedroom in the apartment into a nursery. Without the townhouse's exorbitant property taxes, she had enough of a nest egg that she didn't need to work. She could divide her time between writing and taking care of her baby. It wouldn't be the nuclear family she once pictured with Michael, but she knew she could be a loving mother to a child.

Maybe when the baby grew bigger, she could move out to the suburbs, to be closer to her Uncle Charlie. A house with a yard would be good for a child, and for Max. She could picture her child running on the grass with

Max racing along behind.

Slowly, Kat stood up and walked to the front door to get her coat. Max came bounding up for a walk but she promised him she would take him out later. She took the elevator to the building lobby and exited out onto the street, feeling as though she were in a dream.

Kat walked the three blocks to a nearby Duane Reade and stood for a few moments looking at the different pregnancy tests. She picked a test that claimed to be 99 percent accurate one week after missing a period. Still in a daze, she paid for the test and walked back home.

Once she was back in her apartment, she took off her coat and hung it up in the hall closet.

"No matter what the result is, I'll be okay," Kat promised herself.

She knew she would be okay. Kat had discovered that her life was pretty wonderful, even without Michael. She had her family, her friends, her writing and Max. Her life would still be wonderful, even if she wasn't pregnant.

Kat took the test into the bathroom and closed the door behind her. Her hands were shaking as she opened the box and read the instructions. The instructions were pretty simple to understand: just pee on the stick and wait one minute. A single bar would mean she wasn't pregnant. A plus sign would mean she was having a baby.

After peeing on the stick, Kat placed the test on the bathroom sink. She washed her hands and set a timer on her phone for sixty seconds.

'I won't look until the timer goes off,' she promised herself. To waste some time, Kat left the bathroom and walked into the living room. She sat down and opened the Facebook app on her phone but couldn't really concentrate on what she was reading.

'No walking back into the bathroom,' she admonished herself, putting down the phone with a sigh. She picked up a book that was on the coffee table and set it down again without opening it. She walked over to the refrigerator and got a bottle of water because her mouth had gone dry.

After what felt like ten minutes, she finally heard the ringer as the timer went off. Going into the bathroom, she walked over to the sink and picked up the test.

It showed a big red plus sign. Kat blinked and looked again. No doubt about it – the test showed a plus sign. She was pregnant.

'What a perfect symbol for pregnancy,' Kat thought joyfully. A plus sign to signify she would be Kat Davidson, plus a little one. A wonderful addition to her wonderful life.

Her life with Michael may have ended, but her new life was just beginning. A life that would be focused on the life now growing inside her.

Kat was beaming as she walked back into the living room to call Ren.

THE END

THANK YOU SO MUCH FOR READING

If you enjoyed reading this book, I'd be grateful if you took a few minutes to write a review on Amazon.

When you post a review, it makes a huge difference to help new readers find my book.

Your review would make my day!

Thank you,

V. R. Street

ABOUT THE AUTHOR

V. R. Street lives in Connecticut with her husband, daughter, son and a cheeky cat named Bob.

Lucky is her first novel, although she has published three nonfiction titles under a different name. The idea for *Lucky* came from fantasizing about winning the lottery and wondering what it would be like if a reality TV series was shot about lottery winners. Since publishing this book, HGTV has come out with a show called *My Lottery Dream Home*. Sometimes life imitates fiction!

When not writing, V. R. works for a sports broadcasting company. In 2017, she was the winner of an Emmy for her work on the 2016 Summer Olympics.

ACKNOWLEDGMENTS

There are a number of people I wanted to thank. They helped make this book a reality and I would like to acknowledge them.

To Caroline Leavitt who edited the first draft. She helped craft the work into a better story and was a joy to work with.

To Victoria Skurnick who told me I was a very good fiction writer and encouraged me to keep going. Her words meant a lot when I wondered if the writing was any good.

To Kathleen Zea for being my first early reader. Kathleen, you gave me confidence to move forward and I'm very grateful for your support and friendship!

Finally, to Neil, Jessica and William. Your love and support mean everything to me and I couldn't have done it without you.

Made in the USA
Middletown, DE
28 February 2021